Beautiful BURN

T0204542

ALSO BY JAMIE MCGUIRE

THE PROVIDENCE SERIES
Providence
Requiem
Eden
Sins of the Innocent: A Novella

THE BEAUTIFUL SERIES
Beautiful Disaster
Walking Disaster
A Beautiful Wedding: A Novella
Something Beautiful: A Novella

THE MADDOX BROTHERS BOOKS
Beautiful Oblivion
Beautiful Redemption
Beautiful Sacrifice

Apolonia

Red Hill
Among Monsters: A Novella

Happenstance: A Novella Series (Books 1-3)

Sweet Nothing

Beautiful
BURN

JAMIE McGUIRE

Visit my website at www.jamiemcguire.com

Cover Designer: By Hang Le, www.byhangle.com

Editors: Murphy Rae, www.murphyrae.net, and Madison Seidler, www.madisonseidler.com

Interior Designer: Jovana Shirley, Unforeseen Editing, www.unforeseenediting.com

ISBN: 978-1512284133

To Sweet Cheeks,
Amber Cheeks and Sarah Sweet
Thank you for always putting a smile on my face.

CONTENTS

CHAPTER ONE

W HEN I WAS A CHILD, I'd sit for what seemed like an eternity, staring into an open flame. My family thought it was a peculiar pastime, but almost twenty years later, I was gazing at the end of my cigarette, the ashes as long as my finger, the end burning orange as the fire climbed the paper.

The house was crowded, so full of sweaty, stumbling drunks and debauchery that a deep breath wouldn't matter; all the oxygen had been sucked from the room. My bones were saturated with the sounds of the bass drum, yelling, and cackling girls, most too young to buy a can of beer much less be on the verge of puking the six-pack of Mike's Hard Lemonade they'd just consumed.

I sat back in Mother's favorite overstuffed imported chair, taking in the chaos and feeling at home.

Daddy was convinced I was a good girl, so it was easy to be a witness to bad behavior without guilt, even if I occasionally participated.

A pompadoured beauty with glitter lotion and a purple dye job held out a roach—just an inch of magic grass encased in twisted paper—and I gazed into her eyes for less than a second to assess if the joint was laced before accepting. I exhaled toward the ceiling, watching as the smoke wafting above joined the white cloud already hovering the span of vast space that was our gallery, meant for après ski, wine, and sophisticated guests, not the drunken blue-collar locals who were rubbing against paintings and knocking over vases.

I immediately relaxed, letting my head fall back against the sofa cushion. As recreational cannabis goes, Colorado was one of three states that qualified as my top favorite places to be during a holiday. The fact that my parents kept a vacation home in Estes Park made it my number one.

"What's your name?" she asked.

I turned to face her cherubic splendor, unsurprised that she was at a packed party without knowing the host. "Ellie," I said, barely paying attention to her sleepy, red-rimmed eyes.

"Ellie Edson? Are you Ellison's sister?"

I sighed. This wasn't the conversation I felt like having. "I'm Ellison."

Her eyebrows turned in as confusion shadowed her face. "But … Ellison's a dude, right? The guy who owns this house?" She giggled and rested her cheek on her arm. "Are you like … twins or something?"

I leaned back, grinning as she spontaneously ran her fingers through my long, dark hair. One of her arms had been inked with various sizes of black-lined skulls and bright blue roses; the other was a blank canvas.

"No, I'm Ellison, the dude who owns this house."

She giggled loudly at my joke, and then kneeled on the floor in front of my chair. "I'm Paige."

"How long have you lived here?"

"What makes you think I'm a local?" she asked.

She was focused on my every word, the one-sided attraction making me feel a strange combination of exhilaration and tedium. Paige was more than just beautiful; she wore hope the way she carried her sad stories—out in the open, for everyone to see, vulnerable even when her heart had been broken too many times to repair.

I held out the roach. "Your eyes are absent of a lifetime of failed expectations and the guilt of wasting limitless resources."

She giggled. "I don't know what that means."

"Exactly."

"Is that painting of your parents?" she asked, pointing her short, chipped nails at the portrait across the room.

I sighed. "That's them—attempting to buy immortality."

"They don't look so bad. They gave you all of this."

"No, it's still theirs. I'm just borrowing it. People like us learn early to quit giving things away for free."

"People like you?" she asked, amused. "As in, people who own a gazillion-square-foot house?"

"Several of them," I said.

Her eyebrows rose, and her mouth curved up into a sweet grin.

Some might perceive my comment as bragging, but there was purposeful disdain in my voice I knew Paige wouldn't recognize. She was still smiling. I could probably mention my mother had admitted to me during a Xanax binge that she loved my sister Finley more, or how I deliberately totaled the Ferrari my father had bought me for my sixteenth birthday (mostly as an apology that he'd missed it), or even the time my roommate, Kennedy—also an heiress—brought a Ziploc bag full of her miscarriage along on a women's rights march at Berkeley. Paige would still gaze up at me as if I were professing my love for her instead of detailing seven levels of fucked up.

I breathed out a laugh. "You're definitely a local."

"Guilty. Boyfriend?" she asked.

"You get right to the point."

She shrugged, taking a drag and holding her breath for five seconds before hacking out a puff of smoke. "Is that a no?" she asked, still coughing.

"Unequivocally."

She tried to pass the roach back, but I shook my head. She jutted out her glistening bottom lip.

"Disappointed?" I wasn't sure if she wanted a threesome or a drug buddy.

"You just look like you'd be a fun girlfriend."

"You're wrong." I stood up, already bored with the conversation. A glass broke across the room, and a small group tightened around whatever show was happening in the center.

Laughter turned to yelling and chanting. Peter Max's *Better World* was knocked off the wall, shattering the glass. Cheap beer splashed over the fifty-thousand-dollar brush strokes. I pushed my way to the front, seeing two men throwing punches, making an unholy mess of every piece of art around them.

All eyes fell on me, and the spectators quieted, causing the two in the middle to pause. They were all waiting for me to break up the fight, or yell, or maybe cry over the damage, but my gaze fell on the shirtless man covered in tattoos. He watched me, too, his chestnut eyes scanning my tits and legs, and then the room. His adversary had turned his red ball cap backward, bouncing as he circled Tattoos, rolling his fists back and forth in the air like he was in a Bugs Bunny cartoon.

"Maddox, you've proved your point. Let's go," someone said to the tattooed man.

"Fuck you," he replied. He didn't take his eyes off me. "We'll just take it outside."

Red Cap had at least fifty pounds on Maddox. I pulled out five bills from my cleavage and held them above me. "I've got five hundred on Maddox."

People shot their fists into the air, holding bills, shouting bets and winners. Maddox looked at me with a light in his eye I was sure no one had seen in a while—not even him. He'd just barely broken a sweat; his buzzed hair and dark eyes screamed invincible. Most of the men I'd met were all hat and no cowboy, but Maddox didn't have to pretend. He lived it, and had the balls to back it up. The apex of my thighs tightened, and my panties were suddenly soaked. I took another step, forcing my way closer to the middle. I'd never seen him before, but he looked a lot like my next mistake.

The way he moved, I could tell he was extending the fight much longer than needed. Blow after blow—none by the bulky douchebag in the backward red hat—more glass broken, more blood spilled and beer sloshed onto Mother's custom, Italian shag rug.

It became a pattern of Red Cap throwing a missed punch, and Maddox using the opportunity to land his. He was unbelievably fast, precise, and ruthless. I could almost feel his knuckles against my jaw, rattling my teeth, vibrating down my spine.

Too soon, it was over. The tattooed champion stood over his bloody opponent like it was nothing. Someone handed Maddox his T-shirt, and he used it to wipe specks of blood and sweat from his face.

Someone handed me cash, but I didn't pay attention to how much.

"Tyler ... let's get the hell out of here. I don't want to get fired, man. There's about a dozen underage, wasted kids in here."

Maddox kept his gaze on me. "What's the rush?"

"I don't feel like explaining to the superintendent why we got arrested. Do you?"

Maddox pulled the white cotton tee over his head and the defined curves of his chest and abs. When the V just above his belt disappeared behind the shirt, my shoulders slightly sagged in disappointment. I wanted to see more of him. I wanted to see all of him.

His nervous friend gave him a black White Sox ball cap, and he put it on, tugging it low over his eyes.

A friend patted Tyler on the shoulder. "You made me fifty bucks, Maddox. Feels like old times."

"You're welcome, dickhead," he said, his gaze not leaving mine.

The crowd exchanged money, and then, in mass exodus, left for the kitchen where the kegs were tapped and flowing.

Tyler Maddox approached me in a damp and blood-smeared shirt. His eyes and nose were shadowed by his hat. He began to speak, but I gripped a fistful of his shirt and pulled, planting a hard kiss on his mouth. My lips parted, letting his hot tongue slip inside. He reacted like I knew he would—carnal electricity between us—as he gripped the back of my hair, tilting my head up toward him.

I shoved him back, keeping a grip on his shirt. He waited, unsure of what to expect. With a wry smile, I took a step backward, letting my hand slip from the fabric down his arm, and then pulled on his hand. His hands were rough, his fingernails bitten to the quick. I couldn't wait to feel the coarseness against the soft parts of me.

One side of Tyler's mouth pulled up into a grin, and a deep dimple appeared on his left cheek. He was the kind of beautiful you couldn't buy, with his golden-brown eyes and square, scruffy chin—a symphony of perfection only flawless genes could compose. There were plenty of beautiful people in my circles, with access to the best products, stylists, spas, and cosmetic surgeons, but Tyler was real—effortless and raw.

I quickened my pace, climbing the first step backward.

Tyler glanced up from the base of the stairs. "Where are we going?" I didn't answer, but he still followed. I could have been leading him to his death, but I could tell Tyler Maddox was afraid of nothing. "What's up there?" he asked, still climbing.

"Me," I said simply.

He began to move with purpose, his eyes turning from amused to hungry. I twisted the knob of the master bedroom and pushed through, revealing my parents' California king and two dozen pillows.

"Whoa," Tyler said, looking around the room. "This house is nuts. Whoever lives here must make bank. Friends of yours?"

"This is my parents' house."

"You live here?" Tyler asked, pointing to the floor.

"Sometimes."

"Oh, fuck. You're Ellison Edson. Like the *Edson Tech* Edsons?"

"No, I'm just Ellie."

"Your dad is like on Fortune 500, isn't he?"

"Don't really want to talk about my father right now," I said between kisses.

He held me at bay. "Sorry about the painting, and the table ... and the vase. I'll replace them."

I reached down, cupping the hardness behind his jeans. "Stop talking."

Tyler refocused, reaching down to slide his hands between my leggings and bare skin, his fingers knowing the perfect place to pause and explore. I kicked off my boots, humming while his fingertips glided more easily, slick with my desire for him.

The end of the bed touched the backs of my thighs, and I leaned back, yanking Tyler on top of me. I'd kissed dozens of lips before that night, but none of them had felt like they'd been starving for me, and had been for a long time. Every part of my skin Tyler touched seemed purposeful. He was anything but nervous, as practiced as I was at ripping buttons and pulling at fabric.

The second my bra and panties were tossed to the floor, I yanked down his boxer briefs. He kicked them off the end of the bed, and we rolled. I straddled him, both of us panting and smiling. My red lipstick was smeared on his mouth, and my insides tensed, begging for him.

"Where the hell did you come from?" he asked in awe.

I raised an eyebrow, and then looked over at his jeans hanging halfway off the bed. I reached over, searching his pocket with my fingers and grinning when I touched a foil packet. "Slow your roll, Maddox. I haven't come yet."

Three deep lines formed on Tyler's forehead as his eyebrows shot up. He watched me tear the condom package with my teeth, and then his eyes rolled back in his head as I used my mouth to secure it in place.

"Holy shit," he breathed. He lifted his hips as I put his entire length into my mouth and throat. His fingertips raked through my hair and pulled, and I hummed against the latex. He arched his back, sending his tip even deeper.

I climbed up from his lap, straddling him again, gripping his girth and lowering myself slowly, watching the warmth and wetness of my insides overwhelm him. He had done this many times before, but not with me. Tyler looked like the type to take charge, the kind of guy who pleasured his women until they futilely begged him for more. But he couldn't give them more, and that was exactly what I liked about him—aside from the fact that he was insanely hot and knew how to touch my sensitive parts like he was the architect who'd built me.

His fingers dug into my hips, and I could tell he was trying to relax my pace. He wouldn't admit he wanted me to slow down. He was close, but so was I, and some asshole was knocking on the door, calling his name. He wasn't leaving until he'd finished what I'd started.

I was panting hard, moaning every time my ass slammed against his lap, and when Tyler came, he came hard, gripping my ass as he arched his back. He was so deep it hurt, but I circled my hips until I tumbled over the edge. I dug my fingers into his chest, smiling with an open mouth, unable to control the cries ripping from my throat.

Tyler spread my thighs and tensed his ass, pressing into me further. He growled a string of expletives, and then relaxed, exhaling after catching his breath. He looked up at me, sleepy and satisfied. "God damn, woman."

I leaned over, lifting my leg, and then crawled off the bed. He watched me dress as he lay on his side, ignoring the knocking on the door.

"I, uh … I work a lot. I'm on the Alpine Hotshot crew, and—"

"So?" I fastened my bra behind me, and then stepped into my underwear.

Tyler paused, trying to decide what to say next. "So … are those Calvin Kleins?"

I looked down at the extra small men's tighty whities I'd slipped on. Lace, thongs, cheekies … not my thing. "Yeah?"

He chuckled. "So, uh … I won't be able to … you know—"

"Call? That makes two of us."

Tyler stood up and began collecting his clothes while the pounding from the hall began again. "Maddox! You in there?"

"For fuck's sake, Zeke! Hang on!" he said, pulling on his jeans.

He was waiting for me to dress before opening the door, but I'd barely pulled my T-shirt over my head before his friends opened the door.

One of the men, a bit shorter and a lot bulkier, nodded to me, and then—realizing I was half naked—stared at the floor. "You ready or what?"

"I'm ready, Zeke," Tyler said, grinning at me.

Zeke pointed behind him with his thumb. "They're tearing up the place. Want us to help you get them out of here?"

I shook my head. "I have a great cleanup crew."

"I don't think they can clean your couch. There's down feathers all over the floor."

"I'll buy a new one."

Tyler frowned. "Let's put a stop to that shit."

Zeke nodded. "And then we're going."

Tyler winked at me. "Thanks for the, um … pleasant surprise."

"I'd say anytime, but neither of us call."

Tyler breathed out a laugh, looking down, and then back up at me from under his thick lashes. "I guess. See you around, Ellison."

"It's Ellie. And probably not."

He didn't seem fazed. "Good night." He took a step back and closed the door.

I sat on the mess of sheets, blankets, and throw pillows that was my parents' bed. Tyler's condom was hanging halfway off the rim of my mother's wastebasket next to her vanity by the door. Tyler was a terrible shot.

I curled into the fetal position, shedding tears no one would see. Crying, not because I was ashamed, but because I knew no matter how trashed the house would be, or how horribly I'd disrespected my parents' room, they wouldn't be angry. They would forgive me, and pity me. I would forever be their perfect little girl. The louder I screamed, the tighter they'd mash their hands over their ears.

Someone knocked on the door, and I called for them to come in. Standing in the threshold was Paige, looking lonely and desperate.

"Room for one more?" she squeaked.

I pulled back the blanket and sheets. She smiled and then hurried to lie beside me. I wrapped my arms around her and relaxed as she kissed the inside of my wrist.

"You're beautiful," she whispered. "What is it like? To live in a house like this? To live this life?"

I didn't know how to respond, so I said the first thing that came to mind. "Close your eyes."

Paige reached back, wedging her hand between my wet thighs.

"I saw him come downstairs," she said.

"So you decided to come up?"

"I knew he wouldn't stay."

"I didn't need him to."

"I do," she said, "need people to stay. You can pretend I'm him ... if you want."

"I'll pretend you're you," I said, kissing her temple.

Paige relaxed in my arms, settling in while the bass throbbed through the floor. After a few minutes, the music abruptly turned off, and I knew Tyler and his friends were ending the party and kicking everyone out.

Not long after, Paige's breathing evened. I closed my eyes, pulled her closer to me, and sunk into oblivion.

CHAPTER TWO

I WAS JUST MAKING MY WAY to my father's pristine black Audi when the first van arrived. Men and women filed out, their boots crunching against the snow as they carried buckets, vacuums, and boxes of cleaning supplies into the house. Felix, my father's assistant, had already expedited the new sofa.

My parents wouldn't be in Estes Park from Rome for another week, providing plenty of time to get the house back in order. It wasn't the first time Felix had had to hire crews to clean up after a party, and he was very good at making sure nothing was out of place. Since I was seven, Felix had been the peacekeeper and protector of the family, and doubled as my father's bodyguard when necessary. Sometimes Felix had to protect Daddy from me.

"Miss Edson," Felix said, nodding as I approached the drive.

He towered over the Audi, his suit jacket tight around his thick arms. His metal-rimmed glasses were tinted, protecting his eyes from the same sun that reflected off his smooth head. He held a cellphone in his right hand and a clipboard against his chest with his left. No doubt there was a list several pages long of items to be checked off, repairs and orders to be made, all in an effort to provide Daddy with the life he paid Felix to create.

"Thank you, Felix," I said.

Once I passed, he swept the driver side door open, allowing me to slide inside. The car was warm, already running, making my fur vest and tall boots feel more like overkill than appropriate winter attire.

"All set, miss?" Felix asked. I nodded, and he shut the door.

I gripped the steering wheel and sighed. I hadn't started a car in seven years—since my driving test. I was sitting inside a vehicle I didn't own, in front of a house I didn't own, on land I didn't own … wearing clothes my parents had bought. They owned me, and I let them because it was convenient. Not that I hadn't tried to buck the system in high school, but arguing meant I wasn't appreciative, whether or not I'd asked for the things I had.

I grit my teeth and put the car into drive. My bitter inner monologue was constant because I couldn't say aloud what I was really thinking or feeling. Complaining was offensive to my father and everyone else. I had nothing to complain about. I was the girl with everything. The more money and material things my parents threw at me, the bigger the void became. But I couldn't tell them that; I couldn't tell anyone. To have everything and feel nothing was the worst kind of selfishness.

I pulled into the driveway, motoring slowly for a full mile until I reached the entrance of my parents' chateau. At the press of a button, the copper gate obeyed, swinging toward me, slow and steady. My cell phone buzzed, and a picture of Finley appeared on my screen, her lips pursed in full duck face. She was looking up to fully display her turquoise eyes and thick, authentic mink lash extensions.

I pressed the phone button on the steering wheel, pulling forward through the open gate. "Hey, Fin."

Finley's voice surrounded me. "Tired, Elliebee?"

"A little."

"Good. I hope you feel like shit, you spoiled bitch. Why didn't you tell me you were having a party last night?"

"Uh, because you're in Rio?"

"So?"

"I didn't figure you'd want to waste your Brazilian wax on a random keg party in the mountains with the locals."

"Is it cold?"

"Definitely not bikini weather."

"Our hot tub has determined that is a lie. Did you get laid?" She had already forgotten about the mild offense and settled into sister mode.

Finley Edson was the eldest daughter of Edson Tech, and on a direct path to rule with an iron fist that happened to have perfectly manicured nails. We were heiresses, but unlike me, Finley embraced it. Finley was two years older, but she was my best friend, the only one left from our childhood who I could still stomach. The rest had become vapid clones of their mothers.

"I don't kiss and tell," I said, turning toward downtown.

"Yes, you do. Was it the local you were telling me about?"

"Paige? No. She's sweet. Too fucked up for me to use."

"I'm not sure I believe that person exists."

"She does, and her name is Paige."

"You're getting soft in your old age, Ellie. If we were still at Berkeley, you'd have been all over that just to break her heart. So who was it?"

I cringed at her description, but only because she was right. I'd been the source of pain for most of the people I'd come into contact with, mostly because I didn't care, but a small part of me enjoyed the temporary distraction from my own pain.

"Do you always have to remind me of my dysfunction?"

"Yes. Don't change the subject."

"He's an Interagency Hotshot guy."

"A firefighter? Ick."

"No, not ick. He's the elite. They deploy them like soldiers to the frontline."

"That's kind of hot," she conceded.

"He was refreshing … let me wipe him off and send him on his way without blinking an eye. And he was hot. So, *so* hot. Maybe a ten."

"A ten? Like a solid ten, or barely a ten?"

"Mid-ten. He missed the trashcan when he tossed the condom, but he can fight. Like *really* fight. He beat a guy's ass twice his size in the middle of the gallery last night. He's built like David Beckham. Maybe a little thicker. He's covered in tattoos, and he smells like Marlboro Reds and copper."

"Copper?"

"He had the other guy's blood splattered on his clothes."

"You let them fight in the gallery last night? Was anything broken?"

"The better question is what didn't get broken."

"Ellie." Her tone turned serious. "Mother is going to flip."

"Do not parent me from Brazil. I already have two absentee parents. I don't need you."

"Fine, it's your funeral. Or rather, your trust fund's funeral. I'm intrigued about the boy. I might get on a plane and cover up my wax and pedi with leggings and boots. Oh." She paused. "Marco? I need flannel shirts!"

"Don't bring Marco," I warned.

"He comes with me everywhere. His speaking Portuguese has made the trip here a breeze."

"He's not coming here. You're different when he's around."

"What? Like helpless?" Finley was teasing, but we both knew she was whinier and needier when her ladysitter was around. Marco was hired to be more than an assistant. He didn't just carry bags and keep her schedule; he was also her buyer, stylist, barista, bartender, nurse, waiter, designer, and constant travel companion.

"I hate Finley and Marco. I only like Finley."

"Correction: you *love* Finley. I'm bringing Marco."

"Then he can't stay here."

I could hear her pouting through the speakers. "I'll get him a hotel room. If I need something, I can call."

"Finley, Jesus Christ." I pulled a stale pack of cigarettes out of my father's console and dug around for a lighter. I flipped up the silver cap and pressed, promptly taking a drag.

"Where are you going?" she asked, frustrated.

"Just getting out of the way while the cleaning crew fixes Ground Zero."

"It's really that bad? And you're lecturing me about Marco?" she asked.

"Hold on." I focused long enough to parallel park, and then turned off the car, finishing my cigarette.

"You there?" Finley asked.

"Yeah," I said, blowing out a puff of smoke. The white cloud slipped out through the top of the window I'd cracked just enough that I could tell my father I'd tried.

"You've got to stop this shit, Ellie. Everyone has a limit."

"That's what I'm counting on," I said, taking one last drag before pushing the butt through the window. I stepped out, and then ground the cherry of the cigarette with the heel of my boot.

I bent over to pick it up and then tossed it into the nearest trashcan.

"You're lucky," a voice behind me said.

I turned around to see Tyler leaning against the brick veneer of an automotive parts store with his arms crossed, a US Forestry truck parked not far away.

"Excuse me?" I asked.

"If you hadn't picked up that cigarette butt, I might have had to arrest you."

"Someone should inform you that you're not a cop."

"I'm friends with a few."

"How very cool for you."

"How's the house?"

"Bashed the fuck in. Good to see you," I said, turning on my heels.

I heard his footsteps chasing after me. "I was just … kidding," he said, finally at my side. He held up a black pack of Marlboros.

"What the hell is that?" I asked.

"A peace offering?"

"You're offering me cancer?"

He chuckled and stuffed the pack into the side pocket of his standard issue blue coat. "Where are you headed?"

I stopped and turned to him, sighing. "You're a douchebag."

He blinked once, and then those beautiful creases in his forehead formed, and a smile spread across his face, revealing most of his perfectly white teeth. "What's your point?"

"My point is you were supposed to fuck me and leave me alone."

"Okay?"

He watched me for a while with a disgusted look on his face. His boots were worn but shined, his blue cargo pants pressed but wrinkled from half a day's wear, his shirt faded. Tyler was a hard worker and took pride in his job. He had probably never missed a day of work, but that was where his ability for commitment ended. Tyler Maddox had no doubt broken as many hearts as I had. He was exactly what I deserved, even though I had no intention of going anywhere near him.

"You're talking to me. You said you wouldn't."

Tyler shoved his hands in his pants pockets and shrugged, smiling at me like he'd never had a one-night stand. That kind of charm couldn't be learned. "I said I wouldn't call."

I crossed my arms and narrowed my eyes, looking up at him. Jesus, he was tall. "I have no interest in you."

His dimple appeared, making my thighs tighten. "It didn't seem that way last night."

"That was last night. I'm sober now."

He made a face. "Ouch."

"Run along," I said.

He squared his shoulders. "Do I seem like the running type to you?"

"Only when it comes to women, which is why I fucked you."

He frowned. "Are you like … off your meds or something?"

"Yes. Yes, I am. Emotional trauma, past baggage, you name it. Keep talking to me and I might be your next overly attached girlfriend. Does that sound like a good time to you?"

"Okay, Ellie," he said, holding up his hands. "I get it. I'll pretend it never happened."

"Thanks," I said.

"But it was pretty fucking amazing, and I wouldn't mind a repeat."

"Can't we just be friends-with-benefits without being friends?"

He mulled over my words. "You're kind of a mean bitch. It's strangely appealing."

"Go away."

"I'm going."

"Don't come back."

"It never happened," he said, opening the passenger door to his truck. He was the opposite of offended, which offended me. Most people were more sensitive to my abuse than that.

Zeke came out, pausing when he saw me. He waved, and then jogged around the front to the driver side. They traded a short conversation, and then Zeke started up the engine.

"Who's that?"

I turned to see Sterling standing behind me. He looked like a banking executive, trying his best to emulate his father, the CEO of Aerostraus Corp. He was wearing a dark wool trench coat, a scarf, a three-thousand-dollar watch, and to offset his stuffy look, a blue button-down with no tie—top button undone. He had managed to walk down the snowy sidewalk without getting a single speck of moisture on his Italian boots.

"Kiss me," I said.

"Ew," he said, horrified. "No."

"Kiss me, asshole. Right now. A good one. You owe me."

Sterling grabbed each side of my face and planted his mouth on mine, slobbering all over me, but making the scene I'd wanted.

The truck passed by, and once it sounded far enough away, I pushed Sterling back.

He wiped his mouth, disgusted. "Why did I have to do that?"

"To get rid of a guy."

"Stalker or mooch?" Sterling asked, smoothing his dark hair to the side.

"Neither. Just making sure."

"Are we still doing brunch?" he asked. He wiped his mouth again, looking mildly disgusted.

"Yes," I said, pulling him toward Winona's Café.

We chose a table by the window, and Sterling immediately checked the menu. He ran his fingers over each line, paying attention to every ingredient. He wasn't allergic; he was a snob.

I rolled my eyes. "Why? We eat here all the time."

"I haven't been here in three months. They might have something new on the menu."

"You know they never do."

"Shut up. I'm reading."

I smiled, checking my phone while he searched the decade-old menu. Sterling's family had a home down the road from ours, one of many around the country, left empty most of the year. I knew Sterling was my people when I saw him getting drunk, fourteen and alone, next to a tree beside our property line. He was just another trust fund baby—lamenting how hard life was with millions at his disposal but without an attentive family to anchor him to the real world.

Sterling had invested his entire worth in his father's opinion of his success on any given day, and that made my friend somewhat moody. Sterling's father, Jameson Wellington, changed his mind about his son's significance regularly, depending on the stocks, the attitude of the board of directors, and if his wife was pissing him off that day.

"How did the party go?" Sterling asked without looking up.

"Oh. I meant to invite you. It was sort of impromptu."

"I heard it was a bunch of locals."

"Who else would I invite?"

"Me?"

"Finley isn't home."

Sterling glanced up at me for just a few seconds, and then returned his gaze to the menu. He wasn't reading it anymore.

"Don't tell her about the kiss. I just did it because I owed you one."

"I won't. She'd hate me because whether she admits it or not ... she loves you."

"She does?"

I leaned in, annoyed. "You know she does."

He seemed to relax.

"I invite you to parties all the time. I needed to ... I needed something..."

"Uncomplicated?"

I pointed at him. "Exactly."

"Ellison?"

"Yeah?"

"You're a terrible kisser. You're probably doing that guy a favor."

I glared at him. "Order your eggs-fucking-Benedict and shut your hole. I'm an excellent kisser. That is precisely why I had to scare that guy off with your slobber box."

"Who are you fooling? You didn't just kiss that guy."

The waitress approached, wearing an olive and cream striped apron and a smile. "Hi, Ellie."

"Chelsea, if you had to guess what Sterling was going to order—"

"Eggs Benedict," Chelsea said without hesitation.

"Really?" Sterling asked, genuinely forlorn. "Am I that predictable?"

"Sorry," Chelsea said, sheepish.

I sat back, handing Chelsea my menu. "I'm not judging you. Those are some damn good eggs."

"Same?" she asked.

"No, I'll have the Southwest omelet and some OJ. Do you have vodka? A screwdriver sounds great right about now."

Chelsea wrinkled her nose. "It's ten thirty in the morning."

I stared at her, expectant.

"No," Chelsea said. "We don't sell liquor here."

Sterling held up two fingers, ordering orange juice for himself.

Chelsea walked away, and I pressed my lips together, trying to keep from looking too concerned. "You look tired, Sterling."

"It's been a long week."

I smiled. "But you're here now."

"Finley's not."

"Sterling," I warned. "She's not changing her mind. She loves you more than she loves anyone else."

"Except you."

"Of course except me. But she loves you. She just can't be with you until she takes over Edson."

His face fell, and his eyes lost focus.

"I'm sorry," I said, reaching across the table to touch his arm. "We should have picked a place that has vodka."

My mouth suddenly felt dry. Wanting a drink and realizing it wasn't immediately available created a subtle pang of panic.

Sterling pulled away. "Careful, Ellie. You're beginning to sound like me."

The door chimed, and a family of four walked in, already arguing about where to sit. It was tourist season, and although Sterling and I could be considered tourists, we'd both had homes there for more than eight years. Long enough to be annoyed by the non-resident tourists. We were what the locals called part-time families, and most of the time, if we shared the name of our neighborhood, they didn't even have to ask. Only one of our neighbors was a full-time family, and that was only because they were from Arkansas and moving to Estes Park was a dream not a vacation.

The two waitresses scurried between tables that were filling by the minute. Chelsea's sneakers occasionally squeaked on the apricot and white tiled floor while she collected orders and rushed to the back through the swinging doors of the kitchen. She would reappear with a smile, stopping on her way back to fill large plastic glasses at the drink station behind the bar lined with stools for the snowboarders who frequented the café.

Body heat filled the room, and I noticed everyone peeling off layers. Chelsea was working up a sweat while tourists walked on the other side of the wall of windows bundled up in coats, scarves, knit hats, and gloves. The door would open, offering a blast of cool air, and Chelsea let everyone know when she would walk through a nice breeze with her sweet sigh.

Snow had just begun to fall in delicate pieces for the fourth day in a row. The resort was happy, and business was booming, but there was a storm coming, and I worried about Finley trying to make it in.

"How's Fin?" Sterling asked, seemingly reading my mind.

"She's in Rio. I think she's coming here."

"Oh?" Sterling wiped his nose with his knuckle and sniffed, a telltale sign that he was attempting to be nonchalant.

"You're so far inside the friend zone, Sterling. Time to give up."

He looked appalled. "I haven't tried to get her back in a long time."

"If a month ago is considered a long time."

He frowned. "I'm too tired for Ellie the Bitch. Can you just try to be nice today?"

I jutted out my lip. "Aw, is Sterling on his period?"

He wasn't amused. "I'm going to leave you here, alone at this table."

"Don't threaten me with a good time," I said.

"And leave plenty of room for fire boy to join you."

"What?" I asked, turning to see Tyler Maddox walk in with Zeke and a few more of his hotshot crew. I scooted down in my chair. "Shit," I hissed. I sunk down in my seat. In my family, uncomfortable situations required something a lot stronger than orange juice, and the urge to go home and raid the liquor cabinet became overwhelming.

A warm pair of lips touched my cheek, and Tyler pulled a seat to the table. "Hi, baby. Did you miss me?"

"Are you mental? Do you hear voices?" I said, incensed.

"Just came in for lunch before we head back," Tyler said, directing his crew to sit.

Zeke sat on the other side of me, looking uncomfortable. "We can find another table."

"No," Tyler said. "We can't. Who's your friend?" he asked, motioning to Sterling.

"Fuck," I murmured. I'd meant to run Tyler off. Instead, he'd gotten jealous and saw Sterling as competition he could easily conquer.

Sterling held out his hand, but I slapped it away.

"That was some kiss earlier," Tyler said. "Makes me reminisce about the time she kissed me like that. Last night seems so long ago."

My face twisted into disgust. "Really? You're going there."

"I did, yeah," Tyler said, smug.

"Sterling doesn't care that I took advantage of you in my parents' bed last night."

"That was your parents' bed?" Tyler asked. "Had you already used yours once?"

"As a matter of fact," I began.

Zeke squirmed. "Tyler, c'mon, man. Let's just find another table."

Tyler glowered at Sterling, determined. "I like this one."

Sterling cleared his throat, unsure how to process the situation. "What do you like about it ... exactly?"

Tyler didn't take his eyes off mine. "Your friend."

I leaned in. "If you don't find another place to feed that hole in your face, I'm going to stand up right now and announce to everyone that you have a tiny penis."

He wasn't fazed. "I can whip it out and prove you wrong."

"I'll start screaming at you for giving me chlamydia. You work here. This is a tight-knit town. Stuff like that gets around."

He shrugged. "You live here, too."

"Part-time. And I don't give two shits what the people here think of me."

Chelsea brought Sterling's plate and placed it in front of him, and then mine, along with our drinks.

"We're ready to order," Tyler said.

I placed my palm against his face, my face falling, tears filling my eyes. "It's going to be okay, Tyler. The dripping will stop after a couple of rounds of antibiotics, and the itching will go away."

Chelsea made a face, looked at Tyler in disgust, and then stumbled over her next words. "I'll, um ... be ... I'll be right back."

Tyler looked at me, mouth hanging open.

Zeke chuckled. "She warned you."

Sterling poked around on his plate, tuning us out.

Tyler glanced back at Chelsea, who was whispering to the other waitress and the cook. They were looking at our table, repulsed. "Wow. You just sunk my battleship, Ellie."

I used my fork to cut into my omelet and took a bite, quite pleased with myself.

"Maybe I just want to be friends," Tyler said.

"Guys like you can't just be friends with someone who owns a vagina," I said.

Zeke nodded. "She has a point."

Tyler stood, gesturing for his crew to stand with him. They did, their chairs whining against the tile. "We got rid of all the idiots trashing your house last night, and this is the thanks I get?"

I smiled up at him. "Under the douchebag façade, you're actually a nice guy. I was drunk last night, so my radar was a little off, but I can smell you from a mile away. I don't want to be your friend. I don't want to reminisce about that one-night stand we had that one time. I don't have time for nice guys, Tyler, and I can't imagine a more powerfully dirty hell than to be forced to spend time with you sober."

He nodded to Sterling. "He looks like a nice guy to me."

The hair on the back of my neck stood on end. I was being the meanest I knew how, and Tyler was acting like we were trading pleasantries. "Sterling is a self-loathing, wretched piece of shit."

"She's right," Sterling said casually. "I am."

Tyler's team traded glances, and then Tyler watched me for a long time. "Enjoy your eggs."

"Will do," I said, making sure not to watch him leave.

Sterling waited a second or two before leaning in. "You must like him. I've never seen you so brutal."

I waved him away. "He might be an overconfident prick, but he's not a bad guy. He shouldn't get mixed up with us."

"True," Sterling said, shoveling another bite into his mouth. He patted his mouth with his napkin, and then looked at me from under his manicured brows. "Since when are you accountable?"

"Oh, honey … I hope your day is as pleasant as you are."

He chuckled quietly, and then took another bite.

CHAPTER THREE

Finley ruffled her mink coat and tossed her Chopard Grey glasses on the marble entry table. Finley wasn't careless; she just wanted everyone to know that the six hundred dollars she'd spent to shield her eyes from the sun didn't concern her—never mind they would likely be knocked off a leased yacht into the South China Sea the next week.

She turned her diamond nose ring one-quarter turn counter-clockwise, and then popped a mint into her mouth. "I'm going to have to charter from now on. Even first-class has become filthy. And the airports … *ugh*."

Marco, filling out his charcoal Henley like a Banana Republic model, set their luggage down in the foyer, greeting Maricela and José in Portuguese when they came to collect the bags.

"They speak Spanish, Marco," I deadpanned.

Marco took off his glasses, grinning at me like he knew a story or five he would tell me later, in front of Finley, when we were all drunk. "It's close enough."

I glared at Finley. "You brought him," I said in an accusatory voice.

"He's staying in a hotel," Finley said, barely noticing that Marco was removing her coat. He bent down to untie her fluffy snow boots.

I cringed. "Stop. Marco, stop. Right now."

Marco slipped off her second boot and set them perfectly side by side, standing up and waiting with want in his eyes—not the sort of desire a woman my age would want an exotic, gorgeous man like Marco to have. He was waiting to oblige me, please me, take care of any need I had, and not for me—for Finley. He didn't simply take pride in indulging his employer and anyone who surrounded her—it was his obsession. Appeasing Finley and her entourage at once was his specialty, and he loved to show off his talents.

"Could I just," he began, reaching for her bags.

"No, no you can't," I said, slapping his hands away. "Take your luggage and find your hotel. Finley will be able to breathe for herself this week."

Marco fidgeted, unsure how to grant my demand.

Finley smiled at him with feigned patience. "It's fine, Marco. Go on. Enjoy your vacation."

He nodded a few times, both confident and unsure, clearly unsettled at leaving Finley to her own devices for more than a few minutes.

Marco kissed her hand. "Should you need anything, Miss Edson, I'll be here within ten minutes."

She pulled away slowly, waving him away, indifferent to his charm.

Marco looked borderline devastated as he collected his baggage and closed the door behind him.

I sighed. "That shit is getting out of hand."

She smirked, walking the few steps to hug me tight. "You're just jealous."

I squeezed her once, and then pulled away. "Does he wipe your ass? Only then would I be jealous."

Finley laughed, pulling off her gloves and walking down the hall to the piano room. She tossed them on the chaise and sat, relaxing back and crossing her socked feet. Her golden hair fell in soft waves just past her shoulders, shiny and perfect like it should be after the money she'd spent to keep it that way. "Not that he hasn't tried, my love. You're right, he would probably breathe for me if he could."

"Isn't that annoying?"

"Not really. I worry about nothing except what I have to worry about."

"When do you go back to work? Is Daddy's board still bitching about your promotion?"

She sighed. "Soon, and yes. How's Winterland?"

I looked out the window. It wasn't snowing, but the wind was blowing icy globs from the tree branches. "I think I'll be ready for the sea."

She watched me as her red lips pulled to the side. "You don't look ready."

I picked the navy-blue polish off my thumbnail. "I feel numb. We've tanned on every beach. Skied every resort from Estes to the Alps."

"You're bored?" Finley asked, amused.

"Displaced."

Finley rolled her eyes, disgusted. "Don't do that, Ellison. Don't become a goddamned cliché. The rich girl who is bored with life, surrounded by everyone and no one, feeling all alone."

"Don't patronize me. I recall you going through a phase."

"I shopped and spent a month with you in Barbados. I didn't fuck my way through it. You've always enjoyed your pharmaceuticals—you get that from Mother—but for Christ's sake, Ellie. Pick a hobby. Get a boyfriend—or girlfriend. Find a cause. Find *God*. I don't give a fuck, but don't whine about having too much money and too many options."

I wasn't sure what expression was on my face, but it might have mirrored Finley's. I covered my eyes, and then sat down on the sofa, leaning back. "Fuck, you're right. I'm Sterling."

"You're not that bad, but you're one stint in rehab away. You're not bored, you're empty. Stop trying to fill up with coke and hash. You know that shit doesn't work."

I narrowed my eyes at her. "The fuck, Finley. When did you start adulting? You have a ladysitter who stirs your coffee, and you're coaching me on life choices?"

She stood up, walked the few feet to the sofa, and collapsed next to me, hooking her legs over my lap. She interlaced her fingers between mine. "Betsy OD'd. I don't want that to be you."

I sat up. "Betsy March?"

Finley nodded, rubbing my palm with her thumb. "Nine months ago, she was where you are. We all saw it."

"I didn't."

"You've been MIA, Ellie. No one sees you anymore. Except maybe Sterling."

"We're going to Sanya next week."

"I haven't seen you in six months. Betsy was empty. I don't want to hear about you being found lying in your own excrement on the floor. This is our sister talk. You're fucking up. You need to man up and handle it."

"Mandle it?" I said, smiling brightly.

Finley was trying to keep it light, but she quickly wiped her eye. I reached for her. "Fin. I'm fine."

She nodded. "I know. We're all fine until we're not."

"Come on. You've been traveling all day. We'll run you a hot bath, relax, and order in."

She smiled at me. "No wonder you're bored. That sounds dreadful."

"Fine, take a hot shower, and then we'll go to dinner and find a bar with a bunch of hot locals."

She grinned. "Much better."

The Grove was busy but not packed. Odd for ski season, but I counted us lucky. Finley was dividing her time between her Kir Royale and the surrounding tables, relishing in the curious attention she was getting simply for being beautiful.

"I've always liked the men here. They're a different kind of sexy than what we're used to. Gruff. I'm liking the beards."

"Most of them aren't actually from here."

She shrugged. "Neither are we." Her phone buzzed, and she tapped a quick reply, annoyed with whoever had sent the message.

"Mother?"

Finley shook her head. "Marco's just checking in."

I leaned in, my nearly exposed breasts pressing against the table. Finley noticed, but only allowed them to distract her for a moment.

"Is he in love with you?" I asked.

"I don't know. Probably. Where did you get that top? It makes your tiny tits look freakishly perky."

"My tits are not tiny."

"Please," Finley said as the waiter dropped off our edamame. "You're barely a B-cup."

"Not everyone wants to surgically insert double-Ds, Fin."

She looked up at the waiter. He began to speak, but she cut him off. "Yes, I want another. No, there is nothing else you can get for us right now. Yes, the edamame is superb. Thank you."

He nodded and left for the kitchen.

"He's going to spit in our food," I said, watching him disappear behind a swinging door.

She breathed out a laugh. "I wasn't rude. I just made his drive-by efficient." Her eyes lit up, and she stood, embracing Sterling. "Hello, my love!"

Sterling kissed her cheek, and then again square on the mouth. She didn't flinch.

He looked into her eyes, shaking his head and smiling. "Fin. You're beautiful."

She smiled. "You're right."

Sterling held the back of Finley's chair until she sat, and then he helped push her forward. I turned my face as he leaned down, allowing him to peck my cheek.

"Disclaimer ... I kissed your sister," Sterling said, sitting down next to Finley.

She glanced at him, and then at me. "What's he babbling about?"

"I kind of forced him to kiss me yesterday," I said, already feeling Finley's silent wrath. She didn't want Sterling this second, but he belonged to her. "To get rid of the firefighter."

Finley's eyebrows rose, and she looked to Sterling for confirmation. They were an odd pair, between them wearing clothes and accessories that cost more than the average home, but both emotionally and morally bankrupt. Finley might have been able to talk me out of a spiral, but she had a pocket full of people and a closet full of things: all expendable. Sterling loved Finley, but would never beg for her, and preferred to wallow in infinite misery than admit defeat and try to love someone else. We were friends because less than one percent of the world's population could identify with the sorrow of having too much money and too many opportunities—with the boredom of total freedom of monetary limitations.

We could depend on each other to neither expect anything but time, nor hope that we'd be invited on the next paid vacation. Our friendships would never be more about connections than inside jokes or late night talks. We knew if we were to ever bitch about the throes of money, it was not because we were hinting at needing any. We had nothing in common but the fact that we had one more thing in common than we did with everyone else.

"You really kissed her?" Finley asked Sterling.

He nodded, realizing too late his mistake. He was hoping for jealousy. Finley's anger had always been a slow boil, and she was just beginning to simmer.

"Fin," I began.

"Shush. You don't get to talk."

I sat back in my seat, hoping the night didn't get any more awkward.

We ate our seabass and veal, buffalo ricotta, and chicory. We drank far too many Kir Royales that somehow turned into rounds of Irish whiskey, and then after giving the waiter the largest tip he'd ever seen, we headed out into the cold to light cigarettes and breathe puffs of white into the air.

Finley seemed to have forgiven us both, giggling against Sterling's chest at my jokes, but I knew better. Sterling pulled her in, taking any chance to hold her that she would allow. I guided them down the alley to Turk's, the local dive bar with a back entrance, hard to find on purpose.

"I want to see your hotshot," Finley said, drunk and silly.

"He'll probably be here. I've seen him here before. Most of the locals hang out at Turk's."

We walked in, removing our coats and gloves, and Paige waved to me from the bar. I let her hug me and guide us to a table in the corner. Tyler Maddox was present as expected and had a pitcher of beer to himself, a cigarette tucked behind his ear.

"Holy fuck," Finley said not so quietly into my ear.

Tyler pretended not to hear as he stood, shaking Sterling's hand and sweeping his own toward the empty chairs, including his. Zeke and another man stood until we sat, and then waited as Tyler found an extra seat to pull to our table.

Paige leaned into my ear. "He was just talking about you."

"I bet he was," I said.

Finley introduced herself to Tyler first, and then Zeke. The third man shook her hand when she extended it.

"Daniel Ramos," he said.

"Otherwise known as Sugar," Tyler said with a smirk.

Finley giggled. She was immediately enamored with Tyler, and Sterling noticed. He transitioned too easily from laughter and affection to sitting motionless between the love of his life and Paige.

Paige rested her chin on her hand, smiling at Sugar. "It's just so predictable."

"What is?" he asked.

"All the transplants are from California."

"I didn't come here meaning to stay for six seasons," he said.

Paige's purple pompadour glowed in the neon lights of the bar. "Then why did you?"

"I came here for a girl."

Zeke slapped him on the shoulder. "Isn't Sugar sweet?"

Sugar shrugged away from him.

"And where is she?" Paige asked, attempting her best flirtatious smile.

"Not here," Sugar said, leaning toward her.

"Is there no waitress tonight?" Finley said, annoyed. It was then that I saw it, the truth behind the flash of anger in her eyes. She hadn't forgiven me and definitely not Sterling. She was going to flirt with the hotshot I'd mentioned to punish us both.

Tyler stood up, heading to the bar. "I got it."

I listened to Finley and Sterling chat for a while, at the same time trying not to eavesdrop on Zeke and Sugar. Sugar was complaining about a girl, and then Zeke mentioned another Maddox.

"Tyler has a brother?" I asked.

"Four of them," Zeke said.

"Can you imagine five Tylers running around?" I teased.

"I don't have to," Zeke said. "I've seen it in real life, and it's fucking scary."

I shook my head. "Their poor mother. I would kill myself."

Zeke shifted in his chair. "She passed away when they were little."

I put my head in my hands, looking down. "*Fuck*. That's terrible. I'm sorry," I said, glad Tyler wasn't around to see me stick my foot so far into my mouth.

"It's okay," Zeke said. "You didn't know."

Tyler returned with a tray of shots and passed them around. He held up his glass.

"To good friends and beautiful women," Tyler said. We held up our glasses, almost appreciative of his sweet toast. Then he added, "Sucking my dick." His friends laughed, and we shook our heads, but everyone tossed back the whiskey.

Tyler stood to get another round, and Paige leaned in toward Sugar. "What the hell was that? Why is he acting like a douchebag all of a sudden?"

Sugar glanced at Finley from under his lashes. "Sisters are complicated."

Tyler sat back down in his seat, carefully lowering the tray to the table.

"What is that one?" Finley asked, touching Tyler's arm.

Sugar made a face. "Guess it didn't work."

Paige turned to me. "Is he being an asshole to run your sister off?"

"I'm not sure," I said, watching him watch me.

He returned his attention to Finley and turned his wrist, allowing her to examine the arrow just above his elbow. "That would be Taylor's choice."

"Your girlfriend?" Finley asked.

Tyler and Zeke laughed.

"No," Tyler said. "Taylor is my brother."

"Taylor and Tyler. That's adorable," Finley said, keeping her fingers on his arm.

"Apparently there are three more," I said.

Finley turned her attention to me, wondering how I knew Tyler's personal business. I pointed to Zeke, and she smiled, continuing to brush Tyler's arm. "Are we talking five of you?" she asked. "Is that how you learned to fight?"

"Oh," Tyler said, looking suddenly uncomfortable. "You heard about that."

"Is it?"

"Mostly."

"Have you ever fought over a girl?" she asked.

I was beginning to feel sorry for her. Finley was trying so hard to make Sterling and me jealous that she was looking like quite the desperate tourist girl.

"No," Tyler said. "Never."

"I don't believe it. Surely, at least once, more than one of you has been attracted to the same girl?" Finley asked.

Tyler shifted in his seat. "None of us have ever traded blows over something like that. It helps that we're attracted to completely different types. Most of us, anyway."

"What is your type? Blonde? Rich? Nympho?" Finley asked, leaning in.

I cringed. "Fin…"

Sterling stood. "I think I'll call it a night."

"No," Finley whined, reaching for him. "Don't be silly. We just got here."

Sterling tossed a few large bills on the table that would easily cover everyone's drinks and more, and headed for the door. Finley frowned but followed him.

Tyler watched me for a few seconds, and then leaned in with his elbow on the table. "Are you going, too?"

I lifted my shot and took a gulp, shaking my head. "She'll be back. He won't."

"How do you know?" he asked.

"We've been friends for a long time."

Zeke laughed behind his hand, trying to look everywhere but at me.

I raised an eyebrow. "Something's funny?"

He cleared his throat, sitting up a bit taller. "Nothin'. You're just an odd trio. Is he with her? She's stayin' with you?" He scratched his five o'clock shadow, waiting for me to answer.

"She's my sister. Do you guys ever work?" I asked. "All I see is you partying, fucking, and driving around the company car."

Tyler ordered another round for the table. "It's a company truck. And yes, we work our asses off. It's just been slow. We work for the city in off-season."

Sugar raised his glass to Tyler. "Indeed we do. Saved this town more than once."

I held my glass high. "To fighting fires or whatever!"

"Fight fires or *whatever*?" Tyler said, sounding offended.

I laughed once. "Oh, please. You chose the job. It's not like everyone is obligated to worship you for it."

"Wow, okay," Tyler said, standing. He gripped the back of his chair, the muscles in his forearm tensing below the hem of his Henley sleeve. He adjusted the worn, braided leather bracelets on his right wrist, his nails uneven and his knuckles thick from him cracking them like he'd done twice since Paige had led us to their table. I wanted those fingers inside me, his forearm tensing while he gripped my hips. I wanted something that hadn't occurred to me before—a repeat.

"Easy, Maddox," Zeke said. "She's not wrong."

"Oh, she's wrong. She's all kinds of wrong."

I winked at Zeke. "What are you doing after this?"

Zeke looked around and then pointed to his chest. "Me?"

"Yes. The flannel shirt is doing it for me. I'm loving the lumbersexual thing you've got going on."

Zeke chuckled, and then held his fist up to his mouth, choking on his own spit when he realized I was serious.

Tyler's chair fell forward, propped against the table when he shoved it away from him before walking to the bar. He leaned on the bar with his elbow, chatting with the bartender, Annie. She cackled and shook her head, batting her eyes like Tyler needed.

"I don't know what's going on between you two," Zeke said. "But don't put me in the middle of it."

"Wise man," Sugar said, slapping Zeke on the shoulder.

"Fine," I said, turning to Paige. "What are you doing later?"

"You?" she said with a wicked smile. She didn't mind being plan B, or even plan C.

I smiled. "Good answer."

Zeke's chin lifted, staring at someone tall behind me.

"Hey, Todd. I thought you weren't allowed in here anymore?" Zeke asked.

Todd shifted his weight from one foot to the other, sporting a yellowing splotch on his cheekbone. "Maddox has been kicked out of here more times than I have. Yet you're here with him."

Zeke nodded. "You're right. I don't know why I keep doing this to myself."

Sugar patted his friend on the back. "We should go."

Todd leaned down, touching his temple to mine. I was more curious than offended, so I waited, unmoving.

Sugar leaned forward, waiting to pounce. His navy-blue button-down hid the monster beneath. He was a brick wall, maybe even more than Tyler, and just as tall. They both had a buzz cut, but Sugar was less unleashed bull dog, and more trained soldier.

"Maybe we'll join you," Todd said, turning to look at me. He smiled, far too close to my face, but I didn't recoil. He was reckless,

and I needed to be in the front row to witness whatever happened
next.

"Todd," Sugar warned, "Maddox's been drinking."

"So have I," Todd said, smiling at me. "What's your name,
beautiful?"

"That's it," I said, mirroring his expression. "That's my name."

"Beautiful?" he asked, amused.

"Mercer," Tyler said, his voice booming over the music. He
stood close behind Todd, taunting him with the lack of personal
space he offered.

Sugar stood up. "We're leaving, Maddox."

One side of Tyler's mouth turned up, but he didn't take his
eyes away from Todd's. "Not with all these pretty girls just getting
here."

Paige touched my hand and I squeezed, not because I was
afraid, but because the spike in testosterone was making my lady
parts cry out in the best kind of pain.

Zeke stood up, too, and the bartenders took notice.

Todd and Tyler stared each other down for a solid twenty
seconds until Todd finally spoke. "I'm curious."

"I'm sure I can answer," Tyler said.

"If you're worth a fuck without your brother around."

Tyler's eyes sparked with excitement. "Don't just get my hopes
up, Mercer. Swing or shut the fuck up."

Without thinking, I stood between them, looking up. "Why do
guys do that? Why do they call each other by their last names? Is
saying the first name a pussy thing to do? Is it too intimate?"

Sugar reached out for me. "C'mere, Ellie."

My face twisted. "They're not going to do anything."

"We're not?" Todd asked, unsure if he should be insulted or
relieved.

I touched his shoulders, reaching up on the balls of my feet to
softly kiss his cheek. "You'll thank me later." I lifted my knee,
sinking it deep into his groin. He doubled over, and then fell
forward in the fetal position while everyone stood around in shock.

"Hey! Get the fuck outta here!" Annie yelled.

Tyler grabbed my hand and rushed out, pushing through the
door and running down the alley, and then down the street. Our
shoes crunched through the snow as we cut through a light flurry.

Tyler didn't stop until we reached his white crew cab Dodge truck, his friends close behind.

He pressed his key fob and looked down at me with a surprised grin, his breath visible in the cold night air. He nodded toward the truck as two doors on the passenger side opened and then slammed shut. "Get in. I'm going to take them home, and then—"

"And then what?"

He shrugged. "I'll take you home."

I shoved my hands in my coat pocket and shook my head. "Nah. I have to go back and wait for Fin."

"She's with Sterling."

"We sort of left Paige back there, too."

"Why did you do that?" Tyler asked. "I've never seen a girl do that—ever. Well, maybe once in middle school, but never with so much enjoyment."

"The bruise on his face. Is that from you?"

He nodded. "Two weeks ago. Bar brawl. It was brutal."

"But no bruises on you."

He shrugged. "I don't like getting hit, so I don't."

"No one does."

"But I don't."

"How is that? Are you trained or something?"

"Sort of. I have four brothers."

"I thought you said you didn't fight?"

"Not over girls."

"Are they all like you? Your brothers?"

He shrugged again. "Pretty much."

"Explains a lot."

He took a step toward me with the same look in his eyes he'd had at the bottom of my stairs. "You didn't have to do that. I had it handled."

"I didn't do it for you. I did it for him."

"Because you knew I'd kill him?"

I breathed out a laugh and then licked my lips when I saw him pull out a cigarette. "I'll take one of those."

Tyler held his cigarette between his lips while he lit mine, cupping the lighter as he puffed on his own. We exhaled at the same time, and I felt my body begin to shake.

"Come home with me," Tyler said.

I shook my head. "I'm taking Paige home. She was into Sugar. Now she's back there, sitting alone, feeling deficient when she's really the most beautiful thing to ever grace that shit hole."

"Not the most beautiful," he mumbled, looking away. When I didn't respond, he turned to meet my gaze. "I wanna take you home."

"I'm in the mood for something soft tonight."

He leaned down, kissing my lips once. "I can do soft."

I breathed him in, feeling my thighs tense. "Not like we can."

He slid his fingers behind my neck, backing me against his door, and then pressed his lips against mine, tasting me like he had the first night, with a yearning that made all reason melt with the rest of me.

He pulled away, brushing his thumb across my bottom lip. "Fuck Paige."

"I intend to," I said, walking backward a few steps before turning around.

Tyler puffed, and then I heard his door open and close and the engine fire up. I crossed the street and returned to Turk's. Paige was standing outside in the snow-lined alley, smoking, looking relieved to see me.

"You came back," she said.

My phone buzzed, and the display lit up. I recognized Finley's magazine-worthy selfie and frowned.

On my way. Marco will drive us.

I growled, shoving my phone back into my back pocket.

"Bad news?" Paige asked.

"It's just ... the girl I was with, my sister, Finley. She has an assistant, and she's with him now. They're coming to get us."

"Us?"

My face softened. "Yeah. You have plans for the next three hours? Or until morning?"

Paige swallowed and then smiled, shaking her head. She had such a sweet face. The death of her innocence was still fresh, and I could tell that she still liked to pretend it existed.

Headlights beamed into our eyes, and we both held up our hands. "The fuck, Marco? Turn off the brights!"

"I'm sorry!" he called from the driver seat.

The lights dimmed, and I held out my hand to Paige. "This is not happy ever after. It's just tonight."

She hooked my fingers with hers and nodded, following me to Marco's rental.

"Hi," Finley said as we settled into the backseat. Her lipstick and mascara were smeared.

I recoiled. "Ew, what happened to you? Please don't tell me you guilt-sucked Marco."

Finley's smile faded, and she turned around. "Take us home."

"Yes, Miss Edson."

CHAPTER FOUR

FINLEY WADDLED INTO MY ROOM, swathed in a plush white robe, holding a box wrapped in thick white paper and a bright teal bow. She flipped on the light and recoiled. The smeared mascara was gone and she looked like her usual gorgeous self, sans the makeup she didn't need anyway.

She noted Paige naked and prone in my bed, and then joined me on the bench next to the windowsill.

She handed me the box and leaned against the wall. "Open it."

I did as she asked, pulling at the fussy ribbon and paper, finally getting to the cardboard lid. Inside was another cardboard box. I lifted it, seeing a picture of a camera on the side. "What's this?"

"Not the most expensive camera for beginners out there, but it's the best. Or so Google tells me."

"This was your idea?"

She shrugged. "Marco's. He mentioned the time you were bored in Maui until you stole his camera. He was really impressed with some of the shots you took. He thought it would be a nice present for you."

"I barely remember Maui."

"So a camera is definitely a good idea for you," she teased.

I removed the lens cap and pressed the power button, configured the few settings I recognized, and pointed the lens at Finley. She held up her hands in front of her face. "Don't you dare."

I turned toward Paige, zoomed in on her hand against the wrinkled sheets, and clicked.

The image immediately popped up on the screen, and I turned the camera just enough so Finley could see.

"Marco was right. You're a natural."

"Thanks for the camera," I said. It did feel natural in my hands—something I could hold on to.

Finley nodded toward Paige. "She's a sweet girl. And God … crazy beautiful. She must have been burned pretty badly to be waking up in your bed. More like tarred and feathered. Poor kid."

"I know."

"So, you probably shouldn't …"

"I know. I've warned her."

"You know that doesn't work. We don't get happy endings with people like her. We ruin them."

I pinched off the cherry of my cigarette, and then tossed the butt out the window to rest with the hundreds of others in the hidden Marlboro cemetery below.

"I don't know. I'd consider last night a happy ending."

"I'm serious, Ellie."

"I know that, too."

"And so we're clear, I don't do guilt blow jobs. That's your fucked up talent."

"I shouldn't have said that. I was a little messed up. The firefighter kissed me. I was trying to take anyone home but him."

"The cute one?" When I nodded, her shoulders fell. "Damn it. I wanted him."

"You did not."

"I tried to ignore it."

"Ignore what?" I glanced over at Paige. I could still feel her soft hands all over me, her salty sweetness lingering on my lips.

"That he's into you. Every time I opened my mouth it was like I was breaking his concentration. He wanted so badly for you to look at him, and you were staring at blueberry muffin over there," she said, gesturing to Paige.

"I wasn't her first choice. She'd rather be waking up next to Sugar."

"Sugar was talking to Zeke about another girl. I got the feeling he's nursing a broken heart. Paige is better off." Finley scanned Paige as if she were a dying kitten. "Maybe she'll be okay."

"She'll be okay," I said, standing. I strolled across the room, lying next to the naked masterpiece in my bed, snuggling up next to her.

Paige reached back, tightening my arms around her without opening her eyes.

Finley waved to me, mouthing, *Brunch in two hours,* before she left.

I rested my cheek against the silky skin of Paige's back, inhaling the alluring mix of stale smoke and lotion. She stirred, her blue hair dragging against the pillow like a peacock feather. I didn't fear the awkward goodbye that would inevitably follow, or her feelings. My genuine curiosity for what she would do with her life after me settled in the nonexistent space between us. I hooked my leg over hers, the full, smooth limb sticking out of the expensive wrinkled sheet that only covered her perfectly curved ass—the same one that arched and bucked against my touch until the sun cast pastels across the sky.

"I'm awake," she whispered. "I'm afraid if I move, it will be over."

I placed the camera in front of her face and clicked the display button, showing her the picture of her hand. Everything from her arm out was blurry, but her blue hair couldn't be confused with anyone else. I was prepared for her to ask me to delete it, but she reached back to caress my face.

"It's beautiful."

"Can I keep it?"

"Yes. Is it over now?"

"It's over," I said. "I'll have José drive you home."

"Who's José?" she asked. She sat up and stretched, not at all upset.

"An employee."

She smiled, her sleepy, content twin pools disappearing behind her lashes several times before she focused. "I'll get dressed."

She hopped out of bed, pulling on her skinny jeans and sweater, and then her boots.

"Breakfast is downstairs. Maricela will get you anything you need."

Paige nodded, holding her purse to her chest. She really wasn't going to ask me to join her. She wasn't going to ask anything.

"Maybe I'll see you around," she said.

I propped my head with my hand. "I won't get that lucky twice."

She didn't try to hide that she was flattered. Her cheeks pinked, and she carried her coat out the door, disappearing down the hall. Her footsteps were barely audible as she descended the stairs, but my father's voice carried when he greeted her.

I settled against the headboard, waiting patiently and without fear of his inquisition. He would be angry about the cleaning bill, but more so about his wrecked Peter Max painting than the money. He didn't love anything more than he loved me, and that was fortunate because my mood swings and acting out had cost him millions. The Ferrari, the fire in his partner's Italian villa, and the legal bills—also known as bribes—to keep me out of jail.

He stopped abruptly in my doorway, as if he were a vampire who had to be invited to enter.

"Hi, Daddy. How was your trip?"

"Ellison," he began, his voice thick with contrived disappointment. "We've come home early to chat with you. It's not that we don't love you, bunny…"

"I know you love me," I said. I kept my face smooth, but I was wondering where he was headed with the conversation. He usually began with the *We're so disappointed in you, but we love you and expect you to do better* speech, but this seemed different.

He sighed, already exhausted from parenting me. Two sets of heels clicked down the hall. I sat up taller when my mother entered the room, followed by her life coach, Sally.

"Philip," Mother began, "I told you to wait." She spoke under her breath, smiling at me as she always did, as if her unnatural smile made her words magically imperceptible.

"I just—"

"Mr. Edson," Sally said. "It's important we keep a united front, remember?"

"What is this?" I asked, amused. "An intervention?"

"We love you," Daddy said.

Mother held the back of her hand against her husband's chest and took a step forward, clasping her fingers together at her waist. "Ellison, when your father and I learned about the party and damage, we were already at our limit. We've warned you countless times. You're an adult now. There really is no excuse."

"Why is Sally here?" I asked.

Mother continued, "We're at the point where we're concerned about your safety and the safety of others. How old was the young girl who just left?"

"Old enough," I said, settling back against my pillow.

I stretched to hide how unsettled I felt. This kind of confrontation was a first for them. My parents usually had a heated argument, in my presence, about how to deal with me, and then my father would send me on a lavish vacation—like the one I was about to take with Finley.

Mother smoothed the lines of regret that cut across her forehead. "Your father and I have decided to…" She cleared her throat. Despite her exasperation, she was unsure.

"Meredith … go on," Sally said.

"You're grounded," Mother forced out.

"I'm … what?" I giggled the last word, in total disbelief. I'd never been grounded in my life, not even when I was young enough to actually be grounded.

Mother shook her head, and then retreated to my father. He held her as if they were identifying my body.

Sally took over. "Your trip to the South China Sea with Finley has been canceled, as have your credit cards and access to family homes and employees. You are allowed to stay here for ninety days. You must find employment, and once you reimburse your parents for the amount in damages you've cause to the residence, some of your privileges will be reinstated."

I grit my teeth. "Fuck off, Sally."

Sally didn't flinch.

"Ellison, really," Mother said. "Maricela and José have been instructed to keep food in the pantry and the main quarters clean. Other than that, it's up to you."

"Let me get this straight. You're going to leave me penniless, alone—since I know Fin is going on this trip without me—and without transportation, but you want me to get a job and work off tens of thousands of dollars while also paying for daily necessities and rent? Gas, taxis, toilet paper, food? How am I supposed to do both? Do you have any idea what rent is like in this town? What you're proposing is asinine."

"We're not proposing," Sally said. "This is your life now."

I crossed my arms. "I'm sure my shenanigans have cut into your payments, Sally."

"Bunny," Father began.

Sally held up her hand. "We talked about this, Mr. Edson. Ellison, this isn't about me. This is about you."

"What's in it for you? What do you get out of this?" I asked, seething.

"Nothing. Healing your family is my job."

"Not for long," I warned. "Don't forget who signs the check, Sally. It isn't my mother, and Daddy doesn't subscribe to your bullshit." I pointed to my father. "Daddy, you can't let her do this."

"This is best," my father said without conviction.

"Best for who? You've raised me to be this person. Now you're going to punish me for it? I didn't used to be this way. I've tried being good to get your attention. *Nothing* works!"

"Guilt," Sally said.

"This is a *tourist* town! No available job here is going to pay enough to satisfy whatever it is I owe, *and* rent and bills! It will literally take me years!"

"Reasoning," Sally said.

When my father didn't show any signs of recanting, I pushed out my bottom lip, sitting crisscross to appear child-like. "I know I messed up. I'll be better, Daddy, I swear."

"Bargaining," Sally said.

A tear fell down my cheek. "I will hate you after this. This is not going to bring us closer. I will never speak to you again."

Sally cleared her throat. "Manipulation. Those tears are instruments, Philip."

"Fuck you, you abhorrent cunt!" I clutched the sheets in my fists and bounced once on the mattress as I screamed.

My parents' eyes grew wide. Sally looked relieved. "There. There is the real Ellison. You aren't penniless. You still have use of the house. Maricela will make sure there are basic provisions. The rest, as Meredith has said, is up to you."

My father watched me with pain in his eyes. I knew this was killing him inside. "We do love you. You're right, bunny, we've failed you. This is the only way we know how to fix this."

"I know," I said through my teeth. "Leaving someone else in charge of my fate has always been your go-to."

He winced, and my mother guided him out and down the hall. Sally stayed behind with a smug smile on her face.

"You can go," I said, looking at the window across the room where, only half an hour before, Finley and I had been admiring Paige's beauty and discussing how I shouldn't ruin her.

"You can call your parents, Ellison. But not to torture them. Not to beg. Not to try to change their minds. I will be with them for the next three months. Your phone bill has been transferred to your name and responsibility. You have a basic package until you can afford more, so use it wisely."

I turned to her, hoping to kill her with my glare. "Why are you still here?"

"It is important that you use this time to better yourself. This is going to be life-changing for you, Ellie. Take advantage. What your parents are doing is the hardest thing they've ever done, and they're doing it because they love you."

"Oh my God, Sally. You're right. I'm cured."

Sally breathed out a laugh. "I'm glad to see you've maintained a sense of humor."

"That wasn't humor, imbecile; it was sarcasm. You can fuck right off with my gullible parents, you greedy, scheming snake."

"Best to you, dear. I do hope we'll talk soon."

"I hope you text my parents asking for money, two seconds too long before looking up and being hit head-on by a truck full of toxic waste."

Sally didn't look appalled, but sad, turning for the door without another word. She spoke softly with my parents, Maricela, and José before the front door closed and their car headed for the gate.

I pounded my fists against the mattress, screaming as loudly as I could. The words coming from my mouth didn't even make sense, and I couldn't remember what was said from one sentence to the next, but I had no choices, and it was the only thing to do.

I rushed down the hall to Finley's room. Her bed was made, her room empty, her luggage gone.

"What the fuck?" I said, running back to my room for my phone. I dialed Finley's number.

She answered right away. "Ellie? Oh my Christ, honey, I'm in the car with Marco. They barely gave me time to get dressed. Maricela had my things packed and sitting next to the door when I got back to my room."

"They kicked you out, too?"

"No. They want me to leave for Sanya. They said you need time alone."

"Oh, for fuck's sake. I'm in a time-out?"

Finley grew quiet. "What are you going to do? Mother said you're cut off."

"I ... I don't know. I haven't thought that far ahead. I guess ... I guess I..." If I asked Finley for money, I would be as pathetic as every putrid mule we'd bitched about since puberty.

"They've forbidden me to help you," Finley said, sounding defeated. "But I left all the cash I had in my nightstand. I think it's eight or nine hundred. She's taken your passport and frozen all of your accounts. I'm so sorry."

"Did you know this was going to happen? Is that why you came home?"

"Of course not. You're my sister, Ellie..."

"It'll be okay. Thanks for the cash. When they stop being mad, they'll feel bad and change their minds."

"No," Finley said softly. "They've turned over control to Sally."

"That's ridiculous. Not even possible."

"They've signed a contract. Sally has to sign off on all monies or services extended to you. That's what Mother told me. I don't know what they're going to do if you don't find an apartment. Sally was talking about shelters in Estes Park." I'd never heard Finley sound afraid before.

"That's just ... absurd. Once Daddy abandons this bullshit intervention, he'll tell Sally to kick rocks. He loves me more than his own conscience, more than Mother—definitely more than a goddamn contract with a wannabe therapist."

"Exactly. He loves you more than anything, Ellie. More than his guilt or pride, or your anger. More than me."

"That's not true, Finley. You're the good daughter."

"And you're the one who requires the most attention."

My chest ached. It was the truth, which made it that much more painful. I didn't know Finley thought of me that way, and her opinion was the only one that mattered to me.

She continued like she hadn't just ripped out my heart. "It's too early to call, but I wouldn't count on their help anytime soon. They're serious this time. You've gone too far."

"You have to talk to them."

"I've tried. I've tried to talk to you, too, if you'll remember."

"Fin. You're my sister. Help me."

She paused for several seconds, and then sighed. "I am."

Even though Finley couldn't see me, I nodded, and then touched my fingers to my lips. She was right, but that didn't make it fair. There were less dramatic ways for my parents to make their point.

"Have a good trip," I said.

"I'm so sorry, Ellie."

"Yeah," I said, pressing the END button. The phone fell from my palm onto the bed. I looked out the window at the snow blowing off the trees. *Get a job? I have a degree in ceramics. Where in the fuck am I going to get a job in Estes Park?*

CHAPTER FIVE

"I SAID NO," I said, picking at the wood on Sterling's monstrosity of a dining room table.

"It's perfect for you," Sterling said, sipping his third glass of red wine. He was still licking his wounds from our night with Finley. Contrary to what he'd said when he'd invited me over, Sterling wasn't the least invested in ideas for me to find a job in Estes Park.

"A bartender?" I said. "The people in this town know who I am—most of all the bartenders. They will laugh me out of the building if I go looking for a job. They won't believe that I need one."

"They can't discriminate against you, Ellie. If you're qualified more than anyone else who's applied, they'll have to give it to you."

"That's not how this works. They hire grandsons and nieces in this town. And, no. Not a bartender. I just got kicked out of Turk's. They'll be afraid I'll drink up their stock. Especially now that José has been ordered to remove all the liquor from the house."

"Really?"

"Really," I grumbled.

"What the hell did you do, Ellie? It can't be worse than the time you—"

"It wasn't. A painting was broken. A few vases and a table. Some vomit on the floor ... nothing the cleaning crew couldn't handle."

"Then it's not about the money."

"What do you mean?"

"You're fucked. They're not trying to teach you responsibility or appreciation, Ellison. They're trying to save you from yourself. Betsy March's parents did the same thing to her. You have no way out of this. You might as well give in or end it all now."

My mouth fell open. "You are an unbelievable asshole."

He took another sip of wine. "People keep saying that. I'm inclined to believe it."

I looked up at him, my cheeks already burning from humiliation. "You don't need a ... um ... an assistant or anything, do you?"

"Me? Fuck no. I already have four. Oh. You mean ... hire you?"

My eyes fell to the floor. "Only if you need one. I don't want charity."

"It would never work, Ellie."

"Why?"

"Because we're friends, and I want to continue to be friends."

"You just told me to kill myself."

He chuckled. "I didn't mean it."

"Fine."

He pointed at me. "That's why."

I frowned. "What are you talking about now?"

"You didn't even put up a fight. I said 'no,' and you folded. I don't want a pussy working for me. I was raised with more nannies than I have assistants. One to wipe my ass, one to wash my hands, one to feed me, one to play with me during the day, and one to wake up with me at night. There were more. I don't remember their names. But my favorite? Beatrice. She was meaner than a cat with a firecracker in its ass, and I loved it. No one else talked to me like that. I need people who aren't afraid to tell me the truth. You can, but you can't, and we remain friends."

I sighed, and then nodded, already bored with his speech. He did love to hear himself talk.

Sterling tossed the paper at me, leaned across the table, and turned to the classifieds. There were already red circles in the *Help Wanted* section.

"Mail sorter," I said, reading his suggestions. "McDonald's." I looked up at him. He held up his hands. "Bank teller. I'm broke, and you think it's a good idea that a pot head without money for pot works at a bank?"

He shrugged, standing up and heading for the bar. "I'm trying. You need a drink."

"Desk clerk for a hotel. Nights. Checking guests in and out, light cleaning, and putting out continental breakfast." I looked up at Sterling. "They pay people fifteen dollars an hour to do this?"

"It's a tourist town. They can't get people to work for minimum wage even at minimum wage jobs. The cost of living is too high."

"There's nothing else?"

"An assistant at the local magazine." He chuckled. "*The MountainEar*," he said in a mocking tone. "Guess who owns it?"

"Philip Edson?" I snorted.

"Nope, this is one your father doesn't own. It's the new endeavor of J.W. Chadwick, the owner of Turk's. He's not going to hire you. There's also a server position at the resort, but you'd be dealing with dicks like us all day."

I covered my face, letting the paper fall to the table. "This is what I get for majoring in something I knew wasn't going to come with the expectation of a job. They've fucked me. My parents have fucked me."

"You've fucked yourself. Don't act like you didn't know what you were doing."

I pulled a wadded one hundred dollar bill from my pocket and tossed it on the table. "This is all I have left."

"They left you one hundred dollars?"

"No, they left me nothing. Fin left me eight hundred forty dollars. I drank it all."

"You're not just a lush; you're an irresponsible lush. You deserve this."

"I hate you."

Sterling winked. "Nah. You love me. I can tell you the ugly truth, and we still remain friends. That's why I love you." He put a tall glass of gin in front of me. "Drink up. We've got a long day ahead of us."

"I can't apply for a job drunk."

He held up a small white pill, and then placed it on the table, pushing it toward me. "We're not applying for jobs today. Today, we're saying goodbye to Ellison Edson the rich bitch, and hello to Ellie the blue-collar worker."

"Eat shit and die, Sterling."

He popped his own pill, washing it down with wine. I looked down at the table, turning the chalky white oval with my fingers. He was right. I wasn't going to find a job today.

I threw the pill to the back of my throat, not caring what it was, just hoping it would take effect quickly. I gulped the gin until my throat burned, and then looked at Sterling, wiping my mouth. "This is going to get ugly."

"It always does with us," he said, taking another drink.

I woke up on the floor, naked and barely covered with a tablecloth. Sterling was my pillow, his bare thigh against my cheek. I sat up, wiping my mouth, tasting salt and gagging.

"Oh my God," I whispered, looking at his naked body sprawled on the floor.

He didn't look like Sterling, with the clean-shaven jaw I was used to. His face had begun to darken with whiskers, and his typically slicked coif had pulled free from the gel meant to keep each strand in place. He was no different from anyone else I'd left in my path, messy and ruined, but the sight of him was the physical manifestation of rock bottom—the man my sister loved lying naked on the floor, a mixture of our sweat still glistening on his skin.

Bile rose in my throat, and nausea overwhelmed me. I hadn't thrown up after a day of drinking since junior high. The feeling caught me off guard.

I crawled on the floor to reach my clothes, pulling each piece of fabric to my chest. I breathed out a quiet cry and felt tears burn my eyes. *Finley.*

She would never forgive me—she'd never forgive us. I tried to remember what had happened. The sun was already behind the mountaintops, the sky getting darker by the second. Sterling and I had been fucking for hours, but I didn't remember any of it.

Groggy and humiliated, I collected my clothes, pulling on my bra, shirt, damp panties—more nausea—and then my pants, feeling the coldness of the cotton against my skin. I gagged again, and then ran down the hall to the bathroom. My stomach heaved, and mostly wine and liquor splattered against the door. I pressed my lips together and let my cheeks bulge out, holding in the rest just long enough to lift the lid on the toilet. What seemed like gallons of alcohol burned my nose and throat as it came up and gushed into the toilet. The toilet water sprayed my face, and I closed my eyes, sobbing.

Once it was over, I stood up, washed my hands and face, rinsed my mouth, and tried to rinse mystery chunks from my hair. I looked in the mirror. The girl looking back was unrecognizable. She was gaunt, with dark circles under her bloodshot eyes. She was a junkie. Finley was right. Living this way was going to kill me.

I padded down the hall, picking up the wadded cash and my snow boots on the way.

Sterling stirred, and I rushed to the door, hopping on one foot to pull on one boot, and then the other.

"Ellie?" he called, his voice broken.

"Nothing happened," I said.

He covered his face and turned his back to me. "Fuck. *Fuck!* No, no, no … we couldn't have. We didn't. Tell me we didn't."

"We didn't. Nothing happened. Because if it did, Fin will never speak to either of us again," I said, closing the door behind me.

CHAPTER SIX

THE ALARM BLEATED next to my ear, and I reached up, slapping at it until it turned off. The morning sun was pouring through the open blinds—I'd left them that way on purpose to force me out of bed. My interview with *The MountainEar* was in ninety minutes. Unfortunately, J.W. Chadwick owned the very bar I'd been kicked out of more than once, making my interview a littler trickier.

I opened my closet, wondering what people wore on interviews. When I Googled *What to wear to magazine interview*, it resulted in a thousand outfits I would never wear, including a ball gown with a plummeting neckline and see-through skirt I was sure no one wore outside a runway show.

I pressed my back against the wall and slid to the floor, perching my elbows on my knees and resting my forehead on my fists. I was known for a lot worse things in this town than being the daughter of the local billionaire. No one was going to hire me, and once Finley found out what I'd done, she would never forgive me. I had lost everything, and my future seemed very bleak.

Tears streamed down the bridge of my nose, pooling at the tip and dripping to the carpet. Soon, I couldn't control the sobs rattling my body, and all I could think about was how unfair it was that my parents dropped this bomb on me and took all the liquor in the house. Mother couldn't even pack without consuming two bottles of wine to calm her nerves.

"Miss Ellison!" Maricela said, crouching in front of me. "What is it? Are you hurt?"

When I looked up at her, she used her apron to wipe my eyes. "No one's going to hire me, Maricela. I'm the town drunk."

"Not for the last two days, you're not."

"I can't do this," I cried. "I have no idea how to do this. They're just throwing me to the wolves."

Maricela rubbed my arms. "That's how I learned to swim, muñequita. Sometimes we have to be thrown in, or we'll never do it on our own."

"I messed up," I said, wiping my nose with the back of my hand. "I hurt Finley." I looked up, my bottom lip quivering. "She doesn't even know it yet. All I can think about is getting high to make it go away."

Maricela touched my cheek. "It won't go away unless you face it. Admit to your mistakes, and then make amends."

The little resolve I had left crumbled. "She won't forgive me. Not this time."

"Miss Ellison, is this about the place where José took you? To the Planned Parenthood? What did they say? What did they do?"

I sniffed. The pregnancy test came back negative, and it had been more than two weeks since I'd been tested for STDs, and they hadn't called about results. With Planned Parenthood, no news was good news.

"Finley is your sister. She loves you the most. She wants the best for you."

I began to sob again. "I really fucked up this time. I can't believe I'm that person. Someone who would…" I shook my head again, despondent. "I've thought so many times since it happened that maybe it would be easier if … I can't do this." I looked Maricela in the eyes, solemn.

"I don't understand," Maricela said, worried.

"I just want it to be over." The words sounded insincere, such a powerful statement with so little emotion. I wondered if that's how Betsy felt about her own end—too damaged to feel anything but numb.

Maricela took my chin between her fingers. "Niña, no more of this. The Ellison who is destructive and full of anger … go on. Kill her. But *you* can live."

I tried to look away, but she wouldn't let me.

"If you want to prove that you're not that person, then you have to stop being that person. Let her go. Look at you. She's not making you happy."

I blinked, and then nodded slowly. Maricela always knew what to say when I was upset, but she'd never raised her voice at me before. She was fighting for me. I couldn't let her fight alone. "You're right. She has to go."

Maricela helped me to my feet.

I looked at my closet again. It was full of plaid flannels, hoodies, and ripped jeans, revealing shirts, and concert tees. "The interview is in an hour. I'm going to show up looking like I just left a drug deal."

Maricela stood behind me, touched my shoulders, and whispered into my ear, "She's dead. Go find a new Ellison."

"What if I don't know where to start?"

"You already have." She kissed my cheek and left the room.

I stared at the clothes for a bit longer, and then slammed the doors and ran down the hall to Finley's room, pulling open her closet with the hope she hadn't taken everything fantastic to her Manhattan apartment. Clanging through her hangers, I found a pair of black leather skinnies and a burgundy sweater. With a tall pair of black boots, a bit of makeup, and after raking a brush through my waves, I snarled at my appearance in the mirror. I rifled through Finley's hair products, sprayed some frizz control on my hair, and then brushed it through. I looked at my reflection again and sighed. I was so used to dressing like I didn't care, anything that took more effort seemed like I was trying too hard.

"You look nice, Miss Ellison," Maricela said from the doorway. "Shall I collect your laundry?"

"Thank you. But I don't think you're supposed to. I don't want to get you into trouble."

Maricela's expression fell, and then she nodded, knowing I was right. "I'll teach you when you're ready." She waved once before turning for the hall. "José is sure Mr. Edson forgot to mention that you're to be driven to any job interviews."

A wide grin crept across my face. "Really?"

"Good luck, Miss."

"Maricela?"

She turned.

"I don't know if they've asked you to report on what I'm doing, but I'd prefer you not tell them about the interview."

Maricela had been with our family since I was in grade school, and she looked at me with maternal love in her eyes. "I just want you to get better, Miss Ellie."

"I know. I'm trying."

She closed the door, and I turned to look in the mirror, deciding to pull my hair into a high, smooth bun. Mr. Wick was going to hire me, even if he didn't know it yet.

José glanced into the rearview mirror of the Audi. "You look nice, Miss Ellison."

"Thank you," I responded, turning to look out the window at the buildings passing by.

Our home was hidden away south of Highway 66, and the magazine was almost due north. It took José just over ten minutes to reach the highway, and he turned south, driving the opposite way from everyone else on their way to their jobs, and the tourists on their way to the mountain base. The sand trucks were out in full force, scraping a path toward Estes Park. We passed resorts and inns, a river and a cemetery ... so many things I'd never paid attention to because they weren't bars or restaurants without a dress code.

José turned down Mills Drive, and my heart began to race. I wasn't sure what to expect, but I had a feeling I was about to humiliate myself. We passed several buildings, all brown and filled with matching vehicles. Farther down from the rest, sat a small building with two garages and several emergency trucks parked along a circle drive. I sat up when I saw the sign.

INTERAGENCY CENTER

ROCKY MOUNTAIN NATIONAL PARK

I sat up, touching the glass with my fingertips. I wasn't sure if their crew stuck around throughout the year, but if I was going to be down the street for forty hours a week, I hoped not.

Next door to the fire station was a large RV park, and a quarter-mile of trailers dotted the landscape. Across the street from the station and the park was a new steel building. A driveway curved in front of the entrance, also continuing back toward another, smaller steel building that might have served as a garage, or storage building, or possibly both. The MountainEar office was small, a non-descript steel structure, newly finished on the outskirts of town.

I waved goodbye as José pulled away. He'd already promised to return in an hour. I stood on the sidewalk, inadequately dressed for the plummeting temperature. The clouds hung low over the peaks, and the snow had already spotted my hair like feathers, disappearing on contact.

A dually truck and gooseneck trailer barreled down the road toward the RV Park, all ten tires sloshing against the wet asphalt. I took a quick step back before a wave of water and ice soaked me from bun to boot heel. I walked toward the main building, passing the sign that read: MOUNTAINEAR MAGAZINE. My ankles wobbled with each step, feeling less confident and more ridiculous the closer I came to the front door. My hand hesitated to reach for the door handle, but I opened it, sighing in relief when the heat warmed my cheeks.

The door chimed when I walked through, the pristine industrial rug now wet from my boots. The walls were painted eggshell; the frames hanging in a line between windows contained magazine covers. Besides the front desk, six cushioned red chairs backed against the front wall, and a fake plant, the lobby was a whole lot of blank space.

At first, I could only see the top of the head of the girl manning the front desk. She stood up, acknowledging me with a nod. She looked barely out of high school, wearing braided blonde pig tails hanging from beneath a knit cap. Her name plate on the upper desk read JOJO.

She held a black phone receiver with hot-pink mittens, with far too much makeup on her young face. Although I was sure she only meant to hold up one finger, her entire mitten was erected, silently asking me with a wink and a smile to wait while she finished the call.

"No, Mike. Because Wick is busy, and so am I. He doesn't want your pictures of the parade. Because they suck. I've got someone at the desk. I'm hanging up now. Yes, I am."

She slammed down the phone and looked up at me with big eyes and fake lashes. Her orange skin had been baking in a tanning bed far before the ski season had started. She chomped on her gum and smiled at me with an inch of gloss slathered across her puffy lips.

"How can I help you?" Her tone changed as if she were a different person. She was no longer the cranky receptionist fielding questions for Wick. Jojo was pleasant, eyes bright, waiting to make me happy.

"I'm here for the nine AM interview. My name is Ellison Edson."

Jojo's expression immediately fell. "Oh. You're Wick's assistant."

"No, I … I'm applying for the job."

She stood up, gesturing for me to follow her down the hall. "Trust me, no one else wants the job. You're the first person who's even applied. The ad's been out for a year."

We walked through an extra-wide doorway to an empty room with a desk and a seating area, and stopped in front of a lightly stained door with J.W. Chadwick branded into the wood.

"Is there a reason no one has applied?" I asked.

"Yeah," she said, opening the door. "Because he's a dick."

Mr. Chadwick lowered the paper he was holding. "I heard that."

"From everyone," Jojo said, closing the door behind her. "Love you, Daddy."

Mr. Chadwick sat up, interlacing his hands on his desk. "Love you, baby." He looked to me. "When can you start?"

"I'm sorry, Mr. Chadwick, I didn't hear you correctly. When can I…?"

"Start. And it's just Wick. Everyone calls me Wick but Jojo."

"Maybe we should discuss what exactly being your assistant includes," I said. "Hours, benefits, and pay." I wasn't sure how all of this worked, but I wasn't stupid.

"Do you need a job?"

"Yes."

"Then what does it matter?" he asked, chewing on the toothpick in his mouth.

"It matters."

He sighed, leaning back in his worn chair. "Why?"

"Why what?"

"Your Philip Edson's daughter, ain't ya? You've also been kicked out of my bar twice this year alone. Why do you need a job? I'm not in the business of hiring lazy people who don't need a job."

"Sounds like you haven't hired anyone."

Wick glared at me, and then the corners of his mouth turned up. "I need you to file, keep my calendar, run errands, help Jojo on occasion, schedule ads, and vet any calls I receive. Jojo is tired of hearing from every journalist in the state and everyone who owns a camera thinking they're a photographer. I need someone firm. I need someone organized. Is that you?"

"I can be firm when you need me to, but I can't promise I'm organized."

Wick pointed at me. "But you're honest."

"I guess."

"Thirty-six hours a week, one week of vacation … unpaid, no benefits, this ain't a charity."

I shrugged. "I don't need it anyway. My parents keep my insurance. Or, they did. I need to ask them about that."

"You haven't said why you're here. Everyone knows your sister works for your dad. Why aren't you? Has there been a family uprising, or are you some kind of spy from the paper?"

I couldn't hold back a chuckle. "A spy? No. If you'll notice," I said, reaching over to point at the paper on his desk, "that's not on my résumé. It's also none of your business."

Wick grinned, his crooked, yellowing teeth making me never want to pick up another cigarette again.

"Do you smoke?" he asked.

"Yes?" I said, sitting up and feeling a bit creeped out that he'd mentioned the very thing I was thinking about.

"You're hired. Nine hundred a week. You'll start tomorrow. Let's go have a smoke in the back."

"Oh. Uh … okay, then."

I followed Wick out of his office, down a hallway lined with boxes, and then out a back door. My boots crunched in the snow, and I looked up, letting the flakes fall and melt on my face.

Wick pulled a cigarette from a soft pack in his shirt pocket and a lighter from the back pocket of his Wranglers and hunched over. He cupped his hand around the flame and puffed, then held out his lighter for me to do the same. I leaned in, took a drag, and then startled when two men came around the corner.

"Wick!" Tyler said, slowing mid-step the moment he recognized me.

"Tyler! Zeke! You're late! Where the hell is the other one?"

"Colorado Springs. Again," Zeke said. He pulled two cigarettes from his pack and handed one to Tyler. I recoiled. Menthols were disgusting. That must have been Zeke's preference. Tyler smoked from a black pack.

"Hi, Ellie," Zeke said.

"You know her?" Wick said, pleasantly surprised.

"Yeah," Zeke said with a smirk. "We met at a party."

"She's my new assistant," Wick said.

"Assistant?" Tyler asked. "What does that mean?"

"I'm not sure yet," I said. "We'll figure it out as we go, I guess."

Wick nodded, seeming proud, and then a deep line formed between his brows. "Make sure you don't get her into any trouble, Maddox."

Tyler spoke with his cigarette between his lips, squinting his eyes from the smoke. "You've got it backward, Wick."

Wick pointed at him. "If you get kicked out of my bar again, I'm not letting you back in this time. I mean it."

"You always say that."

"And I'm not going to let you be friends with my new assistant, either," Wick said.

Tyler frowned. "Now you're fighting dirty."

"I'm right here," I said. "And I can hang out with whoever the hell I want." I stabbed my cigarette in the sand of the butt canister and patted Wick on the shoulder. "Thanks for the job. I'll see you in the morning. Nine?" I asked, hopeful.

"Sure. Don't be late. I'm a fucking bastard in the morning."

"He is," Zeke said with a single wave goodbye.

I walked around the smaller building to the front, relieved to see that José was early. I slid into the back and let my head fall back against the cushion.

"Did you get the job, Miss Ellison?"

"I got the job."

"Congratulations," José said, smiling at me from the rearview mirror.

"Don't congratulate me yet."

CHAPTER SEVEN

"THIS," JOJO SAID, placing her hand on top of a five-foot-tall metal cabinet, "is our backup database. The hard copies—when we have them—go here. On the back desk by the wall is the scanner and printer—I'll show you how to work those later—and in the corner is the most important part of your job … the Keurig."

Littered with torn and empty sweetener packages and used coffee pods, the table was water-stained and wobbly when touched. The trashcan beside it, however, was empty. I shook my head.

"No," Jojo said. "He doesn't know how to throw anything away. Dawn cleans in the evenings, but Dad drinks about six cups a day, so try to make her job easier. She's good, but she's not a magician. And, since this is the first room anyone coming to see Wick will walk through, it would be a nice change for it not to look like a landfill."

"Noted," I said, pushing some of the pods and paper into the trash can.

Jojo gestured to Wick's door. "It's closed when he's in a good mood, open when he's not."

I raised an eyebrow at the closed door.

Jojo lifted her hand, holding her fingers next to her mouth. She whispered, "So you can hear him better when he yells."

"Also noted."

She pulled out the chair, and I sat automatically. Jojo didn't know it was second nature for me to sit in a chair pulled out for me, but I felt the blood rise under my cheeks when I realized what I'd done.

She tapped the space bar on the keyboard. "Create your own username and password here, but make sure to keep it written down somewhere so if you're gone I can access this if I need to." She waited while I tapped in my normal *ESquared* username and *DoubleE5150!* password. Despite my father's constant warnings, that login had been created in middle school, and I had since used them for everything. If Jojo had paid attention, she could have signed into my social media or even my online banking if she wanted.

Jojo educated me on the program I would use for Wick's calendar and reminders. It seemed simple enough. By the end of my first hour, I could check my email and Wick's, and had access to his contacts and what to say when his various friends and frenemies called.

Wick opened his door, and I waited patiently for him to yell, but instead he dug inside his front pocket for his soft pack of cigarettes and jerked his head toward the back door.

"Is your brain full yet, Ellie?" he asked.

"No."

"Good. Let's have a smoke."

"Dad…" Jojo said, unhappy. "She's being paid by the hour. We didn't hire her to be your new smoke buddy."

"He already has a couple of those," I said.

Jojo smirked. "Oh. You've met Tyler and Zeke, huh?"

"You know them?" I asked.

"Zeke is a big teddy bear. He looks mean, but he's the kind of guy that opens doors and brings you flowers. Tyler is a bastard."

Wick looked insulted. "Now, Jojo, don't go around telling people that. He's not a bad guy."

Jojo narrowed her eyes at him, and then her gaze turned back to me. "He takes Tyler's side every time. This is a sore subject with us." She looked back to her dad. "So I'm not going to gratify his ignorant opinion of Maddox with a reply, but he *is* a bastard. If you know him, you've already slept with him, so I'm sure I don't have to tell you that."

Wick and Jojo both watched me, waiting for an answer.

"So?" Jojo asked, flattening both her palms on my desk. "Have you?"

"Slept with Tyler?" I said, swallowing. I crossed my arms, fidgeted, and made weird noises with my throat while I tried to find a way to change the subject. Normally I wouldn't mind finding an abrasive, too-truthful answer for such an inappropriate question, but sobriety was a confusing time for me. "Have *you*?"

Wick turned to his daughter and put a cigarette in his mouth, holding it between his chapped lips.

Now Jojo was fidgeting and shifting uncomfortably. She stood upright. "I don't think this is a suitable conversation for the workplace."

"Damn it, Jojo! Now I'm going to have to shoot my favorite smoking buddy, because we all know I can't kick his ass!"

Jojo rolled her eyes and turned on her heels, walking around the corner toward her desk.

Wick waited for me to put on my coat and then led me to the back alley. A small steel storage building behind the magazine's main steel building created a cubby between the drive and us. A concrete pad provided parking spots for Wick and Jojo, but beyond that was a pasture full of snow and the intermittent rock poking through before a landscape full of Blue Spruce and Aspen trees.

"That fire station up the road ... is that the hotshot station?"

"And the city's second station. But some of the guys who work there are seasonal hotshots—like Tyler and Zeke. During fire season they live out at the Alpine barracks."

"What is a seasonal hotshot?"

"During fire season, they eat, sleep, and travel around the country fighting fires. Three to six months of the year."

"Oh," I said, wondering if Tyler was already gone.

Wick sparked the white paper and tobacco and took a puff, then handed me the lighter so I could do the same with one of my father's stale leftovers. The pack had three somewhat mashed cigarettes left, and I had just thirty-four dollars of the money Finley had left for me. Prices weren't something I had paid attention to, but I was sure I couldn't afford cigarettes before my first paycheck.

"Does nine hundred a week mean you pay me every week, or were you just talking wages?" I asked, rubbing my head. I could feel a headache coming on.

"Every week. Just like my bar staff."

"So ... on Friday?"

"Friday."

Seconds after Wick answered, I heard boots crunching against snow. Zeke and Tyler rounded the corner, already smoking and carrying on conversation. They both looked happy but unsurprised to see me, and then both took a turn shaking Wick's hand.

"Taylor!" Wick said. He noticed his street clothes the same time I did. "You must be off today."

I frowned, wondering if Wick was trying to be funny or he'd just gotten Tyler's name wrong.

"I heard you finally found someone to put up with your shit, Wick," Tyler said.

Wick had told Zeke and Tyler the day before I was hired. Now he acted as if he'd found out from someone else.

Zeke took a drag of his cigarette, and then playfully pulled at the sleeve of my puffy navy-blue coat. "Confused?"

I arched an eyebrow, unsure if it was a trick question.

Their laughter was cut off by the sound of Zeke's pager. He pulled the clip from his belt and held it up, squinting. "That's me."

He patted Tyler on the shoulder as he nodded to Wick. "Maybe I'll see you guys this afternoon. It's just a meeting."

I waved to him, and then crossed my arms as the air between the three of us who remained quickly turned awkward. Tyler and Wick traded smug grins, clearly sharing a silent joke at my expense. I glared at them, relieved when Jojo poked her head out through the back door.

"Annie is on the phone for you."

"I'm on a break," Wick growled.

"You should probably take it. It's the refrigerator again."

"Damn it, damn it, damn it!" Wick said, tossing his cigarette and missing the canister.

The back door slammed behind him, and I picked up his still-lit butt and buried the end in the sand.

"Good thing you picked that up," Tyler said.

"I've heard that one already," I said, taking a drag.

Tyler pulled his cap low over his eyes, and then shoved his hands deep in his coat pockets. Before I could ask him how he managed to get the day off, he grinned.

"How is it? Working for Wick?" he asked.

"Not as bad as I thought it would be."

"That's unexpected."

I took another drag, watching him put out a cigarette and light another. "Do you come here every day?"

"During fire season, yes. In off season, if I'm here."

"When are you not here?"

"When I'm traveling."

"Oh."

"Oh?" he asked. I could see that familiar desire in his eyes, even behind the shadow cast by his ball cap. The dimple in his left cheek deepened, and he leaned a millimeter in my direction.

Even that nominal response made the old me wish for a bottle of bourbon and a dark room. I swallowed. The old me was just two days away, and she wasn't buried deep enough to withstand the way Tyler was looking at me. I wanted to hide underneath his body and replace the pain with his fingers digging into my hips and to watch him tense while he thrust himself deep inside me, forgetting everything else but Tyler's rough hands on my bare skin, letting the sweet escape of intoxication carry me through.

"Stop looking at me like that," I snapped.

"Like what?"

"Like you've seen me naked."

"Have I?"

I rolled my eyes, bending down to put out my cigarette.

"Hey," he said, reaching out. He scanned my face, almost as if he was trying to remember. "I'm sorry. I didn't mean to offend you."

I shrugged him off. "I better get back in there. I sort of need this job now."

"Does uh ... does Zeke have a thing for you?"

"*Zeke?*" I said, my voice going up an octave. "No. I mean, I don't think so. No, definitely not."

"Do you have a thing for him?"

My expression twisted. "Why in the fuck are you asking me that?"

"Have you met my brother?"

I stood, completely confused. "You sound completely crazy right now."

"Just making sure before I make a pass at you."

"Make a *pass* at me? Are we in junior high?"

His eyebrows pulled in. He was really concentrating now, looking as confused as I felt. "I went to middle school."

"I don't think you left."

He breathed out a laugh. "What are you doing later?"

"Not you."

He choked on the drag he'd just inhaled, and then smoke and laughter tumbled from his mouth. "Easy, sweetheart. You're going to hurt my feelings."

"Listen, I'm having a hard time going back inside, which tells me one thing: you need to go away, and stay away. I'm trying to be good here, and you're ... not. Good ... for me ... at all."

He touched his chest with his palm. "I'm good," he said, feigning insult.

His confidence made my thighs tingle. "No. You're bad. And I'm bad. And you need to go back to the station or headquarters or whatever you call it so I can keep my job."

"I'm going to Turk's later. You should meet me there."

I shook my head, backing away. "Nope. Definitely not."

He took a step forward, amused by my retreat. He knew the effect he had on me, and he was enjoying it. "Am I making you nervous?"

My back touched the door. I sighed, looking up at the clouded sky. "I'm going to get fired." I reached for his face and planted a hard kiss on his mouth.

Tyler didn't flinch, gripping my coat and pulling me toward him. His lips were vaguely familiar, commanding and purposeful. He slipped his tongue inside, and I hummed, closing my eyes and letting him take me somewhere else—anywhere else—but the surreal, clusterfuck scenario I was currently in.

I pushed him away, breathless. "Is your truck around?"

"My truck?"

"Yeah, the one with the back seat." I reached down for the rock behind his zipper.

"It's ... at the station." He moaned, taking my ass in both hands. He lifted up, pressing me against him.

I was glad I was wearing jeans and a flannel shirt. If I had been in the leather and light sweater I'd worn the day before, no amount of fucking could have warmed me up.

"Does Wick keep that storage building unlocked during the day?" I asked.

Tyler leaned back, looking down at me with labored breath. He grinned. "Are you serious?"

"Just check the fucking door, Tyler."

He tucked his chin and blinked. "*Tyler?*"

"What the fuck?" another voice said behind him.

Tyler's carbon copy gripped the back of his coat and yanked him backward, throwing him to the ground.

Zeke stood wide-eyed behind him before holding up his hands. "Whoa, whoa, whoa! They didn't know! I didn't tell him! I didn't tell *her!*"

I wiped my mouth and straightened my clothes. "What the hell is going on here?"

The Tyler on the ground wasn't sure what to think, while the one standing was clearly ready for war.

Zeke pointed to the Tyler I'd just mauled. "Ellie, that's Taylor, Tyler's twin brother."

"Oh, fucking hell," I said. They weren't just twins, they were reflections. I couldn't see a single difference. "What … *why* didn't you tell me?" I cried.

"Shit. *That's* Ellie?" Taylor asked, holding up his hands, palms out. "You didn't tell me she worked here!"

Tyler pointed at his brother. "You didn't even get her fucking name before shoving your goddamn tongue down her throat?"

"Are you fucking kidding me right now?" Taylor said, sitting up slowly. "Don't act like you haven't done it a thousand times, fuck stick."

"You know better than that shit, Taylor! We always make sure. What the hell is wrong with you?"

"She…" he said, looking at me. "I asked about Zeke! I asked her about you! She didn't act like … she didn't say anything!"

"Did you say my fucking name when you asked her, or did you just ask about your brother? It's not the first time someone's been confused."

Taylor shrugged, sheepish, and Tyler moved toward him.

I held out my hands. "*I* kissed *him!*" I blurted out.

Tyler froze.

"*I* kissed *him!*" I said again, touching my chest with one hand, the other still held out toward Tyler. "This isn't his fault!"

Taylor stood up and brushed snow and mud off his coat and pants, red-faced and teeth clenched.

Tyler glared at his brother. "I owe you one, dick."

"Fine, you owe me one." He glanced at me. "Nice to meet you, Ellie."

"That's it?" Tyler growled.

Taylor's jaws danced beneath the skin. "I'm sorry for the misunderstanding."

My shoulders sagged. "I'm sorry, too."

Taylor disappeared behind the storage building with Zeke not far behind. Tyler rolled back his shoulders and looked down on me with disappointment in his eyes.

"No," I said, pointing at him. "You don't get to be jealous. You barely know me."

"I'm not jealous. That was my brother, Ellie."

"Please," I sneered. "Like this hasn't happened before. Just based on the forty-five minutes I've spent with both of you combined, I'm fairly certain you've shared a dozen or more women at some point. Maybe without even knowing it."

"No," Tyler said, nearly pouting. "We have a system. It usually works."

"I have to go back in."

"Ellie?"

"Yeah?" I said, annoyed.

"Were you telling the truth or were you just trying to avoid a fight?"

"What?"

"You said you kissed him … thinking it was me."

"So?"

"I thought you said you didn't do repeats."

I sighed. "I'm going to be straight with you, Tyler. I fucked up. My parents cut me off. I'm broke, and I need this job. I did something terrible to my sister, and I'm trying to change so if and when she finds out, she'll know I'm not that person anymore."

One side of Tyler's mouth curled up, and the same dimple on his left cheek appeared.

I pressed my lips into a hard line. "This was just a weak moment. I don't do repeats. Especially, *definitely* not now."

Tyler processed my words, nodding once. "Fair enough."

I breathed out a laugh. "Okay, then. Enjoy Colorado Springs."

"Colorado Springs?" Tyler asked, confused. Recognition lit in his eyes, and he seemed embarrassed for me. "Oh. That's Taylor."

My cheeks burned. "I'm glad I'm staying away from you. The twin thing is too much for me sober."

Tyler laughed and reached out, offering a low, small wave as he began to walk away. "Goodbye, Ellie Edson. It's been fun."

"Fun Ellie is dead. All that's left is broke-and-alone Ellie," I teased.

Tyler stopped. "She's not dead. Just transitioning. Like a butterfly."

"That's deep, Maddox."

"I've been deeper," he said with a smirk, pulling his cap down low, just like his brother had less than ten minutes before, and walked away.

I rolled my eyes and shook my head, pulling open the back door. Wick and Jojo nearly fell forward, and then pretended—poorly—to be doing something other than eavesdropping.

"Am I fired?" I asked.

"Fired?" Jojo asked. "Hell no! That's the most fun I've had at work since Daddy built this place!"

Wick held up a cigarette and squeezed by, and I followed Jojo inside. She went to her desk and I went to mine, staring at my computer for a full minute before I could focus.

"Ellie?" Jojo called over the speaker.

I pressed the button. "Yes?"

"Did you quit cold turkey?"

"Um ... yes?"

"Daddy is nine years sober. We're impressed."

"Thanks."

"You're welcome. No more breaks today."

"Understood." I let go of the button and covered my eyes with my hand. The new Ellie's paint wasn't even dry, and I'd already managed to ding the first door that had opened. I rubbed my temples, feeling another headache. I wanted a drink; my mouth felt dry, and my mind toyed with having José stop at the liquor store on the way home.

"Ellie?" Jojo said from the doorway, startling me.

I pulled my hand away from my face. "Yes?"

"You're going the right direction. No one does anything perfectly the first time. It's going to be okay."

No one could have said anything better to me in that instant. Those three simple sentences set my soul at ease.

"Thank you," was all I could manage.

Jojo winked at me and returned to her desk.

I clicked a few times to navigate to the computer's settings, and then selected Change Username/Password.

USERNAME: ELLIE2POINT0

PASSWORD: RIGHTDIRECTION001

CHAPTER EIGHT

BLUEGRASS PLAYED THROUGH CEILING SPEAKERS placed throughout the *MountainEar* building. I thumbed through a stack of pictures from the recent half marathon, shaking my head.

"You don't like the music. I figured you were a rock chick," Wick said, walking into my office.

"I tune out the music," I said, laying the pictures down on my desk, fanned out. "It's the pictures. They're terrible, Wick. Who took them?"

"She's right," Jojo said, sitting on the loveseat across from me. She crossed her legs, her snow boots still wet from her walk inside. "I've seen them. They suck. You've got to quit letting Mike turn in that crap. Just quit using him period."

Wick frowned. "There's no one else."

I nodded toward Jojo. "Her coverage of the art walk was stellar. Why not just use Jojo?"

Jojo smiled and stood. "Because Jojo has an office to run."

"Who took those?" Wick asked, pointing to the frames on my desk.

"Oh," I said, turning them slightly. "I did. Just something to remind me what I'm trying to do."

Jojo walked around my desk, picking up a frame holding a picture I'd taken at my parents' house the weekend before. I had snapped just half of the black and white portrait of Finley hanging in my parents' main hall—taken when she was just fourteen. Even back then, she was stunning.

"You took this? Who is this?" Jojo asked.

"My sister," I said, my voice quiet. I hadn't spoken to Finley since I'd woken up next to Sterling. She had left me a few voicemails, but she also understood that I might not want to chat about her vacation by the sea while I was stuck in a snow globe.

"It's actually pretty good," Jojo said. She looked at Wick, and he agreed. She picked up another frame, and then set it down. "What camera are you using?"

I shrugged. "Just a point-and-shoot my sister bought me. A Nikon, I think. It's over there." I pointed to a bag in the corner.

Jojo strutted over and rifled through my things, pulling out the camera and holding it up. "I started with this one. I can teach you a few basics over lunch. Take some pictures tonight, and show me tomorrow."

"Why?" I asked.

"Because your job description might broaden."

"I'd love to do lunch, but I'm sort of on a budget. I brought a sandwich from home."

"It's your fourth payday. You can't afford lunch yet?" she scoffed. When I didn't answer, she continued, "My treat. Don't bother arguing. I'll win."

Wick nodded. "She's right."

"Okay. I have a few things to wrap up first."

Jojo left for her desk, and Wick disappeared into his office, closing the door. I was glad he was in a good mood. Thoughts of Sterling and the many possible reactions Finley could have about our moment of temporary insanity ran on a loop in my brain, and I was working on maybe three hours of sleep.

I finished answering Wick's emails, and then pushed my roller chair away from my desk. The phone buzzed.

"Ellie, line one," Jojo squawked over the speaker.

"For me?"

"Yep."

I picked up the phone and pushed the button for line one, wondering if it was a bartender complaining about something not working at Turk's, or Mike hoping I'd give him good news about his crap pictures.

"This is Ellie," I said, waiting for several seconds until the voice on the other end began to speak.

"I'm … I'm sorry to call you at work. Congratulations on the job, by the way."

I hunched over, as if that would help to muffle the conversation. "You can't call me here, Sterling."

"I know. I'm sorry. But Finley isn't returning my calls."

I rolled my eyes. "She never returns your calls. Stop being paranoid, and stop calling me. Don't think I don't remember you passing me whatever the fuck that pill was. What did you do? Roofie me?"

"I—this isn't my fault."

"Then whose fault is it?" I hissed. "I don't even remember what happened."

"Neither do I!" he snapped. "You were upset. It was supposed to just make us chill. It was something new I scored from Preston."

"Preston?" I hissed. "You gave me something you got from Preston? You could have killed us both!"

"You didn't have to take it. You can't put this all on me."

"I trusted you," I said, gripping the phone and trying to yell at him as quietly as possible. "But you're right. I accept my part in what happened. You might love her, but she's my sister. I'm trying to turn things around so I can prove to her that—if she does find out—I've changed."

"You can't tell her," Sterling said, sounding desperate.

"I won't. But you know best of all, Sterling. Finley always finds out. She knew I cut her Barbie's hair and she wasn't even home. We hosted a birthday party that weekend. It could have been anyone, but she knew it was me."

Sterling laughed once. "I remember that story." He was quiet for half a second. "You're right. We're fucked."

I closed my eyes. My lips skimmed the speaker as I spoke. "This is not *we*. I don't want to talk to you anymore, Sterling. You're on your own."

"Ellie…"

I hung up the phone and sighed, pushing away from the desk and gathering my things for lunch with Jojo.

She was standing by the door waiting for me when I rounded the corner. I followed her to her Outback and ducked inside, hugging myself for warmth. Jojo seemed oblivious to the cold, twisting the ignition like she wasn't wearing huge sleeping bags for gloves.

"You brought your camera, right?" she asked.

I held up my bag.

"I figured we'd try Camp's Café. The food isn't farm-to-table or organic or any of that shit, so it's tourist free, and one of the

quieter places, so I can show you some tricks on your Nikon. I'm
excited to see what you can do. You seem like a natural."

I laughed once.

"What?" Jojo asked, pulling out onto the road and poking at
the heater setting with her mittens.

"That's what Finley said. My sister."

"Well, she was right. Maybe we can start covering things other
than the farmer's market and wandering wildlife."

Jojo parked in the alley in a space meant for the townhouses
spanning the entire block. She didn't seem to be worried, stepping
out and slamming the car door. We walked together, and I
followed her past dumpsters and oil vats through a dirty screen
door into the back kitchen.

"Jojo!" one of the cooks called.

Jojo waved, and then gestured for me to follow her past the
pantry area, beyond the grill, and then the cash register.

"The same!" Jojo called. "Two!"

The woman behind the counter nodded and yelled back to her
staff. "Two Jojos!"

We pulled off our coats, scarves, gloves, and hats, and sat them
beside us in a booth by the window.

"You have your own sandwich? That's kind of cool."

"Not really. I just order the same thing every time, and you're
going to love it, too. A fried biscuit with avocado, a medium fried
egg on top, and their special sauce. It's Korean or something,
which is weird for a country cooking kind of place, but it's f—it's
good. Trust me."

I frowned. That didn't sound appetizing at all, but it was a free
meal and better than turkey meat on plain wheat bread, so I wasn't
going to complain.

I handed Jojo my camera, and she told me all about exposure,
aperture, shutter speed, and ISO. She had me play around with the
different creative modes on the camera—the P, A, S, and M—
showed me how they were used, and then educated me on why
they were superior to the icon modes.

By the time I scarfed down the weird but delicious Jojo biscuit,
I was already adjusting the camera and taking a few shots of the
café and outside.

Jojo clicked through them, shaking her head. I bit my nails,
waiting for judgment.

"Ridiculous," she said. She handed me back my camera. "You really have an eye. Wick is going to shit, because he's getting ready to lose his assistant."

"No," I said, waving her away. "Really?"

Jojo grinned, putting her elbows on the table and leaning in. "Really. You'll still be helping at the office and cleaning his coffee table, I'm sure, but you're going to be great. I can tell."

"I'm not a journalist. I can't write. I paid someone to do my papers in college."

Jojo made a face. "You had to write papers for a degree in ceramics?"

I closed my eyes, embarrassed. "Yes."

Jojo cackled, and I laughed with her, *really* laughed, for the first time in a long time.

"Thank you," I said, trying to catch my breath. "I didn't know I could laugh like that sober."

Jojo rested her chin on the heel of her hand. "I know you're supposed to be some kind of family fuck-up, but you're not that bad. I can't imagine you've changed that much in a month."

"It's amazing what detox and responsibility will do for a girl," I said, only half-teasing.

"You've been doing so well. Not one slip-up."

"It's hard to drink or buy weed when you're broke. And even if I had, I wouldn't tell my boss."

"I'm not your boss, and you're not a liar. It's not just about the money, Ellie, and it's kind of sad, because I've been watching you work so hard, you're still waiting to get it wrong."

"That's not true," I said, shaking my head and fidgeting with my water glass.

Jojo breathed out a small laugh, and then began gathering her things. "Let's go. You have work to do."

Jojo dropped me off a block from the magazine, and I bent down, glaring at her through the open passenger side window. The exhaust was puffing from the back of her car, and my breath didn't look much different.

"Really? Is this photography *Survivor*? It's like nine degrees."

Jojo waved at me. "There are some interesting things this way. I want to see how you see it."

"Fine."

"See you in a bit," she said with a shit-eating grin.

My camera was cold against my skin, and I struggled to change the settings with my stiff fingers while Jojo pulled away, heading for the back lot behind our building.

I turned around, seeing an old house, and leaned back to see the antennae. I took a practice shot and checked it, tuned the settings again, and took another. When the display filled with my shot, I smiled. Jojo was right. Automatic mode sucked ass. It was a world of difference knowing how the adjustments would affect the picture.

I walked down the road, away from the *MountainEar*, getting lost in taking shots and then watching how the quality changed with the different variations of ISO, shutter speed, and exposure time. I took close-ups of leaves with snow, roofs with snow, broken down cars covered in snow, windows panes with snow ... There was a lot of snow in my shots, but I made it work.

"Did you get fired?" Tyler, or Taylor, said from across the street. "Zeke and I have a bet going how long you'll last." He was squinting one eye against the setting sun, and I turned around, noticing it was peeking behind the mountains. I pulled back my coat sleeve to look at my watch. I'd been outside in freezing temps for two and half hours and had barely noticed.

"Which one are you?" I asked, putting away my camera.

He chuckled. "Tyler. Are you an insurance adjuster or something?" he asked with a smile.

"No. I'm taking pictures for the magazine now."

"They must be hurting for help," he teased.

"Fuck off," I said, turning to walk the three blocks back to my building. Tyler had been standing in front of his station. I hadn't realized I'd walked that far, either.

"Hey," he called. I could hear his boots sloshing against the wet street and crunching against the rock salt before he reached me. "I was kidding."

"So was I," I said, continuing down the sidewalk.

"So, um." He shoved his hands in his tan cargo pants. "You and Paige..."

"There is no me and Paige."

"No? Why? Someone said you and her might be ... You like guys, right? I mean ... you'd have to after the night we had. I just can't figure you out."

"What's to figure out?"

A grin slowly made its way across his face. "You, Ellie. I'm trying to figure you out."

"You're talking to me again."

"I thought maybe this time it would be okay."

"Why?"

His eyebrows pulled in. He was getting frustrated. "Do you, uh … still think about that night?"

"Not really, no."

He sighed. "It's been a month, Ellie."

"I'm aware."

"I still think about it."

I took a breath, hoping I could exhale away how he made me feel. "We've talked about this," I said, continuing my trek to the *MountainEar.*

"Ellie," he said, chuckling nervously. "Could you stop and talk to me for just a second?"

I stopped, lifting my chin to meet his gaze. "So are you interested in me because I didn't just fade away like the rest of your one-night stands, because of my father, or because I may or may not be into guys?"

· "None of the above. Why are you being so difficult?"

"It was one night, Tyler. I was a different person then. I don't want to be attracted to the sweaty fighter willing to take a drunk girl to bed anymore."

He shoved his fists in his pockets and squinted one eye—that damned dimple in his cheek making another appearance. "You don't want to be, but you are."

He was so overconfident my insults didn't faze him. He was too arrogant to believe me.

I kept walking. "*You're* making this difficult. I'm trying to be clear. Just because I may not be at my strongest at the moment doesn't mean I'm trying to send you mixed signals."

"I've already taken you to bed. I was going to ask if you wanted to hang out."

I stopped to scan his face, deciding if he was telling the truth or not. There was hope in his eyes, maybe a little bit of fear. Tyler was tall and bulky and wrestled with wildfires for a living, but he was scared of me, and with good reason. Behind all that muscle and badassery, Tyler was good, and that meant I was bad for him—even if I was better than I used to be.

"I can't hang out with you."

He continued as if he hadn't heard me. "I'm off at ten tonight."

"I'm in bed by ten."

"What about breakfast? You don't have to be at work until nine, right?"

"Because I like to sleep in, genius."

"Are you a bacon and eggs girl? Or pancakes?"

I frowned. They both sounded fantastic. A free breakfast was as good as a free dinner, and Sally had decided she wasn't going to allow Maricela to add to the pantry until I spoke to my parents on the phone—which I didn't plan to do ... ever. I wasn't turning my life around for them; I was doing it for Finley, and that meant I would soon be living on Ramen noodles unless Maricela took pity on me and brought over some of her famous tamales.

Free breakfast sounded perfect, but using someone for food, knowing he was interested in me, wasn't being the good person I was trying to be. "No."

"*No?*" he asked, surprised.

"I'm sort of busy with myself. I'm sure you can find another girl to hang out with."

My feet finally decided to complain about the cold three steps into my walk to the *MountainEar*. The door chimed when I pushed through the front door, fading while I stomped my boots on the mat.

"I was beginning to wonder if you were coming back," Jojo said. Her bright smile faded. "Did you know Maddox is outside?"

I turned to see Tyler standing outside the door, his hands in his jacket pocket, waiting.

I pointed to the windows, demanding that he go back where he came from. He shook his head.

"What are you doing?" Jojo asked.

"How do you get rid of these guys? He's like gum stuck to the bottom of my shoe."

"I couldn't tell you. I'm fairly certain Maddox has never waited outside in the cold for any girl. You should make him wait until he turns blue. You know ... for the rest of us." She held out her hand. "Let's see what you've got."

I pulled the small card from the camera and handed it to her. Excitement lit her face as she inserted the card into the side of her monitor and sat, the wheels whining as she scooted her chair closer.

My fingers were red and frozen, and I wondered how they'd managed to work while outside for that long in sub-freezing temperatures. Quickly getting the right adjustments and shot became an obsession, making it easy to lose track of time. Even standing next to Jojo while she clicked through the hundreds of photos, I wanted to go back out and do it again.

Jojo shook her head and perched her elbow on the desk, cupping her chin in her hand. She covered her mouth with her fingers, the clicking of the mouse getting faster.

"I don't even know what to say."

"The truth. I'll still have the assistant job if they suck, right?"

"They don't suck."

"They don't?"

"These are incredible!"

I took a deep breath. "They are?"

"Daddy!" Jojo called, sounding more like an impatient pre-teen than a young woman capable of managing an entire business.

Wick hurried out of his office, hobbling but motivated. "They're good?"

"See for yourself," Jojo said, still clicking the mouse.

I crossed my arms, feeling my skin burn as it slowly warmed, and shifted my weight, unsure how to take their reaction. Wick put one hand on his daughter's shoulder, bending over to get a closer look at the monitor.

"Ellison," Wick said, staring at the screen. "These aren't bad, kid."

"Yeah?" I said, sniffing.

He stood upright and patted me on the shoulder. "She needs an assignment, Jojo. Not any of the usual boring shit, either. Something both the locals and tourists want to know more about. Something exciting. Sexy!"

Jojo frowned. "Ew. Don't say that, Daddy."

Tyler finally pushed through the door. "I'm not leaving."

I rolled my eyes. "Don't you have a job to do?"

Wick snapped his fingers. "Yes! That's it!"

"What's it?" Jojo asked.

"Ellie's first assignment!" He pointed to Tyler. "She can follow the hotshot crew. We know the basics, but what do they *really* do?

How dangerous is their job? How physically arduous? What does it take to be a hotshot? Who are they? What do they do in their down time?"

"No," I said, more begging than answering.

"Oh my God, Daddy, that's brilliant!"

"Jojo," I pleaded. "I'm not a journalist."

"I'll help you," Jojo said. "I can rewrite it, or write the whole damn thing if I have to. You just take notes and get the pictures."

Wick smiled, all of his yellow teeth on display. He puffed out his chest, proud of his daughter. "This is going to be a feature. Edson and Wick. It could get picked up by the AP."

"Let's not get ahead of ourselves. Are we sure this is even possible?" I asked. "I'm sure there are safety concerns."

Wick pointed to Tyler. "Make this happen, Maddox. I'm calling in a favor."

"Don't call in a favor," I said.

Tyler took a step toward Jojo's desk. "I'm sure I could work it out with the superintendent. I have the day off tomorrow. I could take her in and speak with him."

I sighed and raked my fingers through my hair, pleading to Wick and Jojo with my eyes. "Stop. Let's think about this for two seconds. You want my first assignment—as an amateur photographer—to be a featured story about following hotshots into fires? Really?"

Jojo turned off her computer, slipped on her coat, and winked at me. "Bring me back something amazing."

"It's my second day of taking photographs. You want amazing?"

"I have faith in you," Jojo said. "Get out of here. Work day is over, and José is outside."

I trudged to my office to gather my things. When I returned to the lobby, Tyler was standing in the dark, chatting with Jojo about my assignment. Jojo had already turned off the lights and was waiting for me to leave, keys in hand to lock up behind me.

Tyler walked with me to the curb where the Audi was parked, white clouds puffing from the exhaust. Sally hadn't authorized the use of the car, but José was certain my parents wouldn't want me walking miles in the snow.

I wasn't as sure.

"So … breakfast tomorrow before we go in? My treat."

"This isn't a joke to me," I said. "I need this job. If I screw this up—"

"You won't. I'll make sure you have plenty to shoot. Let me buy you breakfast before we go to the station. We'll talk about presenting it to my boss, and I'll have a better idea of what you want."

"I don't know what I want."

"Okay," he said, the dimple in his cheek appearing. "Either way, after breakfast is over, you'll have a better idea of what you want."

The Audi's back door creaked as I opened it.

"Ellie…"

"Just remember this," I said. "This wasn't my fault. I tried to save you the trouble."

"I'm a firefighter, Ellie. I do the saving in this relationship."

I slid into the back seat and closed the door. Tyler tapped on the window, and I rolled it down. "This is not a relationship."

"I've told you before—I'm open to friends with benefits," he said with a wide grin.

"You're embarrassing yourself."

"Me?" Tyler said, touching his chest. "Nah!"

I rolled up the window as José pulled away. The leather seats were warm, and I rubbed my fingerless gloves together.

José turned left onto the highway for home, glancing at me in the mirror.

"You look happy, miss."

I stared out the window at the lights breaking through the dark. "I think what you're seeing is irritation."

"You have a guest this evening."

"A guest?" I asked. "Please tell me it's not Sterling. Or my parents. Fuck, it's not my parents, is it?"

José chuckled. "Neither. The girl with blue hair."

"*Paige?*"

He nodded.

"How long has she been there?"

"Almost an hour. She brought cookies. They're good."

"You ate my cookies?"

"No, Miss Ellie. She brought four dozen."

"She must know Sally is trying to starve me to death."

José slowed at the gate, and then passed through, driving leisurely down the drive and stopping in front of the house next to an eighties model Hyundai hatchback. The blue paint was chipped, and a long scrape and dent spanned from front fender to back seat. The car was cute but beat up—no more perfect car for Paige.

She greeted me in the foyer, throwing her arms around me. She was wrapped in a blanket that smelled like Finley, nothing but her head, hands, and tattered red Converse visible.

"I hope it's okay that I'm here."

"Yeah. Yeah, of course."

She pulled me into the kitchen. "I brought cookies," she said, pulling off the lid of a plastic tin that looked older than she was.

She held out a round sugar cookie, the white frosting in the shape of a snowflake.

I took a bite. "Wow," I said, still chewing. The cookie melted in my mouth, and the frosting was decadent. "You really made these?"

She nodded. "My grandma's recipe."

Maricela opened the fridge and pointed to a covered plate before zipping up her coat and gathering her things to leave for the night. José's taillights glowed through the frosted glass, too, making Paige's unannounced visit an even bigger relief.

"How's it going? You've sort of disappeared," Paige said, choosing another cookie.

"It's been a rough month."

"Tyler said your parents cut you off. Is that true?"

"Tyler Maddox? You've seen him?" A strange pang of jealousy burned in my stomach.

She shrugged. "At Turk's. He said you gave him the shaft."

"I didn't give him the shaft. He had to have been hanging on to get turned loose."

Paige giggled, her childlike smile prompting me to reach for her hand. She intertwined her long fingers with mine. "I've missed seeing you around."

"I'm still around."

"Is it true? About your parents? Is that why you're so different?"

"Good different, I hope," I said, corralling the crumbs from our cookies into a pile. Paige didn't answer. "Yes, it's true."

"Well, I've come to save you." She bent down, and when she stood up, she pulled a bottle out of a brown paper sack. She rummaged through the cabinets until she found two tumblers, and sat them on the counter. My mouth began to water at the sound of the cap twisting off, and the initial splash of the amber liquid against the bottom of the glass. Paige filled both tumblers to the top.

"Whoa," I said. "I haven't drank a drop in over a month."

She handed me a glass and held hers halfway between us. "To being sober."

"I..." My throat burned, aching for the contents in the glass. It was right there. Just one drink. I'd just have one.

CHAPTER NINE

"YOU LOOK LIKE HELL," Tyler said, holding out my chair.

I sat down, leaving on my sunglasses. "Thanks."

"Late night? I thought you weren't drinking anymore."

"I wasn't," I said, recoiling at the sound of his voice, the sunlight pouring in through the windows, and the squeaking little shit pre-K'er bouncing in the corner like he was on crack.

"What happened?" Tyler asked.

"A friend showed up last night with a bottle of Crown."

He scowled at me. "After what? Five weeks on the wagon? Doesn't sound like a very good friend."

"I'm not riding a wagon. Those are for alcoholics."

Tyler flagged down Chelsea, pointing his finger in the air. "Hi. Can we get some waters, please?" She nodded, and he returned his attention to me. "Can you eat?"

"Maybe."

He shook his head. "Did you at least have good time?"

"Yeah. We talked until around midnight and crashed. She made cookies, and we talked about my parents, and Finley, and…" I trailed off, remembering the tears and blubbering about Sterling before passing out. I'd told Paige. She knew what Sterling and I had done. I covered my eyes with my hands. "Oh, no. Oh, God. *Fuck.*"

"So … not a good time?"

"I don't want to talk about it. Oatmeal. No fruit. Cinnamon." I was determined to eat, not knowing when I would have a non-instant-noodle meal next. "Please."

"You got it," Tyler said, ordering for me when Chelsea returned with our waters. He didn't talk much, and I didn't complain. There was already too much movement and light and sound and breathing going on. Clanking of dishes, talking, some damn kids laughing, car doors slamming shut—everyone needed to die.

"You look like you hate everything," Tyler said.

"Pretty much." I pulled my hoodie over my head, supporting my face with my hands.

"Is this one of those things we'll laugh about later?"

I sunk down in my seat. The sunglasses weren't helping. It felt like the sun was piercing my brain. "Probably not. I'm so sorry."

Chelsea slid my bowl of oatmeal in front of me, the cinnamon wafting to my nose. It actually smelled appetizing until Tyler's stack of pancakes with blueberries, chocolate, whipped cream, and maple syrup hit my nose.

"Christ," I said, recoiling. "Has anyone ever told you that you eat like a toddler?"

"Many, many times," he said, digging at the stack with his fork and shoveling in a bite.

"How do you look like that," I said, pointing at him, "if you eat like that?" I pointed to his plate.

"We have a lot of downtime at the station as opposed to the dormitory during fire season. I don't like sitting still, so I work out a lot."

He had to. He was a mammoth.

I picked up a spoon and dug into the bowl, scooping up a small bite first, just to test the waters. So far, so good. Plain toast, cinnamon, bland oatmeal. I could still party like a rock star but apparently couldn't recover like one.

I finished off my water with the pair of ibuprofen I'd brought from home, and then looked at my watch.

"In a hurry?" Tyler asked.

"I just want to make sure that I get to the office on time if your superintendent doesn't let you talk him into this absurd plan."

Tyler had already nearly put away half of the pancakes. I wasn't sure when. "Photographers follow us out all the time. Not sure how you're going to keep up in your condition, if we get called out, though. The hikes are pretty brutal."

"Shut up."

"Uphill."

"Why are you torturing me?"

"…in the snow."

"You worry about your job, I'll worry about mine."

Tyler laughed once. "How did a billionaire's daughter wind up taking action shots for a magazine? That's kind of random, isn't it?"

"I've told you about my parents, and I know you remember. You told Paige over drinks or whatever."

"Does that bother you?" Tyler asked, amused.

"That you're talking about my business? Or that you were with Paige?"

"Either."

"That was personal. That's not exactly bar talk."

"You're right. I'm sorry. I just figured she was your friend … and I was a little worried about you. I figured she'd know more than I did."

"Paige is a sweet girl. She's not my friend."

"Friends with benefits?"

I glared at him, and he held up his hands, chuckling.

"Are you finished stuffing your face? It's making me nauseous," I said.

He stood, put a few bills on the table, and helped me up. He held me to his side, supporting my weight with ease and looking fairly sympathetic. "You okay?"

I blew an errant long bang from my face, even more pissed at myself than I already was, and if I was honest, pissed at Paige. She didn't know how hard I'd been working, though. She wasn't responsible for my new path; that was all me.

Tyler guided me to his truck and helped me inside. I tried to face forward and keep my eyes on the road, because riding in the back of the Audi on the way to Winona's an hour before was rather brutal.

Less than fifteen minutes later, we turned onto Mills Drive. His truck bounced over the uneven asphalt and ice as he parked in a lot south of the station.

"Sorry," he said. "We've got a short walk."

A vent was bleeding white mist out of the side of the brown building, and I stepped down and looked across the street, squinting my eyes to try to see if the lights were on yet at the *MountainEar.*

"If you need to throw up, now is the time," Tyler said, walking around the front to stand next to me. His thick arm hooked around my shoulders, but I shrugged away.

"I'm fine. Don't baby me. I did this to myself."

"Yes. Yes, you did." Tyler stepped through the blanket of snow covering the broad gap between his truck and the station. We reached the back door, and with a quick twist of the knob, it was open. Tyler swept his arm toward the hallway ahead. "After you."

I crossed my arms to ward off the cold as I walked inside. It was much harder to keep warm when I was hungover for some reason—another thing to be pissed about.

Tyler stomped his boots on a large industrial mat, and I did the same. He gestured for me to follow him down a hallway lined with cheap frames holding pictures of former superintendents and a few fallen fire fighters. The last picture was from the late nineties, and the guy couldn't have been more than twenty-five. I paused, staring at his freckles and sweet smile.

We passed an open doorway that led to a brightly lit garage full of pumper trucks, engines, and equipment. Packs and helmets hung from hooks on the walls, and extra hoses were squared away on large shelves.

"I'll let you get some shots in here after we get the okay from the superintendent," Tyler said. "My squad boss said he's in today, sorting through applications."

After a few closed doors, we crossed the threshold of another doorway. Tyler pointed behind us. "That's the squad boss's office. The superintendent is in there now, cussing at the computer. His name is Chief."

"Is he the chief or superintendent?"

"His name is Chief. His position is superintendent. He's the one who has to clear you to stay at the dorms."

"Gotcha. Wait. I'm staying at the dorms? Where are the dorms?"

"Farther into Rocky Mountain National Park. If you're going to follow us around, we can't come into town to get you every time we get a call."

"Holy shit. So I'm going to have to, like … pack?"

"Yep. These," he said, nodding forward, "are our quarters. TV room," he said, pointing left. Two sofas and four recliners sat in front of a large television. It was a widescreen, but seemed to be its own unit, older than most of the guys watching it. Tyler waved, and they waved back, curious but not enough to move from their chairs. "Another office," he said, pointing to a room farther down on the left. "We do our reports on that computer. And there," he said, pointing right, "is the kitchen."

I walked through the doorway, seeing a rectangular table that seated eight on one side, and a modest cooking area with cabinets on each side, a refrigerator, and a stove. Next to the sink sat a toaster and a microwave. They seemed to have everything they needed, although it was the size of a closet to serve eight or so men.

Tyler continued through a second doorway. "These are the sleeping quarters."

"Seriously?" The room looked like an infirmary, with beds set almost side-by-side, separated only by individual, square, armoire-like pieces. "What are those?"

"They hold our personal belongings—extra clothes, coats, stuff like that. There are two on each side, sort of like lockers."

"You sleep like this? In one big room with a bunch of guys?"

"Sometimes. Yes, some of them snore."

I made a face, and Tyler laughed. "C'mon. Let's go see the superintendent."

We walked back through the kitchen, passing the guys in the TV room. They were just beginning to stir, standing up and stretching.

"Are they going somewhere?" I asked.

"They eat breakfast and watch the news. Then they go down and do chores unless we get a call. In off-season, we work a typical forty-hour week, five AM to four PM or four PM to ten PM."

"No fires at night?"

"Yeah, for the full-time engine guys."

"Chores?"

"Yep. Wash the vehicles, sweep and mop floors, dishes … whatever. We don't have maids here."

I snarled at him, knowing it was a dig at me.

"Downtime—if we get any—is a lot different at the hotshot duty station. We dig new trails and fix fence and signage, run drills…"

"So, not really downtime," I said.

Tyler knocked on the door across from the quarters, and a deep voice growled from the other side.

"Come in, damn it!"

Tyler winked at me and opened the door. The superintendent sat behind his desk, partially hidden by several file folders and an ancient, boxy computer, looking frustrated.

"Hey, Chief. I have a journalist here who—"

"Do you know anything about Twitter?" Chief asked, his black eyes targeting me.

"Pardon?" I said.

"The Twitter. Do you know anything about it? Someone with a lot more time and who makes a lot more money than me decided we needed to have a Twitter account, and I haven't the slightest fucking clue how to ... what is it called?"

"Tweet," Tyler said, trying not to laugh.

He pounded his fist on the desk. "Goddamn it! Tweet!"

"Yes. I could probably help," I said, "but I'm here on an assignment, Mister..."

He looked at me only briefly before shaking his head and returning his attention to the computer. "It's just Chief. What assignment?"

"I'm a ... photographer for the *MountainEar*." Even though it was the truth, I felt like I was lying. "I've been assigned to the Alpine Hotshots. Mr. Wick would like to share with the community what you guys do."

"We tweet," he grumbled.

Tyler breathed out a laugh. "Chief, c'mon. Miss Edson would like to—"

"Edson?" Chief said, finally deciding I was worth more of his consideration than Twitter.

Shit.

Chief narrowed his eyes at me. "As in Edson Tech?"

"Uh..." I began, not sure which was the right answer. My father had just as many enemies as he had friends. Probably more.

"She's just a photographer," Tyler said. "Quit busting her balls and tell her yes or no. I'm in here on my day off."

"Yeah, and why is that?" Chief asked.

"I owe her a favor," Tyler said.

"Is that so?"

"Yeah. Can she shadow the crew and take pics or not?"

"Did she get her red card?"

"Chief," Tyler said, exasperated.

"If she can show me how to send a twit, then yes."

I took off my coat, handed it to Tyler, and walked around the desk, kneeling next to the superintendent. "Tweet, Chief. You tweet on Twitter. And you have to have an account to tweet. Fill this out."

He tapped on the keyboard, following the steps to create an account.

"Click on that button," I said, pointing. "Here, you can upload a photo. I bet you have your logo in your Pictures folder." I clicked a few times, and like I'd thought, the Alpine Hotshot logo was in a file folder. One of their snapshots from the field made for a nice header photo, and then I stood. "All set."

"All set for what?" Chief asked.

"Click on that icon, and type whatever you want."

"Not whatever you want, Chief," Tyler specified. "Type something associated with the hotshots, but no cuss words. And keep it under a hundred and forty characters."

He wrinkled his nose. "A hundred and forty what?"

"Just write about that cleanup we helped with the other day. Or the food drive we're doing this weekend. Tell them we're ready for the upcoming fire season and post the group photo. Short and sweet."

"Cleanups and food drives? You guys do stuff like that?" I asked.

"Yeah. All the time." Tyler said the words as if I should have known.

After a knock on the door, a familiar voice began to speak. "Who's the skirt?"

I turned to see Taylor standing in the doorway. It was downright unsettling how identical he was to Tyler.

I glared at him. "I'm not wearing a skirt, nor am I a skirt. And you know perfectly well who I am."

Taylor winked and smiled. "Be sure to tell all your Tumblr feminists you were offended first," he said before turning for the TV room.

Tyler's jaws pulsed beneath the skin, but then he breathed out slowly.

The superintendent's eyes danced between where Taylor stood, Tyler, and me. "What the hell was that about?"

"Nothing, Chief. Did you tweet?"

Chief clicked the mouse and sat back in his chair, perching his elbows on the armrests. "It's tweeting!"

"Is Ellie clear?"

"She's clear. Keep her in the black or in the goddamn safe zone, and get the hell out of my office. I have work to do."

"Aye, Chief," Tyler said, shooing me into the hall.

"The black?" I whispered from the side of my mouth.

"The area that's already been burned to a crisp," Tyler said, mimicking me.

I breathed out a sigh of relief. "That was more difficult than I imagined."

"He's a good guy. He gets shit done, makes sure we have all the equipment we need, even when the brass don't always think we need it."

"Brass?"

"Government higher-ups. It's a budgeting thing. Constant fight. Not why you're here. Let's go meet some of the guys."

Tyler led me to the truck bay where the rest of his crew was hard at work. Two of them had the hood up on one of the trucks, two were sweeping and mopping the concrete floor, and a few more were in the corner with the equipment.

"What are those?" I asked, pointing to the axe/hammer hybrids hanging from the wall.

"Oh, those are pulaskis. Those," he said, pointing to a shovel-like tool, "are rhinos. We make those here."

"*You* make those?"

"Yeah, with the welder, a saw, a sander, and a few other tools. Whatever we can find, really. We have to get creative sometimes."

I pulled out my camera, took a few shots of the tools, and then aimed at the crewmembers going about their day. Tyler approached the men tinkering under the hood of a vehicle that looked like an oversized ambulance.

"This is a crew bus," Tyler said.

"When it runs," one of the men said.

"The sign outside says Interagency, and you have Interagency equipment here, but also engines, and this is the city fire department?" I asked, confused.

Tyler shrugged. "Double duty. Just makes things easier, especially since a lot of us do both urban and wildland. It's closer to town, too, during off-season."

I nodded, pulling out my notepad and pen.

"This," Tyler said, pointing to a man taller than him, but not as thick, "is Smitty." The short but solid hotshot wore glasses, and was a sophisticated kind of beautiful, with olive skin and a grease smear on his cheek.

They both wiped their hands on their pants and greeted me.

"Lyle Smith," Smitty said, shaking my hand.

Tyler pointed to the other one. "This is Taco."

"Taco?" I asked. His red hair and freckled skin gave me no hint of a reason for the nickname.

"Clinton Tucker. My son is two. When he says our last name, it sounds like taco. Unfortunately, it stuck, but it's not the worst nickname around here."

"Does everyone have one? A nickname?" I asked.

Tyler shrugged. "Pretty much."

"What's yours?"

Smitty chuckled. "He has one, but no one is brave enough to say it to his face."

"You'll have to let me in on that," I said with a smirk.

"No," Tyler said. "He won't."

I jotted down their names. "Is it hard for you, Taco? Being away from your son for days or weeks at a time?"

"I guess. We don't really know another way. It's what I do," Taco said, wiping his hands with a rag. "During fire season, it's months at a time."

"How long have you been a hotshot?"

"This is my fourth season in Colorado."

I nodded and let them get back to their jobs, then stood in the corner to snap a few candids of them working.

"Over there is Watts ... Randon Watson," Tyler said, pausing while Watts waved with one hand, holding a mop in the other. "And that is our squad boss, Jubal Hill. Don't let the silver hair throw you. He's an animal."

"Jubal?" I asked. "What's his real name?"

Jubal dropped the broom and walked over, his light hair setting off his bronze skin and baby-blue eyes. He held out his hand. "Jubal Lee Hill. Nice to meet you."

"Jubilee," I repeated.

He looked down and laughed once. "It's just Jubal. No nickname needed."

"Nice to meet you," I said. When he walked away, I documented him like I was paparazzi. He needed to be in a calendar, or working for *Vogue* in New York and wearing designer glasses and a suit, not pushing a broom in a garage.

"It's okay," Tyler said. "Every female who comes through here has a crush on Jubal."

"He doesn't act like it," I said.

"That's because he doesn't know it."

"Right."

"Seriously. He's loved the same woman his entire life. Since, like, the first grade or something. They got married right after high school, and ... you should see them. They're gross."

"Gross?"

"Like newlyweds. They've been married thirty years."

"That's gross?"

"No," Tyler said. "We just like to give 'em hell. I bet my parents would still be like that, too. It's kind of cool to see. The rest of them are out."

"How many are on your crew? And what do you mean by out? Hurt? Vacation? Out sick?"

Tyler chuckled. "Crews are typically twenty men and women."

"Women?"

"Not very many, but the toughest hotshots I know are women."

I smiled, letting my camera hang from the strap around my neck. "So where are the rest?"

Tyler led me to a group photo in a frame. "Like I said, in off-season, when we're not fighting fires, we're sometimes assigned other jobs like search and rescue or disaster response assistance. We'll also work to meet resource goals on our home units. Some guys have other part-time jobs or just take unemployment and ski or travel or spend time with family." He pointed to the faces I didn't recognize. "Fish, the assistant superintendent. Sage, Bucky, and Slick are squad bosses like Jubal. Sugar. Cat. Scooter. Baggins. Jew. Sancho. Runt. Puddin'. Pup."

I arched an eyebrow.

"I'll get you a list of full names later."

"Real names, please. What are resource goals?"

"Thinning, prescribed fire implementation, habitat improvement, trail construction projects ... stuff like that. Sometimes we go to the schools and do ... you know ... Smokey Bear stuff."

"Who has to dress up?" I asked.

Tyler made a face. "That'd be me."

I snickered. "Thanks for that," I said, scribbling on my notepad. "I'd like to get a picture of you in the suit at some point." He frowned, and I nudged him. "You're a peach for showing me around and an angel for taking me to see the superintendent."

"A peach?"

"So, how many hours do you work on average?"

Tyler crossed his arms. "We're doing this now?"

I looked up at him from my notepad. "Yeah?"

"It depends on if it's fire season or downtime. If we're fighting a fire, we just sleep, eat, and work. We can work up to eighteen-hour days, but working thirty-two hours a stretch isn't uncommon. Up to fourteen-day stretches."

"Holy shit," I said under my breath.

"Used to be twenty-one. Then we get our required days off—a forty-eight hour R & R—and then we're back out. We travel all over ... wherever they need us. Even Alaska, Canada, and Mexico."

"How long have you been doing this?"

"I'm a *peach*? Really?" he said, amused.

"Shut up and answer."

"I can't shut up *and* answer..." He trailed off, recoiling from my glare. "We're on our third season. We were ground crew before that."

"We?" I said, looking up at him again.

"Taylor and me."

"Are you a package deal?"

"Basically," he answered matter-of-factly, and I imagined him doing the same in interviews as well.

I scribbled a few sentences, and then touched the pen to my lip. "I don't see a lot of older guys on your crew. Why is that?"

"You won't see many at all. Wildfire fighting is brutal. If you do it more than five or six seasons, you start seeing some lingering physical issues. The superintendent goes on site, but he's basically restricted to a desk because of his back, knee, and shoulder surgeries."

"Jesus," I murmured.

"What?"

"Nothing. You've mentioned something about the community. What else do you guys do?"

"You mean community outreach? During downtime we have AM and PM physical training built in to the schedule, patrolling, drills, chainsaw work, fence building, signage…"

I jotted down his answers while he spoke, hoping Jojo could somehow produce a story from my random scribbles.

"Do you get time off?" I asked.

"Not during fire season. I took today off to get some shit done."

"Do you need to…" I said, gesturing to the door.

"What? No, no, I'm good."

"You don't want to leave me alone with these guys, do you?"

"No, not really."

"What will you do when you leave until you come back? What does a hotshot do on his day off?"

Tyler's brows pulled in, and he stared at me, confused. "What do you mean?"

"You're leaving, right? You don't live here, do you?"

"No, I'm not leaving."

"So you do live here?"

"No, I have an apartment with my brother here in Estes Park. We typically only stay at the station when we're on shift, but yeah … you're here, so I'm here. I cleared you with the superintendent, so you're my responsibility."

I wrinkled my nose at the thought.

"If the guys get called out, your plan is to ride along, right?"

"Well … yeah."

"Then I'm staying. They'll be busy. They won't have time to babysit you."

"I went to kindergarten. I can follow directions."

"I'm not arguing with you. This is how it's going to be."

"What about when you're on shift?"

"Same thing."

"Oh, so they won't have time to babysit me, but you will?"

"Jojo wanted you to follow us around, right? This is how it's done when we have journalists shadow. Someone has to make sure you don't get hurt."

"You can't be serious. I'm assigned to you, and you're assigned to me? I was just beginning to feel cool."

"I'm not leaving you alone. It's dangerous, Ellie."

"You're just precious."

Tyler frowned. "I'm rethinking this."

I suddenly felt heavy, and then panicked as bitter bile rose in my throat.

"I was just kidding. Are you all right? You look a little green," Tyler said.

"I'm nauseous all of a sudden."

"Bathroom's down the hall, second door on the right."

My stomach lurched, and I gagged, covering my mouth. I didn't wait for it to happen again, sprinting to the bathroom just in time. Just as I bent over the toilet, I thought about my camera being dunked in toilet water and covered in vomit, but it was hovering over my right ear, held by the hotshot I loved to hate.

"Why am I so stupid?" I moaned, my voice echoing off the porcelain.

Tyler was holding my camera with one hand, my hair in the other.

"Is she okay?" one of the guys asked from the hall.

"She's fine, Smitty. She's caught that stomach bug going around," Tyler said.

"What a bad ass," Smitty said. "I was in bed for two days with that shit."

I hurled again. Both men made the same sound, equally surprised and disgusted.

"I'm super excited to have an audience for this on my first day," I said.

"Sorry," Smitty said. "Feel better, Ellie."

"Not humiliating at all," I said, puking again.

CHAPTER TEN

"WHOA," I SAID, taking a step back. I'd been on several house fires and car fires, and even a few grass fires my first week, but Tyler was right. Wildland fires were different.

Tyler kept eyes on everything around him while guiding me to a safer area. I was bundled in a base layer, thermal, fleece pullover, with oversized flame-retardant jacket and pants for a top layer, making it more than difficult for him to keep a grip on my arm. He was in a fire-resistant shirt and tan cargo pants, with maybe thermals underneath, wearing goggles, a gear bag, and a hardhat.

A line of Alpine hotshots—most of whom I'd just met two days before at the fire camp, but who Tyler loved, including his brother—in bright yellow jackets and blue hard hats were digging a line at the bottom of the hill. A symphony of their pulaskis and rhinos clanging against roots and branches bit through the constant drone of radio communication.

Tyler had brought me as close as he could, trying to help his crew while keeping an eye on me. We'd camped for two nights, and excluding any embers jumping the fire line, he predicted we would be packing up by nightfall. No one was more surprised than me that I wasn't looking forward to it.

There were no engines with hoses or pumper trucks full of water. The hotshots fought fires with drip torches, shovels, and chain saws, digging trenches to pull everything out of the ground that could fuel the fire.

I wasn't scared of heights, but a strange combination of fear and exhilaration came over me as I looked down at the valley below. The wind was blowing chunks of my hair into my face, and I realized it was also blowing the fire toward the Alpine crew. Time slowed down as I stared at Tyler. We were stuck in a moment I'd never been in before, not skiing a summit, not on a wave runner off the beaches of Thailand, not hiking Machu Picchu. We were on top of the world, the only force between the fire and the houses I could see from the mountain we were standing on. Holding my camera, freezing, and a mile from flames that could burn me alive, I'd finally found what I didn't know I was looking for.

"Back up, sweetheart," Tyler said, reaching across my chest like my mother used to do when she'd slow down the car too fast.

I was nearly hanging over his arm, leaning forward, hungry to be closer, snapping shot after shot, devouring the adrenaline as fast as my body could produce it. It was better than any high I'd ever had.

The flames made a low roaring sound as they crawled over the dry brush and leafless trees like a line of soldiers pushing forward without fear. The walk to the fire site was a difficult trek. We'd driven almost two hours to the fire camp, and then hiked for nearly an hour through ice and snow, climbing steep inclines and through the aspens. My feet and face were numb before I even smelled smoke, but I'd forgotten about the cold hours ago, looking through the lens of my camera.

Taco ran up the hill, out of breath and drenched in sweat and dirt, stopping in front of Jubal to report. "Fuel break completed on the eastern edge."

Smitty was behind him, panting and holding a drip torch in one hand, his pulaski in the other. Watts was holding a chain saw, his shoulders sagging. They looked equally exhausted and content, every one of them in their element and ready for their next order.

Jubal slapped him on the shoulder. "Good work."

Tyler was supposed to have the day off, but that didn't stop him from helping his team dig a two-foot-thick fire line. I watched him cut at the ground with the pulaski like it was nothing, directing the men around him as if a wildfire wasn't burning the world less than a mile away.

Clicking through previous pictures, I noticed they were Tyler-heavy, but that didn't stop me from zooming the lens and snapping another close-up of his sweaty, sooty profile against the setting sun. He was sort of beautiful—from every angle—and that made it hard for me to leave him out of a shot. The green pines stood waiting to be saved, and with the cool gray color of the smoldering smoke and the warm oranges of the fire on the horizon, tragedy made a beautiful backdrop.

"Helo's coming in!" Jubal yelled, holding the radio to his ear. "Wind turned!"

I looked to Tyler, confused. "There's no wind."

"Up here there's not. A fire makes its own weather. Farther out, we might not have wind at all, but where the fire's burning, it's sucking oxygen and can create thirty or forty mile per hour winds."

More hotshots whom I hadn't yet met had been called in. With chain saws in hand, a small group called sawyers was limbing trees to cut gaps in the canopy above, keeping the fire from hopping from one tree to another. Each sawyer had a partner called a swamper who gathered the cut limbs and bushes and threw them on the other side of the fire line.

The rest of the crew—the diggers—would work in a line, hacking away at the forest floor, creating a three-foot trench—a fire break down the middle of the saw line. The Alpine crew had been split into two groups of ten—sawyers, swampers, and diggers, and then some on lookout, one checking the weather, and the others down the way igniting a back burn. Even separated, they worked together seamlessly, half the time not saying a word. Jubal was communicating with the superintendent, and then barking those orders at the hotshots while elbow-deep in the dirt himself. They all worked for hours to create what they called fuel breaks, cutting and burning away any vegetation, covering miles bent over digging, sawing, all in an effort to starve the flames to death.

A distant *thud thud thud* drew closer, and soon a helicopter was zooming overhead. Just beyond a pillar of smoke, the helo released its load, and a purplish-red powder rained down.

"That's red slurry—a fire retardant," Tyler explained.

"It stops the fire?"

"Slows it down. Buys us more time to dig."

I swallowed, and Tyler touched my cheek with his gloved hand. "We're okay."

I nodded quickly, terrified and excited at the same time.

The hotshots barely took a second to notice the dump of slurry, and then continued hacking at the ground. I watched in awe, exhausted from just the hike to the fire site and the cold.

Tyler breathed out a laugh, and I turned to see him staring at me the way I looked at the fire. He didn't look away; instead, one side of his mouth curled up. Even through the sweat and ash, his dimple appeared. In that moment, Tyler Maddox and his fires filled a hole in my soul I hadn't known existed.

They worked past dark, the fire reduced to a galaxy of glowing orange embers along the hillside.

"All right," Chief said to Jubal over the radio. "Time to call in the ground crew."

"What does that mean?" I asked Tyler.

He smiled. "The ground crew will mop up after us. They'll pull together piles in the black and burn them out until the fire is cold. We're done unless embers jump the fire line."

The hotshots were already packing it in, making the long haul back to the vehicles. I walked with my camera in hand, making it easier to document the return hike of exhausted, ash-covered men trudging through the forest without a single person to thank them for saving countless miles of trees and homes. The public would never know the reality of what had happened here, or how hard the hotshots had worked to make sure no one would. The only evidence was the scorched earth we'd left behind.

A small white flake touched the end of my nose, and I looked up, seeing thousands more falling to the earth. The snow seemed to give the crew a second wind, and they began chatting about the day and what they might do with the rest of their weekend.

"Are you warm enough?" Tyler asked.

"As warm as one can be in twenty-degree weather," I said.

"Did you get any good shots of me, Ellie?" Watts asked, pretending to flip back the long hair he didn't have.

"I'm pretty sure I got at least three hundred of everyone," I said, lifting my camera to click through the shots again. I was impressed with myself. Every time I snapped the shutter, the result was better and better. My adjustment time was faster as well.

The hotshots walked in a single file line to the trucks, the lights on their hardhats piercing the dark. The smell of smoke was all around us—in the air, on our clothes, saturating our pores—I wasn't sure I would ever smell anything else.

An animal scurried through the snow-covered brush just feet from us, and I startled.

"I think it's a bear, Ellie," Taylor teased. "You're not scared of large animals with teeth that could rip the flesh from your bones lurking in the dark, are you?"

"Knock it off," Tyler said from behind me.

I readjusted the straps on my pack, unable to stop smiling, and relieved Tyler couldn't see it. My new love for what Chief called *adventure photography* wasn't the only thing that made me feel I was on the right path. The fires and photographs were a thrill—surprisingly, Tyler's presence had a calming effect. Together they replaced the risks and narcotics I'd been destroying myself with since I was fourteen.

I frowned, unhappy with that revelation. Did I have to replace old vices with new? I was digging one hole to fill another. That didn't seem right, either.

"Do you want me to carry that?" Tyler asked.

I tightened my grip on my pack. "I've got it."

"We've still got a few miles to go. If you need me—"

"I've got it, Tyler. Don't coddle me."

Smitty looked at me over his shoulder and winked, but his expression fell when his gaze drifted behind me to Tyler. I wasn't sure what exchange they'd had, but Smitty turned back around in a hurry.

The hotshots in the long line ahead had already started the trucks and had them toasty warm by the time we reached fire camp. The tents had been broken down and the equipment and generators loaded. Tyler opened the door for me, and I climbed in, scooting close to Taco to give Tyler plenty of room.

The engine revved, and the cab rattled before we pulled forward, heading for the back mountain road we'd taken there. Tyler fidgeted, barely able to sit still, as if each second sitting next to me was torture.

I clicked through the different pictures, deleting the junk and keeping my favorites. After a few miles, Tyler finally tapped my knee and leaned close to whisper in my ear.

"What did I do?"

I looked into his russet eyes. He was confused, and maybe a little hurt, but I couldn't explain something I didn't understand myself.

"Nothing," I said.

I started to mess with my camera again, but he gently touched my chin, tilting my head to meet his gaze. "Ellie. Tell me. Was it when I pulled you back? You know I'm just trying to keep you safe, right? If I was rough, I'm sorry."

"No, I know. It's fine," I said, shrugging from his touch. "I'm not mad; I'm tired. I'm sorry I snapped at you."

He scanned my face, trying to discern if I was telling the truth. He knew I was lying, but nodded, choosing to let it go while we were riding in a truck full of his crew. The hotshots were being lulled to sleep by the rumble of the motor and the vibration of the tires against the uneven terrain.

Tyler looked out the window, vexed and frustrated. I touched his arm, but he didn't move. After another ten minutes, his body relaxed. His head was propped against the glass, bobbing with the movement of the truck. I returned my attention to my camera, assessing the remaining images and hoping Jojo would be happy with at least a few.

Taco was snoring in the front seat, his head tilted back and his mouth hung open. The engine was so loud it almost drowned out the sound, and the others didn't seem to notice.

I tapped on Jubal's shoulder. "You're driving the whole way?"

"I like to drive home. Clears my head."

"It was a good run," I said.

"Any day without injuries or fatalities is a good day."

Jubal was smiling, but I sat back, stunned. The hotshots went out to each call hopeful, but never truly certain, if they would all return. I couldn't imagine a sadder family unit than that, and I finally understood why a group of men from all over the country— some of them strangers—were so close.

"What kind of injuries?" I asked. "Aside from burns."

"I've seen a lot of guys get hurt by snags—the trees still standing in the black. They can topple so silent, you never hear them coming. Lotta guys hurt that way. We work with a lot of sharp equipment—the saws, pulaskis—not to mention the drip torches and flares. Pretty much everything we do can get somebody hurt, and we're operating on little sleep and physical exhaustion."

"Why do it?" I asked. "Loving the outdoors and physical labor is a given to even think about this job. But when you're exhausted and surrounded by fire in the middle of nowhere, what makes you think, 'This is worth it'?"

"My boys. Doing something so difficult for months on end makes for a tight-knit crew. We're family. Some days I think I'm getting too old, and then I remember there's nowhere else you can find what we have. Soldiers, maybe. That's all I can think of."

I scribbled in my notepad, straining to see in the glow of the dashboard light. Jubal told me stories about the different crews he'd been on, how Alpine was his favorite, and how he'd decided wildfire fighting was his calling. Then he recalled the day the Maddoxes walked into the station.

"The closeness and trust level of a crew is paramount, but those boys ... they came in and were the glue. I don't know what we'll do if they move home."

"Where's home?" I asked, a sinking feeling coming over me.

"Illinois."

"Why would they move back?"

"They're dad's gettin' older. He's a widower, you know."

"Tyler mentioned that."

Jubal thought about that for a while. "They've got two younger brothers there, too. They've talked about moving back to help."

"That's sweet, but I can't imagine either of them doing anything else."

"Neither can I, but they're a close family, the Maddoxes. I've just heard Taylor and Tyler talk—I've never met any of 'em. The rest of the family doesn't know the boys fight fires."

"What?" I said, stunned.

"Nope. They don't want to upset their dad. Those boys are rowdy, but they're softies on the inside. I think the twins would light themselves on fire before they'd let anyone they love get hurt."

I looked up at Tyler sleeping deeply, his face peaceful. I leaned over, barely touching my cheek to his arm. Without hesitation, Tyler reached around my shoulders and hugged me against his side. I stiffened at first, but then relaxed, feeling the warmth of his body thaw my frozen bones.

I met Jubal's gaze in the rearview mirror. His smile touched his eyes, and then he looked forward. "Ellie?" he said. Just the reflection of his ice-blue irises seared through me. "Do you know what's coming?"

"Goodbye?" I said, only half-joking.

Jubal smiled, concentrating again on the road. "Maybe not."

CHAPTER ELEVEN

FINLEY'S DUCK-LIP SELFIE popped up on the display of my cell phone, but I pressed END and let my voicemail talk to her instead.

"Your sister again?" Tyler asked, patting his face with an old ratty hand towel. The rest of him was still dirty, as were the rest of us.

I'd forgotten what my hair smelled like when it didn't reek of smoke, or how my sheets felt against my skin. I pulled my camera off my neck and fell onto the raggedy sofa of the Alpine duty station, deep in the Rocky Mountain National Forest. Fire season had started early, and I'd been camping with the Alpine Hotshots for fourteen days while they fought a fire that dug in so deep the smoke jumpers from all over the country were deployed. According to the Alpine crew, it was their biggest fire in two seasons.

The crew headed for the kitchen, and I sat, my limbs sprawled in every direction, watching them pass by. Every muscle in my body hurt, every joint, even my insides. I'd started my period our second day in fire camp, but it was barely present before it went away, most likely from the sudden surge in activity and decrease in caloric intake. My pants were loose. I wasn't sure if I wanted to look at myself in the mirror.

Smitty high-fived Taco before opening the fridge and leaning in to weigh his options, his face smudged with soot.

"That got intense for a second there," Tyler said.

"Thanks for babysitting me ... again. And for helping me with my tent. I can't believe the guys slept on the fire line for three nights. Some of the guys didn't even have coats."

"They're bigger guys. It's called flight weight—sort of like a weight limit. Sometimes, the helos fly us to the more remote locations, so we don't have to hike so far on foot. Between equipment, our fuel, and the crew, the helos can only carry so much. Sometimes, Runt will bring one of those aluminum sheets the mountain climbers use for camping because he's skinny, and he has the flight weight to spare."

"So you huddle?"

"Huddle, share blankets, spoon … it's fucking cold up there. Whatever works," he joked.

"Then why do it?"

"Sleeping on the fire line means hazard pay. Some of the guys prefer it to sleeping at fire camp."

"The generators were pretty loud," I said.

"You should have said something. We could have hopped in a truck and driven a little farther out, away from the noise."

"It was fine. I was fine."

"For a rich kid, you don't complain, do you?"

"I loved it out there. I really did."

Tyler leaned over and sniffed my shoulder. "You smell amazing."

"Shut up."

"I'm serious. Wildland smoke is my favorite smell. On a girl? Makes you strangely appealing."

"I've been called worse."

Tyler frowned. "Not in front of me."

I managed a tired smile. "My hero."

The hotshots had already peeled off their suits and packs in the truck bay, but we all smelled like old cheese that had been smoked in a giant campfire. Tyler kneeled, pinching the laces of my snow boots and pulling apart the knots. He slipped them off, one by one, and I leaned back even further, wiggling my toes a few times to celebrate their freedom. He pulled off my socks slowly, grimacing at the new blisters, the seeping blisters, and the healing blisters.

"Christ, Ellie. We talked about this."

"I don't mind. Makes me feel like I'm earning it."

"Gangrene isn't an award." He jogged over to fetch the first aid kit and began doctoring the mangled mess I'd been walking on for ten days.

I tried to blink, but it took a while for my eyes to open again. They felt like they weighed a hundred pounds. I could have taken a nap right there.

Tyler finished slathering antibiotic cream and taping gauze to my wounds, then took a blanket from the back of a recliner and unfolded it, spreading it over me. I bounced when he plopped on the sofa next to me, wearing jeans and a long-sleeved thermal, the three buttons at the top open. I preferred him in his ill-fitting, flame-retardant clothes and blue hardhat, but he would never let me forget it if he knew.

"You never complain. No training, you just jumped in there and hiked miles and camped out in the dirt and snow in freezing temperatures," he said, relaxing next to me. "I'm impressed. All the guys are."

"I don't care," I said, resting my cheek against his shoulder. I was frozen and exhausted, unsure how my fingers continued to function as the days went on. True to his word, Tyler had kept me close. It was a beautiful but difficult trek, up inclines and through the aspens. In some places, the snow was still ankle-to-shin deep, and we walked for almost an hour to the site through the underwood and slush. My feet and face were numb before we ever reached the fire, but I was distracted from any discomfort when I looked through the lens of my camera.

I could barely move, and the rest of Tyler's crew were chatting and making sandwiches. After fourteen days on the mountain, they were owed forty-eight hours of mandatory R & R. Even though they were all worn down, their version of a weekend had arrived, and they were restless.

"How are they so … peppy?" I asked, my words slow, my voice hoarse.

"Adrenaline," Tyler said, picking up my camera and clicking through the various shots.

"How can they still have an adrenaline high? The ride home took forever. I thought we were never going to get back."

"Every time we leave for a fire, there's a chance one or all of us might be injured or worse. Returning as a complete unit means a lot." He handed me the camera. "Nice pics."

"Thanks."

He rested his chin on my hair. "Jojo is going to be happy."

"Thanks. She texted me today. She wants to see what I've got."

"So you're going to show them to her now?" His eyebrows pulled in. "Does this mean you're done?"

"I guess we'll find out."

Tyler was watching his friends wrestle and joke in the kitchen, but he looked unhappy. "Ellie?"

I heard him call my name, but I was at the bottom of a barrel full of water, warm and unwilling to move. The sound of the guys in the kitchen faded away, and all I could hear was the sound of my own heart and the steady rhythm of Tyler's breath. I sank deeper into myself, comfortable under the blanket and against Tyler's arm.

"Shut the fuck up!" Tyler hissed. He jerked, and I blinked, seeing a blurry Watts jump over whatever Tyler had thrown at him.

I sat up and rubbed my eyes. "Wow. How long was I out?"

"Three hours," Jubal said with a smile. "Tyler didn't move a muscle the whole time so he didn't wake you up."

"Did you get dinner?" I asked, looking up at him.

"I brought him a sandwich," Watts said, throwing the small square pillow back at Tyler. "He'll live."

Tyler caught it and held it to his chest, pouting.

"What's up with you?" I asked.

Watts jutted out his lip. "He's pissed we woke you up."

"Knock it off," Jubal said, handing me a glass of ice water.

"Thanks," I said.

Smitty turned up the television, and Taco fished for his ringing cell phone, standing up to take the call in the office.

Tyler stood. "We should probably get those shots to Jojo and you home, huh?"

"Yeah. I should probably call José."

"I'll take you," he said immediately.

Jubal watched us with amusement, although I wasn't sure why. The rest of Tyler's crew seemed to be going about their business, while still keeping an ear open to whatever I might say.

"Uh, sure," I said. "Thanks."

All nineteen hotshots, from Fish to Pup, gave me a bear hug before I left, all asking me to come back soon. Chief made a rare appearance outside of his office to tell me goodbye, and then Tyler walked me to his truck, patiently keeping pace with my sloth-like speed.

"Fuck," Tyler said under his breath. "I should have started the truck so it was warm."

"It's fine. Really, no big deal. I think I've proven myself by now not to be high maintenance."

"That you have." He opened my door but paused when he noticed me staring. "What?"

"What are you doing?"

He shrugged. "Opening the door for you."

"Why?" I said. His gesture made me feel awkward.

"Just get in."

I climbed inside, hugging myself to keep warm while Tyler slammed the passenger door and jogged around to the other side. He was brooding, unhappy about something.

He drove us down to the magazine so I could drop off my flash drive to Jojo. She greeted me with a smile, eager to upload the pictures to her computer.

"Daddy is loving these," she said.

"Yeah? Does that mean I'm done?" I asked.

"Maybe. I need you to write up what you've learned so far, and I'll clean it up for you. We might need some pork."

"Um ... pork?"

Her finger tapped the computer mouse. "You know ... material we might use later." She scanned me from head to toe. "Go home and get some rest, Ellison. You look like hell."

"On my way," I said, taking back my chip and heading for the door.

Tyler's truck was still running, the exhaust fumes billowing into the night sky. The moment he saw me walking toward him, he leaned over the console and pushed open my door. I climbed up again, and he rubbed my leg quickly.

"We need to get you home. You're exhausted."

"You've been working a lot harder than me."

"But I'm used to it. Jojo should give you a few days off. You're going to get sick."

"I feel better than I have in a long time, actually."

Tyler put the gearshift into drive and pulled away from the curb, heading toward my house. He lit a cigarette and handed it to me without me asking, and then lit his own. We didn't talk much. Instead, I left Tyler to the seemingly millions of thoughts in his head.

Tyler pulled his truck into my drive and slowed to a stop at the gate. I leaned over him to press in the code, and the gate whined, beginning its slow journey open. Tyler pulled forward and drove the mile-long path to the house.

It was dark, and I assumed Maricela and José had gone home for the night.

"Thanks for the ride," I said, gathering my things and climbing down to the concrete below. I walked around the front of the truck, took a few more steps, and then froze.

"What are you doing here?" I asked.

"Ellison, she knows," Sterling said. He stepped out from the shadows, looking thin, his whiskers a few days past a five o'clock shadow. He stumbled down the steps, his tie loose and his shirt stained.

Tyler's door opened and closed, and his footsteps crunched against the snow and rock until he stopped just behind me.

"Hey, Sterling," Tyler said. "Good to see you."

Sterling's eyes were wet. I could smell the whiskey from ten feet away. "She fucking knows, Ellie. She won't answer my calls."

"I've told you, she never answers your calls when she's on holiday."

"She fucking knows!" he spat.

"Hey," Tyler said, stepping between us. "I'm not sure what's going on here, but I bet it will make more sense in the morning. Let me take you home, Sterling. You look like you've had a rough day."

"Fuck you," Sterling said, still staring at me. "And you, too."

"Fuck me?" I said. "Who's the one who passed me the mystery pill?"

"She's never going to speak to me again. What am I going to do?"

"You're overreacting, Sterling," I said. "You're being paranoid. Whatever you're on isn't helping."

"I know this is your fault!" he snapped, his voice carrying through the trees between our homes. "You're not just the town whore; you're the world's whore. Everyone knows who to call for a fuck if Ellie's in town," he said.

"Wait just a goddamn minute," Tyler said, taking a step. I grabbed his coat, holding him back.

Sterling laughed. "What are you going to do, lieutenant bad ass? Change my mind?"

"Keep talking," Tyler growled. "You'll find out."

Sterling held up his hands in mock terror. "Put that blue collar to work."

Tyler took another step, but I put my hand on his chest. I turned to face him but looked down instead, ashamed. "He's drunk. He's upset. He lives next door. Just let him go home."

Tyler's jaw muscles danced beneath the skin, but he let Sterling pass, even after Sterling nudged him with his shoulder.

I trudged up the steps, using my keys to gain entrance to my parents' home. It was quiet, every step and movement we made echoing through the halls.

Tyler closed the door behind us, and then followed me to the kitchen. "Your house looks a lot different this time."

"Nearly empty?" I asked.

Maricela had left me a covered plate in the fridge with a toothpick flag on how many minutes it should cook in the microwave.

"Wanna share?" I asked. "It might be a day or two old, but at least it's not an MRE."

"Nah. You go ahead."

I removed the foil and pressed the three. The light turned on and the plate began to spin, slow and steady. I was glad someone else was in the house besides me, but I didn't want to turn around, afraid of the expression on Tyler's face.

"What happened with you and Sterling?" Tyler asked. "Weren't you friends a few weeks ago? Why was he saying those things about you?"

"Because it's the truth," I said simply.

"Bullshit. I don't believe that for a second."

"Why wouldn't you?" I asked, turning around. "You've experienced it firsthand."

"I just consider myself lucky that I happened to be here at the right time. We had fun, and we were safe. Anything beyond that is no one's fucking business."

I laughed once, surprised at his response.

"What do you want me to say?" he asked. "If you're a slut, I'm a slut."

"You're a slut, Maddox."

"Not lately."

I fought a smile just as the microwave beeped again. Tyler stood, removing my plate and setting it on the black and white marble island. "And you're clearly trying to make some adjustments in your life. It's just fucking wrong for him to throw your past in your face."

"Does eight weeks ago qualify as my past?" I asked, pulling a fork out of the drawer. I sat down, swirling the silver points around in the baked potato.

"This morning is the past," Tyler said. "We can be totally different people today if we want. Fuck Sterling if he resents that you've changed. People like that are usually dealing with their own shit, anyway, and what they're pissed about really has nothing to do with you."

I felt a hot tear fall down my cheek, and I immediately wiped it away.

"Hey," Tyler said, reaching across the island. "You can talk to me."

"My sister? Finley? She's in love with Sterling. That first-love love doesn't go away."

Tyler pointed his thumb behind him. "That douche? Why?"

"It doesn't matter. He's kind of a certifiable head case, but she loves him. She would be with him, but she's holding off. She's taking over my father's business and doesn't have time to be in a relationship. They want to be together. She's fighting it, and he's been miserable."

"So how is that your fault?" Tyler asked, confused.

I wiped my nose with my napkin. "He had a ... I don't know ... I was over there, talking about finding a new job. We were already drinking, and he had these pills. We took them ... I don't remember much after that, but we..." I nodded.

Tyler nodded, too, letting me know I didn't have to continue. His face flushed, his teeth clenched. "He drugged you, fucked you, and now he's blaming you for it."

I closed my eyes, and more tears fell down my cheek. So many hours of the day had been spent trying not to think of what I'd done and how it could have happened, that hearing Tyler describe it so bluntly made my chest ache.

"I shouldn't have taken the pill. I didn't even ask him what it was. I just popped it in my mouth." My breath faltered. "Sterling loves Fin. If he knew that was going to happen, he wouldn't have taken it, either. He's just as scared as I am that she'll never speak to us again."

"That's why you're..." He gestured to me.

"Yes, why I'm trying to do better. I'm hoping if she ever does find out, she'll forgive me because..." I choked. "I'm not that person anymore."

"You're not. I'm not sure you ever were," Tyler said, putting his hand on mine. "Eat. You haven't eaten all day."

I took a bite, chewing as I cried—as it turned out, that was surprisingly difficult.

Tyler rummaged through the cabinets until he found some Keurig pods. He watched me eat, clearing his throat when he finally got the courage to ask his question.

"Did you ... you know ... go to the doctor? I imagine neither of you probably thought to use protection."

I nodded, wishing I could crawl into a hole and die. "Yeah. I've had an IUD in one form or another since I was fifteen. I checked out."

"Good. It could have been a lot worse. Piece of shit," he grumbled.

"It would be easier to blame him, but it's not just his fault." The tears began to flow again. Tyler set a steaming mug in front of me, and then made another for himself. We sipped tea until I stopped crying, sitting together in comfortable silence. We had barely said anything since our initial conversation an hour before, but I felt better just knowing he was there.

Dark circles began to form under his red eyes, and he tapped his keys. "Ellie..."

"Stay," I blurted out.

"Here?" Tyler said, pointing down at the island.

"Can you?"

"I mean ... I guess I could. It's my day off, anyway. Chief owes me."

"It doesn't have to be like last time."

He made a face. "I know. I'm not a complete asshat."

"So you'll stay?" I felt so weak, so vulnerable, but that was preferable to being alone.

"Yeah. I mean, I can if you want me to. On one condition, though."

I studied him, unsure what he was going to require.

"What if we tried another breakfast?" he asked. "Tomorrow morning."

I breathed a sigh of relief. "That's it?"

"That's all."

"I'm assuming you don't want me to attend hungover this time?"

He chuckled, but he seemed preoccupied. "I don't know. I kind of liked holding your hair."

"I bet you did," I teased. I looked over at him, not a trace of humor in my expression. "Full disclosure ... I'm pretty sure this is a terrible idea."

"Yeah," Tyler said, looking down. "You've mentioned that. I know you're trying to get your shit together, and I'm probably a risky friend to have during a transition ... but, I don't know, Ellie. I just like being around you."

"Why? I'm mean to you."

He grinned. "Exactly."

I shook my head. "You're weird."

"You're sort of beautiful with dirt on your face."

I managed to use my remaining energy to breathe out a laugh. "I'm just going to say that's a compliment and call it good, but I'm still going to take a shower."

"I'm next," he said.

I put my dirty plate in the sink, and then led Tyler upstairs, this time to my bedroom. He sat on the end of my bed while I undressed and turned the knob on the shower.

"I was thinking," he called from the other room. "I'm getting pretty sick of the bar scene. There are so many other things to do here. All my friends drink, though."

"Take it from me, that makes it difficult."

"Maybe we should form a club."

I stepped under the water, moaning as it washed over me. Hot showers in the middle of a national park with twenty other people were rare. Just because I didn't complain didn't mean I didn't miss it. "Two people don't make a club, Tyler."

"Who cares?" he said, poking his head through the door. He faced the wall but spoke loud so I could hear. "We can do what we want."

"A no drinking club? That sounds like the lamest thing ever."

"Any club I'm in is fucking awesome."

"If you say so."

"So ... breakfast?" he asked, a new spark of hope in his eyes.

I sighed. "I would be really, really bad for you."

"Nah," he said, waving me away. "Anyway, I'm a big boy. I can handle it."

"I don't need you to save me. I've got this."

"Any other excuses?"

My eyebrows pulled together. "You're sort of a dick when you're not in the woods."

"Rinse off already. It's my turn."

I wrung out my hair and pulled the towel off the rack, stepping out onto the mat. From the corner of my eye, I could see Tyler pulling his shirt over his head. He pulled his belt from the loops, and the buckle clanged against the tile before his jeans hit the floor. He walked across the room and opened the shower, stepping in under the water.

"Christ, this feels good," he said.

I smiled, pulling a brush through my wet hair. I watched his reflection in the mirror lather the soap over his skin, and felt a familiar tingling between my thighs.

"What if this gets ugly?" I asked. "What if you hate me when it's over?"

"Not gonna happen."

"It did with Sterling."

"I'm not going to make you trip balls, and then have sex with you."

"So ... friends?" I asked.

The water cut off, and Tyler stepped out, wrapping a towel around his waist. His Adam's apple bobbed when he swallowed, and then he cleared his throat like he was about to make a promise he didn't want to keep. "Friends."

"Will you still stay?" I asked.

Tyler managed a small smile, the thoughts swirling behind his eyes clouding his irises. "I wasn't going to try to sleep with you, anyway, Ellie."

"No?"

"No. It's just different now."

I stood, stunned, unable to form a response. Whatever the ache was in my chest, I was sure it was something similar to a broken heart.

"C'mon," he said, standing. "Let's crash. I'm beat."

He followed me to the bed, but there was a difference in the air between us. Tyler seemed more relaxed, as if the question was gone, the pressure eliminated. With the towel still wrapped around him, he crawled into my bed, turning onto his side.

I opened my dresser drawer and slipped on a pair of Calvins under my towel and then walked over to bathroom doorway, picking his T-shirt off the floor.

"Just leave it, Ellie. I'm going to wear it home in the morning."

He watched me with confusion and then surprise when I slipped it over my head and padded over to the bed, climbing in next to him. He wrapped both arms around me, burying his nose in my hair, and sighed.

"You're half naked, wearing my shirt. This isn't exactly fair."

I reached into my nightstand, and then turned to face him, staring into his eyes while I peeled open the package in my hand. "We can still be friends," I said, reaching down, sliding my hand between the towel and his skin. He immediately hardened in my hand.

"I don't know how to do this," Tyler breathed, leaning in to graze his lips across mine while I slipped the latex over his skin. "This in-between shit, Ellie. I don't think I can. You're either mine, or you're not."

"I'm not anyone else's."

He planted his mouth on mine, kissing me hard and deep.

"We don't have to fit into any special box," I said. He pulled away, looking for more answers in my eyes. "It is what it is. Can't we just do that?"

Tyler slowly climbed on top of me, scanning my face for half a minute before leaning down to claim me with his mouth.

I tugged on his towel until it slipped away, and it fell somewhere next to the bed.

"You're right," he whispered. "This is a bad idea." He swept the fabric of my Calvins aside, just enough for him to slide inside me.

I took a deep breath and sighed. Tyler felt too good ... too safe. I could see in his eyes that he was willing to try me like poison; even after the first taste, we were already wondering how excruciating the end would be.

CHAPTER TWELVE

TYLER SEEMED TO BE in an uncharacteristically cheerful mood, chomping on his pancakes and smiling at everyone who passed by our table at Winona's, waving with his fork.

I'd woken up in his arms, his nose pressed against my neck. Once he began to stir, I half expected our night together to end in this awkward walk of shame, not sweet kisses and cuddles while he schooled me on doing a load of laundry. He'd loved removing his shirt from my body to drop it in the machine. He'd taken a lot longer to do that than he had chucking in his pants, underwear, and socks.

We'd barely gotten through the first cycle before he lifted me on top of the machine and settled between my legs, reminding me why I'd woken up so wonderfully sore.

In spring fresh clothes, he'd held my hand out to the truck and opened the door for me at Winona's. Now he was looking down at his nearly empty plate, grinning like a fool.

"What's funny?" I asked.

He looked up at me, trying to subdue the smirk on his face and failing. "I wasn't laughing."

"You're smiling. Like, a lot."

"Is that a bad thing?"

"No. I was just wondering what you were think—"

"You," he said immediately. "The same thing I've been thinking about since the night we met."

I pressed my lips together, trying to keep them from curving upward. His good mood was contagious, making it easy to forget what Sterling had said on my front steps the night before, and the worry that he was right.

Finley hadn't called or texted in twenty-four hours. Maybe Sterling was right. Maybe she did know.

Tyler's phone chirped, and he held it to his ear. "Hey, dickhead," he said. His expression changed as he listened, at first concentrating on whatever was being said. Then his eyebrows bounced once. He glanced up at me for half a second, and then looked down, blinking.

"But he's okay," Tyler said, listening again. "He ... he what? No they didn't. Are you fucking *serious*? Wow ... Yeah, no. I won't. Who might come here? What kind of questions? About Trav? What do you mean? Oh. Oh, fuck. Do you think it'll work? All right. Yeah. Yeah, I'll tell Taylor. I said I'll tell him. I get it. We'll circle the wagons. Love you, too, Trent."

He put down the phone and shook his head.

"Did you say Trav?"

"Travis," he said, deflated. "My baby brother."

"Everything all right?" I asked.

"Uh ... yeah. I think so," he said, lost in thought. "He just got married."

"Really? That's great, right?"

"Yeah ... Abby is ... she's amazing. He's crazy in love with her. I'm just surprised. They've been split up."

"Oh. That's um ... that's kind of weird."

"They're like that. I guess there was a fire at the college where I graduated. It's in my hometown."

"Anyone hurt?"

"It was pretty bad. Broke out in a basement, and a lot of people were trapped."

"In a basement?"

"Uh ... that college is sort of known for underground floating fight rings."

"Underground what?"

"It's kind of like a betting ring. Two guys are set up to fight. No one knows where until an hour before. The coordinator calls the fighters, their guys call ten people, then they call five, on and on."

"Then what?"

He shrugged. "Then they fight. People bet. It's a shit ton of money."

"How do you know so much about it?"

"I started it. Taylor and me with the coordinator, Adam."

The look in Tyler's eyes when I'd bet on him at my house the first night we met now made sense. "So was Travis there?"

Tyler's expression fell, and he looked at me for several seconds before answering. "He eloped to Vegas."

"That's good."

"Yeah," Tyler said, rubbing the back of his neck. "More OJ?"

"No, I'm good. We should probably head in."

Tyler paid the check, and then held my hand to the truck like it was the most natural thing in the world. When he dropped me off at the *MountainEar*, the air between us felt heavy and awkward. It was that *should we or shouldn't we kiss* moment and *what does it mean if we do?*

I reached for the handle.

"Hang on a sec," Tyler said, reaching for me. He slid his fingers between mine, and then lifted my hand to his lips.

"Thanks for staying with me last night," I said.

"I'm glad I was there to run off your uninvited guest."

"Me, too."

He took my phone, tapping in numbers and then letters. "If he bothers you again," Tyler said, the crease between his brows deepening. "Call me. But just … you know … call me, anyway."

I stepped out of the truck and waved to him as he pulled away. He bumped up the volume on his radio, and I could hear the bass thumping until he turned onto the highway toward the hotshot dorms.

The door chimed as I walked in to the office. "Morning," I said, waving to Jojo on my way to my desk.

Not only was Wick's door was closed, but a stunning bouquet of butter-yellow and vivid violet roses reached out from a simple glass vase. I circled my desk, crossing one arm across my waist, touching my lips with my fingers, trying not to let my entire face erupt into a smile. Flowers, romance, and theatrics were last on my list of things I wanted from Tyler, but I sat down, soaking in how absolutely giddy it made me.

Jojo poked her head in the doorway. "Who are they from?"

I leaned forward once more to confirm and lifted my hands, letting them hit my thighs. "I couldn't find a card."

"No card? Do you have a guess?" she asked, sauntering into the room and planting her backside on the love seat. "Maybe the guy who just dropped you off?"

I reached down to turn on my desktop, taking a few seconds to get the ridiculous expression off my face before sitting upright. "Maybe."

Jojo crossed her arms, looking quite smug. "I thought this might happen, with you spending so much time at the station. I just didn't realize it would happen so soon."

"Nothing is happening. We're friends."

"Clearly," Jojo said with a smirk. "You look like you've lost weight. Did they feed you?"

"Barely."

She stood. "I brought donuts to celebrate your first day back. They're in the break room."

"You're a saint, but I've already had breakfast. I'll eat some for lunch."

"I have a lot to do today. Are you doing that write-up for me?"

"As best I can. Remember, I'm not a writer. I'll just write what I know, and you can turn it into a story."

"Yeah, yeah ... I heard you the first time," she said, disappearing around the corner.

I opened a new document and stared at the blank page for a while before my gaze wandered to the bouquet. I'd been sent flowers before, mostly from my father, but thought had been put into this bouquet. The colors were straight from my room, the roses meaning more than just 'thanks for last night.' Maybe I was reading too far into it, but Tyler wasn't one to make dishonest gestures.

I shook it off, focusing on Jojo's request. I recounted my first day, the basics like the names of the tools, what they looked like, and the crew's funny nicknames. They all respected one another, but, in my opinion, looked up to Tyler. He settled arguments, led them on the mountain, and they respected the decisions he made when Jubal wasn't around to make them. I talked about fuel breaks and mineral soil and vegetation. Packs, supplies, flight weight, and ten codes. I included my limited knowledge on slutter, fire towers, coordinates, and weather. Then I added stories like the one about the best helo pilot Tyler had ever worked with—an Aussie redhead named Holly who could back in her Huey and swing it around at the last minute to get them on the side of the mountain so they didn't have to hike so far in—and the time Tyler ate a fat, juicy grub worm for two hundred dollars.

Two hours had passed without me realizing, and Jojo knocked on the doorjamb before walking in. She moseyed across my office to her father's door. She knocked on it twice and then took a step back.

Wick walked out, his cheeks red and his eyes bright. Jojo stood next to my desk, crossing her arms.

"What's going on?" I asked.

"Daddy and I have been in awe over your pictures, Ellie. You've sent us some amazing stuff. You went out in the field and camped in freezing temps with those heathens for nights on end. You were born for this."

"For what?"

"To be a field photographer," Wick said.

"A what?" I asked, feeling uneasy.

"Daddy is going to hire another assistant."

"What?" I said, panicking.

Jojo touched my arm. "It's okay. Your new job with the magazine will pay more."

"More?"

Her eyes widened. "A lot more. Daddy wants this to be an ongoing feature for the magazine. He wants you to follow the Alpine Hotshots through fire season."

"But if you hire someone else, then what?"

Jojo rolled her eyes. "Who are we kidding? Daddy isn't going to find anyone. I've been doing it for this long. I can wait until fire season is over. You have to do this, Ellie. It's going to be amazing."

"I … don't know what to say," I said, both unsettled and flattered.

"Say bye," Wick said. "I want you back out there starting today. We'll need a continuing story for next month. We've already cleared it with the superintendent. Pack your bags. You'll be bunking at the Alpine's dormitory until October."

"Oh, thank God," I said, closing my eyes.

I could practically hear Jojo smiling. She had no idea I was going to be kicked out of my parents' home next month. I had barely saved enough for my cell phone bill, much less a deposit and first month's rent, even on houses or apartments up to half an hour outside of town. Shadowing the hotshots until October gave me six to seven more months to figure out living arrangements. Even if I was sleeping in a truck or tent most of the time, it was preferable to moving into a shelter.

"We knew you'd be happy! I told you she'd be happy, Daddy."

"Am I done?" Wick said.

Jojo sighed. "You're done. Go back to resting your feet on your desk."

I pulled out my phone and texted Tyler.

> *Did you hear the news?*

>> *Just now. I'm your official babysitter. Pretty pumped.*

> *Thanks for the flowers. They're beautiful.* ☺

It took a while for Tyler to respond.

>> *I didn't send you flowers. I can't decide if I feel like a dick or if I want to kill whoever sent them.*

> *You didn't send the flowers?*

>> *No. There's no card?*

> *No.*

>> *I wanna know who sent them.*

> *Me, too.*

>> *Not for the same reason.*

> *… which is?*

>> *I'm having violent thoughts. All I can say.*

> *Quit.*

>> *I have a bad temper in general. Sending my gf flowers is not a good idea.*

... I am not your gf.

Yet. You're not my gf yet.

I set my phone to silent and put it in my drawer, shaking my head, a dozen conflicting emotions swirling in my head and heart, including curiosity about the flowers. Who else would send them but Tyler?

"Ellie?" Jojo's voice came over the speaker, and I jumped. "You've got a call on line one."

"Is it a guy?"

"Yes."

"Is his name Sterling?"

"No."

I pressed the button for line one and picked up the phone, fully expecting Tyler's voice to be on the other line. "This is Ellie."

"Bunny?" My father's deep voice boomed through the receiver, so loud that I had to hold the phone away.

I slowly pressed it against my ear, speaking softly. "Daddy?"

"I heard the news. I'm so proud of you," he said, his voice breaking. "I knew you could do it."

"Th-thank you. Daddy, I can't talk right now. I'm at work."

"I know. I spoke to Wick this morning. He's impressed with you. He says you're the best assistant he's ever had."

Wick didn't tell him about the assignment.

"I actually just got a raise, so I'll um ... I've found a place. I'm moving out this week."

"Nonsense, bunny. You've proven yourself. Maricela is packing for you now, and your passport and plane ticket is at the house. We want you to join your sister in Sanya. Your plane leaves in the morning."

"Who's we?"

"What's that?"

"You said we want you to go to Sanya."

He cleared his throat. "Your mother..."

After a short scuffle, my mother had possession of the phone. "Really, Ellison, you couldn't have found something less ... desperate?"

"Excuse me?"

"A secretary? For J.W. Chadwick, no less. That's just embarrassing."

The blood beneath my cheeks began to boil. "You didn't really give me a choice, Mother."

"You're going to thank them for the opportunity, and you're going to meet your sister like your father wants, and then you're going to start with his company, under Finley. Do you understand?"

"Is this what Sally wants?"

Mother sighed. "Your father felt Sally was too … restrictive."

"What about the contract?"

Mother chuckled. "Well, it wasn't a legally binding contract, Ellison. It was more of an agreement on paper."

I took a deep breath, relieved that I could be lying on the back of a rented yacht in thirty-two hours, soaking up the sun and drinking mimosas and eating my weight in lobster and Peking duck. The question was whether Finley wanted me there.

"Have you told Finley?"

"Not yet. It's the middle of the night there."

"You just decided this morning that I wasn't dead to you?"

"Honestly, Ellison. Don't be so dramatic. We forced you to get a job, you did, so you're being rewarded for your hard work, and then you'll work under your sister. No one's dead."

"Someone's dead."

Mother tripped over her words. "What do you … who are you … what on Earth are you going on about, Ellison? Who's dead?"

I swallowed. "Please thank Daddy for the tickets, but I'm not going to Sanya. I have a job here that I love."

"You love being a secretary," Mother deadpanned. I could hear my father asking questions in the background.

"I'm actually taking pictures for them, too, and I'm really good at it."

"Ellison, for goodness' sake. You're a secretary slash photographer? Listen to yourself."

"I'm staying."

"This is about a boy, isn't it? You've met some local, and you're not thinking straight. Philip, talk some sense into her."

"I'm going to be unreachable at times. If it's an emergency, call the magazine. They know how to get in touch with me."

"Ellison," Mother warned. "If you hang up the phone—"

"You'll cut me off?" I asked.

While my mother stumbled over what to say next, I hung up. I was afraid that if I spoke to my father again, I would change my mind.

CHAPTER THIRTEEN

THE LIGHTS WERE DIM at headquarters. Half the hotshots were sitting around the kitchen table, playing cards, while the others were showering.

The only noise was the water pipes funneling through the dorm to the ten showers plus my fingers clicking on the keyboard. I had pretty much become part of the sofa since we'd arrived back to our temporary home, simultaneously resting and uploading the latest pictures. After the last picture sent, I began typing out the next installment of the *MountainEar*'s "Fire and Ice" series.

Tyler walked out, his hair freshly buzzed and his cheeks red from the hot shower. When he was clean, the tan line around his eyes from wearing his goggles all day in the sun was more prominent. He was wearing a heather-gray Alpine Hotshot T-shirt, navy cotton shorts, and—from the looks of it—nothing underneath.

"My turn?" I asked as he fell onto the sofa next to me.

Tyler frowned. "The shower stalls are side by side."

"So? I'm just one of the guys, right?"

Tyler didn't answer, but I could tell the thought of me showering next to his crewmates bothered him. Initially they'd all offered to let me shower first, but I wasn't about to make all twenty of them wait after nearly two weeks on the mountain for me to take a shower.

I chuckled. "Just kidding. Puddin'!" I called. "You're up! Wash the stink off!"

"Yes, ma'am," Puddin' said, hopping up from his padded foldout chair.

Tyler breathed out a laugh, and I nudged him with my elbow. "What's funny?"

"You've somehow become the boss around here. They take orders from you like they do from the superintendent or Jubal."

"Maybe they just need a big sister."

Tyler watched Puddin' walk across the room toward the showers with his bath bag swung over his shoulder. Puddin' ducked under the doorframe, his arms standing out from his body because his muscles were so massive. He was the largest crewmember, followed by Cat and Sugar. Although they had arrived looking like powerlifters, the hiking and arduous labor for twelve to sixteen hours a day had made them leaner. Tyler had said that by the end of fire season, they would all look more like cross-country runners. Puddin' had already lost forty pounds.

"You think he needs a big sister?" Tyler asked.

Puddin' poked his head around the corner. "Ellie? Think you could make me another grilled cheese? They're the best I've ever had."

"I'll make you one," Fish said from the table.

Puddin's sheepish expression made him look like a little boy. "Nah. That's okay, Fish."

I smiled. I wasn't the best cook, but I could make a mean grilled cheese. Puddin' didn't mean they were *the best*; I just made them a lot like his mom had when he was young. "Three?" I asked.

"If it's not too much trouble," Puddin' said. His voice was so deep it carried like he was speaking through a muffled megaphone, the way a giant might sound.

"Okay if I do it after my shower?" I asked.

"Beggars can't be choosers."

He disappeared around the corner, and I stretched my neck toward Tyler, looking up at him with a knowing smile. "Yes, I think they all need a big sister."

"Or a mom," Tyler said. "They might not let you leave."

"If I don't find a place by October, I might not." I was joking, but Tyler watched me for a long time.

"You need a place?" he asked. "I'm looking for a roommate."

"I thought you and Taylor lived together."

"Part-time. After fire season, he travels."

"I need someplace permanent."

"Maybe we could look into a three-bedroom. This is Slick's last season. He and his wife have a three-bedroom condo that will be up for sale."

I thought about it for half a second. "I can't afford to buy."

"I can. I was thinking about it, anyway."

I shook my head. "We can't be roommates."

"Why not?"

"You know why."

He nodded a few times, pretending to watch the television. Every few minutes he would smile and start to say something, but think better of it.

Puddin' came out in a fresh pair of comfortable clothes, and the remaining ash-covered crew looked to me.

"Really?" I asked.

They kept staring.

I sighed. "Go, Cat."

Cat jumped up, smiling. "I'm her favorite."

"Bullshit," Tyler said, pointing at him.

Everyone at the table laughed, and Cat jogged by, smooching his lips at me. "I love you, too, Ellie," he lilted, winking.

"I'll punch your cock," Tyler said, slapping at him.

Sage came out, and I sent Jew in. Bucky came out, and I called on Sancho. Soon, all the guys were finished, and it was my turn. I rolled my eyes at Tyler—he insisted again on standing by the door. It wasn't the first time I'd taken a shower at headquarters, and the guys would never peek, but they loved to tease him.

I stepped in front of the long line of sinks and mirrors, snuggled in my robe—the only thing I had packed that reminded me of the luxuries of home. I scrubbed my hair with the towel, feeling a little more human. Sometimes we would have access to a tractor-trailer full of shower stalls, but when we were too deep in the mountains for the trucks to reach, it was living dirty or bathing in a pond, river, or waterfall. At fire camp, I was a different person, ignoring the dirt and sweat on my body and the grease in my hair. Once, Tyler had taken me down to a waterfall to rinse off, but the water was freezing. For me, at least, being dirty for a few more days was preferable to the sting of just-melted snow that didn't warm, even at the height of summer.

Tyler knocked on the doorjamb.

"I'm decent," I said.

He leaned against the wooden frame, crossing his arms. "You are grossly underestimating yourself."

"What?" I said, rubbing moisturizer on my face. Spending so much time in the dry mountain air, my skin felt like sandpaper. It didn't help that I'd forgotten my sunscreen one day, and my nose was beginning to peel.

"Nothing," he said. "I meant what I said earlier. If you need a place, one way or another, we can make it work."

"We can't live together, Tyler. We've already got this weird friends-with-benefits thing going on…"

"Not lately," Tyler said, almost pouting.

"And it would make things really complicated. Look at you. You're standing outside the bathroom door so the guys don't walk by."

"I'm protecting your virtue," he teased.

"You're jealous. They like messing with you when it comes to me. Everyone knows—"

"Everyone knows what?" he asked.

I cleared my throat. "You know."

"No, I don't know. Tell me."

"That something is going on between us." He smiled, his dimple sinking deep into his cheek. I narrowed my eyes. "Stop smiling."

"No," he said.

I wet my toothbrush, squeezed out a dot of paste on the bristles, and then wet it again before scrubbing my teeth.

"I do that," Tyler said.

"Do what?" I said, my mouth full of suds.

"Wet my toothbrush twice."

I rolled my eyes. "We must be soul mates."

"Glad you agree."

I bent over and spit in the sink, and then Tyler grabbed me, sealing his lips onto mine. When I pushed him away, he had a circle of toothpaste around his mouth.

"What are you doing, Tyler? Gross!"

He wiped the toothpaste from his mouth and licked his finger, winking at me. "I kind of miss you."

I stood next to the sink, the water running, watching Tyler turn the corner, a bounce in his step. I shook my head, wondering what the hell had gotten into him. Since I'd been at headquarters, he had been professional. No late-night sneaking around, no ass grabs or even a stolen kiss—until now.

I looked in the mirror at my sunken cheeks and the happiness in my eyes. A giddy feeling swirled in my stomach, different from the tingling I usually felt when Tyler was around. The summer was flying by. He was talking about sharing an apartment, but reality was different in the middle of nowhere, surrounded by trees and seeing the same twenty people every day. I wasn't sure if Tyler would feel the same when fire season was over.

I changed into a pair of flannel pajama pants, sweatshirt, and fuzzy socks, and then stepped out into the TV room. Nineteen hotshots were standing behind the sofa, listening to Tyler talk to a stranger in a dark suit and tie. The man was sitting on one of the recliners with a notepad and pen.

I approached the crowd, listening in.

"So, you haven't spoken to your brother about the fire?" the man said.

"I mean, yeah," Tyler answered. "I'm an alumnus of Eastern. He's a student. We belong to the same fraternity, and we lost brothers in that fire."

"But you're sure he wasn't there," the man said. "I would like to remind you that I'm a federal agent, and it's imperative that you're honest."

"He already gave you an answer, Agent Trexler," Taylor said, his voice firm.

I swallowed. Tyler had gotten the phone call about the fire back in March. I wondered why they were just now questioning him.

The agent looked up at Taylor. "Did he speak to you about it?"

"No," Taylor said. "I heard about it from Tyler."

Trexler pointed his pen at the twin on the sofa. "And you're Tyler."

"Correct," Tyler said.

Trexler looked down at his notepad. "It's interesting that you're a…"

"Interagency hotshot," Fish said. "And a damn good one."

Trexler suppressed a grin. "Your father is under the impression that you're an insurance agent. Were you? An insurance agent?"

"No," Tyler said.

"Why does your father think that you are?"

Taylor shifted his weight from one foot to the other, tightening his grip on his arms. I could see his biceps tensing.

"Our mother died when we were kids," Tyler said. "It would upset our dad if he knew what we did."

"So," the agent said, "do you think it's a safe assumption that he wouldn't be aware that Travis fought in an underground fight ring for the purposes of illegal gambling on his college campus?"

"Travis wasn't at the fire," Tyler said, his expression blank.

"Is that all you need, agent? These boys just came off almost two weeks on the mountain. They need to rest." Sage said, his red beard twitching when he spoke.

Agent Trexler scanned each face of the hotshot crew, and then nodded. "Sure. I'll be contacting your superintendent to let him know I'll need open communication. This is an active investigation, and your brother is a person of interest. Your cooperation will be the best thing you can do for Travis now."

"Whatever," Tyler said, standing. "Good night, Agent Trexler."

After Trexler left, and his truck could be heard driving away from headquarters, Taylor and Tyler's crew patted them on the backs, offering their silent support.

I stood back, watching the twins engage in an intense conversation in the corner. Taylor walked off with his hands on his hips, and then returned to his brother, shaking his head. The rest of the crew crowded around the table, resuming their card game. They were Taylor and Tyler's family, too, but they knew the twins needed to figure out their other family at home.

Taylor retreated to the barracks, and Tyler glanced at me before looking down. I'd seen that look before, many times, mostly in the mirror. He was ashamed.

I padded across the room, stopping just a few feet from him. "What can I do?"

He frowned, trying to focus on the floor.

"Okay," I said. "You don't have to tell me. I can ... you know ... just be around."

He nodded, keeping his eyes on the carpet. I backed away, settling into the corner of the sofa closest to the wall. I pulled a knit throw over my lap and sat quietly. Tyler crossed the room, sitting on his knees at my feet.

I ran my hand over his buzzed hair, pausing on the back of his neck.

"I lied to you," he whispered. "But if I tell you the truth, you'll be dragged into this mess."

I shook my head. "You don't have to tell me."

He looked up at me from under his brow, angry. "Didn't you hear me? I lied to you."

"No, you were protecting your brother."

Tyler looked up at me from under his brow. "And now I'm protecting you."

CHAPTER FOURTEEN

ALL BUT TAYLOR AND TYLER were gone when I woke. After
fourteen days on the mountain, the crew had woken up to their R
& R and scattered. For two days, they would travel to any friends
or family who were close, going into town to hit a bar or an
outfitter or to a mom-and-pop café to eat real food.

I rubbed my eyes, squinting at Tyler as he sat on my bed, his
elbows resting on his knees. He was wearing a pair of red
basketball shorts, a white tee, and a navy blue baseball hat. By his
attire and bare feet, it was obvious he wasn't planning on going
anywhere, but he was miles away. His twin was wearing boots,
cargo pants, and an Alpine tee, a duffel bag at his feet.

"What's wrong?" I asked.

Taylor was leaning against the large wooden square that held
the few things I'd brought with me to the dormitory. He was
frowning, his arms crossed.

"Taylor's leaving," Tyler said.

I sat up. "What? Why?"

"After R & R, we're going to Colorado Springs to join a crew
to work on a fire down there."

"You're not?"

Tyler shook his head. "I'm waiting on the Aussies to get here,
and then we'll drive down. It's better that Taylor goes first,
anyway."

"Why?"

He glanced over at me before looking down. "Taylor's a better
liar than I am."

"The federal agent is going to be down there," I said. It wasn't
a question; I knew the answer.

Taylor nodded. "I'm going to answer all his damn questions—again—and hopefully he'll leave Tyler alone."

"Because Tyler was the one who spoke to Travis."

Tyler shifted. "Actually, it was Trent."

I frowned. Without having met them, it was hard to keep the brothers straight. "Which one is he again?"

For some reason, that brought a smile to Tyler's face. "Second youngest."

"Oh yeah," I said. "The tattoo artist. It makes sense why you're both covered."

"We all are," Taylor said. "Except Thomas. I have to get on the road. I'm going to try to get there first. Maybe get Trexler's third degree out of the way before we go back to work."

"Something seemed … off about him," I said. "Watch yourself."

Taylor winked at me. "I got this, Ellie. Don't worry about me. Ever since I found out we were going to Colorado Springs … I dunno. I've had a good feeling about it."

"You just like that damned cowboy bar down there," Tyler said.

Taylor arched an eyebrow. "Colorado Springs has a considerably higher percentage of attractive women, and most of them hang out at that bar."

Tyler rolled his eyes. "They're looking for fly boys. The Air Force base is there."

"Yes, but it's me we're talking about," Taylor said, pushing off from my armoire. He bent down to grab his duffel bag, and then slung the strap over his shoulder. "I'm out, dick head."

Tyler stood up, hugging his brother. It wasn't a side hug or a hand-shake-slash-shoulder-bump. Taylor and Tyler wrapped their arms around each other and squeezed. The customary hard slapping on the back followed, but they were a sweet sight.

Taylor's keys jingled in his hand as he rounded the corner. The front door opened and slammed, and Tyler sighed.

"You're going to miss him."

He sat down on my bed again, leaning over and lacing his fingers together. "It's kind of a pussy thing to say, but Taylor and I haven't been apart a lot. It feels weird."

"Understandable. The twin thing."

"I'm just glad he's not going to Australia with Jew."

"*Australia?*"

"Yeah, we switch out. A couple of our guys go over there for a season to learn their way of doing things, and we get a couple of their guys to see how we do it."

"So those are the Aussies we're waiting on? Isn't that going to mess with your groove or whatever to get two new guys?"

"The Aussies are machines. They always come here to work. We're dragging ass to headquarters, and they're antsy, wishing for the next call. What?"

"I don't know ... I feel irrationally betrayed."

Tyler wrinkled his nose. "You feel what?"

"You should have told me. One minute I'm the big sister making grilled cheese, the next I'm left out of the loop."

Tyler thought about that. "Wow, I'm sorry. You just fit in so well I forget you don't already know this stuff."

"I suppose I can forgive you." I sat up, running my hand over my face. "Oh my God."

"What?"

"My mouth. It tastes like a trashcan." I stood, opening the armoire to grab my toothbrush and a tube of toothpaste before rushing to the bathroom. After spitting the suds into the sink, I rinsed and grabbed a towel. My sinuses felt congested, so I grabbed a tissue.

"Oh my God!" I said again.

Tyler jogged across the barracks, stopping in the doorway. "What's wrong?"

"I'm dying," I said, blowing my nose again. "My insides are rotting."

"Black in the tissue?" Tyler asked.

I nodded.

He chuckled. "That's normal. When fire season is over, you'll still be doing that for weeks. It's from the smoke and ash."

"Isn't that ... I don't know ... unhealthy?"

Tyler made a face. "You smoke, Ellie."

"So do you," I snapped.

"But I'm not whining about the hazards of inhaling wood smoke. We're sucking a lot worse every time we light up."

"But I don't blow charcoal out of my nose after I smoke."

Tyler shrugged. "So wear a filter mask next time."

"Maybe I will."

"Good. Are we going into town or what?"

I shook my head and shifted, holding up one foot off the cold floor. "I can't right now. I have to get my notes emailed to Jojo."

"I don't know why you don't just write it yourself. She used most of your manuscript for the magazine. She didn't even credit herself."

I smiled, filling my hand with water and rinsing out the sink. "That was pretty cool. I thought it was crap, but she cleaned it up a little bit and called it good."

"Chief said he's gotten a lot of phone calls about the story. The brass like the positive press it's brought to the crew."

"It didn't get picked up by the AP like Wick had hoped."

"Yet," Tyler said as I turned off the faucet. "So you're going to work?"

"Yeah ... go ahead."

"Nah, I'll wait. It's kinda nice being alone with you."

I fetched my laptop, and then sat with Tyler in the TV room. He lifted the remote and turned on the television, keeping the volume down while I typed. The process was a bit easier this time, matching numbered photos to corresponding accounts.

Not quite an hour after we'd sat down, Tyler reached down and lifted my legs, lowering them over his lap. He settled back against the sofa cushions, looking sleepy but content.

"Hungry?" I asked, clicking SEND.

"All done?" Tyler said, watching me close my laptop.

"Yes. Finished. Let's eat."

We rode into town in Tyler's truck, his ridiculously loud exhaust pipes announcing to everyone within a three-mile radius that we were back. He stopped in a small café I'd never been to, but where he seemed to be familiar.

The waitress looked both surprised and overly enthusiastic about seeing him, but Tyler didn't seem to notice.

"Uh, just waters for now. You want OJ, Ellie?" Tyler asked, still reading over the menu.

"Yes, please," I said.

"Two," Tyler said, holding up his index and middle finger. When the waitress left, he lowered his index finger, leaving me a charming gesture for a few seconds before putting it away.

"Back atcha," I grumbled. I pretended to be annoyed, but it was hard to stay mad at him when his dimple was working its magic.

"Orange juice. Two," the waitress said, setting down two glasses. "Who's this, Tyler?"

She was smiling when she asked the question, but a familiar glint was in her eye. She took in my clothes, my hair, even my jagged fingernails and chipped polish, wondering what it was about me that had enticed Tyler Maddox enough to buy me breakfast.

"This is Ellison," Tyler said, the grin on his face breaking out into a full-blown smile.

"Ellison?" the waitress asked. "Edson?"

I cringed, wondering which story she'd heard and how satisfying to her it would be to realize I wasn't competition after all.

"Yes?" I said, trying to meet her condescending gaze. Life was a collection of stories, and I couldn't let her judge me for a few chapters.

"You know my cousin, Paige. She talks about you a lot."

"Oh. Yeah. Tell her I said hi," I said, surprised at how relieved I was.

"Hi? That's it?" the waitress said, her voice tinged with disdain.

"Emily, c'mon. Can we order?" Tyler said, impatient.

Emily pulled out her pad and pen, her lips pursed.

"The waffles," Tyler said.

"Peanut butter and whip with warm maple?" she asked.

"Yep," Tyler said.

Emily looked to me.

"Oh, uh … I'll have two eggs, over medium, and bacon. Burned."

"Burned?" Emily asked.

"Crispy fried."

She shook her head. "I'll tell the cook. Anything else?"

"That's it," I said. Emily walked away, and I leaned against the table. "She's going to spit in my food."

"Do you know her?" Tyler asked.

"No. I'm not sure if she hates me because of something she thinks I did to Paige, or because I'm with you."

"Maybe both. Girls are weird that way."

"Oh my fuck, Tyler. Could you be more of a misogynist?"

"Am I wrong?"

"About what? I'm not even sure I know what you meant."

"But you knew enough to be offended."

"I hate you today."

"I can tell," he said. "I would say you need a drink, but…"

"No. My luck, we'd get called to a political fire, and I'd be puking my guts out."

Tyler smiled at the jargon. A political fire was anything big enough to make CNN, something everyone was dispatched to, and the only reason I would ever know that was by living with the twenty-man crew who would be sent to one.

"I didn't realize you knew that term," Tyler said.

"I sort of have to pay attention for my job."

"You're really good at it, Ellie. I'm glad Jojo gave you a raise, but I saw on the Internet the other day that they're paying photographers six figures a year to shoot pics of national forests."

"Really?"

"I was looking into *National Geographic*, too. That seems a little harder to get into, but not impossible."

I arched an eyebrow. "You trying to get rid of me, hotshot?"

"No fucking way. Not even a little bit."

We looked at each other for a moment in a silent exchange. We had an understanding that I needed, and Tyler was satisfied with whatever it was that we were doing. Part of me wanted to thank him for not pushing, but that would defeat the purpose of our rule to avoid labels, or really to even discuss the nature of our relationship—if it could even be called that.

Emily returned with our plates, interrupting our little staring contest. "Waffles. Eggs," she said, turning around before Tyler could ask for a refill.

"Okay, then. Not sure what you did to Paige, but her cousin is pissed about it."

"I honestly don't know this time."

"Weren't you two, uh…"

"No. As a matter of fact, I was very clear. Many times."

"Many times, huh?"

"Shut up."

Tyler chuckled, finishing his waffle. He paid, and we walked downtown, stopping into various shops. It was strange to see something I liked and not buy it. I found myself looking at price tags for the first time, and once, when I came across an exceptionally soft black turtleneck, calculating my bank balance and upcoming bills in my head to see if I had the extra cash to spend. I didn't.

I walked around the store, peeking at Tyler through the shelving. He had a few items in his hands, so I waited for him to check out, and then we popped into a candy store. We spent the day walking around, talking about the crew, a lot of playful bickering, trading family stories, and trying to one-up each other on what shocking illegal activities we'd participated in.

I won.

The day wore away, and as the sun ducked behind the green mountaintops, I felt myself already mourning *The Day Tyler and I Did Nothing*. Wandering aimlessly in downtown Estes was one of my best days.

After a light dinner, Tyler and I walked down the block toward a familiar alley. He casually reached for my hand, at first swinging our arms, and then gently squeezing my fingers when he realized I wasn't going to pull away. He was wearing jeans, black boots, and a short-sleeved white T-shirt with something about a motorcycle in black ink. It went well the tattoos covering his arms, and I smiled when I thought about the reaction my parents would have if they saw us.

"What do you think? Want to share a Shirley Temple?"

"I thought you said you were tired of the bar scene."

"We don't have to go. I don't want to encourage old habits."

I pulled my hand away. "I'm not an alcoholic, Tyler. I can be around liquor without drinking."

"I didn't say you were."

I narrowed my eyes. "You don't believe me."

"I didn't say that, either."

I squeezed his hand, tugging him forward. He resisted for the first few steps, and then gave in. A woman pushed through the door, her heels clicking down the concrete the same way we'd come. Her ankle rolled, and she nearly fell but regained her balance, grumbling curse words until she turned the corner.

Tyler pulled back as I reached for the door with my free hand. I stumbled backward, leaning against him before pushing him away.

"I was kidding, Ellie," Tyler blurted out. "I don't think we should go in there. We can find something else to do."

"At ten o'clock in this town? We go in here, or we go back to headquarters," I said, pointing at the door. Its chipped black paint was the perfect prologue to what awaited us inside.

I reached for the door again, but Tyler resisted. Just as I began a scathing review of his reluctance, he touched my cheek, looking down on me with concern in his eyes. "Ellie."

I turned my face away from his touch. My new job and my new life were due to my stubborn pride. Not even being disowned by my parents could make me get my shit straight. My luck was better when I made my own decisions apart from external influences, but I found myself wanting to do things just to make Tyler happy—the sort of stupid, vapid shit Finley did when she liked a guy—things that definitely weren't me. But then again, I wasn't sure who I was anymore. Maybe Ellie two-point-oh would skip the bar to play it safe and hide from temptations at headquarters.

I frowned. "C'mon. O'Doul's, mocktails, and people watching. We can laugh really loud like we're drunk and slap the table a lot. No one will ever know."

Tyler was still unconvinced, but I pulled him through the door anyway. A small group of barely legal women sat at a table by the door. A few couples were at the end of the bar near the bathrooms, and a few older local men were peppered across the bar stools. Tyler pointed to the table we had sat at when I was here with Finley and Sterling. The thought of Sterling made my skin crawl. He hadn't intended to fuck me any more than I'd meant to be fucked when I went to his house that day, but Sterling was the embodiment of rock bottom for me, and I was okay with never seeing him again.

"Hey, you okay?" Tyler asked, sitting next to me. He patted my thigh, bringing me back to the present. I both loved and loathed when he touched me like we were that familiar, as if I belonged to him. Tyler was my new addiction, like flirting with fire on the mountain, loving the danger and waiting for the burn.

"Yeah, why?"

"You just look a little uncomfortable."

"A couple of O'Doul's and I'll be fine."

Tyler smirked. "Good luck getting some liquid courage with non-alcoholic beer." He stood, leaving me alone to order at the bar.

I picked at the last bits of polish left on my nails. Finley had always been the one to make sure I had a regular manicure, even if she had to make an appointment from the other side of the country, but now that I couldn't afford one, I sort of missed it.

My phone buzzed in my back pocket, and I pulled it out, seeing Finley's silly, beautiful face. I pressed the red button for the second time that day and put my phone away.

"You're looking awfully forlorn," Tyler said, setting a bottle on the table in front of me. "Here. Drink up. Annie told me that Wick had already warned her that if we came in together to remind me not to get kicked out."

"What an asshole. He ruined our entire night."

Tyler breathed out a laugh. "That's exactly what I said."

"Really?" I asked, dubious. Tyler nodded. "We are spending way too much time together."

"I was just thinking we needed more days like today."

"Tyler…"

"Don't say it. I know."

"Ellie?" a high-pitched voice called from across the room. "Oh my God! Ellie!"

I turned to see Paige weaving through tables to get to mine. She bent down and threw her arms around me. Her blue hair was now fuchsia, and she was beautiful as ever. Her tiny features remained soft as she smiled sweetly at me. She was still searching for someone, wearing a cropped tank top and frayed denim shorts to display her tattoos. Her right arm, the blank canvas, was now marked with black lace serving as leaves to a coral-colored rose.

"That's new," I said.

She grinned and then pointed to her nose. "So is this."

I frowned, unable to ignore the thought that Paige was changing too much, too fast. She was already drunk, her eyes were bloodshot, and purple circles darkened the thin skin beneath her lower lashes. She wasn't more than twenty-two or -three, but already tired of the bullshit life kept throwing at her. We were going in opposite directions, and I wondered if I'd been the last straw. Finley had always said that I ruined people, and I could see the turns Paige was taking, all downhill.

"I'm so glad to see you," she said, a new nose ring shimmering as it reflected the multi-colored lights above. "I went to your house. José said you took a job and moved out."

"True."

"Where? New York City? L.A.?"

"The Rocky Mountain Alpine Hotshot barracks, actually."

Paige turned her head like a confused puppy. "The what?"

"I'm a photographer for *The MountainEar*. I'm following the hotshots this summer."

Paige giggled and nudged my arm. "Seriously. Where did you move to?" Her eyes bounced between Tyler and me, and then recognition lit her expression. "So you're ... living together?"

"Not exactly," Tyler said. "Unless we say we're also living with nineteen other guys."

Paige tightened her bottom lip, but then she tried to relax, forcing a smile. "You couldn't call?"

"I don't have your number," I said.

"Really? I thought I gave it to you." I shook my head, and she blinked. "Well, I can give it to you now. Where's your phone?"

"In my pocket."

Paige shifted her gaze from me to Tyler, and then back. She sat in the chair next to me, her shoulders sagging. "I've missed you. You look great. You look happy."

I smiled. "Thank you."

Her eyes glossed over. "What are you doing later?"

"I rode into town with Tyler, actually," I said, feeling guiltier with each word that came out of Paige's mouth.

"Oh. Well ... I could take you back. I have a car."

"I'm on call, Paige. I'm really sorry."

I could see the hurt all over her face, in the way she looked to the floor, the way her mouth twitched.

"You warned me, didn't you?" She looked up. "I've been waiting for you this whole time and you told me not to. So stupid," she said, shaking her head and looking away. She wiped her cheek quickly.

"Paige," I said, reaching for her.

She pulled away. "There is only one person who's a bigger whore than Tyler Maddox in this town."

"Taylor?" Tyler said. I could hear the amusement in his voice, and my cheeks burned with anger.

"Me," I said.

Paige laughed once. "You don't even try to deny it. What does that feel like?"

"Pretty shitty," I said. "Happy?"

Paige's face crumbled, and an escaped tear fell down her cheek. "No. Not for a long time." She stood and walked out, and I grabbed my pointless beer and took a long swig.

"Ignore her," Tyler said.

"It's not funny," I snapped. "There is nothing funny about me using her and casting her aside like everyone else in her life."

"Whoa. I'm sorry. I thought I was on your side."

"You should go back to yours," I said. "People get hurt over here."

"You don't scare me," Tyler said, leaning in. "Stop being so damn stubborn. I'm good for you."

"What if I'm bad for you?"

He tipped his bottle until it clinked against mine. "Just what I look for in a girl."

I sighed. "I feel like I need to drink something stronger."

"Just one?" Tyler asked. He wasn't really offering, and I could see the patience in his eyes as he waited for me to make my own decision.

I considered his question, and then perched my elbows on the table, holding my head in my hands. "You're right. I shouldn't."

"All right, time for us to head out." Tyler stood, bringing me with him.

By the time we reached the alley, Tyler had already given me a cigarette from his black pack and was fishing for a lighter.

"What the hell?" Tyler said, stopping mid-step.

He was staring at the sky, and I retreated beneath his arm when a loud boom echoed across the sky like thunder. A rainbow of colors rained down, and I gasped. Another rocketed up, exploding in golden sparkles.

Tyler looked at his watch, pressing a button that ignited the face so he could see the date. "I'll be damned."

"July 4th? How did we miss that?"

"Shit, I've gotta call Trent. It's his birthday."

Tyler led me to the street, his arm still hooked around my shoulders. We watched the fireworks for close to an hour before the finale lit up the night sky.

Tyler hugged me to him.

"Is it lame that I'm thinking about how many fires the fireworks could potentially start?" I said, looking up at the incredible bursts of light.

Tyler turned to look at me. "Is it lame that I want to kiss you right now?"

I could still see the fireworks in my peripheral, feeling a bit sentimental. This was a particularly poignant Independence Day.

I closed my eyes, and Tyler leaned down, touching his lips to mine. What had started out as sweet and innocent quickly changed, and I gripped his T-shirt in my fists. When I pulled him against me, I could feel him harden inside his jeans, making me moan in his mouth.

He took a step back, still holding me in his arms. "That was awesome and unexpected."

"We should definitely go home," I said, breathless.

He held up his keys. "I was thinking the same thing."

CHAPTER FIFTEEN

MY BODY JERKED ME AWAKE, my eyes wide and staring at the ceiling above while I panicked for just a moment, trying to recall where I was, and whose arms were around me. In my dreams, I had been on a yacht in Sanya with Finley, feeling the hot sun on my olive skin and looking at the world through a pair of five-hundred-dollar sunglasses.

I touched the heel of my hand to my forehead, already mourning the carefree feeling I had on the imaginary boat with my sweet sister.

My cell phone buzzed, and I reached over to retrieve it from the wooden nightstand someone had cut from a log. Finley was texting me. The previous texts were of her looking bored on a beautiful beach, slathered in suntan lotion on the bow of *Andiamo*, or effortlessly beautiful while she shopped on Hainan Island. The last few texts were the increasingly impatient requests for me to contact her. I read over the saltiest one that she'd sent since she'd left, and couldn't help but smile.

> *Ellison, text me back. I want proof of life, or else I'm getting on the next plane to Denver so help me god.*

I typed a response but let my thumb hover over the SEND button. Sending *I'm alive, I'm happy, I miss you* wouldn't be enough.

Tyler's lips touched my temple. "Send it." He cleared the hoarseness from his voice. "She's worried."

"She'll want to call me."

"That's a bad thing?"

"She'll know something's wrong. She can read me, even halfway across the world."

"Ellie," Tyler said, holding my body against his. "You can't duck this forever. You're going to have to talk to her sometime."

I sent the message, and then turned off my phone, sitting up. My muscles ached as I stretched, complaining from the strange position we'd slept in all night, trying to fit on a twin-sized bed.

"I got an invitation in the mail the other day. My brother is getting married again."

"Again? He's already divorced?"

"No, they eloped, so they're making it formal so the family can attend. It's going to be in St. Thomas mid-March next year."

I sighed. "I love St. Thomas, but that's not enough time for me to save."

He touched my lower back with the tips of his fingers. "I've got it. Wanna go? With me?"

I looked over my bare shoulder at Tyler. "Like … as your date?"

He shrugged, stretching his arm above his head. "You can call it whatever you want. I just want you there."

I looked forward, pulling the blanket up over my chest. "I don't need a passport for St. Thomas." I sighed. "I hate this. I feel like this," I said, gesturing between us, "is paying for whatever."

He chuckled. "It's not. I had already planned to ask you to go."

I offered him a small, regretful smile. "We can't do this again."

His sleepy grin was infectious. "You keep saying that. Why don't you just admit it?"

"Admit what?"

He waited.

"Fine," I said. "We have a … thing."

"That wasn't so hard, was it?" he said, but the grin was wiped from his face when I stood, taking the blanket with me to the bathroom and grabbing my bath bag and robe from the knob of the armoire on the way.

"Shower?" Tyler called.

"Yeah."

"Want company?"

"Nope."

I hung the robe on a hook that was nailed into the divider between showers and let the down quilt fall to the floor, reaching behind the plastic curtain to twist the knob. The water sprayed from the head, instantly steaming. I stepped under, letting the water run over my head and down my face.

My mascara burned my eyes, and I reached for the soap, quickly scrubbing it away. Tyler had kissed me all the way to the bed and undressed me, and neither of us had left that spot the rest of the night. His tongue had tasted almost every inch of my body, making me come over and over until my legs twitched with exhaustion.

Once it was over, though, and I was lying in his arms, I could feel his relief. He practically radiated how at home he felt against me, and all I could think about was that it was getting harder to pretend what we had was just sex. Underneath his thick armor, Tyler cared about me, and I wasn't sure I deserved that—at least, not yet.

I stepped out of the shower, fully intending to talk to Tyler about where he saw our benefriends relationship going, but a stranger was standing in the doorway, stunned but not at all trying to shield his eyes from my bare skin.

"Does this outfit have sheilas, or are the Alpines allowin' conjugal visits?" he said.

I pulled my robe from the hook and wrapped it around me. "I'm the photographer. Who the fuck are you?"

He laughed, delighted with my answer. "I'm Liam. This wog is Jack." Liam was at least six feet two inches, but Jack was taller, and very blond.

"What the hell is a wog?" I asked.

"Ow ya goin'?" Jack said. "We're just in from Oz."

"Great," I said, knotting the robe belt and pulling it tight.

Tyler padded in, glowering at the two men. I'd never seen his expression so severe.

Liam held out his hand to Tyler. His bicep was as big around as my head, and I wondered how he carried all that muscle mass on a hike to a fire.

Tyler stared at Liam's hand until he took it back, but the Australian didn't seem fazed.

"There's an undressed woman in your midst, gentlemen. I suggest you excuse yourself to another room until she's otherwise."

Jack slapped Liam on the shoulder. "They're a bit uptight about nudity. Let's not piss off the crew on our first day."

Liam didn't take his gaze from Tyler's, but he wasn't challenging him. With his unrelenting stare and amused grin, Liam was letting Tyler know he was far from intimidated, which only pissed off Tyler more.

The Aussies left, and Tyler joined me at the sink. "You okay?"

"Yeah," I said, waving my hand dismissively. "You're no longer the only Alpine hotshot crewmember who's seen me naked."

Tyler clenched his teeth. "We should have just had them go straight to Colorado Springs."

"Then we wouldn't have had last night."

He smiled, gently pinching a few strands of my hair. "It's a political fire. They need all hands on deck. Maybe you should stay."

I frowned. "And what the hell am I going to do here? Take pictures of flowers? The barracks? Jojo will be pissed if I don't go."

"There's a different TAC team. It's not just Chief making the decisions. They might not let you up there."

"I have a press badge. I can go wherever I want."

Tyler breathed out a laugh. "That's not exactly accurate."

I pulled a brush through my wet hair.

"My God, you're beautiful in the morning."

"No longer strangely appealing?"

"I never said that about *you*. I was talking about how much I liked that you smelled like a wild fire."

I squeezed out toothpaste on my toothbrush, making Tyler grin. I pointed my brush at him. "Don't even think about it. We've got crew here now."

Tyler seemed unhappy. "They just got here."

"They're still crew."

"Or maybe you heard his accent and suddenly you don't want us to have a thing."

I wrinkled my nose. "You're not serious."

He shrugged. "Chicks dig that." He walked off, and I brushed my teeth like I was punishing them.

We packed our bags, and Tyler called Chief, letting him know the Australians had arrived. The guys loaded up in a forestry truck and began the hundred and thirty miles south, down Highway 36 to Colorado Springs.

"How long a drive is it, mate?" Jack asked.

"About two and half hours," Tyler said. "Give or take."

Jack adjusted a few times, and I turned. "You must be sick of traveling. When did you get in?"

"Late last night. We drove over first thing this morning," Jack said. He smiled a lot, making him seem younger, even though he was all muscle.

"Hit the ground running?" I said.

"What's that, darlin'?" Jack said.

I laughed, knowing it was going to be an interesting drive. We both spoke English, but the slang was going to be a challenge. "Just that you started working the second you landed."

"That's the way we like it," Liam said.

I faced forward, adjusting my seat belt. Tyler had both hands on the wheel, his knuckles white.

"What?" I said. We were sharing the cab of the truck, but the Aussies were chatting, and the engine helped to muffle anything I didn't direct at them.

"I'm just thinking of this morning."

"You're not the only one who's ever seen me unclothed."

"I know," he said, closing his eyes. "I know, but I wasn't there to witness it."

"You're going to have get over it," I said. "You have to work with these guys."

"Maybe I could if I knew what the hell we were doing."

I wrinkled my nose, caught off guard by his sudden ire. "It's not like you've brought it up."

"Actually, I have. I was trying to be patient."

"What happened to that?" I asked.

"A man can only be patient for so long."

"And what does that mean, exactly? Did I miss the deadline I didn't know I had? Everything was fine two hours ago. Why are you so pissed off?"

He didn't answer, his jaws fluttering beneath the skin.

Liam leaned up, patting Tyler's shoulder. "Sorry about your girl."

"She's not my girl," Tyler said.

I curled my shoulders forward and looked out the window, trying hard to seem unaffected. The Aussies were instantly quiet, making the awkwardness even worse. I didn't realize how much Tyler's dismissal would hurt. The entire time we'd known each other, I had thought I was the one being pursued, but in that instant I understood why I'd held back: Tyler had left his dad, his friends, his brothers behind. Deep down I knew he was going to leave me, too.

The engine revved, and the tires spun on the asphalt, creating a high-pitched hum. I couldn't talk, so I folded my arm against the window and closed my eyes, pretending to sleep.

Tyler spoke when the Aussies asked him questions about the Alpines, keeping silent while they chatted in the back seat, discussing their enthusiasm for the hikes in the mountains and the cooler climate.

Liam paused, and then called up to Tyler. "What's the story with the sheila?"

"Her name is Ellison."

"Okay, what's the story with Ellison, then?"

"She's a photographer for a local magazine. She's following us around for fire season, documenting what it is that we do."

"She's a beaut," Liam said. "She's got the lightest blue eyes I've ever seen."

Tyler stayed quiet, but I didn't have to open my eyes to see his expression.

"Does she have a boyfriend?" Liam asked.

"Crikey," Jack said, disgusted. He clearly understood what Liam didn't, that something was going on between Tyler and me, even if he wouldn't admit to it.

"You're barking up the wrong tree, pal. She's into girls," Tyler said.

Technically, he wasn't lying, but it didn't make me feel any less pissed. Up until that moment, Tyler had been forthcoming and unapologetic about his feelings for me. Now he was acting like a prepubescent who was trying to act cool in front of his buddies.

The two and a half hours felt like an eternity, and by the time we pulled into the hotel parking lot, my body was stiff and screaming for me to move.

I stepped out onto the asphalt, and then scrambled to pull my camera out of the bag and slipped the strap over my head, snapping pictures of the pink ball of fire behind the thick layer of smoke in the sky.

"That's nothing, darl," Liam said. "You should come back to Oz with me."

Tyler grabbed his duffel and slammed the driver side door, walking quickly into the lobby. Liam and Jack followed, and I walked behind them, standing back while Tyler and the Aussies checked in.

The lobby was drab, decorated in beige and fake plants, and full of firefighters, some of them gearing up to go out, others standing around with a beer in their hand. A chalk sign by the bar read *Welcome, Firefighters! Half-price IPAs and appetizers!*

Tyler began arguing with the female desk clerk, and then he pulled out his cell phone.

I frowned when he produced his wallet, slapping his credit card on the desk. The clerk ran his card and handed it back with two small envelopes. He looked around for me, and then walked across the room to where I stood.

"Here," he said, handing me one of the envelopes.

"What was that about?" I asked.

"I got you a room."

"I could have done that," I said. "I have a card from the magazine."

He sighed. "I didn't know that. Anyway, I took care of it." I started to walk around him toward reception, but he took my arm. "What are you doing?"

"I'm giving them my card so you don't have to pay for my room."

"I told you I took care of it."

I pulled away from him, glancing around at the different faces in the room. Most of the firefighters hadn't noticed our exchange, but the Aussies had.

"What is your deal?" I hissed.

"I'm just trying to get you a fucking room, Ellie."

"No, why are you so mad? You're like ... I don't even know this person."

Tyler sighed, looking at everything in the lobby but me. "It's me."

"The jealous, asshole you?"

He laughed once, fidgeting. "Who the fuck am I jealous of?"

"Liam saw me naked. So what? It would have ended there if you wouldn't have not only told him I was single, but fanned the flame of every man's fantasy."

"Huh?"

"You told him I like girls," I snapped.

"It's the truth."

"Well, don't be surprised if Liam asks me for a threesome one of these days."

Tyler snarled. "Right up your alley."

"I can't believe you're so intimidated by him."

Tyler took a step closer. "Let's get something straight, sweetheart. No one intimidates me."

"You've sure been pissy since Liam walked in."

"I saw you," he seethed.

"Saw me what?"

"When he walked in on you. You just stood there. Took you a full three seconds to even cover yourself."

"Oh? So I'm supposed to rush to protect my lady parts because some rude dick walks in on me? You walk around with your ass out all the time at the barracks."

"That's different."

"Why? Because I have tits? When have you ever known me to be modest?"

"Exactly."

"Fuck you."

I snatched the envelope out of his hand and stomped to the elevators, mashing the button several times until the door opened. The family already inside slipped past me to the hallway, the daughter wearing a bathing suit and holding a flamingo inner tube around her waist.

I rode up to the third floor, walking down the hallway and around the corner to my room. My shaking fingers fumbled with pulling the key card out of its casing, and then I held up the card to the sensor, but a large hand covered mine, pushing it down.

"Goddammit, Ellie," Tyler said. "You're right. I'm jealous as fuck. You're sending all these mixed signals and some guy walks in on you, sees you naked, then he's asking about you … I have a million fucking feelings swirling around. I don't know what the hell I'm doing. I've never felt like this before."

I held up the card again, and the lock buzzed. I pushed down on the handle, looking up at Tyler. "Grow up," I said, shoving through the door and then slamming it behind me.

CHAPTER SIXTEEN

I UNPACKED THE FOUR SHIRTS, five rolled pairs of socks, three pairs of cargo pants, two oversized nightshirts, a toothbrush and toothpaste, a brush, mascara, and lip gloss from my backpack. The Alpines could have been called out at any time, and I wanted to be ready. It wasn't lost on me that I was arguing with the only hotshot assigned to keep me safe, or that Tyler needed to be focused on the growing fire and not our ridiculous predicament.

Tyler and I weren't an *our*. We weren't a *we*, meaning no jealousy, no expectations, and no deep discussions about our relationship status or where it was headed. I was a recovering drunk, and he was a recovering whore. Any therapist I'd seen over the last five years would say the same thing I was thinking: we had no future.

I picked up the remote and turned on the television. The news channel was already reporting on the fire, the latest updates scrolling across the bottom of the screen. I only listened for a few minutes before turning it off.

My phone buzzed, lying in the same place on the bed where I'd tossed it earlier. Even from ten feet away, I could see it was my sister. It rang a few times before going dark, and then the display lit up again.

I walked the few steps and reached for my phone, unsure of whether I would throw it across the room or answer it until I held the speaker to my ear.

"Hello?"

"Ellison?"

"Hi, Finley."

She sighed. "I thought you were dead. Mother and Dad thought you were dead."

"I guess to them I sort of am."

I could hear her wrath building, cringing when she yelled into my ear. "Not to me! I haven't done shit to you, Ellie, and you've been ignoring and avoiding me for months! Do you think I've been hanging out on the beach just hoping you were okay?"

"No, but I hoped..."

"Fuck you! Don't hope nice things for me right now. I'm mad at you! I don't deserve this from you!"

I froze, wondering if she meant more than just being ignored.

"Say something!" Finley's voice broke, and then she began to sniffle.

I wrinkled my nose. "Are you crying? Don't cry, Fin, I'm sorry."

"Why won't you talk to me?" she cried. "What did I do?"

"Nothing. You didn't do anything. I just didn't want to ruin your vacation. I didn't want you to feel guilty, and I didn't want you to worry."

"You've failed on all counts!"

"I'm sorry."

"I don't want you to be sorry!" she snapped. "I want you to answer your fucking phone when I call!"

"Okay," I said. "I will."

"You promise?" She was calmer now, taking a deep breath.

"I promise. I'll answer when you call ... if I'm not working."

"What are you doing, anyway? Mother said you're a secretary or photographer or something for the magazine there."

"Yes."

"Are you using the camera I bought you?"

I could hear her smiling. She had already forgiven me. She didn't know about Sterling, and when she found out, she would remember this conversation and feel even more betrayed. All I wanted to do was get off the phone, but that would only make her suspicious.

"I am. It's a really good camera, Fin, thanks."

Finley didn't talk for a few seconds. "I feel like I'm talking to a stranger."

"It's me," I said.

"No, it's not you. You've changed."

"I'm sober."

She breathed out a laugh. "How is that going?"

"Well, actually. Well ... one fuck-up. How's Sanya?"

"I wouldn't know. I've been in Bali the last three weeks."

"How's Bali?"

"Beautiful. I'm coming back to the States to see you."

I panicked. "I miss you, Fin, but I'm traveling a lot with this job. I'm following around the interagency hotshots, and we're all over the place until early October."

"The hotshots? As in Tyler's crew?"

"Yes."

"You're fucking him, aren't you?"

"Occasionally."

"I knew it!" She giggled.

I was going to miss this Finley, the one who was never shocked, and who always let my misdeeds slide off her shoulders. Finley always made excuses for me; she led me around life holding my hand, and bossed me around without a second thought because that was what older sisters did.

No matter how much I wanted to prevent it, there would come a time when we would be sisters but no longer friends. Even if Finley forgave me, she would forever feel the pain of my betrayal and never know if she could trust me again.

I chugged one of two bottled waters in the room, wishing it were something stronger, and then paced a few laps before deciding to go back downstairs. My reflection in the mirror by the door caught my attention, and I stared into the round, icy-blue eyes staring blankly back at me. My reflection wasn't kind. Dark strands of wavy hair hung from my messy bun. I was sober, and working, doing everything normal people did ... was I happy?

A part of me hated Tyler for having to ask myself that question. If I couldn't be happy doing something I loved, sleeping next to a patient man trying to care for me the only way he knew how, did I deserve to be? I was autonomous, making my own money and my own decisions—but staring at Ellie two-point-oh in the mirror, the sadness in her eyes was hard to ignore. It was infuriating.

The heavy door slammed behind me as I made my way down the hall. The elevator took me to the lobby, which I was surprised to find nearly empty.

"Hi," I said to the desk clerk.

She smiled, pushing away the doodle she was working on.

"That's pretty good," I said, taking a second look.

"Thanks," she said. "What can I do for you?"

I placed my credit card on the front desk. "Can I change the card on my room?"

"Sure," she said, taking the silver rectangle from the desk. She used her mouse, clicking a few times, and then slid the card through the scanner. "For incidentals, too?"

"Yes. Everything."

"Got it," she said, handing it back to me. "Just sign here."

"Thanks—" I looked at her name badge "—Darby."

"No problem, *MountainEar*."

I walked over to the bar and sat on the stool, alone except for the man behind the counter washing dishes. He had smooth, swarthy skin, and he was too young for his full head of silver hair and sideburns.

"Afternoon," he said. He stuffed his cloth-covered fist into a glass tumbler, twisting quickly before picking up another glass from the sink. His dark eyes made him seem to be staring at me with much more intensity than he meant to.

"Hi. Just a … um … a Sprite for now."

"On the rocks?" he teased. His smile faded, and he got to work, realizing I wasn't in the mood for jokes.

He filled a tall glass, sliding it in front of me. His eyes sparked when someone sat on the stool to my right. It wasn't hard to guess once he spoke.

"Toss me a Victoria's Bitter, mate!" Liam said.

"You're going to drink the first day on the job?" I asked. "Don't you have a meeting in fifteen minutes?"

"No worries. I'll have what she's having."

"Another Sprite," the bartender said, disappointed.

I tore at the edges of my napkin, a million things bouncing off the edges of my mind.

"So how did you end up with this outfit?" Liam asked.

"I started at the magazine answering phones, and ended up taking some pictures that impressed the owner. He sent me out with Tyler, and my pictures got some local attention. So, here I am, shooting a series."

"Worked your way up. I like that," Liam said, drinking his soda as if it were a pint. He even tipped his plastic cup to greet other firefighters as they walked by.

"I hadn't been at the magazine long when I was sent on my first assignment."

"Even more impressive," Liam said.

"Not really." I shook my head and looked down.

"What did you do before?"

"Nothing. I went to college, barely graduated, and then traveled for a while. My parents have a house in Estes Park, so that's how I ended up there."

"Oh. What do you Americans call it? You're a trust fund baby."

"I guess I was."

"But not anymore?"

"No, I was disowned, actually."

"The longer I talk to you, the more interesting you are. It's usually the opposite."

I looked over at Liam, studying his features. He was such a stereotypical Australian man, with the strong chin, broad shoulders, and massive frame. His jaw was covered in light brown stubble, and his emerald irises were beautiful, albeit barely noticeable because of his narrow eyes. My first instinct was to invite him up to my room and forget about my fight with Tyler for an hour or two, but if the past five months had taught me anything, it was that I couldn't screw, drink, or smoke away my problems. They would still be there in the morning, even worse than before.

Liam took another gulp of his soda, finishing it off. I'd barely touched mine.

"Starting over can be a bit depressing," he said. "No one tells you that. You think you're supposed to instantly feel better, and not knowing why you don't can be bloody rough."

"Don't tell me you're a trust fund baby," I said, dubious.

"No. Working clears my head, but even that wasn't helping anymore. I needed some distance."

He looked around, over each shoulder, like whatever he had left behind might have followed him.

"But you feel better eventually, right?" I asked.

"I'll let you know when it happens," Liam said, standing.

Tyler rounded the corner but stopped when he recognized Liam and me sitting at the bar together.

"Best be off to the meeting," Liam said.

"Good talk," I said, raising my cup.

Liam clinked his empty glass to mine, and then left for the conference room.

Tyler paused for just a few seconds before making his way over to me. "What are you drinking?"

"Sprite. Get your own."

He shook his head, scanning the lobby. "I'm a Cherry Coke guy."

"Where's Taylor?" I asked.

"Not here. Not yet, anyway. He called me earlier. He met a girl."

"Here? A local?"

He shrugged. "He didn't have a lot of time to talk. I guess she's a waitress or something."

"Interesting. Oh, fuck. Tyler," I said, seeing Agent Trexler stop at the front desk. He flirted with Darby the desk clerk for a few seconds before heading toward the automatic doors, noticing Tyler as he passed through. When he didn't stop, I exhaled a sigh of relief.

"Taylor's got a handle on it," Tyler said.

"How?"

"He just does. Gotta go."

To my surprise, Tyler leaned down to kiss my cheek before following Liam to the conference room. When he opened the door, I saw a lot of official-looking people standing at the head of the table, holding down the newly unrolled papers fighting to return to their previous position. There were phone calls being made, tapping on iPads, and typing on laptops. The hotshots were standing around, waiting for orders while the TAC team gathered information. I saw some of my boys for half a second before the doors closed, arms crossed and looking tough until Puddin' caught a glimpse of me and waved like a kid seeing his parents from the stage at a school recital.

"Hanging in there, Stavros?" Darby asked, leaning on the bar. Her white button-down was perfectly pressed, her red lips matte and perfectly lined, her black slacks lint-free, and her honey-colored mid-ponytail pulled tight, not a single hair out of place.

With her curves and million-dollar smile, I wondered if Darby was a former pageant queen. Every movement she made was elegant, every smile planned.

I glanced over at her, immediately suspicious. Trexler had been flirting with her earlier. Maybe she was an agent, too.

"The firefighters don't tip," Stavros grumbled. "And so far, all of them are straight."

"It's been like this for a week," Darby said, resting her chin on the heel of her hand.

I felt my body stiffen, worried to say or do anything that might help Trexler with his investigation of Tyler's family.

"Are you all right?" Darby asked.

"Who was that guy who just left? The one who talked to you before rushing out the door?"

"Trex?" she asked, her eyes instantly sparkling at the sound of his name on her lips.

"Yeah," I said.

"He's a firefighter, staying here until the fire is out. He's like … some kind of special crew. He's not a hotshot or ground crew. He doesn't really talk about it."

"Like fire secret service?" I asked, only half-teasing.

She giggled, although the sound seemed awkward coming from her, as if she wasn't used to laughing. "Probably. He's about that uptight."

"So you don't know him?" I asked, wondering why he'd lied to her.

"A little."

"Just a little?" Stavros said with a smirk.

"What about you?" Darby asked, combing through her hair with her fingers. Her brown eyes reminded me of Tyler's: warm with gold tones and a lot of hurt behind them. "I'm guessing you're a reporter from your card."

"Photographer. I'm following the Alpines around."

"Oh. I've met Taylor Maddox and Zeke Lund. They're sweethearts. They've been hanging out with Trex."

"They have?" I asked, confused.

"Yeah. Been up in his room almost every night since they got here."

"How long has Trex been here?"

Darby shrugged, glancing behind her to check that no one was at the desk. "Two weeks. He got here before the fire started."

My eyebrows pulled together. "That's kind of weird."

She smiled. "Maybe it's not the fire secret service. Maybe it's fire secret psychic."

A family of four breezed in through the automatic doors, approaching the desk. Darby hopped up and returned to her station, greeting them with her red-rimmed smile.

The conference door opened, hemorrhaging hotshots and TAC team officials. I saw more than just my crew in there, and I wondered how many had been called to the Colorado Springs fire.

Tyler and Runt stood next to me, looking like father and son instead of crewmates. Runt was two heads shorter than Tyler, but just as strong. Like the other guys, Runt had leaned out over fire season, but even though he was the newest and smallest, he was usually the last one in the truck at the end of the day.

"What's the verdict?" I asked.

Tyler crossed his arms, scanning the crowd forming in the lobby. "It's deep. We're going to ride in as far as we can, and then take a helo to the fire site. Alpine has the eastern edge."

"Should I get my gear?" I asked.

Tyler cringed. "No."

"What do you mean *no*? When are we headed out?"

"We're not."

I shook my head. "I don't understand."

"You're not cleared to go. It's a fast-moving fire. They've already had some close calls. The winds are changing by the hour, and it's just not safe, Ellie."

"It's never *safe*," I hissed.

"The only safe zone is the black."

"Then I'll shoot the black."

"I won't be in the black. They need me on the fire line."

I turned my back to him, fuming. The decision wasn't his, but knowing that didn't help. "Did you at least stick up for me?"

"He vouched for you, Ellie," Runt said. "We all did."

"I could probably get my red card by now. This is some sexist bullshit," I growled.

Tyler sighed. "There are half a dozen women out there right now. It's not sexism; it's a safety issue. No civilians on the mountain. They'll reconsider when it's closer to being controlled."

I turned to him. "Are you fucking kidding me? Are you saying if I had a dick they wouldn't let me up there with my press pass? A fire is never controlled. It's never safe. You don't know what it's going to do. We all just hope it goes our way up there. Now I'm going to be shooting the horizon and the ground pounders mopping up when it's over."

"I told you not to come," Tyler said, impatient with my tantrum. "We have to go. I'll see you when I get back."

"Get me out there," I called after him. "Maddox!"

The crowd in the lobby quieted and watched Tyler walk away from me toward the elevators. I turned to face Stavros, trying to hold back angry tears.

"You said 'dick,'" Stavros said. "I like you already."

"Pour me a vodka tonic."

Stavros smiled. "Really?"

"Really."

CHAPTER SEVENTEEN

MY FINGERS WERE SPREAD OUT in my lap, all ten ink-stained and covered in dirt. I intertwined them, touching the knuckles of my thumbs to my forehead and closing my eyes but praying to no one. Echoes of movement traveled down the hall to my cell, and my knee began to bob again. This was the first time I'd been arrested without knowing my father would have me freed within the hour.

Tears stung the gash on my cheek, just one of several wounds the forest had left on my body while I'd tried to trudge through the thick trees and dry, razor-sharp branches. My head was still swirling from the countless vodka tonics that had helped me decide to sneak into the black.

The bars rolled to the right, and the sheriff's deputy caught the gate just before it crashed into the wall.

"You got some friends in high places, Edson," he said.

I stood, holding my hand in front of my face to block out the bright light. "Who?" I asked.

"You'll find out soon enough," he said.

I stepped out, hoping to God the person on the other side of the wall wasn't my father.

The deputy guided me by the arm to a small room where Trex sat in a folded chair. He stood, reaching out to take me from the deputy's grasp.

"Don't speak," Trex whispered.

"We're releasing Miss Edson into your custody, Agent Trexler. We assume you'll make sure she's not in a restricted area again?"

"She'll be up north. Nowhere near the fire," Trex said.

We walked down a long hallway into the front of the county jail. Tyler was sitting in one of the dozen or so chairs lining the white wall, his head in his hands. When the door closed behind us, he looked up.

"Oh, thank Christ," he said, standing up and pulling me against his chest. He kissed my hair, breathed me in, and then held me at arm's length.

I cringed, knowing what he would say.

"What the fuck were you thinking, Ellison? I mean … what in the actual *fuck*?"

"Not here," Trex said, holding open the front door.

Tyler grabbed my hand and pulled me through, following Trex down the sidewalk to an Audi much like my father's. Trex opened the back door for me, and I sat, sliding over when Tyler began to climb in next to me. Once the door shut, the yelling began again.

"Do you have any idea how scared I was when I got the call?" he seethed. "Do you have any fucking clue how much trouble you could have been in—how much trouble we *all* could have been in—if Taylor hadn't gotten Trex involved? Do you know what that would have done to me if something had happened to you?"

"I'm sorry," I said. "I wasn't trying to get you fired."

Tyler grabbed my shoulders. "*Fired?*" He shook his head, releasing me before sitting back against the seat. "Goddamn it, Ellie, I thought you were dead."

Guilt overwhelmed me, and the past six hours of wandering in the black, slightly intoxicated, and then getting fully booked into the system after my arrest finally hit me. "I'm really, *really* sorry. That was so stupid. I wasn't thinking."

"That tends to happen when you're drunk," he snapped.

"I'd only had two drinks," I said, immediately feeling guilty for lying. It didn't take long for me to resort to old habits.

Tyler raised an eyebrow, dubious. "You're really going to lie me? After I just pulled a hundred strings to get you out of jail?"

"I'm not." I paused, shrinking from Tyler's glare. "Lying."

"Wow. Okay, then," he said, facing forward.

"Technically, I was the one who pulled all the strings," Trex said.

I frowned at Tyler. "How did you get him to do it?"

Tyler looked down, frustrated. "Don't ask how, Ellie. Just say thank you."

"To who? The FBI? I want to know. What's in it for you, Agent Trexler?" I feared the worst: that Taylor or Tyler had agreed to share information about their brother in return for Trex's help.

"It's not agent anymore," Trex said. I wasn't sure if he sounded deflated or relieved.

"What?" I asked.

Tyler nodded. "He's serious. He no longer works for the bureau. Apparently his boss is a real dick."

Trex breathed out a laugh, somehow finding humor in the situation.

"How did he pull strings, then?" I asked.

Tyler sighed. "He just did, Ellie."

"*Why?*" I insisted. "What did you do in return, Tyler?"

"It's what you're *not* going to do," Trex said.

"All of us," Tyler said.

I crossed my arms and narrowed my eyes. "What are you talking about? What do you mean?"

"Darby," Trex said.

"Darby?" My nose wrinkled. "She thinks you're a hotshot," I said, my tone accusatory.

"I'm aware. Did you tell her otherwise?" Trex asked.

"No," I said.

"Good. We need to keep it that way," Tyler said. "That's the deal."

"That we let Trex lie to Darby?" I asked. "Who is she?"

"Just a girl," Trex said. "But you blow my cover with her, and you're back in that cell."

I settled back into my seat, unhappy about his conditions. "You're not going to hurt her, are you?"

He grimaced, his thick eyebrows pulling together. "That's the point, Ellison. Do you agree or not?"

I looked up at Tyler. "Do you trust him?"

"He got you out of jail, didn't he?"

I pressed my lips into a hard line, shaking my head. "You're not investigating her?" I asked.

"No," Trex said simply.

"Fine," I snapped. "You're a hotshot."

I could see Trex smiling in the rearview mirror. "Thank you," he said.

When we arrived at the hotel, I passed Darby. She waved at me, and I smiled, hoping Trex was telling the truth. I had talked her again during my fourth-ish drink, and from what I could remember, she was in Colorado Springs to start over, running away from someone or something. Darby didn't need more trouble. She'd been hurt enough.

Tyler walked me to my room, pausing just outside my door. He looked pained over what he was about to say. "I know you've had a long day, but I need you to go in and pack your bags."

"What? Why?"

"Because Trex might have gotten you out of jail, but Chief is beyond pissed. He wants you back in Estes Park. He's already called Jojo."

I covered my face. "Fuck. *Fuck* ... Because of one mistake?"

"Sneaking into a restricted area, and then getting arrested is a big one." He looked down the hall at nothing, having a hard time looking me in the eye.

"Am I out for good?"

"I don't know. Give me some time to talk to him. I'm going to let him cool off first."

I exhaled, wishing I could rewind the day and start over. "What about you? Are you still mad?"

Tyler's jaw clenched, and then he folded his arms around me. I closed my eyes, pressing my cheek against his chest. There was nowhere safer for me than Tyler. "I'm just glad you're okay," he said.

"Stay with me," I whispered.

He kissed my hair. "A car will be waiting for you outside in fifteen minutes. Chief wants you on the road heading north. I'm just here long enough to make sure you're packed, checked out, and on the road. Then I have to get back to fire camp."

"You're not coming with me?"

His eyebrows pulled together. "I have a job to do, Ellie. You have to go home."

My eyes filled with tears. "I don't have anywhere to go."

He reached into his pocket and pulled out a single key, the light glinting off the silver. "Lone Tree Village in Estes. 111 F. We're never there, so it's mostly storage. I'm not even sure if there are sheets on my bed. It's not a penthouse, but it's a place to stay. My bedroom is the last door on the left."

I took the key, sniffing. "Tyler…"

"Just … take it," he said. "I'll be home in a couple of weeks. We can figure it out then." He stepped back, waving to me before turning for the elevator.

"I thought you were supposed to make sure I get in the car?" I asked.

He stopped in his tracks but didn't turn around. "I'm sorry. I don't think I can watch you leave."

My bottom lip trembled, and I held the key to the sensor, hearing the lock click before I pressed down on the handle and pushed through. My clothes were still laid out, ready to go, but I would be lucky to ever get to go on a call again.

The wall felt cold against my back as I slid down the scuffed white paint to the aged orange and brown carpet. My phone buzzed, and I held it to my ear.

"Ellie?" Jojo said.

I covered my face with my hand. "I fucked up, Jojo," I said, pressing my lips together to stifle a sob.

"You're right. You did. Now you need to pack your things and get right back on the wagon. Do you hear me?"

"Do I still have a job?"

"You know you do. I'm not saying what you did is okay, but it's an uphill battle. You lost this one. Come home, and let's start preparing for the next one."

My face crumbled, and I took in a deep breath. "I don't deserve it, but thank you," I whispered.

"Hang up, pack, and get downstairs. The car will be there soon. When you get home, go straight to bed and I'll pick you up for work first thing in the morning. Got it?"

"Got it."

"Stand up. Clean slate starts now."

I took a deep breath, simultaneously standing and pressing END. It didn't take long to pack the few things I'd laid out, and then I was out the door, taking the stairs instead of the elevator.

Darby dropped the marker she was using for her newest doodle masterpiece, and stood up. "Ellie? Are you okay?"

I paused at her desk, placing my key card in front of her. "Yeah. I have to leave."

"You have to? Why?"

"I screwed up. I'm being sent home."

Darby shook her head in disbelief even when she'd heard it from me. "Screwed up how? Just because you were drinking?"

"It's a long story," I said. "Trex can explain it to you."

"If you ever come back … be sure to stop by and say hi."

I smiled. "I will."

A man older than my father, who dressed like a Baptist preacher and smelled like cheap aftershave, offered a contrived smile before taking my backpack. The cowlick on the top of his white hair was misbehaving, despite what looked like a quarter cup of gel he'd combed through it.

I waited for him to open the door, but he opened the trunk and threw in my bag. I opened the door myself, thinking the sticky carpet and trash tucked in the back of the passenger seat was the perfect ride for a woman who'd just left county jail.

The two and half hours to Estes Park seemed especially long when having to breathe in the smell of mothballs and possibly a fart or two. When we reached city limits, the driver turned his head while still keeping his eyes on the road.

"Do you have an address?"

"Lone Tree Village. Building F."

He sighed. "Do you have an address?"

"Hang on," I said, looking through my phone. "Thirteen-ten Manford Avenue."

The driver poked at his GPS and then sat back, resuming his mission to ignore me.

We passed through a part of town I was unfamiliar with, and then turned onto a side road, driving for another two minutes. The Lone Tree Village sign made me feel excited for half a second, but then I remembered most of the things I'd taken from my parents were still at the Alpine barracks, and all that I had was inside my backpack.

The driver drove straight to the back where Tyler's building sat. He rounded the back and then pulled into the first free parking space he found.

I stepped out onto the asphalt and waited for the driver to fetch my backpack. He handed it to me and turned for his door.

"Excuse me?" I said, following him.

He turned, annoyed. "It's been taken care of."

"Oh," I said, watching him open the door and sit behind the wheel. I took a step back when he reversed, watching him drive away and then looking up at building F.

111 was upstairs, so I climbed the first set, turned at the landing, and climbed another. Some of the clay-colored slats of the vinyl siding were missing, but it was in a nice neighborhood and the outside lawn was manicured—not that I was in any position to be fussy.

I pulled Tyler's key from my pocket and twisted it in the bolt lock. The mechanism clicked, and my heart began to pound. Standing in front of Tyler's apartment, preparing to enter his personal space for the first time without him there, felt wrong.

The knob felt cold and unwelcoming in my hand, but I twisted it anyway, pushing through the beige door to a living room full of furniture and boxes. Tyler had warned me that the apartment was serving as a storage unit, but there were several stacks, leaving a walkway to a kitchen on the left and a hallway straight ahead.

I followed the path to the hall, feeling along the wall for a light switch. When my fingertips touched the toggle, I pressed up, illuminating a twenty-foot-long hall with eggshell walls and beige carpet—two doors on the right, and one on the left. I pushed through the closest to find a bathroom. I dropped my backpack and quickly unbuttoned my jeans, shoving them down to my knees, sitting on the cold toilet seat and moaning as I relieved myself for the first time in almost twelve hours.

The faucet took a while to offer warm water. I looked around before resorting to drying my hands on my jeans. I gripped the edge of the sink as I tried to wait out the nausea and dizziness overwhelming me. I breathed in and was instantly comforted—the apartment smelled like Tyler.

With my bag in hand, I stopped at the end of the hall between two doors. I pushed the one on the right, seeing a room with more stacks of boxes, a stripped bed, and a nightstand. The door Tyler said was his was closed, so I twisted the knob and walked through, the door hitting a stack of boxes and knocking all but two of them to the ground.

"Shit," I hissed, dropping my bag to reassemble them.

I wiped my brow, and then walked across the room to open a window. A fresh breeze blew into my face, and I closed my eyes, taking in a deep breath. I had been banished from the only place

I'd felt at home, cast away from the only people who felt like family. I was alone inside a dusty storage house of a man whose dick I was more familiar with than his hopes and dreams.

I rested my elbow on the windowsill, unable to fight the fluttering of my eyes. From that vantage point, I could see the mountains that huddled around the barracks. My eyes filled with tears, and they spilled out and over my cheeks, unrelenting until my entire body began to shake. I wanted to be in that rickety building with cold showers and uncomfortable beds so bad it hurt. I sniffed a few times and wiped my nose with my wrist, licking my lips, wishing for another five or six rounds of vodka tonic—hell, I'd have been happy with a twelve-pack of cheap beer, anything to make the pain go away.

I leaned against the wall, trying to keep the landscape in sight, but the only thing to do was to thirst for what I couldn't have, and close my eyes.

CHAPTER EIGHTEEN

JOJO CLICKED HER SEAT BELT and pulled away from the curb, mostly silent as she drove me to the *MountainEar*. Just a block away, she finally sighed and began to speak, but thought better of it. Her silence was welcomed. I knew what she was going to say, and she knew that I knew what she was going to say. People spoke too much and said nothing, which was the only conversation Jojo and I would have if she hadn't closed her mouth.

She parked and gestured for me to follow her in. "Desk is still there. You remember how to do this?"

"I don't see Wick's truck," I said.

"He'll be in later. He has a meeting with some vendors."

"For Turk's?" I asked, swallowing. My throat begged for the burn of whiskey—anything to quiet the craving I'd had since my eyes opened that morning.

"Yeah. You didn't go straight to bed, did you?"

"I tried."

"You fucked up. Believe me, I'm not excusing what you did. But Daddy has been getting a lot of calls about your feature. I bet the Forestry Service is, too." She opened the door, and I followed her inside, pausing until she switched on all the lights.

"Chief was right to make me go home. I wasn't of any use there, and I made him look bad. I wouldn't blame him if he banned me from ever shadowing them again."

I walked into my office and Jojo followed, leaning her platinum locks against the doorjamb. "Me neither. But I wouldn't be surprised if he didn't. When are they due back?"

"It's a political fire. A lot of news stations covering it. They'll be out the full fourteen days."

She stood. "If there are a lot of stations covering, maybe I should go down there."

Anger and jealousy ignited every vein in my body. Jojo had a family ... She needed to stay the fuck away from mine. "They wouldn't let me up there, Jojo, and I'm seasoned. I know their procedures and a little bit about fire behavior. No offense, but they're not going to let you on the mountain."

She winked at me. "When have I ever taken no for an answer?"

I forced a smile, glaring at the space she stood in before she rounded the corner to her desk. Just minutes later, I could hear her on the phone, squaring away the details of her coverage of the Alpine crew.

My eyes burned, but I willed away the tears, refusing to cry in front of Jojo. I typed in my password, feeling like the day I'd updated it was a lifetime ago—so full of hope that I was capable of change.

Jojo's phone slammed, and she peeked around the doorway again. "Can you hold down the fort this week? I'm going south."

"Are they going to let you cover the Alpines?"

She smirked. "They don't know it yet, but yes. The Colorado Springs hotel, right?"

I nodded, holding a brave face until Jojo waved and the back door slammed shut. My face crumbled, and I covered my face with my hands, sucking in deep breaths.

It wasn't so surprising that I had fucked up, but that I had ruined something for myself that I loved. That thought led me to Tyler, and I knew I was ruining that, too. There was a dark part of me that just couldn't let myself be happy, and sabotaged anything good before I could lose it.

The phone warbled, and I sat up, cleared my throat, and picked up the receiver. "*The MountainEar*," I said, my voice breaking a bit.

"How's your first day back?" Tyler said. His deep, smooth voice made everything else disappear.

I wiped my wet cheeks, clearing my throat again. "It's great. Home sweet home."

"How's the apartment?"

"It's great. Thank you."

"Did you go there?" he asked. I could almost see the look of disbelief on his face.

"Yeah. Yeah, I went there. You do have sheets on your bed, and they're clean."

He sighed. "Ellie…"

"I know."

"No, you don't know. I miss you like crazy. Being on the mountain, wreaking of smoke, exhausted and covered in dirt is my favorite place to be, but it's not the same without you. Something's missing now."

"The sheriff?" I teased.

He breathed out a laugh. "I'm serious. I wrote you a letter. All the guys are giving me so much hell."

"Taylor most of all, I'm sure."

"The fire's so close, we're taking shifts and staying at the hotel."

"You're not sleeping at fire camp?"

"Nope. Taylor's been taking off into town somewhere. I think there's a girl."

"There's always a girl."

"Not one intriguing enough to hang around during the few hours we have off from a fire."

"You probably haven't heard yet, but you will. Jojo's on her way to cover the Alpines."

"Jojo?" Tyler said her name with disdain. "Why?"

"I told her about all of the news outlets covering the fire. She thought the magazine should have someone there."

He sighed. "Fuck, Ellie, I'm sorry. I know that has to hurt."

My chest felt heavy, and my eyes began to burn again. "I did it to myself."

"Doesn't make it suck any less."

"You're right."

He was quiet for a moment. "I wish I was there."

"Me, too."

"Twelve days, Ellison. I'm coming for you in twelve days."

"Tyler?"

"Yeah?"

"I've been thinking about drinking. A lot." When he didn't respond, I continued, "I don't think this is going to be as easy as I thought it would be."

"Who is that woman who kicked you out of your house?"

"My mother?"

"No, the other one."

My cheeks flushed just thinking about her. "Sally."

"Yeah. Her. You should call her. You have her number, don't you?"

I rubbed my temple with my index and middle fingers. "She doesn't work for my parents anymore."

"Even better."

"I'm not asking her for help, Tyler. I loathe her. I refuse to give her the satisfaction."

"You're saying it's wrong for her to feel satisfied about helping you? I think that's the nature of her job."

"Satisfied in the way a scheming, smug, rat-faced cunt would be satisfied, not a life coach."

"Well … maybe you can just try to stay busy. Keep your mind off it until I get there."

I considered his suggestion, one project immediately coming to mind. "Your apartment needs some work."

"Don't you dare."

"I'm serious. That will take me at least twelve days. Can I unpack for you?"

"No."

"Please? It will look like a real apartment when you get back."

"Absolutely not."

"Why not? Are you afraid of what I'll come across in those boxes? What? Is there like … skin suits or shrunken heads or something? Don't tell me you're ashamed of your porn."

He chuckled. "No, I just don't feel right letting you do that."

"You're letting me stay in your apartment. I'd say it's a fair exchange."

The line was quiet for a few seconds, and then Tyler sighed. "You don't have to, but if you want to, and it'll keep your mind off things, be my guest."

My smile faded. "Tyler?"

"Yeah?"

"Don't fuck Jojo."

"What the fuck, Ellie? I didn't fuck Jojo when I had the chance a year ago. I'm definitely not going to now."

"You've never been with Jojo? I thought…"

"Yeah, she's still offended … but no. Never."

I sighed, surprisingly relieved.

"So what are you trying to say?" he asked.

"Nothing. I just don't want you making things awkward with my boss."

"Right," he said, self-satisfied. "I'm telling all the guys we're exclusive. I'm telling Liam first."

"We're not."

"You just told me not to sleep with someone."

"Doesn't mean we're exclusive because I don't want you fucking my boss."

"So is it all right with you if I fuck anyone else?"

I clenched my teeth. "I don't like this game."

"Answer."

"I don't care who you fuck," I snapped.

Tyler became quiet. I only felt victorious for a few seconds, and then it was gone. My pride and guilt both seemed to stem from the same hollow, but they filled nothing. I wasn't sure where the need to keep Tyler at arm's length came from. Part of me wanted to believe it was to focus on sobriety that was shamefully failing, the other that as individuals we were too fucked up to function. I let him just close enough to feel loved, and then threw him into the corner like dirty laundry. For someone who at most times was scared he would leave, I was trying incredibly hard to push him away.

I was getting one thing right: being undeserving. The shame sent me into another cycle of guilt and need and feelings of worthlessness. I wasn't getting better; I was getting worse.

"Is it so fucking hard for you to admit, Ellie? Can't we just be happy?"

I swallowed. "We aren't a *we*. I've told you that from the beginning."

"Then what are we doing?"

"We're fucking and fighting, Tyler. That's what we do."

"Fucking and fighting." Clearly shocked and frustrated, Tyler stumbled over his words. He finally laughed once out of frustration. "That's it?"

"That's it."

"We'll talk about it when I get home."

I hung up, instantly feeling sick to my stomach. I couldn't keep busy to stay sober, deal with everything going on in my life, *and* pile on a serious relationship, no matter how much I wanted to.

The phone rang, and I answered, mostly scheduling meetings and fielding ad questions for Wick. He left once and then came back, putting his fist on my desk as he read my report over my shoulder.

He stood up and sighed, then turned on his heels, slamming his door behind him. The frames on the walls rattled, and my shoulders shot up to my ears. I'd worked for the magazine for a little over five months and had yet to experience Wick's wrath. Maybe it was time.

The door was yanked open, and then I heard Wick sit in his leather chair. "Ellie!" he yelled.

I stood, pausing in the doorway, expecting a minor verbal assault.

"You're a good kid. We've pushed you too hard," he said, staring at the bookcase behind me.

"P-pardon?" It was almost more unsettling that he wasn't screaming at me.

"I don't want to lose you. I don't want to facilitate your … issues. I'm not sure what to do. I'm not the type to just ignore this kind of behavior, Ellie. You could've gotten seriously injured, or worse. Is that cut…?"

I touched my cheek. I'd forgotten about the slap nature had delivered to my face—not that I'd felt it until hot blood dripped down my cold skin. "Yes."

Wick shifted in his seat, and then looked at his watch. "Have you eaten? It's almost lunchtime."

"Uh … no?"

"I'll order pizza. Think about what I said."

"Okay," I said, giving him a thumbs up. "Good talk."

He winked at me, and I closed the door, shaking my head. If that was an example of Wick's parenting skills, it made sense that Jojo was a walking carrot-colored Barbie doll who held grudges against any man who'd told her no.

The phone rang the moment I sat down, and I held the receiver to my ear. Just as I opened my mouth to greet the person on the line, Jojo spoke.

"It's me. I'm here."

"Oh. Have you seen my boys?"

She laughed once. "*Your* boys? No, I haven't. I've secured a room—which wasn't easy, by the way. Literally, every room was booked except for a guy who suffered some burns today. He's out for a while, so they're sending him home. I'm going to hang out in the lobby to see if I can catch the Alpines when they get in."

"They might be out there all night. I'm not really sure what their schedule is going to be. They've never stayed in a hotel before—at least, not this season."

"I'll figure it out. The damn news stations are everywhere. We have an in, though, if you didn't..."

"If I didn't screw it up. I know."

"Sorry," she said.

"Just be careful, Jojo. Do exactly what they tell you, when they tell you, and dress warm. It gets cold up there at night."

"Thanks, Ellie."

I hung up, wishing there was a polite way for me to ask her not to fuck my not-really-boyfriend.

I finished my report and emailed it to Jojo. I was surprised to see some shots she'd taken of the firefighters loitering around the hotel lobby. She was gifted, no doubt.

As the sun set behind the peaks, Wick rifled around in his drawers, and then his coat skidded along the sleeves of his sweater.

"Only two smoke breaks and no news from Jojo. Today was mighty fucking boring," Wick yelled from his office.

"Speak for yourself," I said.

He stepped out, straightening his scarf and pulling on his gloves. "Not all of us are spry enough to follow hotshots up mountains for a living. Are you back at your parents'?"

I cleared my throat. "No. I'm actually staying at Tyler's apartment. I haven't found a place yet."

Wick frowned. "Did a story on the affordable housing here. You might find something in the spring if you time it right."

"Yeah," I said, feeling even more hopeless than I had ten seconds before.

"Don't call your man. I'll take you."

"Really?" I said, more surprised that he thought I was still using José than at his offer.

Wick let me smoke in his truck as he puffed on his own cigarette and exhaled out the crack of his window.

"You and Tyler, huh?" Wick said.

"Kind of ... not really."

"He's a good kid, too. I figured you two would end up falling for each other. I could see it in his eyes."

"Yeah?" I said, amused.

"I've never seen him look at anyone the way he looks at you. I know you've got other things going on, though. Probably feels like a lot on your plate."

"It was his idea for me to stay here. And it's just temporary."

"Uh huh."

"I'm not using him. He insisted, and I didn't have another choice."

"Ouch. I hope you didn't say that to him."

"No," I said, looking down. "I didn't."

"You know there's an apartment above the *MountainEar*, right?"

"No, I didn't."

"It's vacant and new. I built it the same time I built the building, in case Linda kicked me out. I'm an old blow hard, you know. Lost my looks. She's still as pretty as ever. Jojo would look just like her without that clown makeup on her face."

I choked out a laugh, coughing smoke and waving my hand in front of my face.

Wick pulled into Lone Tree Village, familiar with where to go. He parked, and I stepped out, bending down. "Thanks for the ride, Wick. I'll figure out some reliable transportation ASAP."

He waved me away. "I'll pick you up in the morning. Not like the shuttles run out there. Just keep busy tonight, and I'll see you in the morning."

"Jojo said the same thing ... to keep busy."

"She's told you. I've been through it. It's probably the only reason I didn't fire your foolish ass for stumbling out into an active fire zone. That, and you're a damn good action photographer. Even better than Jojo."

"Thanks again for the ride."

Wick waved to me, and then backed out, braking just long enough to see me get into the apartment safe.

I locked the door behind me and flipped on the light, sighing at the sheer size of the task. The apartment wasn't dirty, but I was about to unpack an undetermined year's worth of belongings of both brothers. After changing into more comfortable clothes, I returned to the living room and opened the first box. I used every cabinet, shelf, dresser, and closet to put away clothes, photo albums, sports memorabilia, books, magazines, dishes, and cooking utensils in their proper place.

Once I cleared the last box from the living room, a pair of yellow gloves under the sink inspired me to clean the kitchen. Wick had told me to stay busy, and I was still two hours from bedtime. I wiped down the counters, scrubbed the sinks, and ran a load of dishes in the washer.

I opened the fridge, mentally prepared to see mold that would make an antibiotic lab envious, but all that was present on the pristine shelves was a six-pack of locally brewed beer.

I closed the door and sat on the floor with my back to the fridge, looking up. I had worked hard and felt lonely; there was no better excuse for a cold beer than that.

"Just go to bed, Ellie," I said aloud. But I wasn't tired.

I opened the fridge, and then closed it again, my fingers creating that comforting pop and fizz sound I loved so much. The living room looked like a real apartment, with actual decorations and lamps on the end tables at each end of the sofa and one beside the recliner. The dishwasher was still running with the last half of dishes and silverware, and there was a knife block and full salt and pepper shakers just out of the box on the counter.

I tilted my head back, and then licked the foam from my upper lip, smiling at the small victory while trying to ignore my utter failure.

CHAPTER NINETEEN

I WAS SITTING ON THE SOFA with my feet propped on the coffee table, wiggling my toes in my knee-high fuzzy socks and wearing one of Tyler's sweatshirts that was big enough to be a nightgown. I breathed in the smell of the pumpkin caramel latte candles I'd just lit, feeling comforted by the lines in the carpet from the vacuum and the gleam from the wood polish on the end tables.

It had taken me nearly two weeks to unpack each box and find a place for everything the twins owned. Tyler had been busy, home just long enough to see his things unpacked and get a hot shower before heading back to the barracks. After their belongings were put away, I cleaned every inch, and then used some of my savings to buy a few inexpensive finishing touches for the smaller tables, like the candles and antique firefighting books I'd found at Goodwill and had stacked flat next to the lamps the boys already had. Standing on one end table were vintage fire hose couplings from a New York firehouse that had been welded vertically on eBay for cheap and a hundred-year-old copper and brass fire extinguisher that I'd sat by the door.

A photo album from Taylor and Tyler's childhood was sitting in my lap, opened to my favorite picture of Tyler and his mother. She was squatting next to him, surrounded by their baseball team, the Crushers. She was the coach, her right arm hooked around his middle, her left arm around Taylor with a wide, toothy smile. They looked happier than my family had ever been. I couldn't imagine what her death had done to them.

I removed the picture from the album and walked across the room to the empty frame on the mantle that sat beneath the flat screen hanging on the back wall. I inserted the photo, careful to only touch the edges, and placed it next to one of the small lanterns with an antler base I'd found in a box in Taylor's room. The metal flecks in the frame made it stand out, and I hoped it would make them smile like it did me.

I sat down on the sofa again with a mug of hot buttered rum and cider, leaning back and letting my muscles relax. Tyler's absence had helped him focus on missing me instead of our last argument, and our nightly phone calls made it harder for me to deny that I missed him.

The changing leaves on the Aspen trees around Estes Park were beginning to show early signs that fall was upon us. Fire season was just weeks away from being over.

My phone was connected to Taylor's Bluetooth speaker in the corner with Halsey's album on loop, and I was waiting on Tyler's call. He'd stayed in Colorado Springs during his first R&R because the fire still wasn't contained. He'd said the night before that they were close to calling the ground crews, and I was hopeful that this R&R they could come home.

The lock shimmied, and the door opened, and I startled, then turned around to see Tyler standing in the doorway in shock.

"Honey, I'm … holy shit." He leaned back, looking at the number on the door. "Am I in the right place?"

I stood, holding out my hands and letting them fall to my thighs. "Welcome home."

Tyler looked at me for the longest time, a dozen emotions scrolling across his face.

"What?" I giggled nervously, setting my mug on a coaster.

He dropped his bag and took three long strides before wrapping his arms around me and planting a deep kiss on my mouth. He cupped my jaw, and then the kisses slowed, less passionate and more careful, giving me a few more pecks before pulling away.

He bit his bottom lip, tasted the cider on his lips, and looked down at the mug. "What is that? Rum?"

I smiled. "Just a little with my cider. It's been a long day."

"It's been a long month. A really long month." He took turns looking at both of my eyes, his warm brown irises bouncing back and forth while he thought of something adequate to say. He scanned my face, sliding his thumb along my bottom lip.

He shook his head. "What is that amazing smell?"

"The candles."

"Candles." He breathed out a laugh. "In my apartment. Taylor is going to shit a wildcat."

"I can get rid of them. I just thought—"

"They're great. You didn't have to do all this."

"Yes, I did."

He seemed like he was deciding something, and then his eyebrows pulled in. "I kept thinking on the mountain that I needed to focus on the job and stop thinking about you. That's the wrong place to be preoccupied. For twenty-eight days, I've laid awake at night thinking about your lips, your hands, and the way your eyebrows raise when your bullshit detector goes off and you call me on it. I've missed you like crazy, Ellie. And then coming home to you…"

I offered a small smile, not knowing what else to say. "Do you want to see the rest?" I asked.

He chuckled and looked down, not bothered to be frustrated with my answer. When he looked up, his dimple dug into his cheek. "Yeah. Show me the rest."

I took his hand and pulled him into the kitchen, showing him where the plates were stacked and which drawer was the silverware, and then we went down the hall, and I relished in his reactions with each room.

When we got to his, he intertwined his fingers on top of his head and sighed in awe. He didn't have a bed frame, so I'd used some lattice boards sitting by the dumpster for headboards. I'd cleaned them up and painted them with leftover white paint from when the magazine was built.

"This is crazy. Where did you get that?"

"I made it." I shrugged. "Wick helped."

He shook his head. "You didn't have to do all this, Ellie. This doesn't even look like the same apartment … it looks like…"

"Home." I looked around at all my hard work, grinning.

Tyler kissed me again, pulling my oversized sweatshirt over my head as he backed me toward the bed. His tongued danced with mine, and when I sat, I kept him at bay with my right leg, pointing my fuzzy-socked foot at his chest. He flattened both hands on each side of my ankles, sliding them up past my knees to my thighs, and then pulled back, rolling the socks down and tossing them perfectly into the hamper in the corner.

He took my feet in his hands, kissing my toe, the side of my arch, and then moving up to my ankle, trailing up the inside of my leg with tiny kisses, each one leaving behind a second of warmth before it cooled.

He set my foot flat on the mattress and then reached back with one hand, pulling his T-shirt up. The bottom hem revealed his stomach and then chest, before he yanked it off his head and tossed it while keeping his gaze on me. He had leaned out during fire season, making all six tight muscles of his abs stand out, and the small V protrude, making the path that lead to the bulge behind his cargo pants even more noticeable.

He kicked off his boots, and then shoved down his pants, crawling on top of me wearing just his boxer briefs. His hair was longer, his cheeks a bit sunken in, his jaw more prominent, but his skin was still rough over mine, his tongue still as soft and warm as I remembered.

The weight of him between my thighs made me dig my fingers into his back, bringing him closer, begging him to ram me and come before my heart could feel anything more. Instead, his kisses slowed, and he hovered over me while he balanced himself with one elbow, helping me remove the only two pieces of fabric between us.

I reached above me with one hand to point, holding him against me with the other. "Condoms in the nightstand."

He grazed my jawline with the tip of his nose, breathing me in. He was contemplating something, deciding just when he reached the skin beneath my ear. "Have you been with anyone but me since Sterling?" he asked.

I shook my head.

"IUD still around?"

I nodded.

"I want to feel you," he said. When I didn't protest, he held his breath, sliding his bare skin inside me. He closed his eyes, exhaling as he moaned.

An intense euphoria seared through me, crawling just under the skin to the edges of every inch from my head to my toes. He fit perfectly, like he'd been molded just for me. His skin against mine was more powerful than any rush I'd felt before, whether from self-medicating or being on the mountain. Tyler Maddox was the ultimate high.

I pulled the belt of my robe tight and leaned against the doorjamb between the hall and the living room. Tyler was on the other side of the small breakfast counter, standing over a sizzling skillet on the stove.

"He cooks," I said.

Tyler flipped a pancake, catching it in the pan, and then set it down to pick up the tongs and flip the bacon. He turned to look at me over his shoulder, flashing the dimple I was falling for, and nodded for me to join him.

I sauntered across the floor, leaning my backside against the counter next to him, my arms crossed. He leaned over to kiss my cheek and returned to breakfast as if it were the most normal thing in the world. I took stock of my feelings, wondering why I didn't feel like bolting for the door.

"You snore," Tyler said with a snort.

"I do not," I said, rolling my eyes.

"No, but you're the most beautiful thing I've seen in the morning sun."

I looked down, letting my hair fall into my face.

The dishes clacked together as he loaded them up with greasy food, and then he took them to the tiny bistro table against the wall. Our two plates barely fit, but he put them down, directing me to sit while he poured us two small glasses of orange juice.

He sat down, took a big gulp, and then set the empty glass on the counter behind him. "I don't want you to look for another place. I want you stay here."

"It's a two-bedroom, and Taylor is going to eventually want his bed."

"No, I want you to live here with me."

"With you," I said, watching him wait nervously for my reaction. Feeling so much power over a man would normally be thrilling for me, but a man the size of Tyler squirming was uncomfortable to watch.

"I'm sorry, Ellie," he blurted. "I couldn't help it."

"Couldn't help what?"

"I woke up this morning with you in my arms." He chuckled. "Your fucking hair was everywhere. I had a hell of a time getting it out of your face. Then all the strands were fanned out, framing you from the shoulders up. You looked so peaceful. It just happened."

I frowned. "What are you talking about?"

His face fell, desperation in his eyes. "I fell in love with you. It's been coming for a while. I tried not to."

"You're in love with me," I said.

"I'm in love with you," he repeated, more confession than declaration. We both knew what we agreed our relationship was meant to be, and he was shitting all over it.

"Tyler…"

"I don't want you to look for another place. I want you to stay. I can't think of one fucking thing better than coming home to you." He paused. "Why are you looking at me like that?"

My chin was resting against my fist, partially covering my mouth. All I could do was shake my head.

"You don't love me," he said, devastated. He dropped his fork and fell against the back of his chair.

"I don't know," I said, my eyes glossing over. "How do you know?"

"Because I'm scared to death if I lose you I'll never feel like this with anyone else."

I swallowed, knowing what would happen next. It was the reason I'd worked so hard on the apartment. I wanted to leave something good behind.

"I already know that. When I lose you, I know I'll never feel this way with anyone else."

One side of his mouth turned up, but when recognition hit, his grin faded. He nodded and pressed his lips together, looking at every point on the floor before standing and leaving me for his room. The door slammed, and my shoulders tensed, my eyes closed tight.

I walked down the hall, knocking softly on the door. "Tyler? I just … if I could just get my things…"

He didn't answer, and I pushed open the door. Tyler was sitting on the floor with his knees up, his back against the foot of his bed.

"Just getting my stuff, and I'll go."

"Where are you going to go, Ellie? Just stay."

"That's not fair to you."

He looked up at me with the same tired and ruined eyes I had seen so many times before. "You're the only woman in the world I know could tell me half-ass that she loves me while breaking my heart."

"I'm doing you a favor. You just don't know it yet."

"Bullshit. Quit fucking running."

I pointed to the door. "Have you seen your cupboards? Your fridge? Crown, rum, vodka, cheap wine, and beer. I fall asleep wherever I pass out."

"Not last night," he said.

"I put Crown in my coffee and take it to work. I'm a drunk, Tyler."

He shrugged. "So let's make a call. Get you into a program. Doesn't mean I can't love you."

"We had an agreement."

He shook his head, looking to the floor. He closed one eye, the entire conversation more hurtful than he anticipated. "What if falling in love doesn't break your heart, Ellie? We're happy when we're not fighting about being happy."

"That's not true," I snapped.

"It damn sure is. Every time you think we're feeling too much or too happy, you tap the brakes."

"I'm just trying to stop before we start."

He crawled to his feet. "Before we start? I just told you I'm in love with you!"

"You don't know that," I said, picking up my bag and filling it with the few things I owned.

Tyler walked over and grabbed my wrist. "You know how I know? Only love could hurt like this."

I twisted away from him, thinking about the little boy in the photograph I'd placed on the mantle. "I was honest with you from the beginning. I told you I couldn't. You said you were fine with it."

"Well, now I'm not." He held out his hands, gesturing to the room. "Why did you do all of this? You made us a home just to leave me alone in it?"

"I wanted to you to remember that I'm not completely awful."

"Why do you fucking care?" he seethed.

Tears spilled over onto my cheeks. "I don't deserve anything you have to offer, Tyler. I loved being with you while you let me, but anything past this…"

He laughed once in disbelief. "You don't think you deserve me. Ellie…" He cupped my shoulders. "I'm a dick. Trust me, I'm the one who doesn't deserve you. But I'm trying. I told myself a few weeks ago when I … that I was going to keep trying until I did deserve you."

I looked up at him, my eyes narrowed. "When you what?"

He clenched his teeth. "It was after you told me we were just fucking and fighting. I went to a local country bar to meet my brother."

"So?"

"So," he sighed. "A girl showed up. I didn't know she knew Taylor."

"I understand. You don't have to tell me."

"I didn't go home with her or anything; I just kissed her. I intended to, though. She was nice to me. I didn't have to try so fucking hard just to feel rejected."

I swallowed, angry at how hurt I felt. "It's fine. She sounds great."

"She wasn't you," he said.

I wiped my cheek. "I bet she wasn't fucked up."

"We're all a little fucked up. Not all of us use it to push everyone away."

I lifted my chin. "So you decided you were in love with me after you tried to take someone home. Indicative of our dysfunction, don't you think?"

"Ellie …"

I closed my eyes. "I never meant for us to get in this deep. I never meant for this to mean anything more. Let me leave. One of us has to."

He dropped his hands from my shoulders, exhaling like the wind had been knocked out of him. "Where?"

"Jojo's."

He nodded toward the door. "Go."

I bent down to get one last shirt, and then rushed to the laundry room at the end of the hall and grabbed some folded clothes. My backpack was full, so I began filling a small plastic laundry basket.

I reached for the door, but his hand was on mine. I breathed out a cry, knowing if he said one more word, I would stay.

He touched his cheek to mine, then kissed my temple. "Let me drive you."

I shook my head.

He let go of the knob, waiting for me to look up at him. When I did, his expression crushed me. "You're still my friend. Let me drive you."

I nodded, watching him fetch his keys. He led me to his truck, and then I directed him to the magazine. We didn't speak. Tyler gripped the steering wheel so tight his knuckles turned white.

When I pointed to the back lot, he frowned. "Why did you tell me to come here, Ellie? Jojo doesn't live here."

"There's an apartment above. I have a key," I said, pulling Tyler's off my key ring.

He took it, glowering at the metal in his palm. He closed his eyes. "Ellie, I still want you to come to Illinois with me next month."

I laughed once. "I can't meet your family, Tyler. Are you insane?"

"I already told Dad you were coming."

I frowned.

"Please?"

"We can't just be friends now. Not when *I love yous* have been thrown around. We can't go back. You've ruined it."

"You've ruined me."

"It was your turn."

He managed a small laugh, looking down. "Get the fuck outta my truck, Edson."

"Done," I said with a smile. "See you around."

I fished the key out from the small, fake rock by the back door, and then waved to Tyler as he reversed his truck and pulled away. Once inside, I lugged my bag and the laundry basket up a set of stairs, seeing the perfectly clean apartment. No décor, no candles, no pictures of anyone I loved.

I sat on the floor and sobbed—emotionally exhausted, heartbroken, and relieved.

CHAPTER TWENTY

THE ONLY DOWNSIDE to living in a brand-new apartment above the *MountainEar* for almost nothing was that once fire season was over, Tyler was working down the street every third day. The unseen benefit was that Jojo liked to hang out upstairs after work, and sometimes she'd take me with her to Turk's—and the owner's daughter got a nice discount.

We sat at a table in a corner, sipping on Hurricanes in the dim light. Christmas decorations were already hanging from the ceiling, and red and green tinsel garland spiraled around the wooden beams standing at each corner of the bar.

"Good God these are huge drinks," Jojo said, her words slurred. "I'm only to here," she said, touching the middle of her glass, "and hammered."

"The quicker the better," I said, irritated that I wasn't even buzzed.

The door blew open, and in walked a line of familiar faces, chatting and smiling.

I sunk in my seat. "Shit."

"What?" Jojo said, turning to see the source of my reaction. "Liam!" she said with a wide grin.

Liam heard his name and turned toward our table. Jojo waved like an idiot, and he switched direction, heading straight for us.

"Jojo! Damn it!" I hissed.

Jack, Fish, Jubal, Sage, Zeke, Bucky, Sugar, Cat, Taco, Watts, Smitty, Runt, Puddin', and Pup followed, filing into our booth and pulling up chairs when the space was filled. I was squished between Jojo and Liam, and she looked unhappy he'd gone left instead of right to sit next to her.

"You couldn't bring the whole crew, huh?" I said, elbowing Liam.

He laughed and rubbed his ribs. "The rest are coming. Except the twins. Taylor stayed in Colorado Springs, and Tyler went home."

"What's the occasion?" Jojo asked.

"Fire season's over. Most of the guys are getting on a plane in the morning," Jubal said, patting Pup on the shoulder.

They all looked exhausted, skinny, and content.

"Tyler didn't want to come out on everyone's last night?" I asked.

Watts pulled out his phone. "He will if I tell him you're here."

Everyone laughed but me. "Please don't."

"Too late," Watts said, replacing his phone in his pocket.

My shoulders sagged.

Liam leaned into my ear. "So you dumped him, did ya? That's rough."

"I didn't dump him. We weren't together," I said.

Sage spoke up. "He's sure been moping around the last two weeks. I don't think I've seen him so miserable."

Jojo looked at me with sleepy, glazed eyes and jutted out her bottom lip.

"Stop," I warned.

"Chief said he's going to let you back next season," Liam said.

"Really?" Jojo asked, her eyebrows lifting so high they threatened to skim her hairline.

"Yeah," Liam said. "The poor bloke heard about it every day from twenty crewmen."

"Are you and Jack going to the airport tomorrow?" I asked.

"Nah. We're gonna do some sightseein'. You should come." He looked to Jojo. "Your photographer should do a feature on the Great American Road Trip. She could cover your travel section."

"We're not that kind of magazine," Jojo said, annoyed with Liam now that he wasn't flirting with her.

He turned to me again. "You should come."

"I can't."

"Why?" he asked.

"Because I have a job, and bills, and I can't just pick up and leave. I've seen the States. Most of them, anyway ... and the rest of the world."

"Oh. World traveler, are ya?" Liam said. He was beautiful—
even twenty pounds leaner, cheekbones more pronounced and eyes
a bit sunken in—but the part of me that wanted to act on attraction
had been stolen by Tyler, and he wasn't giving it back anytime
soon.

"Yes."

"Her dad owns Edson Technologies, genius," Jojo said.

The men at the table all covered their mouths and said *Oh!* in
unison. I wasn't sure why. Her comeback wasn't that great.

"Your father is Philip Edson?" Liam asked, shocked.

"You've heard of him, huh?" I said, twirling the straw in my
tall glass.

Jack laughed. "We've had Paris Hilton following us around in
the woods all this time?"

I wrinkled my nose. "Take that back, fuck-knuckle. Right.
Now."

Everyone at the table but Jack and Liam looked confused.
They'd heard the term plenty in Australia; it was my favorite Aussie
insult.

"I'm ... I'm sorry," Jack said.

Liam burst into laughter. "Ya soft cock! You're just gonna take
that from her?"

Jack pouted. "Maddox takes a helluva lot more from her than
I do."

I sunk in my chair, blown back by equal parts guilt, shame, and
humiliation.

"For fuck's sake, Jack!" Cat chided.

"No, he's right," I said. "I don't know why."

"I do," Jubal said with a knowing grin. "But you can be damn
sure he wouldn't do it for anyone else."

After a long minute of awkward silence, the crew turned to
their pints and whiskey, chatting about their favorite stories from
the ending season. Once in a while, they would belly laugh, always
at someone's expense. I scanned over the faces of the boys I'd
come to love, wishing my favorite one were among them, but at
the same time, relieved that he wasn't.

Liam leaned in, tapping my nearly empty glass. "You need
another, love?"

"Yes, please," I said without hesitation. Someone else offering to buy me a drink wasn't new—having to wait to drink until that happened took some getting used to.

Liam raised his index finger into the air, signaled to the waitress, and then held up my empty glass when she looked his way. She smiled at him, already enamored with his accent and the trademark hotshot tan line around his emerald eyes.

He leaned in, his lips grazing my ear when he spoke. He talked about where he and Jack were planning to drive to first, pretending to need traveling tips and laughing at my sarcasm. I'd just finished the drink he'd bought me, and was just beginning to feel a bit lighter when his gaze fell to my lips.

"I've been patiently waiting, ya know," he said. "It's been almost an hour. Your boy hasn't come for you yet."

I looked down. "Probably because I'm not his to come and claim."

"Yeah, but he's yours. I can see it all over the poor bastard's face."

I noted the pink tint of Liam's lips against his bronzed skin. A faint echo deep inside me suggested I grab his face and pretend not to care that Tyler hadn't come like Watts had said he would. The taste of Liam's drink on my tongue wouldn't be the worst distraction. The more I imagined his strong hands on my skin, the unhappier I felt. Sterling was supposed to have been my rock bottom, but Tyler had given up on me, just like I had—there was no lower feeling than that.

Just for one night I wished I could return to the pathologically selfish asshole I once was. Even drinking back-to-back Hurricanes couldn't erase Ellie two-point-oh. Jojo was happily sloppy drunk, but guilt and an ache for Tyler consumed me. Exhaling, my back hit the hard wood of my chair as I wondered if more experienced company could have helped me lose myself. I needed someone supremely manipulative, heartless, and cruel—someone like me.

"You're terrible at flirting," I said, deflated.

Liam seemed surprised at my retreat, and then he closed one eye and wrinkled his nose, almost like he was in pain. "I really fucked that one up, didn't I? Just forget I said that. Let me help. I'll buy you another drink."

"I'll take it."

The door swung open, and Tyler walked in alone, shoving his hands in his pockets and looking around. When his gaze landed on me, he paused. My breath hitched, and my heart banged against my ribcage. It was all I could do not to leave my seat and run across the room and tackle him.

Tyler casually strolled over to the bar to greet Annie and grab a beer before navigating the tables to stand next to our corner booth. Each step he took seemed to take an eternity, but finally he was there, standing just a few feet away.

He eyed Liam before smiling at me. "Hey."

"Hey," I replied, nervous and embarrassed, knowing we sounded ridiculous in front of the crew.

Tyler grabbed a chair and sat next to Jubal, who patted him a few times on the back for encouragement. "Glad you decided to join us after all, Maddox."

Watts smirked. "I'm sad to know we weren't good enough for a sendoff, but add Ellie to the mix…"

"Shut your hole, Watts," Cat growled.

Tyler took a swig of his bottle and leaned back, looking unaffected until Liam lifted his arm and rested it across the back of my chair. Tyler's eyes darted to Liam's extended arm, and then to Liam, a murderous glare in his eye.

"We were just talking about you, Maddox," Liam said.

I let out an involuntary, awkward chuckle. "No we … no we weren't."

Tyler stayed guarded, unsure of Liam's intention but clearly undaunted. He took another sip of his beer, then leaned forward, his elbows on the table. "Is that so?"

"No, it's not so," I insisted, trying to wade through the Hurricane to be present enough to avoid humiliation.

Tyler smiled at me, and I melted. "It's okay if you were. I was just thinking about you."

"And there we have it," Liam said. "Told ya, love."

Tyler's gaze left me and targeted Liam, a line between his eyebrows forming. "I don't know what you're trying to do, Liam, but if you want to leave here with both arms, stop."

Liam laughed, genuinely amused.

"Liam," I warned.

"I'm just having a go at you, mate. You make it too easy."

Jack's chair whined against the floor as he leaned forward. "Liam. Enough."

Liam held up his arms. "I'm sorry. I was just trying to get her to take a trip with me. I don't think it's Colorado she'll miss."

Three lines on Tyler's forehead deepened when his eyebrows pushed upward. The crew shifted in their seats, uncomfortably witnessing the exchange.

"Another round!" Jubal said, lifting his half-empty glass. The rest of the crew lifted their glasses and hollered their agreement in unison.

Tyler leaned in, lowering his chin as he stared at Liam. "What are you doing, man?" He took the tone he did with Taylor when he was disappointed in his behavior.

Liam smiled his most charming smile. "I've tried, mate. She doesn't want me. I'm an excellent wingman. Ask Jack."

All of Jack's teeth gleamed when he smiled. "Truth."

One corner of Tyler's mouth curled up, and then he looked at me. Just as he opened his mouth to speak, a man I vaguely remembered stumbled into the table.

"Maddox!" he slurred, slapping Tyler's shoulder. His fingers curled over the top of Tyler's flannel shirt and dug in.

"Look!" he said, spittle flying from his mouth when he spoke. "It's the girl who kicked me in the balls!"

"Todd Mercer," I said, his clue helping me recall. "I'd love to do that for you again."

A sour look came over his face. "Ellie, right?"

Tyler shrugged away from Todd's grip and sighed. "I'm busy, Mercer. I'll kick your ass later."

"Why?" Sugar asked, exasperated. "You get your ass kicked every time, Mercer. Every. Time."

Liam's eyes sparked, amused. "You kicked him in the balls, Ellie?"

"I was trying to keep him from getting killed by Tyler."

"Killed." Todd snorted.

Liam wasn't impressed. "Who invited this drongo?"

Todd's nose wrinkled. "What does that even mean? Speak English!"

Liam stopped smiling, trading a look with Jack.

"Move along, Mercer. Your balls will thank me," I said.

The crew chuckled, and Todd stood up tall, puffing out his chest and suddenly lucid. "You're pretty fucking mouthy for a seasonal whore reduced to begging locals for drinks."

After a short stunned silence, chairs squealed against the floor as the Alpine Hotshots rose to their feet. Todd scanned the crew, taking a step back.

The crew's faces were severe, none more menacing than Tyler's.

"Maddox!" Annie yelled over the music.

"It's okay," I said, standing. I leaned across the table, tugging on Tyler's shirt.

"The fuck it is," Tyler said, glowering at Todd.

"No need to be rude, mate," Liam said.

"Maddox," Jubal said. He shook his head. "We're having a good time, and this drunk idiot isn't going to ruin it for everyone." He pointed at Todd. "Get the hell out of here. Final warning."

Tyler glanced at Liam. "Keep the girls over there."

Liam nodded once.

Todd opened his mouth to speak, but before he could form another word, Tyler lunged at him. Suddenly, the entire bar was a swarm of violent commotion, swinging arms, yelling, and entire groups of men moving one way or the other as they shoved against one another.

Liam pulled Jojo close and stretched his arm across my chest, angling his body in front of us for protection but clearly entertained.

"No!" Jojo yelled as a table buckled and crashed to the floor. "Oh, Daddy is going to be so pissed."

Jack was standing on a chair, directing whoever was at the bottom of the pile. Cat, Sugar, and Puddin' were tossing anyone who wasn't a hotshot out of the mound of thrashing bodies like toddlers eagerly searching a toy box.

"Stop. *Stop!*" I yelled, pushing against Liam's arm.

Tyler's head popped up from the sea of chaos for a brief moment. I escaped the safety of the wall just in time to grab his shirt with both fists. Just as Tyler landed a devastating blow to Todd's jaw, he noticed I had hold of him and hooked his arm around my shoulders, ducking and dodging the various fighting groups until we were safely in the alley.

I shook my head. "That was … unnecessary."

"You're shaking," he said, reaching for me.

I pushed him away. "Mercer could barely stand, and you attacked him."

"Ellie ... no one was going to let him say that and walk out of there. I was trying to knock him out before anyone else got ahold of him."

"Oh, so you were doing him a favor," I deadpanned.

He shrugged. "At least he didn't get kicked in the balls."

I paused and then looked down, unable to stop from smiling. The rest of the crew burst from the door, half of them laughing, the rest pulling their still-swinging brothers out.

Liam and Jojo were holding hands, the fight giving them an excuse to break the personal boundary barrier. After a few drinks, one touch was all it took for most, and Jojo couldn't have been happier.

Jubal exhaled. "That was a much-needed release of tension, I guess."

Fish frowned. "Wick's not going to let us back in until next season. Some of us live here."

"I'll talk to him," I said. "So will Jojo."

They all grinned, patting and hugging me as they passed. "Thanks, Ellie," each of them said. "See you next season."

Liam kissed my cheek, winking at Tyler. "Take care, you two. Quit fuckin' around, would ya?"

Jojo jingled her keys. "Need a ride?"

"I've got her," Tyler said.

I glanced up at him, appreciative. He hadn't given up on me. No matter what I said or did, he was right there, waiting to take care of me.

Jack patted Tyler on the shoulder, and the crew walked out to the cars parked in the street, chatting excitedly about the brawl.

Tyler waved to them and then turned to me, beginning a full minute of silence in the alley in front of Turk's. I folded my arms across my middle, feeling the sweat on my skin chill in the autumn air.

"You cold?" Tyler asked. "My jacket is in the truck."

"I'm fine."

"So ... I'm confused," he began. "Liam and Jojo?"

I laughed out loud, holding my hands out to my sides and letting them fall to my thighs. "I guess. I'm just as surprised as you are."

"Watts said he asked you to go on a road trip with him."

I nodded.

"What did you say?"

"A road trip costs money that I don't have."

"Is that the only reason?"

"Tyler..."

His shoulders sagged. "It doesn't matter what I do, does it? I just can't..." He gestured to the space between us. "Get past whatever's in the way."

I pressed my lips together and clamped down with my teeth. I'd been doing so well staying away from him. It would only be cruel to admit the truth.

"What?" he said with a half-smile. "Say it."

I shook my head.

"Don't be a pussy, Ellison. Say it," he repeated.

"I shouldn't."

"Yeah. You should."

"I miss you," I blurted out.

He scanned my face, a new light in his eyes.

I closed my eyes. "I think about you all the time … mostly wondering why you put up with so much of my shit."

"You and me both."

I looked away, trying to find something that warranted my attention so Tyler wouldn't see the hurt in my eyes.

"But, when I'm around you, Ellie … it doesn't matter why. It doesn't matter what you did to piss me off or push me away. I can't explain it. I can't shake it. Some days I wish I could. I come from a family of proud men, but I'm not the first to falter when it comes to the one woman he can't walk away from."

"You should … walk away from me."

He chuckled. "You think I don't know that? You're the female version of me."

I glanced up at him, pleased with his confession. "When you showed up tonight, I was happier than I've been in a long time."

He didn't hesitate, taking my cheeks in his hands. He leaned in, but I pulled back.

He furrowed his brow. "Then what? What do I have to do?"

My eyes burned as I clutched the mid-section of his shirt with both fists. "I've already told you. I've told you a hundred times. I'm fucked up. I'm drinking again. I'm taking spiked coffee to work."

He shrugged. "So we start over."

There was that word again. *We.* It didn't sound so foreign anymore, and that scared the hell out of me. "It's not that simple. I'm not in any shape to try to manage a relationship."

Tyler looked into my eyes, and then yanked his shirt from my grip and walked away with his hands on his head, breathing hard.

"I know I'm a dick," I said. "You don't deserve this. But I tried to warn you."

"Warn me about what?" he yelled, holding his hands in front of him. "That it feels amazing to be with you? That it'd be incredible to watch you give up everything and fight your ass off just on the hope your sister will notice from half a world away? Or maybe you warned me that you'd make me laugh like an idiot?"

I used my sleeve to wipe away an escaped tear. "You could find that with any nice, normal girl."

"I don't want a normal girl, Ellie. I want you," he snapped.

A laugh tumbled from my lips, but my smile quickly faded. "I warned you that I would make you feel like shit. I warned you that you were too nice to get involved with someone like me."

"Someone like *you?*" he said, both frustrated and desperate. "You should have warned me that I'd smile every time I think about you—which is all the damn time! You should have warned me about that, too. You should have warned me that you're beautiful in the morning, in the moonlight, just out of the shower, or with ten days of dirt on your face."

"It's not funny."

"No! It's not! Goddamn it, Ellie, I'm standing here saying I wanna be with you and you want it, too. I know you do. Your reasons don't even make sense."

"They don't have to make sense to you."

He breathed out a laugh. "All this time I thought you were a masochist. You're a fucking sadist."

"I warned you!" I cried.

"You didn't warn me that I'd fucking fall in love with you!" Tyler's veins bulged in his neck, and he put his hands on his hips, catching his breath.

"What?" I choked out.

"You heard me," he growled. Immediately the anger extinguished from his eyes, replaced with remorse.

"I've been trying to stay away from you, Tyler. I really have. I don't want to drag you down with me."

"Too late!" he yelled. He rubbed his forehead. "I didn't come here to fight," he said, exasperated. "I'm so tired of trying to hate you."

His words cut deep, the pain settling in my bones. I could barely form the words. "Then why did you come?"

"To see you," he said, rubbing the back of his neck. "I had to see you."

I reached for him again, this time slower, testing the waters. Tyler kept his hands on his hips, his gaze bouncing everywhere but on me. I pulled him close, sliding my hands under his arms, hugging his middle, and then pressing my cheek against his chest. His body heat radiated off him like a fever, a thin sheen of sweat dampening his skin. I breathed him in, knowing if I just gave in we might be just a little less wounded, a little less broken, but I was stuck between being too selfish to let him go and too contrite to let it go too far.

The door to Turk's was opening and closing in a steady rhythm. People were walking by, quiet and curious. Until that instant, I hadn't noticed we'd gained a small audience. Tyler acted as if we were the only two people in that alley.

"I'm glad you came," I whispered.

He'd been frozen since I first grabbed him, his arms held stiffly at his sides. After a few seconds, he hugged me back. "Are you sure about that?"

"I miss my friend."

His chest rose and fell as he inhaled and then breathed out, letting go of whatever he was holding on to. "Your friend."

"I know. I know it's so fucking selfish," I said, closing my eyes.

"I guess I'll take what I can get." I couldn't see his face, but he sounded crushed.

"You promise?"

He touched the back of my hair, and then kissed the crown of my head. "No. No, I don't promise. Fuck this, Ellie. I don't want to be just friends."

I took a step back, fidgeting. "Yeah. I get it. I mean … of course. Who would after…? It was a stupid thing to say."

"I told myself I wasn't going to push it, and I pushed it. I know you're fucked up. I'm fucked up, too. I have no clue how to navigate this, and you … goddamn, you make this a thousand times harder than it has to be. But I'm not going anywhere. I can't. I don't want anyone else."

"Don't say that."

"Too fucking bad. We can figure it out later when you're ready. I'll back off, but we're not just friends, Ellie. We never were."

"What if I'm never ready?"

He shoved his hands into his jeans pockets, hope glistening in his eyes. "I've seen what you're capable of when you wanna be. I think you will be."

"Why are you doing this?" I asked in disbelief. "I'm a lost cause!"

"Then so am I."

I covered my eyes, trying not to cry. "It's like talking to a fucking wall! You're not hearing me, and I'm not that good of a person to pretend I don't want you in my life. I'm trying to do you a favor, Tyler. You have to go away. You have to be the one to do it. I've tried. I can't."

"I've already told you," he said. "I'm in love with you. That's not going away." He cleared his throat. "Are you going to Wick's for Thanksgiving?"

I blinked, shaken by the sudden swing in conversation. "What? No."

"Not home? Not somewhere with your family?"

"Finley asked. I'm just not … ready."

"Why don't you come home to Eakins with me?"

"Come home with you."

He breathed out a laugh, frustrated. "It's going to be tough. It'll probably be awkward. But no matter how hard it is, it'll be easier than you being alone—and easier on me than worrying that you're alone on Thanksgiving."

I considered his offer. "I feel like this is a crossroads."

He grinned, holding out his hand. "So cross with me."

CHAPTER TWENTY-ONE

"WHAT'S WRONG?" Tyler asked, nudging my knee with his.

I shook my head, staring at the back of the driver's head. Travis's window was cracked while he smoked and chatted with his wife, neither of them thinking to adjust the heat while the frigid air filled the car.

Travis was too big for the tiny silver Toyota Camry he was driving, smiling far too often at his wife. They were holding hands, chatting about their break from their sophomore year of college, and how this Thanksgiving would be better than the year before.

She lifted their hands and slammed them down on the console, feigning insult. "Really? You had to bring that up."

He grinned, smug. "If it gets me some sympathy points, baby, you're damn right I'm bringing it up."

She made a show of settling back into her seat, failing miserably at pretending to be angry. "No points for you. Be nice or I won't marry you again."

He lifted her hand and kissed her fingers, staring at her as if she were the most beautiful star in his universe. "Yeah, you will."

The two of them were engulfed in their own world, barely noticing Tyler or me, even though Travis had nearly tackled us at the terminal. He and his wife, Abby, had picked us up from the airport in Chicago, and I was freezing in the backseat, dodging the occasional flicked cigarette ash. The handholding and incessant happiness was making me slightly nauseated, and I was beginning to regret agreeing to come.

"Hey," Tyler said, gently patting my knee. "It's going to be great."

Travis rolled up his window, and *then* turned up the heat.

I fantasized about flicking the back of his ear and blaming it on Tyler.

"Are you nervous?" Abby asked, turning around to face me. She looked me directly in the eye, beautiful and confident. Her caramel hair was long and effortlessly beautiful, her gray eyes so intense anyone else would have squirmed under her stare. I wondered if it was because her husband was the most intimidating person I'd ever met, or that she had her own badassery to offer.

"No. Should I be?" I asked.

"I was a little nervous at my first Maddox Thanksgiving."

Tyler punched the back of her seat. "That's because you were pretending to still be with Travis."

"Hey!" Travis said, reaching back to swat at his brother.

"Quit! Stop! Now!" Abby commanded. She reminded me of me at the barracks with twenty misbehaving boys.

"Oh, you weren't together last year?" I asked. "I thought you were married this past March."

"We were," Travis said, a ridiculous grin on his face.

Abby smirked, inviting me to judge them. "We got in a huge fight—a lot of huge fights, actually—broke up, and then eloped to Vegas. We're renewing our vows in St. Thomas in March on our anniversary."

"Ellie's coming to that, too," Tyler said. "She's my plus one."

"We talked about it," I said quickly. "I don't think I've RSVP'd just yet."

"Is that a camera?" Abby asked, looking down at the bag in my lap.

"It is."

"So are you a professional photographer, or is that just to capture the Maddox family Thanksgiving shenanigans?"

"She's the photographer for the magazine in Estes Park. She follows the local hotshots around—did a whole write-up."

"I'd like to see your work," Abby said. "We need a photographer for the wedding. What do you charge?"

"I don't," I said.

"You don't charge?" Travis asked. "You're hired!"

"She's really good," Tyler said.

"Now you have to come," Abby said.

Tyler elbowed me, satisfied.

Abby narrowed her eyes at her brother-in-law. "How did you two meet?"

"At a party," Tyler said, clearing his throat.

"What kind of party?"

"My party," I said.

"So you live in Estes Park?" she asked.

"Yes."

"Did you graduate from there?"

"Abby, for fuck's sake. What's with the third degree?" Tyler asked.

"I'm just making conversation," Abby said with a relaxed smile. She was very good at something. I just wasn't sure what.

I lifted my chin. "My parents have a house there. I lived there until recently. Now I work at the magazine and have an apartment in Estes Park."

"How did you end up at her parents' house for a party, Tyler? Are they clients of yours?" Abby asked.

"Nope," Tyler said, staring out the window.

Abby glanced over at Travis. "He's lying."

Tyler shot her a look.

"Okay, Pidge," Travis said, amused. "Enough detective work for one day."

"Is that what you do?" I asked. "Are you a cop?"

Everyone laughed but me.

"No," Abby said. "I'm a college student. I tutor math a few nights a week."

I arched an eyebrow. "Maybe you should look into that."

Abby seemed pleased. "Did you hear that, Trav? I should be a cop."

He kissed her hand again. "I don't think I could handle that."

"Me either," Tyler said. He leaned over and whispered in my ear. "He gets a little crazy when it comes to her."

"I know someone like that," I said.

Tyler mulled over my words, and then smiled, clearly taking it as a compliment.

We pulled into the drive of a small house with a detached garage and a hideous red Dodge Intrepid in the drive. A round, older gentleman stepped outside with another muscled brother, the same buzz cut and inked arms as Travis and the twins.

"Trent?" I asked.

Tyler nodded.

When Travis parked the car, Tyler hopped out and knocked on the trunk until Travis popped it open. He dug out our backpacks and slung them over his shoulder.

"You pack lighter than me," Abby said. "I'm impressed."

I smiled, still unsure if she planned to be friend or foe.

"Come in, come in," Mr. Maddox called to us.

Tyler bear-hugged his father and punched Trent in the arm before hugging him, too.

"Trent," he said, shaking my hand.

"Ellie," I replied. "It's nice to meet you."

"We're so glad you decided to come," Mr. Maddox said.

"I appreciate you having me, Mr. Maddox."

He chuckled, flattening his palm over his belly like a pregnant woman fawning over her ripe baby bump. "It's just Jim, kiddo. Come in out of the cold! We've had a mean cold snap this week."

Trent held open the creaking screen door as we passed, and I stepped into their tiny home, the worn carpet and furniture an ode to the house from *A Christmas Story*. I half expected Ralphie to be standing at the top of the stairs in a pink bunny suit, and then smiled as I remembered watching that movie on numerous Thanksgiving evenings from my father's lap, swaying as he belly laughed for over an hour.

I inhaled stale smoke and the smell of old carpet, feeling strangely at ease. We paused in the kitchen, watching a girl washing dishes at the sink dry her hands and reach her ink-covered arms for Tyler. He hugged her, and then she shook my hand. Her fingers were pruny from the sudsy water, but I could still make out the word *baby doll* across her knuckles. A diamond stud sparkled in her nose, and beneath the thick eyeliner, she was stunningly beautiful. Everything from her razored bob to her timid smile reminded me of Paige.

"This is Cami," Trent said.

"Or Camille," she said. "Whichever you prefer. Nice to meet you."

"Cami belongs to Trent," Abby said, pointing to the correct brother.

"Actually … I belong to her," Trent said.

Camille lifted her shoulder, standing on the side of her foot. "I think I'll keep him."

"You better," Trent said, winking at her.

Tyler cleared his throat. "Where are we sleeping?"

"I'll take you," Abby said.

She kissed her husband on the cheek, and then led us upstairs to a bedroom with a bunk bed and a dresser. Dusty frames with dirty boys and school pictures of Taylor and Tyler with oversized teeth and shaggy hair hung on the paneled walls. Baseball and football trophies crowded a bookshelf.

"Here you are," Abby said, tucking her hair behind her ear. She perched her hands on her hips, taking one last glance around the room to make sure it was suitable before we settled in. "Clean sheets on the beds. Bathroom is down the hall, Ellie."

"Thank you."

"See you downstairs," Abby said. "Cami and I are starting some of the food if you want to come down. Poker later."

"Don't play with her," Tyler said, pointing at Abby.

"What? Does she cheat?" I asked.

"No, she's a fucking hustler. She'll take all your money."

"Not all of it," Abby said, glaring at him. "I give some of it back."

Tyler grumbled something under his breath, and Abby left us alone, closing the door behind her. The room suddenly felt tiny, and I peeled off my coat.

"Ellie."

"Yeah?"

"You look wound pretty tight."

"I need a beer and a cigarette."

He held out his soft pack and his lighter, walking a few steps to crack the window. I flicked the lighter and breathed in deep, holding in lungs full of smoke until I kneeled beside the window and exhaled.

Tyler lit his own, reaching behind the dresser and pulling out a small red bowl with cutouts on the rim.

"Secret ashtray?" I teased.

"Yeah. He never found it. We were pretty proud of that."

"Rebels."

Tyler took a drag and blew it out the window, looking down at his old neighborhood. "I beat the shit out of Paul Fitzgerald on that corner. And Levi ... damn ... I can't remember his last name.

Weird. I thought I'd remember those kids forever. Do you remember all of your childhood friends?"

"They're mostly all still around. Some of them OD'd. Some of them committed suicide. The rest are around. I see them at charity galas now and then. Well … I used to … when I went to charity galas."

"What is a charity gala, exactly?" Tyler asked.

We both laughed, and I shook my head, taking one last drag before mashing the end of my cigarette into Tyler's secret ashtray. "An asshole magnet."

"Well, it's for a good cause, right?"

I snorted, and then stood, putting my pack on the lower bunk and opening the zipper. "Dibs," I said, setting my things on the bed. When Tyler didn't answer, I turned to catch him staring at me. "What?"

He shrugged. "It's just cool … you being here."

"Thanks for inviting me. I'm sorry for being a cranky bitch." I swallowed, and my throat felt dry and tight. Jim seemed like a beer guy, and I hoped he would have a six-pack or two in the fridge downstairs. It was all I could do not to run down and yank open the door to find out.

I ran my fingers across the spines of the few books that stood next to his trophies.

"*James and the Giant Peach*?" I asked.

"Hey. That's a damn good book."

"Calling you a peach seems fitting now."

"Shut it," Tyler said, holding the ashtray out the window and turning it upside down to empty its contents. He pushed the windowsill down, latching it closed.

"So … what's with Abby the cop?"

I sat on the bed, and Tyler sat next to me, taking my hand and sliding his fingers between mine. "We never bring anyone home, so she's hypersensitive about it. She's our sister … overprotective."

"It's fine. I like her."

He stared at the carpet, breathing out a laugh. "Me, too. She really saved this family … saved Travis … in more ways than one."

"They really love each other. It's kind of gross."

He chuckled. "Yeah. They used to fight all the time. Broke each other's hearts. When they broke up, I thought Trav was gonna lose it. Now look at them. They are crazy happy."

"They make it look easy—like anyone could make it work."

"It is easy, Ellie."

"I'm not Abby."

"She's had a lot happen, too. If you heard her story, you might feel a little differently about things."

"I doubt that. I thought we weren't going to talk about this."

"Talk about what?"

I glared at him, and he smiled at me, his dimple appearing and making it impossible for me to stay mad.

"I wanna be gross with you," he said.

"Well ... when you put it that way..."

He leaned in, grazing his lips across mine. My body instantly reacted, craving nothing else but him. I reached under his shirt, running my fingertips up his back.

"No," he whispered. "I don't mean that." He pulled away, fishing my hands from his shirt. He sighed. "It'll be a year ago tomorrow night that I saw my baby brother in more pain than I'd ever seen him in before."

"Looks like it all worked out, though."

"That's what I keep telling myself. I look at them and remember what it took to get there, how confused and stubborn Abby was and how Trav never gave up."

"Tyler..."

"Don't say it. We've got a whole weekend left."

He kissed the corner of my mouth and then stood, pulling me up with him. We walked downstairs, hand in hand. Abby eyed us until Tyler let me go to join his brothers in the next room.

"Still just friends?" Abby asked.

"You get right to the point, don't you?"

She shrugged. "No sense in beating around the bush. These boys have been through a lot. For some reason they're also gluttons for punishment."

"I guess you'd know," I said, pushing up on the counter to sit and grabbing an apple out of the fruit bowl. I rubbed it on my jeans and took a bite. "Who interrogated you for Travis?"

Abby arched an eyebrow. "Touché."

"Easy, girls. We're all on the same side, here," Camille said while I crunched.

Abby smirked. "Are we?"

"Tyler is a friend," I said.

Camille and Abby traded knowing glances, and then Abby leaned on the counter next to me. "That's what we all say. So … are you going to bring that camera to my wedding?"

I looked at the two of them gazing back at me expectantly. Finally, I nodded twice, slow and emphatic. "I'd be honored."

"America is going to shit," Camille warned.

"Who's America?" I asked.

Abby seemed amused. "My best friend. She's planning the whole thing. She doesn't like it when I interfere."

"With your wedding?" I asked.

"Travis and I eloped, so I sort of owe her one. I don't want to plan it, anyway, but if we have a photographer in the family now…"

"They're just friends," Camille teased.

"Oh yeah," Abby said with a wink. "I forgot."

"Baby!" Travis called.

Abby excused herself to the next room where the Maddox boys were sitting around a table staring at the cards in their hands. Abby leaned over her husband's shoulder to check his hand of cards and whispered in his ear.

"Fucking cheating assholes!" Trent yelled.

"Goddamn it!" Jim snapped. "Watch your mouth!"

"They're cheating!" Trent said, pointing all four fingers at Travis and Abby.

"We quit playing your wife, Trav," Tyler said. "If you don't knock it off, we'll stop letting you play, too."

"Fuck all of you. You're just jealous," Travis said, kissing Abby's cheek.

Tyler glanced at me for half a second before returning his attention to his cards.

My stomach sank. Travis and Abby, disgustingly happy and shameless in their PDA, were where Tyler thought we were headed. That was why he refused to believe me or even listen. He knew Travis and Abby had survived whatever they'd been through and thought we could do the same.

I hopped off the counter and tugged on the handle of the fridge, seeing bottles of Sam Adams lined along the shelf in the door. I grabbed one and popped the top, taking a swig. My body instantly relaxed, and I let my worries and guilt slip away.

"Are you coming back for Christmas?" Camille asked.

I shook my head, beginning to voice my doubts, but Tyler interrupted. "Yep. We'll be going back to Colorado for my birthday, though. Taylor's decided he wants to throw a party."

"Am I invited?" I teased.

Abby's mouth pulled to the side. "I hate that you guys live so far away. You could sell insurance here, you know."

Tyler shifted, and I saw recognition flicker in Abby's eyes. She was a human lie detector. She knew they weren't being honest.

"Yeah, but what we do is good money, Abby. And we like Colorado."

"You boys are doing well. Keep doing what you're doing if it's what you love," Jim said. He and Abby traded glances.

Holy shit. Jim knew, too.

"Does anyone know the Latino gentleman who's been parked out front in a rented Lexus for the last half hour?" Jim asked.

Abby ran to the window to see, and the boys' expressions immediately turned severe. Chairs grated against the faded, chipped tile floor of the dining room as they stood to walk across the small house, between the sofa and television, to look out the windows. They discussed the driver for a moment, none of them recognizing who it was, but they all seemed sure their dad was correct that he was staking the house.

I wondered if it was Trex, and Tyler was feigning ignorance, but he wasn't that good of a liar, and Abby didn't seem to pick up on it.

I walked up behind Tyler, peeking over his shoulder, immediately cringing. "Holy fuck."

"What?" Tyler said, turning to face me. "You know who that is?"

The Maddox family turned their attention on me, and I recoiled, sick with embarrassment. "It's Marco."

"Who's Marco?" Abby asked.

I looked up at Tyler from under my lashes, humiliated to even say the words. "My sister's lady sitter. She must have sent him to keep an eye on me."

Tyler pointed at the window. "I've seen him before."

"Yeah, he took Finley and me home from the bar once."

"No, I've seen him outside the magazine ... outside my apartment. He's been watching you for a long time."

My expression morphed from confusion to disbelief to rage in a matter of moments, and I pushed past Tyler and out the door, stomping toward the Lexus. I could see the panic in Marco's eyes as I crossed the street and yanked open his door.

"What in the ever-loving *fuck* are you doing here?"

Marco tossed the tabloid magazine in his hand. "Ellie! What a surprise!"

I shook my head, pulling my phone from the back pocket of my jeans. I held it to my ear, getting angrier with each ring.

"I can't believe you're not coming to Thanksgiving," Finley answered. "I can't believe you're washing your hands of this family! They're just trying to help you!"

"Send Marco home. Now, or I'm calling the police."

"What are you talking about?"

"I'm standing right next to him … in Eakins, Illinois! What is wrong with you?" I yelled.

I heard quick footsteps coming closer, and turned to see Abby jogging across the street, before she draped Tyler's coat over my shoulders. She crossed her arms across her middle, glaring at Marco. Her breath puffed out in a white cloud like a bull ready to charge. For the first time since I'd left the Alpine barracks, I felt like there was an army behind me.

"Ellison," Finley began, "you won't call us. Half the time we're asking each other if anyone has heard from you or if you're even alive. If you won't answer or return my calls, you force my hand! I won't apologize for loving you!"

I sighed, holding my hand to my face. "You're right. I haven't called. You still don't get to send your goon to stalk me. Do you have any idea how humiliating this is? Tyler's entire family is witnessing this!"

Abby touched my shoulder. "This isn't the worst thing they've seen. Don't be embarrassed."

Finley sniffed.

"Damn it, Fin, don't cry."

"I miss you. You're my best friend. I feel like I don't even know you anymore."

"She's crying?" Marco said, horror in his eyes.

"Tell Marco to come home. I'll check in at least once a week, I promise. I just … I'm not one hundred percent yet. I've relapsed."

"Ellie … we can help you with that. We want to help. There are amazing places you can go. Just say the word…"

"I can do it on my own."

"Maybe you can … but why, if you don't have to?"

I mulled over her suggestion, wanting it as much for me as I did for the people who loved me. I glanced back at the Maddox house. "I'll think about it."

"Happy Thanksgiving, baby sister. We miss you. We wish you were here … even Mom."

I choked out a laugh. "Send home your slave."

Marco held up his hands. "She pays me very well, Miss Edson, and I love so much what I do."

I rolled my eyes. "Send him home. I'm sure he misses you."

"Okay," she said. "I love you."

I hung up the phone, shut Marco's door, and made sure his phone rang before tucking my own phone in my back pocket. Abby hooked her arm in mine as we walked across the street.

"Edson, huh? Like Edson Tech?"

"Yeah," I said, cringing and squinting in the afternoon sun.

"Relapse?"

I sighed. No point in denying it any longer. "I'm a drunk, Abby. My parents invoked the last resort of tough love. I was pretty out of control."

"My mom's a drunk, too. I remember when she tried so hard not to be."

"She couldn't kick it?"

"Not alone, and she's too proud to ask for help."

I looked down at the ground, kicking at the uneven sidewalk with my boots. "I don't deserve Fin's help. I don't deserve anyone's help."

"Did Tyler tell you about Travis and me?"

"Not a lot."

She tucked her hair behind her ear, glancing back at the house. "I was sure he was wrong for me. My family was worse than dysfunctional. My father nearly got me killed. I pushed Travis away, thinking he was bad for me, and then I pushed him away again, thinking I was bad for him. Turns out, when I finally let him in, all the bullshit fell away, and we could just be good together."

"I've known all along I was bad for Tyler. He won't listen."

"When a Maddox boy falls in love, he loves forever..." Abby mused.

"What?"

"If he's in love with you—and just the fact that you're here tells me he is—he's not going to give up on you. I can see that you care about him."

I nodded. "He's a good friend."

She narrowed her eyes. Her radar was going off. "Right."

"I do," I blurted out. "I care about him. I might even ... I feel guilty that I can't seem to let him in or let him go. Either way feels wrong."

"I know exactly how you feel," Abby said without hesitation. "But your sister is right. You don't love yourself right now. That's why you can't get things right with Tyler. That's why you don't want to."

I breathed out a frustrated laugh. "I need a drink."

"I'll make you one. But if I were you, I'd take all the help I could get if it meant happiness was on the other side. And believe me ... these boys ... when they're happy? It's like living in a fairy tale. They don't know how to half-ass anything, and loving someone is no exception."

The brothers stepped out onto the porch with Camille just as Marco pulled away from the curb. Tyler descended the steps and crossed the yard, hooking his arm around my shoulder. "You okay?"

I nodded.

"Finley?" he asked.

"We're good. I haven't called. They were worried about me."

He kissed my temple. "C'mon. You're freezing."

Tyler guided me inside with Abby trailing behind. Travis instantly hugged her and rubbed his hands along her upper arms. Then he cupped her hands and blew on them. They stared into each other's eyes like they were privy to a secret. Suddenly, gross didn't seem so bad.

CHAPTER TWENTY-TWO

TYLER HELPED ME WITH MY COAT, and then we settled in to watch documentaries on Netflix—Jim's favorite pastime, apparently.

Tyler and I sat on the sofa next to Travis and Abby. Trent and Camille made a pallet on the floor and whispered while he drew on the palm of her hand with a Sharpie. Jim was sitting in his recliner, his eyes getting heavier by the minute.

I leaned in to Tyler's ear. "Where's Taylor?"

"On his way. He had to take care of some things, first."

I nodded. "And the oldest? Is it Thomas?"

"Yeah, he was invited to his boss's house this year. Couldn't say no."

I nodded again. Tyler relaxed back against the worn sofa cushion, resting his hand on my knee. No one bugged us about our ambiguous friendship like I worried they would. We all just sat around, spending time together in what seemed to be an uncharacteristically peaceful Maddox moment.

Just as the credits of our second documentary of the night began to roll, the front door swung open, and Taylor dropped his duffel bag.

"Wake up, dick heads! I'm home!"

Trent and Travis jumped up and immediately tackled their brother, all three of them falling outside onto the porch with a thud. After a few seconds of scuffle, Tyler sighed.

"I'll be right back."

He rushed over to aid his twin, and I winced a few times when I saw the grappling escalate.

With some effort, Jim pushed himself up from the chair, making his way to the door. "All right, all right! That's enough!" He used his foot to poke at the writhing pile of Maddox boys, and then Travis finally broke out of the dog pile and began separating the others.

Abby shook her head, unfazed. Camille watched from the floor, not the least bit worried.

The boys walked in, breathing hard and chuckling, red blotches on their faces and arms. Trent used the back of his hand to dab his bleeding bottom lip, and Travis pointed at him and laughed.

"Don't grab my nuts next time, dick licker," Tyler said.

Camille went to the refrigerator and returned, giggling as she held a small ice pack covered in a dishtowel to Trent's lip.

"God almighty," Jim said, returning to his chair.

Travis didn't seem to have a scratch on him, but Tyler limped to the sofa.

"Whoa," I whispered.

Abby patted my knee. "Might as well get used to it. It's a regularly occurring thing."

"You okay?" I asked.

Tyler tugged at the crotch of my jeans. "That fuck knuckle tried to rip off my balls."

Trent cocked his head. "Nice. I like that one."

"It's Australian," Tyler said.

"Cool," Trent said, nodding.

"It means Trenton," Tyler added.

Trenton frowned while everyone else laughed—even Camille and Jim. He reached for Taylor's duffel and tossed it to him. Taylor jogged over to his dad, leaned down to kiss the top of his head, and then made his way up the stairs.

"You boys are going to give me a heart attack," Jim said.

"No, you eating a pound of bacon every morning is going to give you a heart attack," Trent said.

"He's a Maddox," Travis said. "He's invincible."

Someone knocked on the door, and then it opened, revealing one younger couple and one older. The older gentleman looked very similar to Jim.

All but Tyler and Jim stood again, including Abby. She threw her arms around a stunning, long-legged blonde, and they chatted non-stop for a solid two minutes.

Tyler pointed. "That's America. She's Abby's best friend and Shepley's girlfriend. Shepley is our cousin. His dad, Jack, is my dad's brother, and his mom, Deana, is our mom's sister."

I turned to look at him. "I don't follow."

He grinned, expecting my reaction. "Shepley is our double cousin. Both sets of parents are siblings. Dad and Jack. Mom and Deana."

"So, Jack and Jim ... Deana and...?"

"Diane," Tyler said with reverence.

I glanced at Deana, wondering how much she looked like Diane, and if that was hard for Jim and the boys. He seemed to be happy they were there.

"What is with the names?" I asked.

"I dunno," Tyler said. "I guess it's a Midwestern thing? My parents were named with the same first initial, so Mom did it with us, too."

Taylor tromped back down the stairs and fell in between Tyler and me. Tyler elbowed his twin—hard—and Taylor yelped. "Fucking Christ!" Taylor yelled.

"Goddamn it! Language!" Jim said.

Jack helped Deana with her coat, and she kissed him on the cheek before he left her to hang it in the closet. Trenton fetched chairs from the dining room with Shepley's help.

The second Shepley sat down his cousins began harping on him.

"No ring on Mare's finger yet, Shep? Don't you love her anymore?" Taylor asked.

"Shut up, dick. Where's your date?" Shepley snapped back.

"Right here," Taylor said, hooking his arm around me. He kissed my cheek, prompting Tyler to yank him to the floor.

Jim shook his head.

"America can only plan one wedding at a time," Deana teased, winking at Abby.

Taylor rubbed his elbow. "Have you met Ellie? Her dad is Philip Edson. Edson Tech."

"Whoa," America said. "So you're like ... a billionaire?" She grabbed Shepley's arm. "She's an heiress! I think I've seen you in *People* magazine!"

"That would be my sister, Finley. My dad is the billionaire. I'm quite broke, I assure you," I said.

"Oh," America said, looking sheepish.

"Ellie is the photographer for *The MountainEar*," Tyler said.

Taylor piped in. "She takes action shots. Her stuff has been featured in five issues of the magazine over the summer."

"Impressive," Deana said with a sweet smile. "Sounds like you're making it on your own just fine. I'll have to look up that magazine for your work."

Suddenly, Taylor and Tyler were nervous.

"It's not online. I'll see if I can send you some copies," I said.

Deana nodded, appeased for the moment. Of course I couldn't send her anything, not with Taylor and Tyler's dirty faces plastered all over the feature, digging and setting back burns with drip torches.

The twins seemed to relax, listening to the family catch up. Shepley's parents would celebrate with Deana's family this year, and they were going to miss Abby's pies. In the middle of their visit, Thomas called, and the phone was passed around while insults were made as greetings and instead of terms of endearment.

Jim and Jack yawned at the same time, and Deana stood. "Okay, we've got an early morning and a long drive. Let's head home, my love."

Jack stood. "How do I argue with that?" He kissed his wife, and Shepley and America stood as well. They hugged me and everyone else, waving as, one by one, they stepped out onto the porch and made their way to Jack's car.

Travis and Abby stood at the window with their arms around each other, watching them leave.

Jim stood. "All right. I'll see you kids in the morning."

The boys stood and hugged their father. Trenton was in the kitchen and back with a glass of ice water before Jim had even made it to the hall.

"Thank you, son," he said, taking a sip on his way to his bedroom.

"Kiss ass," Taylor hissed.

"I just know what he likes since ... you know ... I'm here to take care of him."

They all groaned. "Too real, Trent," Tyler said. "Let's leave that shit for another holiday."

Trenton lifted his middle finger, gathering his and Camille's things. "See you tomorrow, ass hats."

"Goodnight, Trent," Abby said.

Tyler stood and held out his hand. "I think I'll head upstairs. You coming?"

I nodded, standing and stretching. I glanced at the fridge, and Abby nodded just enough for me to notice.

"I could use a beer," she said. "Want one?"

"Yeah, I'll take one before I head up," I said.

Abby strolled across the room and opened the refrigerator door, pulling out two bottles and popping the tops with her hand and the counter. I took one from her as I passed, and she winked. Tyler winked back.

Neither one of them was trying to enable me as much as they were trying to get me through the visit without outing my addiction. Something only the children of an alcoholic could understand.

Tyler led me up the stairs by the hand, and then down the hall to his bedroom.

"Where will Taylor sleep?" I asked.

"The couch," he answered.

I tipped the bottle in my hand. "Abby doesn't miss anything, does she?"

"Nope. She's definitely the matriarch of the family, and once you're in, she has your back."

"She's keeping your secret, too," I said.

Tyler reached back with one arm and pulled his T-shirt over his head. My eyes scanned the rise and fall of each muscle in his torso. He was already gaining back the weight he'd lost hiking countless miles in the mountains over the summer, looking like his old self and filling out nicely.

"What do you mean?" he asked, tossing me his shirt.

"She knows you're not in insurance. You basically outed yourself when you told her about my feature."

"Nah," he said, unbuttoning his jeans.

I set down my beer and undressed, slipping his shirt quickly over my head. By the time Tyler had stripped down to his boxer briefs, he looked at me with a half-smile.

"I was hoping you'd do that."

"Well, I knew you didn't give it to me to wash."

He laughed once, but his smile quickly faded. "What did you and Abby talk about outside?"

I shrugged, fidgeting with the bottom hem of Tyler's shirt. "She knows." I picked up the beer and took a big swing. "That's why she made sure I had this. She told me to take Finley up on her offer."

"Which is what?" he asked.

"Help. As in…" I trailed off, feeling my cheeks flush crimson. "I'm a functioning alcoholic, and my family wants to send me to a rehabilitation center."

"What do you think about that?" he asked, zero judgment in his eyes.

"I think I want to be happy. I think there are a lot of things I want, but I'm afraid to say it out loud in case I screw it up."

His eyebrows pulled together, hope and desperation weighing down his expression. "Say it, anyway."

I swallowed, nervous. "I want to be gross with you."

He laughed once, taking a step and gently pulling me against his chest. He didn't speak for the longest time, but held me in his arms, touching his cheek to my hair. "Can't you just say it? Just once?"

I looked up at him, thinking about the way the words would feel on my lips, and what it would do to me if I said them. I wasn't brave enough for two huge confessions in one day. I lifted up on the balls of my feet, touching my lips to his.

Tyler stood still, letting me kiss him but nothing more. I reached for his hands and guided them up under my shirt until his warm palms were cupping my breasts. His thumb grazed my nipple, and I closed my eyes, letting out a soft sigh.

"I know what you're doing," he whispered.

"So?" I said, kissing his neck.

He leaned down, running his tongue from the tender skin behind my ear to the collar of my shirt, then planting tiny kisses all the way up. His hands slid to my back, and he pulled me closer, lifting the shirt so our stomachs touched.

His fingertips ran along my spine, then down to my ass, pulling me closer to him with a gentle squeeze. "Say it, Ellie. I know you do."

I kneeled down in front of him, and he blew out a flustered breath, perching his hands on his hips. He was instantly hard, stretching from the confines of his boxer briefs. I gripped the elastic waistband and tugged, wet my palm with my tongue, and then reached for him. He groaned as I began from the bottom and licked my way to the base of his shaft.

He involuntarily arched his back and leaned his pelvis forward. My tongue slid, smooth but firm, all the way to his tip, and then I took him into my mouth, humming when I felt his tip graze the back of my throat.

I cupped the base with my right hand, and as I leaned back, I followed with my fingers.

"*Fuck*," Tyler said, dragging out the word.

I smiled, leaning down again, taking all of him into my mouth, gagging a bit when his hand cupped the back of my head to press himself deeper. I lightly scraped his skin with my teeth as I came up, relishing the low, guttural sounds he was involuntarily making.

Before I could really get started, he pulled away, sitting on the bed. He shook his head. "You sure know how to change the subject. But I'm not letting you do it this time."

I took the few steps to stand in front of him, tucking my thumb under the waistband of my underwear, pushing them down and grinning when they gently landed on the floor.

Tyler didn't move, so I reached for his hand, sliding his fingers between my skin. As I moved his fingers in circles, I leaned my head back and moaned. His fingertips slid more easily the wetter I became, and I could tell his resolve was weakening.

I inserted two of his fingers and two of mine, moaning loudly. He grabbed my ass, and in one motion, turned us and fell on top of me in his childhood bed.

"Say it," he said, his tip grazing my tender skin.

I looked away from his intense gaze and closed my eyes, my body begging for him to be inside me. "Fuck me," I said, returning my eyes to his. I reached around, pressing his backside toward me, but he resisted.

"Do you care about me at all?" he asked. "Do you hate me? Is it lukewarm feelings, or we're really just friends? Whatever it is, Ellie, fucking say it."

"Why can't we just do this?" I said, lifting my hips.

He reacted, pulling away. He grazed my jaw line with his lips. "I'll make you come all night," he whispered into my ear. "I just need a little honesty."

"I love you," I breathed. Before I could finish my sentence, he was sliding inside me and moaning at the same time. I bit his shoulder, trying to muffle my cry as he rocked into me.

His rhythm slowed as he leaned down to kiss me. "Say it again."

"I love you," I said without hesitation.

Tyler lifted my knee until it was propped against his chest, sinking deeper inside me. He licked two fingertips and then reached down between my legs, circling my tender skin while his thrusts accelerated. Something began to build inside me, familiar but somehow different. As my insides relentlessly spasmed, Tyler cupped his hand over my mouth to muffle my cries, at the same time overcome and growling into the crook of my neck.

He shuddered, his breath as labored as mine. My neck was arched back as my chest heaved, trying to pull in as much air as I could. Tyler shifted his weight, setting my sensitive insides on fire, causing me to whimper.

He kissed the corner of my mouth, collapsing next to me.

"You promised me all night," I breathed.

"You can have it. You can have every night."

He buried his face in my hair, and I stared at the wooden underbelly of the top bunk, hoping Abby was right. I didn't want to be too crazy to love.

CHAPTER TWENTY-THREE

"I FEEL LIKE WE LIVE HERE," I said. I hung my legs over Tyler's lap and wiggled against the uncomfortable armrest digging into my back.

We sat in the terminal with full suitcases in addition to our backpacks, Christmas gifts from Travis and Abby. It was a brilliant gift idea, because neither Tyler nor I had thought about needing extra space for the gifts we would inevitably receive from his brothers.

"Did you call Fin?" Tyler asked. He said the words like second nature, reminding me at least once a week since Thanksgiving to check in with my sister.

"Before we left the house."

"They still mad that you didn't come east for Christmas?"

"I did go east for Christmas."

"Ellie. When are you going to see them?"

"Don't start," I said.

"You can't avoid them forever."

"I'm just not ready. I will when I'm ready."

"That's the tenth time I've heard that in three weeks," he grumbled.

"Really? I've already told you. I like my apartment, and Wick isn't going to let you move in."

He nodded, plugging an earbud into the ear farthest from me. I smiled, knowing he wanted to keep the other free in case I had anything more to say. He tapped on his phone display with his thumb, chose a song, and then leaned back, holding my legs on his lap with his free hand.

The attendant at the desk called for anyone needing extra time to board, and then for first-class. That was strangely amusing to me, remembering the days when I would already be standing in line with my family, waiting to occupy one of the first seats—and that was before our private jet.

When she called our group, Tyler stood, grabbing my backpack and his, and his rolling luggage. I pulled up the handle on my suitcase and pulled it behind me, giggling at how weighed down Tyler looked.

"You got it?" I asked.

"Yeah."

"You sure?"

"Yeah, baby, I got it."

I stopped mid-step, watching him take a few steps before he realized what he'd said and turned back. "What?"

"You just ... haven't said that since at the diner with Sterling."

"When I kissed your cheek?" He chuckled, lost in the memory.

"Yeah, when I told the waitress you had the clap?"

He frowned. "She still thinks that."

"Good," I said, shouldering past him.

We checked our luggage at the gate and then followed the line down the jetway and onto the plane. We were herded like cattle to 20C and 20D, and Tyler struggled to find empty spaces for our backpacks. He resorted to stuffing mine into the overhead bin across and one row back, and then putting his under the seat in front of him. He collapsed into his seat and sighed.

"What's wrong?" I asked.

"I'm tired. You kept me up all night."

I pressed my nose gently against his cheek, giggling. "You weren't exactly objecting."

He raised an eyebrow. "Why would I do something stupid like that?"

"It's not about flying. You've been on edge all morning."

He thought about what he wanted to say and then sighed. "Just something on my mind."

"About me?" I asked, sitting up.

"Sort of. Well, yeah, but something I want to talk about later."

"Well now you have to tell me," I said.

Passengers were still filing in, struggling to find space for their carry-on luggage. A man a few rows back was swearing under his breath and then barking at the flight attendant.

Tyler looked back, assessing the situation. "It just sucks spending a long weekend with you, and then going home alone to my apartment."

"You have a roommate."

He frowned. "He's never home. He's always at Falyn's. Besides, he's not the roommate I want to come home to."

I blinked, instantly realizing where the conversation was going. "Is she still coming to the party?"

"She's supposed to," he muttered, used to my deflection.

"What?" I said, nudging him. "You don't like her?"

"They fight a lot."

"Hmm, I know a couple like that."

"We don't fight. Not anymore," he said. "Not for another few days, anyway."

"What does that mean?"

"I want you to move in," Tyler blurted out.

"Where is this coming from? We're one month in. Baby steps, Maddox."

He glanced around, trying to keep his voice down. "Maybe I just need a little more commitment."

I was no longer amused. "What the fuck, Tyler? You're becoming an overly attached girlfriend. Get a grip."

"What? It's not like we just met. Every time I go home, all I see is you. The headboard you made, the decorations ... that's all you."

"So?"

He spread his knees apart, slumping in his seat. He looked like a pouting child.

"You are being so weird right now I don't really know how to respond."

His jaw muscles danced beneath his skin. "I'm not looking forward to this party."

"Okay...?"

"I'm worried that things will get awkward. And we're in a fragile place anyway."

"A *fragile* place? Who are you? And why would things get awkward?"

The flight attendant began her announcements, going over the safety information and asking passengers to put their electronic devices into airplane mode. Tyler's mind was spinning, but not about anything to do with the flight.

"The girl I kissed in Colorado Springs?"

"Yeah?" I asked, bracing myself for what he might say.

"It was Falyn," he said finally. "I kissed Falyn." He turned to me, desperate. "It's like what happened with you and Taylor. She thought I was him, I thought she was flirting with me…"

"You kissed Falyn so you're asking me to move in with you?"

"Yes."

I shook my head. "You kissed Taylor's girlfriend?"

"She wasn't his girlfriend then."

"I'm so confused. What does that have to do with me moving in?"

"I don't know, Ellie, I'm freaking the fuck out. I've never—" He grabbed my hand and kissed it. "I'm in love with you. You haven't said it since Thanksgiving. You balk every time I mention moving in. Okay, yeah, I might be a little desperate, but I don't know what I'd do if you told me to kick rocks."

"I see."

Tyler waited for me to say more.

"You're asking me to move in with you because when I found out about Falyn at the party it would have been easier to keep me from dumping you?" I snapped. "Are you fucking kidding me right now?"

He winced.

"That's so … so … romantic," I growled.

His shoulders sagged. "Do you hate me?"

"Yes, but not because you kissed Falyn."

He looked down, a little lost. "The last month has been amazing, Ellie. Exactly what I thought it would be. I've been sweating New Year's Eve since I found out she was going to be there."

"Then maybe you should have told me the whole truth the first time. If you remember, I didn't care then, either."

"Yes, you did."

"Okay, I did, but it wasn't a deal breaker."

"You're right," he said, angry with himself. "You're right. It won't happen again."

"Kissing Falyn, lying, or asking me to move in with you?"

He turned to me, his eyebrows pulling in to form a deep line between them.

"Wow," I said. "I think this is the first time you've actually been mad at me."

"It's not a good feeling," he said, still frowning.

The plane taxied out to the runway, and within five minutes, the engines pushed us forward, racing down the asphalt and then into the air.

Tyler slid his hand over mine, resting back against the headrest. "I didn't realize how scary this would be," he whispered.

"I told you," I said.

His eyes popped open, and he turned to face me. Even with circles under his eyes and yesterday's scruff on his face, he was ridiculously beautiful.

"And I said it'd be worth it." He squeezed my hand. "And it is."

I grinned. "Just because I don't say it doesn't mean I don't."

"That you love me? Why is that so hard for you?"

I shrugged. "Your family says it a lot. Mine doesn't. It just doesn't feel natural to say. But I do. Love you." I had to force out the words, but not the feeling behind them.

He kissed my forehead, and then I leaned over, snuggling against his arm and hugging him to me. He rested his cheek on my head, his breathing evened out, and he slept until the flight attendant began her final announcement.

"Ladies and gentlemen, as we start our descent, please make sure your seat backs and tray tables are in their full upright position. Make sure your seat belt is securely fastened and all carry-on luggage is stowed underneath the seat in front of you or in the overhead bins. Thank you."

Tyler stirred, rubbing his eyes. "Wow. How long was I out?"

"Well, we're landing, so a little over two hours."

"Holy fuck. I must have been more tired than I thought."

I stretched my neck and leaned in to kiss his cheek, then settled back as we began our descent. The Denver airport was busy and chaotic as usual, but we navigated our new roller luggage through the terminal, to the tram, and finally to level five toward the exit.

Tyler slowed just as we passed through baggage claim, recognizing the couple waving to us before I did.

"Isn't that...?"

"Oh, fuck," I said as my stomach sank.

Finley pulled her newest sunglasses from her face and walked quickly to me in six-inch Louboutin heels, her arms outstretched.

She threw her arms around me, and I looked to Tyler in a panic.

"Finley," he said, opening his arms to her. "Good to see you."

"You too, but I'm hugging my sister for the first time in almost a year," she said, continuing to squeeze the life out of me. "You can wait."

"Fin," I said, trying to keep the contempt from my voice. "What a surprise."

"I know," she said, finally releasing me. She wiped her cheek. "I didn't warn you. But I knew you'd say not to come. It's been ten months, Ellie. I couldn't give you one more day of space. You're my sister."

"I've been calling you like you asked."

"I know," she said, glancing at Marco. "But it's not enough. You're my best friend." Her eyes danced between Tyler and me. "What? What aren't you telling me?"

Tyler looked at me, and my mind raced for a believable lie.

"We're uh ... we're moving in together," I said.

Finley and Tyler shot me identical expressions.

"We were going to try to move my things before the New Year. It's just a really bad time for our first visit."

"Oh," Finley said. She looked a bit lost, and then a grin spread across her face. "Well, congratulations, you two!" She hugged both of us, and Tyler choked when Finley squeezed his neck into her shoulder. "That is so exciting. Our parents can't wait to meet you," she said, pointing at him with her glasses. "They'd love to see your new place. *I* would love to see your new place!" She clasped her hands together. "In Estes?"

Tyler looked at me with his mouth hanging open, unsure how to respond.

"Yes, it's in Estes Park," I said. "He has an apartment across town from mine."

"Can we go now?" Finley asked.

"Fin..."

"I just came to Colorado to see you. I literally have nothing else going on."

"...great. That's great," I said with wide eyes and a forced smile. I looked to Tyler. "Um ... uh ... *honey*, I guess they can follow us to my apartment? You can just drop me off. I know you have a lot of things to do."

He mouthed *honey* with a disgusted look on his face behind Finley. I shot him an expectant smile that surely made me look like a lunatic.

"Sure ... honey," he said. "Are you familiar with this area?" he asked Marco.

"I have navigation," he said with a proud smile.

"We'll meet you off Peña Boulevard at the Avis rental place, then you can follow us from there."

"Are you guys hungry?" Finley asked. "You must be."

"No," I said, shaking my head quickly. "Not really."

"Oh. Okay, then ... we'll meet you at Avis in ten minutes."

"Perfect," I said, smiling at them until they walked out the door.

Tyler and I didn't speak until we made it to the truck and he slid into the driver seat and shut the door.

"This is awful!" I cried.

"This is fucking great!" he said with a wide smile.

I glared at him. "They're coming to my apartment. I'm stuck with Fin for an entire evening. She'll find out about Sterling by dinnertime. I'm *fucked*."

Tyler wrinkled his nose. "I don't understand your strategy, Ellie. You haven't seen your sister in almost a year to avoid her finding out something that may or may not make her never want to see you again."

"Exactly."

"If you never see her again, what does it matter?"

"At least she won't hate me."

Tyler drove us to Avis, and I waved at Finley from behind the passenger side window of the truck. They followed us north on the toll road toward Estes Park.

I sighed for the fourth time in ten minutes.

"Ellie..." Tyler began.

"I have less than an hour and a half to figure this out. What are you doing?" I screeched.

"What?" he cried.

"You're speeding! I need time to think of a way to keep her out of my apartment!"

Tyler eased back on the accelerator, looking annoyed. "What if you tell her it's being fumigated?"

"Then she'll go to your apartment."

"So?"

"She'll expect me to come, too."

"Okay, then you get car sick on the way to Estes."

"I like it, but it's a temporary fix to a permanent problem."

Tyler sighed. "Maybe ... maybe you should just tell her."

"Are you out of your mind? Do you want Finley to hate me?"

"If it were me—" He hesitated. "I would be more upset that you kept it from me. She'll get over it if you're honest with her."

"No," I said, shaking my head. "You don't know Fin like I do. She holds grudges, and Sterling ..."

"Is a whiney little cunt nugget."

I closed my eyes. "Don't say that to her."

When we pulled into the parking lot of the *MountainEar*, my heart began to pound in my chest, and my palms were slick with sweat.

"You're sure you don't want me to come in?"

"Just long enough to follow me into the bathroom and..."

Marco knocked on Tyler's window. He looked at me and then pressed the button, waiting until it rolled all the way down.

"Hey, Ellie's not feeling great. I think she's a little car sick."

"My sister doesn't get car sick," Finley said from behind Marco. "Why are we at her work? I thought we were going to her apartment?"

"This is her apartment," Tyler said. "Above the office."

Finley smiled. "Fantastic. Let's go."

Marco pulled an extra-large roller suitcase with several duffels and bags stacked on top down the sidewalk.

I scrambled from the truck. "What are you doing?"

"Oh," Finley said. "Do you need assistance with your luggage?"

"No. It's a one-bedroom apartment. Why aren't you staying at the house?"

Finley seemed annoyed. "Because our parents are there, and they don't know I'm here. If they knew, they would be at your door because they are desperate to see you, too."

Finley turned on her heels, waiting for me at the door with Marco.

I chewed on my thumbnail, gazing up at Tyler who was still in the driver seat. "It's times like these I regret not being religious."

"Should I come?" he asked. "At least let me help with your bags."

I shook my head, defeated. "I don't want you to see this."

With worry in his eyes, Tyler waved to me, waiting until I reached the door before he backed away.

I led Finley and Marco upstairs, directing Marco to the sofa and Finley to my bedroom.

"This is gorgeous! I was worried what you would be able to afford on your wages, but this is exquisite! Well done, baby sister!"

"Well," I said, watching her unpack as if she had lit herself on fire, "my boss gave me a great deal."

"What is Tyler's apartment like? Is it this nice?"

"No," I said, shaking my head. "But it's decent."

"Then why not just move him here? And why haven't you started packing yet?"

"We just decided over Christmas."

"Thank God I'm here," Finley said. "Marco can help you pack."

"I'm really … I'm okay. Tyler will be over later. We were kind of going to do it together."

"Don't be silly…." Finley began, but she finally looked at me long enough to see what I knew she would. "What aren't you telling me? Oh my hell, Ellie! Are you pregnant?" she screeched.

"What? No! I can barely take care of myself." I left her for the kitchen, yanking open the fridge and popping the top of my favorite cheap beer.

"Ew, what the fuck is that?" Finley asked.

"Beer," I said, holding up the can. "Want some?" I asked, some of it still in my mouth.

"No. You've developed some atrocious habits Mother will definitely not be impressed with."

"Well, I don't plan on seeing her, so I'm good."

"Ellie," Finley began.

"I told them. They're dead to me."

"That's harsh. They were only trying to help you."

I finished the can and opened another.

Finley's nose flared. "I can see it worked."

I gripped the top of the open refrigerator door with one hand and held on to my can for dear life with the other. "Fin. I love you, but you can't stay here. Find a hotel, go to the house, but I need you to go."

Finley stared at me, stunned at first, and then heartbroken. "How did this happen? How did we grow so far apart? I feel like I'm standing in front of a stranger."

"We can talk tomorrow, but I need to do this in small doses. At least at first. I have to start packing. I have a lot to do, and it's not fair for you to just drop into my life right now."

She nodded, gesturing to Marco. He packed up his things, and then rushed into my room to do the same for the few items she had unpacked on her own.

The wheels banged down each step as Marco pulled the rolling luggage down the stairs to the car. I hugged my sister, and she held on an extra second before turning for the door.

Once she grabbed the knob, she glanced back at me over her shoulder. "There's something else. You're trying to protect me from something. Don't think I don't see it."

I closed my eyes. "Please leave, Fin."

She bit her lip, and then disappeared behind the door.

CHAPTER TWENTY-FOUR

THE PARTY WAS ALREADY IN FULL SWING when I stepped inside Taylor and Tyler's apartment. I recognized a few faces— Jubal and who I assumed was his wife. Watts, Smitty, Taco, and Sugar from the fire station were there, too.

Tyler jogged up to me, offering a hug and a long kiss. "Wow. You look amazing. Stunning."

"Thank you," I said, looking down at the strappy, sequined romper and high heels Finley had let me borrow. "I'm sorry I'm late. I was messing with all of this," I said, gesturing to my hair and makeup, "and then Finley called. She wants to talk to me tonight."

"Uh oh," Tyler said.

"She sounded happy, actually."

"Oh. That's good, right?"

"I think so," I said, grabbing his arm when one heel wobbled.

The apartment was dimly lit, undecorated except for a single light in a corner casting a rainbow of tiny circles on the walls and ceiling. The speakers were booming what I recognized as music from Tyler's playlist, and I wondered if the neighbors would call the police or let the thumping of the bass slide because it was New Year's Eve.

"Not a bad way to bring in your birthday every year," I yelled into Tyler's ear.

"It's like the whole world is partying with us!" he said, pulling me through the crowd by the hand to where Taylor stood with Falyn.

She was gorgeous; the sparkles in her ivory dress were reflecting the light from the corner, her full, blonde hair and freckles giving her the perfect balance of sex kitten and girl next door. I tried not to stare at her lips and recall that Tyler had tasted them once, even though there had been a time not so long ago that I wouldn't have minded tasting them myself.

Just as Tyler moved to introduce us, the crowd parted and Paige appeared, looking nervous but hopeful. Her hair was silver now, in a freshly trimmed pompadour. She had more tattoos and piercings than I remembered, the sweet innocence long gone from her eyes. She handed me a beer in a red Solo cup, tapping hers to mine.

"It's been a long time," she said.

"How've you been?" I asked.

"Shitty. How have you been?"

"Still a drunk," I said, taking a big gulp. "But the Internet says I'm a functioning drunk, so I've got that going for me."

She shook her head and smiled. "Always so funny."

Tyler kissed my cheek. "I don't mean to be rude, baby, but Taylor's…"

"Baby?" Paige said, tucking her chin. "What are you? A couple now?"

I cocked my head, surprised at the sass coming from such a tiny package. "Actually, we are," I said.

Paige choked out a laugh, and then continued to giggle, covering her mouth and then waving her hand in front of her face.

Tyler and I traded glances, and then he leaned in to whisper in my ear. "I didn't invite her. I guess she lives in this building now."

"Oh," I said, nodding with wide eyes. "Great." I downed my drink, and then Paige took it, reaching behind her and then producing another.

"Baby," Tyler warned. "There's a fine line between functioning and just drunk."

"It's New Year's Eve," Paige said. "What is your problem?"

The door opened, and Finley walked in, staring wide-eyed, fascinated with all the bodies in the tiny space. I took another drink, tossing back half the glass before I saw Sterling step inside, too.

I choked, and Tyler patted my back while I swallowed the contents still in my mouth and then coughed.

"Jesus, Mary, and Joseph fucking Stalin," I said, shaking my head in disbelief.

Finley waved emphatically and then pulled Sterling through the crowd. He looked as sick about the impending disaster as I was.

"What do I do? What do I do?" I said, panicking.

"Keep me from killing Sterling?" Tyler said. "That should keep your mind off Finley."

I looked up at him, watching him glower at Finley's date. I gulped down the rest of the beer Paige had brought me and handed my cup to Tyler. No amount of alcohol was going to get me through the next few minutes.

"Ellie!" Finley said, throwing her arms around me.

"Fin … you've been drinking," I said, making great effort not to make eye contact with Sterling.

"A bit of celebratory champagne," she said, holding out her left hand. A large diamond sparkled on her ring finger.

I grabbed her fingers and pulled them closer, and then I narrowed my eyes at Sterling. He shook his head, begging me not to make a scene.

"We're getting married!" Finley squealed.

"I don't understand," I said. "You're not even dating? You haven't since college."

Finley's smile faded, and she pulled her hand from my grasp, returning to her reserved self. "Sterling and I have known each other for a long time, Ellison. Daddy and Mother are extremely pleased. I thought you would be, too."

"Maybe if this made any sense," I said, still glaring at Sterling.

"You haven't talked to me in a long time, Ellie. Sterling and I have become quite close and…"

"Hey!" Paige said, bringing me a fresh cup. I chugged it, handing it back to her.

"Baby," Tyler warned.

"Thank you, Paige," I said, wiping my mouth.

I touched my sister's arm. "Finley, there's something you need to know, first."

"Fin, we should go. This clearly isn't a good time for Ellison," Sterling said.

"What does that matter?" Tyler seethed. "Not like it made a difference before. Don't you have any pills for that?"

Sterling cleared his throat. "Let's go, sweetheart."

"This is Finley?" Paige said, pawing at Finley's expensive dress. "Oh, yeah! I remember you! From the bar! You were trying to fuck Tyler!"

Paige's sudden interest in the situation made me nervous.

"I most certainly was not," Finley said, smoothing her hair. "You must have me confused with someone else."

"No, no, it was you. You and your Latin lover gave us a ride home that ni—oh my God!" She grabbed Finley's hand and examined her ring. "What is this? Are you engaged?"

"Yes," Finley said, pulling back her hand.

"To this guy?" Paige pointed, unimpressed. "Isn't this the guy you were trying to get rid of at the bar?"

"No," Finley said, blinking. She wasn't used to being in such an uncomfortable situation.

"Paige," I said.

"No ... no," she slurred, patting my left breast, "I get it now. I thought it was just me." She pressed her palm against her chest. "But it's you guys." She swung her index finger around, pointing at Finley, Sterling, Tyler, and then me. "You're like ... fucked up, sexual deviants with no regard for anyone else's feelings. Just like you two." She gestured to Tyler and me. "What the fuck are you even doing together? I was nice to you, Ellie. He just walked out on you, and we shared a bed ... I made you cookies," she lilted. Then she grimaced at Sterling. "Then you fucked him, and now your sister is engaged to him after she tried and failed to fuck Tyler. You're all very messed up and should seek counseling. Immediately."

"What is she babbling about?" Finley said, tucking her chin.

I closed my eyes. "Fin..."

"Did she just say you fucked Sterling?"

"Actually," Paige said. "He fucked her." She pressed her lips together and nodded, clearly a regretful tell-all.

My eyes burned, and I reached for my sister. "Finley..."

Finley pulled away from me, and then turned on Sterling. "You fucked my sister?"

Sterling held out his hands. "No. I mean, yes, but, darling ... it was a mistake. She was upset, and we took something we shouldn't have ... I'm not even sure what happened. I don't remember any of it, and neither does she."

Finley looked at me, appalled. "Is he telling the truth?"

I hesitated, and then nodded, my eyes filling with tears. "I was going to tell you."

"You..." Finley looked around. "You were going to tell me? Is that supposed to make it okay?"

"No," I said, shaking my head. "Not at all."

"That's why you haven't talked to me in so long? This is what you've been hiding from me?"

I couldn't speak, so I nodded.

Tyler pointed to Sterling. "You need to leave."

Sterling reached for Finley, tears streaming down his face. "Fin. Please. I know you're angry, and you have every right to be, but it was a long time ago."

"How long ago?" Finley asked.

"Not long after you left for Sanya," Sterling choked out.

Finley pulled out her phone and furiously tapped out a message.

"Who's that?" Sterling asked.

"Marco," Finley said. "I've asked him to pick me up."

"Sweetheart, no. We have to discuss this." He touched her arm, but she held up her fists.

"No!" she screamed, her hands shaking.

Everyone around us turned to listen.

She took off her ring and stuffed it in Sterling's tux pocket, patting his chest. "You son of a bitch. You were going to let me marry you without telling me."

Sterling's bottom lip trembled. "Finley, for God's sake..."

"And you," she said, pointing to me. A tear escaped down her cheek. "You just wait. I'm going to fuck Tyler, and then you can see how it feels."

"I wanted to tell you," I cried. "But I couldn't take it back, and I didn't want you to hate me."

"I don't get to hate you," she said. "You're my sister. But you," she said, glaring at Sterling. "You, I can hate." Finley's phone lit up, and she smiled and waved. "Happy New Year, bitches," she said, slamming the door behind her.

Sterling quickly followed, and Tyler hooked his arm around my shoulder, kissing my hair. "Baby, I'm so sorry."

I closed my eyes, feeling the streaks of mascara drying on my face. "It's your birthday, baby," I said. I took someone's cup and slammed back the contents. "Let's party."

When my eyes peeled open, all I could see were mounds of unfamiliar comforter. I blinked a few times to focus, seeing a frame on the nightstand of Taylor and Falyn.

I sat up, trying to swallow, but feeling like there were pine needles in my throat. I was lying in the middle of Taylor's bed, alone. I walked down the hall to the bathroom, stopping when I heard the shower, and then continued to the living room, not recognizing anyone else still passed out and draped over pieces of furniture.

"Tyler?" I called, looking around. I stumbled into the kitchen to get a glass of water. The instant the cool liquid touched my throat, I felt a second of relief before vomiting violently into the sink. Just when I thought it was over, my stomach heaved again, and then again, splashing a mixture of beer, wine, and possibly tequila all over the dishes and trash that had been left in the stainless steel basin.

I turned on the water, rinsing out my mess and throwing away the trash. I started the dishwasher and then plodded down the hall toward the bedroom.

"Tyler?" I said, pushing open the door.

Tyler lifted his head, rubbing his eyes. "Hey, Ellie." He blinked a few times, trying to focus on my expression. "What's wrong?"

"Morning," Finley said next to him.

Tyler nearly leapt out of the bed, but then scrambled for sheets to cover himself. Finley casually stood in her perfect form and stepped into her dress, zipping it up and grabbing her heels.

"What the fuck?" Tyler yelped, looking mortified and confused.

"I so deserved this," I said, my voice breaking.

Tyler shook his head, touching his palm to his forehead, trying to remember what had happened. "No. You … you were drunk and went into the wrong bedroom. We just left you there so you could sleep, Ellie. I did not fuck your sister. Where's Falyn?"

I shrugged. "Why would I know where Falyn is?"

"I swear to God, Ellie," he begged. He pointed to Finley. "Nothing happened! I have no idea why she was in the bed naked."

Finley winked at Tyler and then stopped next to me in the doorway. "How does it feel?"

I let out a faltering breath, feeling my eyes burn with tears. "Like death."

"Then we're even. Marco is waiting for us outside. He'll give you a ride home."

She shouldered past me, and I looked up at Tyler. He dropped the sheets, furiously looking for his clothes. "Don't leave. Ellie," he warned. "Don't you fucking leave with her. We need to figure this out."

"I deserved this," I said, my face crumbling. "But you didn't. I'm so sorry you were mixed up in this … in my fucked up universe. I really did think…" I blew out a slow breath, trying not to sob. "It doesn't matter."

Tyler found his boxer briefs and yanked them on. "Ellie, wait."

I turned on my heels, rushing down the hall and pushing out the door. As promised, Marco was waiting for me in a rented Lexus with my sister looking freshly fucked and content in the passenger seat. I slid into the back, and Marco pulled away just as Tyler burst through the door with just a towel wrapped around his waist.

"Don't stop," I said, hearing Tyler scream my name until we turned the corner a block away.

"You might as well turn off your phone until you can change your number," Finley said. "That's what I had to do with Sterling. Are you going to your apartment, or the chateau?"

"My apartment," I snapped, staring out the window.

My phone buzzed, and I scrambled to turn it off.

"Told you so," Finley said. She sniffed her hair and made a noise, disgusted. "*Agh*, I still smell like him."

"Shut the fuck up, Fin. Just shut up."

Marco drove me to the *MountainEar*. By the time I climbed the stairs, put on a T-shirt and sweatpants, and washed my face and brushed my teeth, Tyler's truck had slid into a parking spot, and he was banging on the back door.

I looked down at him from my window. He was wearing just a T-shirt and jeans, his boots on but untied. I could see his breath puffing out in white clouds, and he rubbed his hands together between knocks.

"Ellie!" he yelled. "I'm not fucking leaving. Open the door!"

I unlatched the window and pushed it up without effort, leaning on the windowsill as I peered down at Tyler. "I'm not mad."

He looked up at me. "Then let me come up."

"Go home, Tyler."

He held out his hands. "It's fucking freezing out here."

"Then get in your truck and go home."

"I didn't fuck your sister! I was in the shower this morning. You stumbled to Taylor's room, so I slept in there with you. I held you in my arms all fucking night. Taylor must have slept in my room and your psychotic sister must have crawled in bed with him, thinking it was me. You caught Finley with Taylor!"

I frowned, knowing I could tell them apart by now, but I had just woken up and was upset. Maybe...

"Just let me come up. Please? I'm gonna start losing fingers soon."

"You're going to let Taylor take the fall for you? This is beyond fooling your teachers in school, don't you think?"

"I swear to God. Just let me come up so I can explain. We'll call Taylor if you want."

"He would lie for you."

"Ellie, please? It's my birthday." His dimple appeared, but I stayed strong.

"Then go find your brother and celebrate it."

He shook his head, smiling. "I want to spend it with you. Even if that means I spend the day trying to figure out what the hell happened last night."

"It's two degrees, Tyler."

"Then let me in," he said, his smile fading. "I can't leave. It'll ruin my whole day."

"I think *you* ruined your day when you *slept* with my sister!"

"I didn't sleep with your sister! Goddammit!" he yelled, kicking the door.

"Stop! Wick will kick me out!"

Tyler perched his hands on his hips, breathing hard. He shook his head, and then looked up. "Open this door, Ellie, or I'll kick it in, I swear to God."

"You're a bastard," I said.

He held out his hands. "And your sister's a bitch."

I closed the window and stomped downstairs, twisting the bolt lock and opening the door. Tyler passed me, jogging up to the apartment. By the time I walked into the living room, he was shivering on my sofa, wrapped in the comforter off my bed.

I rolled my eyes and turned on the Keurig.

"I almost got hypothermia over this," he said.

"You should have dressed warmly," I snapped.

"I didn't have much time, considering my brother busts into the bathroom to tell me a half-ass version of the story, and I had to run after you in a towel down the block and then back. I grabbed the first clothes I saw, put them on, and ran out the door. The only woman I touched last night was you. You have to believe me."

"I'm making you a cup of coffee, and then you're leaving."

Tyler stood. "C'mon! You know this isn't right! Think about it!"

I let my hands fall to my thighs. "So what? My sister came back and deduced it was your room because of our pictures on the wall, undressed, and climbed into bed with a sleeping, naked Taylor?"

"Maybe! I have no idea, but that's more likely than me mistaking her for you."

I stood tall. "Finley wouldn't do that."

"Oh, but she'd revenge fuck your boyfriend?"

My face twisted into disgust.

The Keurig beeped, and I placed a mug under the spout and a K-cup in the holder, pressing the BREW button. I opened the fridge, grabbing a beer and Tyler's favorite hazelnut creamer.

I handed him the mug, cracking open my beer. "I didn't stir it," I snapped.

"Goddamn," he said, offended. "I thought you said you weren't mad."

I glowered at him while he sipped the coffee with a tiny grin on his face. "There is nothing funny about this!"

He laughed once in disbelief. "I would never do that to you. Thank God your sister can't tell us apart, but I'm a little concerned that you can't either."

I crossed my arms. "I'd just woken up and walked in on you and my sister. I might not have been seeing clearly."

"So you believe me."

"Stop talking."

"You gotta know that. I carried you to bed. You were wasted. I wouldn't have left you. The only thing I can't figure out is where Falyn was."

His phone rang, and he answered. "Did you find her?" He nodded, looking at me. "Putting you on speaker."

"Ellie?" Taylor said as Tyler held out the phone. "Falyn went to the store to get a few things for a birthday breakfast. She let

Finley in. She doesn't know everything, and I'd appreciate it if you didn't tell her. I didn't sleep with your sister, and this could get really complicated trying to explain."

I covered my eyes with my hand. "I won't say anything. I'm sorry, Taylor."

Tyler hung up the phone and slid it into his back pocket. "Come here," he said, holding out his hands.

I kept my face covered. "I'm so sorry."

"This isn't your fault," he said. He walked over to me and wrapped the blanket around us both.

I pressed my forehead against his chest, breathing in stale cigarette smoke and his cologne.

I left him to sit on the couch, lighting a cigarette. He sat next to me, letting his head fall back against the wall. "I'm not sure which one of you should hate the other more."

"You heard her. We're sisters. We can't hate each other."

"I can hate her," he grumbled. "I have to know how she crawled into bed with Taylor without him knowing. He must have thought she was Falyn coming back to bed."

I took a drag and then handed it to Tyler. He took a drag and handed it back.

"My fucked up family has officially poisoned yours."

Tyler took the beer out of my hand. "You were black-out drunk last night, and you're drinking again. I thought you were going to quit? Do I need to quit with you?"

"I've just lost my sister. Not the best time to stop drinking."

"There will never be a good time if you have to drink every time you're upset. Shit happens. You have to learn to deal with it without alcohol. I love you no matter what, but you need to wake up, Ellie."

My eyebrows pulled together as I stared at the wall. "I can't wake up. This isn't a dream."

CHAPTER TWENTY-FIVE

GLOWING WHITE LIGHTS hung from the ceiling, strung along the muslin looped loosely from the rafters. Fat candle votives were surrounded with elaborate green and white floral centerpieces on each table.

Abby and Travis were slow dancing in the center of the room, whispering and smiling, deliriously happy. I was lying on the floor, snapping pictures and looking for other angles. I'd already taken shots of the wedding party, the families, the couples, and the first dance. Next would be the cutting of the cake, but Travis and Abby didn't seem to be in any hurry.

I pushed to my feet, feeling someone tap on my shoulder. Tyler stood behind me, clean-shaven and gorgeous in a tux, his top button undone and his bow tie hanging off kilter.

"Wanna dance?" he asked.

"I should probably stay focused. I'd hate to miss anything."

He slid his hands into his pants pockets and nodded.

"Oh, go on!" Camille said, pulling up on my camera until the strap slipped over my head. "I'll take your picture."

"I prefer to be on the other side of the camera," I said.

"Please?" Tyler said, tugging me toward the dance floor.

I followed, but Camille clicking my camera like paparazzi was maddening. Tyler and I smiled for a few pictures, and then Camille decided to try her photography skills on Shepley's parents and Trenton.

Tyler stared at our hands while he swayed with me a few feet away from the not-so-newlyweds. He touched his smooth cheek to mine, breathing me in and savoring the moment.

"This is a good song," he said. "I've heard it a hundred times and never thought I'd be in St. Thomas dancing with you to it."

"It's beautiful here. I'd forgotten. If I haven't told you thank you yet ... thank you."

"If I hadn't, America's parents would have paid your way."

"Maybe they would have gotten me my own room," I said with a smirk.

"Doubtful. No one believes that we're just friends, despite your insistence."

I glanced at my glass of "ice water" I'd left at our table. Before the wedding, I'd emptied a water bottle and gone downstairs to fill it with vodka. Every sip I'd taken during the course of the day made me feel physically better and emotionally worse.

"The second they smash that cake in each other's faces, I'm done. Fourteen hours is enough for one day. This is more stressful than being on the mountain at the head of a fire."

Tyler's mouth pulled up into a half-smile, and he kissed my temple. I didn't pull away, barely giving it a second thought. Earlier, his family had mentioned that I would give in to Tyler eventually. I wasn't even sure what we were anymore. We had started a series of two steps forward and four steps back since the beginning and couldn't seem to kick it.

Beads of sweat were forming between my skin and my dress, and dampening the hair at the nape of my neck. It wasn't so much hot as it was humid. The air was thick and heavy, draping over my skin like an electric blanket.

The song ended, and Travis led Abby to the cake table by the hand. I left Tyler on the dance floor to find Camille and my camera, trying not to feel too irritated that she'd taken over a hundred pictures in the five minutes it had been in her possession.

I focused the lens while Travis and Abby pushed down on the knife to make the first slice. Everyone chuckled while Abby threatened him as he inched the small square of cake toward her mouth. An instant later it was over, sealed with a kiss. Everyone clapped, and then the music began to play again. I snapped a few more pictures and then made my way to our table, swiping my drink and finishing it off before I reached the small bar in the corner.

"Rum?" the bartender said, sweat streaming down his temple.

"Vodka cranberry. A double, please … mostly vodka." I watched him closely as he poured, nodding with satisfaction as he poured three-fourths vodka and the rest cranberry juice. I'd realized vodka was cheap and the least smelling of spirits, and it was easy to mix with most things, making it easiest for me to take to work or most functions. "Better go ahead and make me another," I said, glancing over my shoulder. I finished off the first drink before leaving, turning with a smile on my face, hoping anyone watching would think I'd just come away with one drink.

Hiding, concealing, and strategizing to seem normal. I wasn't sure how much longer the functioning part of my alcoholism would continue to be true.

"Easy," Tyler said. "Everything okay?"

"Just relaxing," I said, watching Travis kiss his wife and then lift her into his arms, waving goodbye. I grabbed my camera and captured that moment, happy for them and me, that I could finally put away my camera and mean it.

It wasn't long before Camille and Trenton, Taylor and Falyn, and Tyler and I were the last of the wedding guests left. The parents had turned in early, and Thomas and Liis seemed to be fighting.

I sat at the table, holding ice on my neck with one hand and a new drink in the other. Trenton and Taylor were twirling to the music with their dates, joking and giggling. The flaps on the outside restaurant that had been unrolled to keep out the rain were flapping in the breeze. I lifted my head, letting the air roll over my damp skin and the liquor sink in.

Tyler brushed a few wet strands of hair from my forehead. "You okay?"

"I'm good," I crooned, keeping my eyes closed. It wasn't often that I could get drunk anymore. "I want to swim in the ocean."

He lit a cigarette, but before he could blow out, I grabbed his cheeks and inhaled, filling my lungs with his smoke. I sat back, exhaling into the thick air.

He perched his elbow on the table and cupped his chin with his hand, shaking his head. "You make it so fucking hard to do the right thing."

"Take me swimming," I said, biting my lip.

"What about tomorrow?" he asked. "It's been a long day. Not sure if swimming at night in a storm is the best idea when we're drunk and tired."

"Whatever," I said, leaning back and closing my eyes again. Air cooled by the rain caressed my skin, and the heaviness from the vodka was comforting. I reached out for Tyler, blindly finding his arm.

"What are you doing?" he asked, amused.

"Just making sure you're still there."

"I'm here. For as long as you'll let me."

My lids popped open, and I let my head fall forward, looking at him with sleepy, dry eyes. "I want to make a pallet on our floor and lie with you naked."

"That sounds like a dirty trick," he said, grinning.

I lifted my hand to the waiter, signaling for another drink. He glanced to Tyler, who I could see shaking his head from the corner of my eye.

"Hey," I said in a moment of clarity.

"Ellie ... you're drunk. You're on like your tenth drink ... not including the shit you've drank all day. You're going to hurt yourself."

"Better me than someone else."

He frowned. "Wow. Are we at the pity stage of the night? Or is that you being a bitter drunk?"

Camille was showing her engagement ring to Falyn for the dozenth time of the evening, and I rolled my eyes. "It's a fucking diamond, and a small one. Stop bragging."

"Ellie, that's enough," Tyler said.

My face twisted. "She didn't hear me."

"You're talking louder than you think. C'mon. Let's go back to the room."

"I'm having a good time."

"No, you're sitting in a corner getting drunk."

I sighed. "I'll go. You stay here with your family. I don't want you to miss this."

"So you can end up in the ocean? No. C'mon."

I reluctantly stood, pulling away when Tyler tried to take my hand. He waved to his brothers and their significant others, and Tyler only touched me when I stumbled off the sidewalk.

We climbed an excessive amount of stairs to our room, and I leaned against the wall while Tyler opened the door. The lock clicked, the door opened, and had Tyler not caught me, I would have fallen inside.

He lifted me into his arms, carried me to the bed, and lowered me gently to the mattress.

"Come here," I said, reaching for him.

He pulled off my heels and then turned me onto my side, long enough to unzip the back of my dress. He slipped the fabric down and then slipped a T-shirt over my head.

"Much better," I said. "Now come here." I reached for him again, but he turned off the light and the bathroom door closed. The pipes whined as he turned on the shower. I thought about joining him, but I was so comfortable, and dizzy, and maybe a little nauseated. After a few minutes, the heat became hotter and the comfort went away. Nausea took over, and I rolled off the bed, crawling to the bathroom and reaching for the knob.

I barely made it to the toilet before my stomach rejected the day's worth of vodka I'd consumed. The curtain pulled back, and Tyler's deep voice filled the room.

"Christ, Ellie. Are you all right?"

"Yep. Ready for round two in no time."

The curtain closed just in time for me to heave again. The water turned off, and I could hear Tyler shuffling a towel over his body before starting a bath. He held my hair until I was finished, and then undressed me, lifting me off the floor and then lowering me into the tub.

He used a washrag to wipe my face, and then he sighed.

"This has stopped being exciting, hasn't it?" I asked, feeling mascara sting my eyes.

"Yeah," he said, sounding sad. "I think it's time."

I nodded, wiping the black from my cheeks. "It's okay, Tyler. I knew it was coming."

"You knew what was coming?"

"Goodbye."

He shook his head. "I've told you … I'm not going anywhere. Maybe it's not perfect, but I'll love walking through hell with you just the same. I'm just not to going to watch you get worse. It's time we start going in the other direction."

"I think we both know we're past a support group and twelve steps."

He wiped my forehead with the rag. "Maybe. Whatever it is, I'm with you."

My bottom lip quivered, nodding.

I picked at my nails, feeling strange to have been sweating from the Virgin Islands humidity in the morning and have Tyler's truck heater blowing in my face to battle the chill of Colorado air twelve hours later. The windshield wipers were creaking across the glass, wiping away the snowflakes falling quietly from the night sky.

"I'm not trying to be difficult. I think I just need some time to get my shit together."

He sighed, frustrated. "And why can't we do that together?"

"Because everything I've tried up to this weekend hasn't worked. It's been a year. I think it's time for something new."

"Or someone new?" he asked.

I blinked, offended. "I can't believe you just said that."

"I just want to help you with your luggage. It doesn't have to be a big deal."

"When you get upstairs, I'll want you to stay."

"Is that so bad?" When I didn't answer, he gripped his steering wheel so tight his knuckles turned white. "You want to drink, and you don't want me to see you."

"Something like that."

"So is this going to be the new thing you're trying? Choosing to get drunk over being with me?"

"No."

"That's what it sounds like to me."

"You're not coming inside," I snapped.

"Why?"

"You know why!"

He slammed his palm down on the dash. "Goddamn it, Ellie! I'm fucking exhausted!"

"Then go home!"

"I don't wanna go home! I want to be with you!"

"Too fucking bad!"

He clenched his teeth, staring straight ahead. The headlights of the truck highlighted the *MountainEar* building and the snowflakes, adding to the already white blanket on the ground.

He slammed his gearshift into reverse. "I can't do this."

I grabbed my backpack and put my hand on the door handle. "It's about time you admitted it."

"You were just waiting for that, weren't you? I give up, so it's not your fault. Or maybe you can go upstairs and pretend you're drinking because you feel sorry for yourself. Fucking brilliant."

I opened the door, and then opened the back door, grabbing my rolling suitcase and yanking it to the ground. I slammed the back door, and then the passenger's.

Tyler rolled down the window. "I've put up with a lot of shit to make this work, and you don't give a single fuck."

"I warned you!"

"That's bullshit, Ellie! Just because I warn a bank I'm going to rob it, doesn't mean the bank had it coming!"

"Be sure to tell everyone at the bar that when you're crying in your beer," I seethed.

"I don't have to go to the bar every time something in my life doesn't go right. It's called being an adult. And I'm damn sure not crying over you," he said, rolling up the window. He stomped on the gas, squealing backward in a half-circle, and then spun out of the back lot and into the street, barreling toward the highway.

I stood alone for a while, stunned. In the year I'd known him, Tyler had never spoken to me that way. Love made people hate in a way they never would have before.

The snow made the world quiet, but even silence made a sound. I tugged my luggage through the snow, up and over the curb to the back door. My key was ice cold, burning my fingers while my hand trembled. In a steady rhythm, the wheels banged against every stair, and then I let it all fall forward when I made it to the top.

I took the few steps to the fridge and grabbed the last can of beer, noticing the only thing left was moldy cheese and a bottle of mustard. The beer hissed at me when I popped the top, the bitter liquid feeling cold and comforting in my throat. There was half a pint of vodka in the cabinet, but payday was a week away.

My phone buzzed in my back pocket, and I scrambled to answer.

"Hello?"

"It's Jojo. You back?"

"I am," I said, brushing the snow from my hair.

"You bored?"

"What did you have in mind?"

"Cheap drinks at a dive bar?" she said. "I'll pick you up."

"Sounds perfect."

CHAPTER TWENTY-SIX

JON BON JOVI PLAYED FROM THE JUKEBOX in the corner, its yellow, green, and blue glow one of the only sources of light in Turk's besides the fluorescents over the bar.

A small group of local snowboarders were shooting tequila in the corner, and despite my occasional flirtatious glances in their direction, they weren't going to share.

Annie stayed busy behind the bar, raking in the last of the ski season's share of tips. I was sitting on a stool in front of her soda gun, watching her mix drinks I couldn't afford. Jojo had already bought me two, and I wasn't going to ask for another. Unfortunately, no one was looking to flirt with a jetlagged, hungover party girl too broke to party.

I looked around, feeling more desperate as the minutes passed, listening to Jojo go on about Liam and his invitation for her to meet him in North Carolina.

A shot was placed in front of me, and I turned to thank whoever it was. My smile faded when I saw a platinum pompadour and sweet grin.

"You look like you've had better days, Ellie," Paige said, straightening one of her enormous gold leaf earrings.

I faced forward. "Go away, Paige."

"That's not very nice. I just bought you a drink."

I craned my neck at her. "My sister won't speak to me because of you."

Jojo leaned forward. "I can't believe you did that, Paige. What the fuck were you thinking?"

"I wasn't," she said without apology. "I was drunk and maybe a lot high."

Jojo wrinkled her nose. "What happened to you? You used to be so sweet. Now you're full of holes and covered in cheap artwork."

"Go fuck a kangaroo, Jojo."

"You're a cunt rag, Paige. Your fake, innocent smile fools no one," Jojo said, turning to watch the television overhead.

Paige seemed unfazed, resting her cheek on her palm. "I wasn't trying to be mean. I didn't realize it was a secret."

"If you're going to pull something that heinous, at least own it. I'd respect you more," I said, grabbing the shot and throwing it down my throat.

"Want another one?" she asked, arching an eyebrow. She had plans for me, and I didn't care what they were. I just wanted to get drunk and not care for a night.

"It depends. What did you put in that shot?"

"Nothing fun, unless you're making a request."

"I'll just take another drink."

Paige signaled to Annie, who nodded.

"Where's your boy?" Paige asked, lifting her leg to climb onto the stool to my right. She was wearing tight jeans and a tank top under a flannel shirt, showing off her curves and cleavage all while staying warm.

"Not here," I said, throwing back the next shot Annie sat before me.

"Hey," Paige said with a giggle. "Wait for me." She lifted her chin and the dark liquid left the glass, emptying down her throat. She placed the glass upside down and slid it toward Annie, ordering two doubles.

I drank them as fast as Annie could make them. Finally, Paige cut me off. "You're going to drink my paycheck. I came in with a fifty, and it's gone."

"Thank you," I said, holding up my empty tumbler.

"Pace yourself," Jojo said. "When Dad falls off the wagon, it's easier for him to climb back on without a hangover."

"I'm already hungover," I said. "Or I was ... six drinks ago."

"You're keeping track?" Paige asked. "That's impressive."

Jojo snorted. "Only counting to six would be impressive to you, Miley Cyrus."

"Why did you bring her to a bar if she's on the wagon, Jojo?" Paige asked, leaning forward.

"Why did you bring her Crown to her house? Why are you buying her shots now? I just wanted to have a couple of drinks and chat, not get her wasted so I could talk her into ungodly things."

"You sure?" Paige asked with a sweet smile.

"Go fuck yourself, Paige."

"Now, ladies," I said, smiling when I felt the warmth settling into my muscles. "No need to fight over who is the best enabler."

"It's not funny," Annie said, glaring at us with her round, chocolate eyes while she furiously dried a glass. "You're both assholes if she was trying to get sober." She looked at me. "You're cut off, Ellie. Get the hell out of here."

My mouth fell open. "What did I do?"

"You let me serve drinks to an alcoholic. I better not see you in here again or I'll call Wick. Jojo … shame on you."

Jojo made a face. "Oh, please. Like Daddy doesn't come in here and get drunk when he fights with Mom."

"Not for a long time," Annie said, her shoulder-length brown curls shaking as she scolded and worked at the same time. "Take her home."

"Okay … okay, we're going," I said, standing to gather my things.

"I'll take you home," Paige said.

"No." I shook my head. "You still haven't apologized for New Year's Eve."

Paige took a step toward me, six inches too far into my personal space. "What do you think I'm trying to do?"

She leaned in, tilted her head, and pressed her lips to mine. The snowboarders in the corner cheered like their favorite hockey team had just scored.

"Buy those girls a drink!" one of them yelled, pointing at us.

I looked to Annie, but she pointed to the door.

Paige led me out by the hand, but once we stepped into the alley, she backed up against the wall and yanked me toward her. Her tongue ring banged against my teeth, her hands firmly on each side of my face.

I heard someone giggle to my left, and I turned to a woman in the same position as Paige, pulling Sterling's face against hers. Her knee was hitched to his hip.

His red-rimmed eyes drifted, and when he recognized me, I could see that he was just as drunk as I was, if not more. We watched each other for a long time, and then Sterling's friend pulled him to face her again, demanding his attention.

Paige tried to do the same, but I backed away.

"Ellie?" Paige said, confused.

I walked toward the street, passing Sterling and his new friend and turning right toward downtown. I stopped on the corner, looking down when a police cruiser rolled by. The light changed, and I hurried across the street to the only twenty-four-hour convenience store in town.

"Bathroom?" I asked.

The clerk pointed to the back, and I ran.

"Hey. Hey! No puking in there!"

I burst through the door and leaned back against it, sliding down to the floor. Pieces of toilet paper and paper towels were lying all around me, and I could feel the ass of my jeans getting wet from one of the many small puddles on the floor. I reached back for my phone, my thumb hovering over the display.

Before I could change my mind, I pressed the last name I ever thought I'd dial—a number Finley had programmed into my phone three months before.

It rang twice before she picked up. "Ellison? My God, it's so good to hear from you."

"Sally," I began. "I'm in the bathroom of a convenience store. I think it's the only open one in town."

"Where?"

"Estes Park. I'm going to need a car to the nearest rehabilitation center. I've tried to stop drinking ... I've..." I took a deep breath. "I can't do it on my own. I'm drunk right now."

"Someone will be there in fifteen minutes. Sit tight, Ellison. We're going to get you well."

I set the alarm on my phone and waited on the dirty floor. Before the chime went off, the clerk knocked on the door.

"Hey, lady? You all right in there?"

"I'm okay," I said, sniffing. I crawled over to the far wall and pulled some toilet paper off the roll, wiping my eyes between sobs.

"There's a guy out here. Says he's picking you up."

I scrambled to my feet, stunned by my reflection in the mirror. Twin thick black streaks of mascara stained my cheeks from my eyes to my jaw line. My hair was in rats, my eyes dull and glassed over. I yanked open the door to see Tyler standing next the clerk, looking very large next to the short, scrawny boy.

He sighed, relieved. "Ellison ... I've been looking everywhere."

I wiped my hands on my jeans and tried to walk out without stumbling. Tyler followed me outside, ready to catch me if I fell. He draped his army jacket over my shoulders and fidgeted.

"I'm so fucking sorry," he blurted out. "I didn't mean it. I didn't mean anything I said."

"I know."

"No," he said, reaching for me. "No, you don't know. You don't have a fucking clue how much I love you. I'm just ... I'm out of ideas. Things were so good before my birthday. I just want to get back there somehow."

I swayed backward, but he pulled me against his side.

"How much have you had to drink?" he asked.

"A lot," I said, my bottom lip trembling. "I saw Sterling."

Tyler's expression changed from worry to rage. "Where? Did he say something to you? How did you get here? Him?"

I shook my head and crossed my arms. "I walked."

"Jesus, Ellie, it's freezing."

"I don't want to be like him."

"Sterling?" he asked, caught off guard. "You're not. You're nothing like him."

"I'm exactly like him. I'm a drunk, selfish asshole who cares about no one." I turned to Tyler. "I can't love you. I don't even love myself."

Tyler looked like the air had been knocked out of him. He shrugged. "What am I supposed to say to that? You keep knocking me down and I keep getting back up, thinking one of these times you'll stop throwing punches. I love you. And I know you love me, but ... I'm not a punching bag. I don't know how much more I can take."

"It's not up to you to save me. I have to do it myself. Somewhere else."

He blanched. "What are you talking about?"

A black car pulled up, and the driver stepped out. "Miss Edson?"

I nodded.

Tyler frowned. "Who the fuck is that?"

"My ride."

"I can take you. Where are you going?"

I shrugged. "I don't know."

"Who is he? Does he work for your parents?"

"Not exactly," I said. Sally knew as well as I did that my parents would pay for any ride taking me to rehab.

I pulled off his jacket, but he held out his hand. "Keep it. Bring it back to me when you come home."

I reached for his face, leaning up on the balls of my feet to kiss him, and he threw his arms around me, closing his eyes tight and holding me like it was the last time.

"Come back," he said against my lips, keeping his eyes closed.

"What if I come back different? What if it takes a long time?"

He shook his head. "I've loved every version of you there's ever been. I'll love whoever comes back."

My face crumbled, and I nodded, waving goodbye.

The driver stood next to his car, opening the door when he saw me heading toward him. He shut the door as I slid into the backseat. The leather and new car smell reminded me of my other life, of the old Ellison who wouldn't have noticed that she was dirty while the car was so clean. I didn't belong in that car, or that life, but there I sat, willing to submit so that I could fully heal.

"Buckle up, Miss Edson," the driver said. "We have a long drive."

I nodded, reaching for the shoulder strap and pulling it across. I wasn't sure where the driver was taking me, but I cried the whole way there.

CHAPTER TWENTY-SEVEN

The cold stone railing felt good against my palms as I steadied myself on the balcony of my private room. The ocean was calm that day, finally settled after a week of storms. The waves calmed me at night, and the salt in the air made me feel safe, but I was leaving. I still had to face my sister, and Tyler, and the boys. I had apologies to make, and a lot more work to do.

A soft knock prompted me to walk across the marble floor. I tightened the belt of my cream silk robe and reached for the brass handle. My stay at Passages was like a luxury vacation. When I first arrived, I thought it was another attempt for my family to buy my sobriety, but I had learned so much, and changed even more. My heart was healed and my soul was at ease—at least in the confines of the walls of the most luxurious rehabilitation center in the world.

Sally walked in with my counselor, Barb, holding a cupcake and a certificate. Sally winked at me, aware of how lame the certificate was, but it meant that I was going home. She hugged me, her genuine pride evident in her embrace. We had spent a lot of late nights in private talks during my sixty-day stay, and she had somehow convinced my parents to respect my boundaries while supporting my rehabilitation with grace and money, even though their demands to see me were repeatedly refused.

Barb had already filled out the discharge papers, and handed me a pen. I read over the large print and small print, and then signed. Sally patted my right hand as I scribbled with my left, and then I said my goodbyes to Barb.

When my counselor left the room, Sally shot me her signature lips-pressed-together smile, pride practically radiating from her hooded eyes. Sally wasn't at all the snake in the grass I had thought her to be. Now that I was sober, it was easier to see people for who they really were. A clear head helped to distinguish who wanted the best for me and would fight me to reach that goal, and those who had good intentions but would be the first to enable me—like my parents. I wasn't strong enough to see them yet, and even though it was hard to take anything from them knowing the damage I'd caused our family, I was committed to my sobriety, and their support would mean the difference between success and a relapse. I had to swallow my pride and accept any helpful support those who loved me would give.

Sally rode with me to the airport, and then hugged me goodbye with a promise to check in often. I fought my resentment about riding in first-class, wearing new clothes and the expensive perfume Finley had sent me. I was so far from the sloppy drunk I had been just two months before, and even the ash-covered, smelly adventure photographer I loved to be, but everything looked different sober, even me.

Just as the plane taxied to the runway, my phone lit up, and Finley's face kissing at me shone bright on the display.

She had come to Passages just once, long enough for us to have a three-hour counseling session and dinner. She'd tearfully admitted to me that she'd walked past Falyn into the apartment, seeing a picture of me on the nightstand and assuming it was Tyler she was crawling into bed with. She recalled him calling her Falyn when she settled into the bed, but she was so jealous and hurt she could only think of retaliation. She was too ashamed to speak to me after that—until the day she sat in a beautiful room with beautiful flowers, marble floors, and expensive paintings chosen to promote calm and comfort while our ugliest sins spilled from our mouths.

"Hello?" I said, holding the phone to my ear. "Getting ready to take off, Fin."

"You should call Tyler. He's a little anxious."

"That makes two of us."

"He wants to see you."

"I want to see him, too. I'm just not sure if it should be tonight."

"He wants to pick you up from the airport. José can do it. It's completely up to you."

"I'm a recovering alcoholic, Fin, not a child."

"I'm sorry. I'll tell José to meet you in baggage claim at seven-thirty."

"It's okay. Driving from Denver will make for a nice chat."

"With Tyler?" she asked.

"Yes. I have to go, Fin. I love you."

"I love you, too, Elliebee."

I pressed END and placed my phone in the console between me and the older gentleman in a Prada suit and eyeglasses. He reminded me a bit of Stavros, the bartender from the Colorado Springs hotel, with his silver hair and style. As the plane took off, I thought about my last moments with Tyler, the choices that I had spent sixty days trying to let go, and the way Tyler had looked at me. I wondered if he would see me that way, as the weak, lost little girl he had to babysit. Ellie three-point-oh was neither weak nor lost, but she was carrying a lot of guilt and not enough forgiveness.

When the wheels set down in Denver, my head fell forward, my chin sliding off my fist. I smacked my lips, taking a sip of water as the flight attendant began her speech about disembarkation procedures. Once the plane came to a full stop and a bell chimed over the PA system, seat belts clacked in quick succession, sounding like the clicking of a keyboard, and then the rustle of everyone standing at the same time resonated throughout the fuselage. I had checked all of my belongings, so I squeaked past the silver-haired businessman and stood in the aisle, waiting for the door to open.

The walk up the jetway seemed longer than usual, as did the train ride to the baggage claim terminal. Everything felt different— I felt different. When I reached the escalator and ascended to baggage claim, I saw Tyler standing at the bottom, getting shouldered and nudged by people getting off the stairs and passing by. He looked up at me, never pulling his gaze away until I was standing in front of him.

"Hi," he said, nervous.

"Thanks for coming all the way here to pick me up."

"I've been everywhere and called everyone to find out where you went. I was going to be here when you came home."

Someone pushed from the back, forcing me to take a step forward.

"Hey," Tyler said, pushing the guy back. He guided me farther away from the top of the escalator, and the warmth of his fingers on my skin made me more emotional than I'd anticipated. "I didn't realize two months could feel like such a long time."

"Probably because you didn't have a coat," I said, handing him his jacket.

He looked down at the fabric in his hands. "I'd forgotten about the coat. Couldn't forget about you."

"Just needed some time to get my shit straight," I said.

Tyler smiled, seeming relieved at my choice of words. I was wearing the cream dress and tall, high-heeled suede boots Finley had sent. My hair fell in soft waves to the middle of my back, smoke free and clean. I looked very different from the last time he'd seen me, but he appeared reassured that I at least sounded the same.

The conveyor belt buzzed, alerting the passengers from the flight just before it began to move. They crowded around the baggage carousel.

"Here," Tyler said, taking me by the hand and leading me closer. Bags were already tumbling to the long oval that surrounded the chute. My bag was the third, the handle wrapped in a bright red priority tag.

Tyler lifted the large luggage without effort, then extended the handle. "It's a hike," he said, apologetic.

"We've hiked together before."

"Yes, we have," he said with a smile. He was still nervous, quiet, as we made the journey to the parking garage. Denver International wasn't the easiest airport to navigate, but Tyler was focused, getting me to his truck as quickly as he could.

Once he loaded my bag into the back seat, he opened my door and helped me climb in. My high-heeled boots made it difficult, but with one arm, Tyler lifted me into my seat.

He jogged around, hopped into his seat, and twisted the key in the ignition. He fussed with the air conditioner and then looked to me for approval.

"Yes, it's good … I'm fine."

Tyler backed out and navigated the maze of the parking garage until we saw daylight.

"So, uh," he began. "Guess who's going to be a daddy?"

I craned my neck at him, bracing myself.

"No! Oh fuck, no, not me. Taylor," he said, laughing nervously. "Taylor's going to be a daddy. I'm gonna be an uncle."

I breathed out. "Great! That's great. How exciting. Jim must be thrilled."

"Yeah, he's pretty stoked."

I nodded, turning toward the window and closing my eyes, exhaling slowly. I'd been looking forward to seeing him for so long, and not knowing what to expect, I was already emotional and feeling frazzled. I tried to do the breathing exercises I'd learned while away.

The tires buzzed against the road, the tone sounding a bit higher when we reached the highway and Tyler kicked up the speed. Waiting for him to have the inevitable conversation about my sudden departure was too much pressure, so I decided to do it myself.

"Tyler…"

"Wait," he said, wringing his hands on the steering wheel. "Let me explain."

I swallowed, worried that it was going to be much worse than I had imagined the last eight weeks. Tyler had cast me aside, left me, broken my heart, and yelled at me a thousand different ways in my dreams. Now, all he had to do was show me which one would be our reality.

"I was pissed. I admit it," he began. "But I didn't know you'd gotten on a fucking plane. I'm an unbelievable dick, Ellie. I didn't realize you were in such a low place. I don't know what we're doing, but if it's just friends with benefits, I can't even call myself a good friend. I should have seen it. I should have known."

"How?" I said. "I didn't even know."

He was fidgeting, taking off his ball cap and pulling it low over his head, then lifting it again so he could properly see to drive. He rubbed the back of his neck, shifted in his seat, and adjusted the radio.

"Tyler," I said. "Just say it. If it's too much for you, I get it. It's not your fault. I put you through a lot."

He turned, shooting a glare in my direction, and then he pulled the truck over onto the shoulder of the highway, shoving the gearshift into park.

"You wind up on the filthy floor of a gas station bathroom. You kiss me goodbye, and then you just fucking disappear. I've been stuck on a mountain, worried sick, Ellison. I had no way to get to you, no way to call around to find out if you were even alive, and even then, I didn't sleep because every phone call I made led nowhere."

I closed my eyes. "I'm sorry. I've done a lot of selfish things, and I owe you more than one apology."

"No," he said, shaking his head. "I shouldn't have left you at the apartment. I saw you struggling. You've been struggling for a while. I've taken you to a fucking bar, I pulled some strings to get you out of jail because you were drunk and looking for the fire, I've taken you to parties, and knew you were spiking your coffee at work … I'm your friend first, Ellie, and I've failed you on every level."

Barb had explained to me the hurricane I would walk into when I was released from Passages. I wouldn't only have to navigate my own guilt, but the guilt of everyone who loved me as well.

"Tyler, stop. We both know you couldn't have stopped me if you wanted. I had to be the one to make the decision, and you loved me right up until I did."

His warm brown eyes were glossed over, full of desperation. "We were both messed up the night we met, but the more time I spent with you, the more normal I felt."

I breathed out a laugh. "Me, too."

He paled, reaching for the glove box. He popped it open, clutching a small, dark red box. "Open it."

The box creaked open, and I exhaled, searching for words that never came.

"You know what it's like up on the mountain. Even when I'm digging ditches, there's a lot of time to think. When Jojo told me you were coming home … I went straight to the jeweler's. I can't imagine anything else but being with you and coming home to you and … Ellie, will you—"

"This is a lot my first day back."

He nodded a few times, and then snatched the box from me. He faced forward, hitting his steering wheel with the heel of his hand. "Goddamn it! I wasn't going to say that. I told myself a hundred times on the way here not to tell you. You don't need this right now. You just got home, and I'm throwing all this heavy shit at you."

My chest felt tight. "I've put you through hell," I said, sinking into guilt so deeply I wasn't sure I could crawl out.

He looked up at me. "If you're the fire, Ellie ... I'll burn."

A tear tumbled over my cheek, and I could see him waiting for me to decide what my tears meant. I reached for him, and he pulled me over the console into his lap, wrapping his arms around me and planting tiny pecks on my neck and cheek until he reached my mouth.

His hands cupped each side of my jaw, and he kissed me deep and slow, telling me he loved me without saying anything at all.

He pulled back, touching his forehead to mine, his eyes closed, his chest rising and falling with every quick breath. He looked up at me, his eyebrows pulling in, but before he could ask, I blurted out the answer.

"Yes."

"Really?" he asked with a small, hopeful smile.

"But," I began. His face fell, the hope in his eyes extinguished. "I have a lot of things I need to work on. I'm going to need a lot of time, and a lot of patience."

He shook his head and sat up, ready to fight for me. He opened the box, plucking the small silver band with a single round solitaire diamond. "I know it's not as big as Finley's..."

"I don't care about that. I just care about what this means."

He slipped the band onto my finger and choked out a laugh. "Holy shit."

I thought about his words, letting them bounce around in my mind along with everything I'd learned over the past two months. Returning to old relationships or starting new ones was a recipe for a relapse, and Tyler and I qualified as both. Knowing that, I knew no one could teach me how to love me better than him.

"Can we just...?" I began.

"Whatever you need, baby," he said, holding my hand to his lips.

I settled back into my seat, and Tyler's hand encompassed mine for the rest of the way back to Estes Park. I didn't feel added stress or worry or anxious—quite the opposite. Everything had seemed to fall into place in the same day. The new Ellie was home, in love, engaged, and happy. I couldn't imagine anything emotionally healthier than that. Not that I expected everything to be smooth sailing, but when I looked at Tyler, the only thing I felt was content.

CHAPTER TWENTY-EIGHT

JOJO POKED HER HEAD around the corner, looking like she'd fallen asleep in a tanning bed. Her long blonde braid hung from the nape of her neck, swinging a bit in front of her shoulder. "Got a minute?"

"Sure," I said. "Just let me finish up this…" I typed out a few more words, saved the document, and sat back in my office chair.

"How does it feel to be back?" she asked, collapsing into the love seat in front of my desk.

"Um … fine," I said, nodding.

"And how do you like your new place?" she asked.

I nodded again. "That it's not mine, nor anything that's in it."

"I know this is hard. It'd be harder without their help. Right now the focus is on getting well."

"I know. Tyler says the same. He's not even pushing me to move in with him, which is … weird."

"But smart. Congratulations, by the way." The synapses of Jojo's mind were clearly firing, and I waited while she twisted the platinum strands hanging from the clear elastic band securing her braid. "Chief called today. He asked how you were doing."

"The Alpine crew's superintendent?"

"Yes, that Chief. He asked a few questions about your recovery."

"Awkward."

"He wants to give you another chance."

"He does," I said, dubious.

"The Alpine crew is on R&R now."

"I know."

"They're leaving for Colorado Springs in two days."

"I know that, too."

"When they're back, Chief asked me if you'd be ready."

"Why would he want me to come back?" I asked, suspicious.

"He saw your latest feature on the forestry service. It's getting great reception, and they would like to see it wrapped up on a positive note."

"I guess the AP picking it up helped him make that decision?"

Jojo smiled. "I'm pretty sure Daddy would adopt you if he could. You put this magazine on the map. Ad space is booked up for six months. Subscription numbers set a new high every day. That was all you, Ellie. I can't even take the credit for the last write-up. I used almost every word you wrote."

"I noticed your name was absent."

"With good reason," she said, leaning forward. "Getting you well is our first priority. If you think it's too much, too soon, we'll push it back to next year's fire season. Daddy wanted to make sure you knew that."

I turned, seeing that Wick's door was closed. It had been that way since I'd returned to a full-time desk job.

"No, I can do it," I said, my heart thumping against my chest. I tried not to make my excitement too obvious.

Jojo's entire face brightened. "Really?"

"Yeah. Just stop saying *well*. It makes me feel sick."

She stood, shaking her head. "Absolutely. Won't mention it again." Not two seconds after she turned the corner, her orange face popped back in, her hot-pink lipstick bordering her bright smile. "That's not true. I'll mention it if necessary."

"Understood."

Jojo left me alone, and I leaned back, taking in a deep breath. The surface of my desk was still as empty as it had been on my first day, but for the three photographs I had framed. I picked up the metal five-by-seven, looking over the hideously cropped retake of a picture of Finley hanging on the wall of the chateau. It was ironic that that very picture had landed me the photography job in the first place, and just eighteen months later, it looked so amateur I had to lay it flat on its face several times a day.

The front door chimed, and Jojo greeted whoever approached her front desk. I could tell by the familiarity and condescension in her voice that it was Tyler.

"Ellie?" Jojo's voice squeaked over the intercom.

I pressed a button. "Yes?"

Tyler was in the background, complaining that Jojo should just let him come back to my office.

"Tyler Maddox is here to see you. Shall I allow him back, or would you like me to suggest he return to the sea of venereal disease where he came from?"

I spit out a laugh. "Send him back."

She sighed loudly. "Fine."

Tyler appeared, holding two fountain drinks. "Sprite for you," he said, sitting it on my desk. "Cherry Coke for me."

"Thank you," I said, wrapping my lips around the straw. "So, Chief called today."

"Did he?" Tyler asking, feigning surprise. He sat on the love seat in the exact spot Jojo had been, bouncing a few times.

"How did you talk him into it?"

"Now how in the hell am I going to talk Chief into bringing you back after what you pulled in Colorado Springs?"

"Don't lie."

"You're right. We all talked him into it."

"Who's we?"

"The guys. They miss you. Puddin' laments your grilled cheese at least twice a day."

"I said yes."

His eyebrows shot up. "You did?"

I nodded, and he popped out of the love seat, leaning over my desk and grabbing my cheeks to plant a kiss on my lips.

"Wow, I should say yes more often."

"I agree. Remember what happened the night of the last time you said yes?"

"Yes, I do."

He smirked. "You said yes a lot that night."

"Shut it. What are you doing tonight?"

"Besides you?" he asked.

"Hilarious. Any plans?"

He chuckled, itching the side of his nose. "No, baby. You're the only plans I have."

"Good, because we've been invited to dinner at the chateau."

"What's that?"

"My parents' vacation home."

He blanched. "Say what?"

"My parents would like to meet you."

He blinked, his entire body frozen in the position it was in when I broke the news. "Oh."

"*Oh?*"

"I just thought ... you know ... we weren't going to any parties."

"Not a party. Dinner. And they're serving sparkling water. Finley will be there."

"So, what you're saying is ... this will be the most awkward dinner ever."

"Pretty much."

"I'm in," he said, standing.

I smiled, lifting my chin to meet his gaze. "Yeah?"

"Of course. Gotta meet the in-laws. Looking forward to all of those judgey eyes and questions about my meager salary."

"Glad you know what to expect."

He leaned over and kissed my cheek, waving before he rounded the corner. "Love you!" he called back just before the door chimed.

"We don't love you back!" Jojo yelled.

The room was quiet except for the forks scraping against the plates and Daddy sipping his water from a wine glass. Felix was standing by the door like a militant waiting for Tyler or me to attempt escape, and mother hadn't looked me in the eye since we'd arrived.

Finley was busy texting on her phone, just as embarrassed to be in the same room with Tyler as he was with her.

Sally looked up to wink at me occasionally to make sure I wasn't too stressed. Tyler was cutting through his lamb shank, happily eating the fourth course of a five-course dinner.

"Ellison," Mother began in her voice that warned of impending doom. "Your father has spoken with the board, and they're very interested in using your newfound talents within the company. I'm sure you'll find the salary very agreeable in comparison with your current pay."

I swallowed quickly, and then cleared my throat. "I like the job I have now."

"You can do the same job at Edson Tech, sweetheart," she said.

"I can't hike mountains and photograph wildfires at Edson Tech."

Mother pursed her lips, deepening the wrinkles around her mouth. "Precisely. Your father and I feel that your higher wages will better assist with the cost of your new condo, and—"

"Uh … you insisted on that condo, and I complied."

"But it still costs money, dear. Money that, as an adult, you should provide."

"I was living in a great apartment that I could afford."

"We agreed a move would help create the feeling of a fresh start."

"I could have found a more affordable apartment, I—"

"Meredith," Sally interjected. I had grown to love her calm, soothing voice—a voice I once believed was manipulative and fake. Now that she was someone I trusted to call when in trouble, Daddy thought it would be a good idea to hire her back "Ellison likes the job she has now. It might be counterproductive to her path to wellness if we pull her away from a place where she feels comfortable and push her into an employment that may pay more, but is something she's not quite as happy with."

"She'll like it just fine," Mother said, blatantly dismissive.

"Meredith," Daddy began.

"Philip," Mother snapped, her voice rising an octave. She smiled, regaining her composure. "We agreed that it would be good for Ellison to find her place in the company and be an active participant in paying her bills."

"Ellison disagrees," Sally said. "And she's doing very well." She smiled at me. "She was paying bills before we moved her to the condo."

"Ellison doesn't have a choice," Mother said.

"Actually, she does," Sally responded. "She could just as easily move into a different apartment if you insist on holding it over her head. I'm sure that's not what your intention was when you secured it for her. I recall you being very concerned about her recovery and wanting to offer something to reduce her stress level."

"Sally," Mother said with a stiff smile. She patted her mouth with her napkin. "You work for me, not for Ellison."

Sally didn't flinch. "I'm an independent service, one which you sought out to help you guide Ellison to a better life. She's happy. What you're proposing is the opposite of that. Especially now, in the beginning of her recovery ... Meredith. You can't honestly think this is what's best for your daughter at this time."

Mother glared at Daddy, waiting for him to interject.

He sat up, clearing his throat and chewing quickly. "Your mother"—she glared at him—"and I ... feel that now that you've moved past your college ... *ways* ... that your place is at Edson Tech. She's taken great care to create a station that includes photography, and she wants you to have the position and respect you deserve. It's been very difficult for her to think of her daughter as a secretary, or this ... dirty, camping, forest person snapping pictures of squirrels."

Tyler leaned forward. "I'm sorry, sir ... have you seen Ellie's work? She's not photographing squirrels, she's documenting the containment of large wildfires around the U.S., and she's very, very talented. She's published, and she's sought after. She's given up a few offers, including *National Geographic.*"

"Really? That's so great, Elliebee," Finley said, a proud smile stretching across her face.

"Thanks," I said.

Tyler grabbed my hand under the table, and I sat up tall. "If you want me to move out of the condo, I'm happy to do that. But I'm not quitting my job."

Mother narrowed her eyes at Tyler. "I suppose this has something to do with him."

"No, actually, it's just about me loving my job. But I also love him, and taking a job with Edson Tech would mean moving to the East Coast, and I want to stay in Estes Park."

Mother rolled her eyes. "It's a tourist town, Ellison. It's not somewhere you plant roots."

"That's not true," I said. "My roots are pretty firmly planted."

Tyler squeezed my hand.

Mother put her elbow on the table and pinched the bridge of her nose. "You're really marrying a firefighter, Ellison? No offense, Mr. Maddox, but how do you plan to provide for our daughter?"

He tossed his napkin on the table, his shoulders relaxed. "Ellie doesn't really need me to support her financially, but I make six figures annually, Mrs. Edson. That ain't bad."

"Really?" Daddy said, intrigued.

Tyler shrugged. "I make a lot of overtime, and hazard pay is the tits."

"Is the…?" Mother began.

"He means it's lucrative, Mother," Finley said, glancing at me.

"Well," Daddy said, loosening his tie. "I think it sounds like they've got it nailed down."

"No, it most certainly does not," Mother said. "This boy—"

"Meredith," Daddy barked. "That's enough."

Finley looked down, her mouth infinitesimally curving upward. It didn't happen often, but we both loved it when Daddy finally reined Mother in.

"I don't see why Ellison can't stay in the condo as long as she likes. We've purchased a New York apartment for Finley, after all."

"Finley's not an addict," Mother hissed.

"Neither am I," I said. "I'm a recovering addict."

Maricela brought out a tray full of crème brulee, passing out a small white bowl to my parents, Finley, Tyler, and me.

"Mother," I said, taking one bite of Maricela's specialty before I spoke. "Maybe it's time you accept that your dreams for me are not mine. I've made a lot of mistakes, and broke your heart, and for that, I'm sorry. I have a long way to go and much to make up for, but I won't apologize for wanting to keep a job I love and being engaged to a man who has been everything to me. We might have to get our hands dirty for a paycheck, but … I love being gross with him."

Tyler's mouth pulled into a half-smile.

"I want to see some of those features, young lady," Daddy said.

"Yes, sir." I smiled.

"Dinner was amazing. Thank you," Tyler said.

Daddy stood up as we did. "It was nice to meet you, Tyler. Looking forward to hearing some of your stories."

Tyler walked around the long table to shake Daddy's hand. "I'm looking forward to you seeing the pictures."

Tyler returned to me and held out his hand. I followed him for a few steps until Mother called my name.

"Ellison? I just want you to be happy."

I smiled. "Believe me when I say that for the first time in a long, long time ... I am happy. Maybe the happiest."

She nodded, and Tyler led me down the hall and out the front door to his truck. He held open the door, and I climbed in, settling in while he slid in behind the wheel.

"That was..." I began.

"Intense." He chuckled. He slid his fingers between mine, lifting my fingers to his mouth. "I think it went well."

I wrinkled my nose. "Really?"

"Yeah. Everything's going to be all right."

I held my hand in front of me, admiring my diamond. "Think happy-ever-afters can happen for someone like me?"

Tyler's phone went off, and he pulled it out, squinting to read the message. "Fuck."

"What?"

"Called in. Colorado Springs. Oh, no."

"What?"

"Taylor's already there with Zeke and David Dalton."

I frowned, not recognizing the second name.

"Jew," he explained. "They haven't reported back. They're getting ready to list them as missing."

I covered my mouth. Tyler looked at me.

"Let's go," I said.

"Baby..."

"I'll stay at the hotel. Drive. Drive!"

"Promise me you'll stay put."

"I'll stay at the hotel." I recoiled from Tyler's stern stare. "I promise!"

Tyler yanked the shifter into drive, surging forward. He called Chief on the way, letting him know we were heading south.

The drive down seemed to fly by—probably because Tyler was driving twenty miles over the speed limit. As soon as we ran into the lobby, Tyler joined the other hotshot crews in the conference room.

"Ellie!" Darby said with a smile. "I was hoping you'd come."

"I'm here. Need a room."

While Darby checked me in, I turned to wave at Stavros.

"Do me a favor," I whispered to Darby.

"Sure," she chirped, staring at the computer monitor and clicking on her mouse.

"I'm not going anywhere near Stavros while I'm here."

Darby's head popped up, and she stared at me, confused.

"I don't drink anymore," I said.

"Oh ... oh! Yeah. Last time was ... that was bad."

I nodded once. "And it didn't get better after that."

Darby's eyes widened, and she reached over the desk to grab my hand. "Chicken nuggets, it can't be too bad! Congratulations! Tyler?"

"Yeah," I said with a smile.

She released my hand. "Hot damn, that is pretty. I'll let Stavros know you're on the wagon."

"Thank you," I said, deciding in the moment that I hated that euphemism.

She gave me two cards and winked, and I glanced down at the envelope to check the room number. I glanced over my shoulder, catching a glimpse of Tyler standing in the conference room, his arms crossed.

I carried my camera bag to the elevator, pressing the button for the second floor. Our room was at the end of the hall, a corner room, and I looked down to see the lot lights illuminating the news and hotshot vehicles crowded around Tyler's truck.

I sat on the bed and tapped the remote. It didn't take me long to find a news channel covering the fire. News of the missing Alpines was already scrolling across the bottom of the screen in yellow letters.

I called Jojo to let her know I was south covering the fire. Just as I plugged my phone into the charger, it chimed.

Going to get Taylor. Love you.

Be safe. I've got plans for you. Love you, too.

CHAPTER TWENTY-NINE

THE SUN WAS GETTING LOW in the sky when the main lobby doors slid open and Trex walked through. He didn't seem surprised to see me, but he was surprised to see the ring on my finger. "Congratulations," he said.

"Have you heard anything about the Alpine crew?" I asked.

"The rescue crew was helo'd in. That fire's a beast."

I stood behind the sofa, watching the large flat screen next to Darby's desk. Stavros brought me a glass filled with something clear and fizzy.

"Sprite," he said. "Just Sprite. Are you hungry?"

"No, thank you."

Stavros returned to the bar, and I returned my attention to the television. CNN was reporting that the smoke plume could be seen from the space station, and then they interviewed the US Forest Service Chief, Tom Tidwell.

"This is bad," I said, folding my arms across my middle.

"My people say they have eyes on the rescue crew," Trex said, checking his phone for the dozenth time.

After another meeting was held in the conference room, officials filed out and converged around the television. My stomach growled, but I didn't move. Darby had clocked out at three, but she stayed with me, knowing I was worried and alone.

"Turn that up!" someone called from across the room.

Darby scrambled for the remote and pressed the volume several times. A female reporter was standing in front of tall grass and burning trees holding a microphone. My heart ached, knowing Tyler couldn't be far.

I turned around in my seat, looking to the TAC team. They were talking quickly in hushed voices, and I turned around, watching the television with my fingers over my mouth.

"The last reported communication with the Estes Park crew was at six o'clock this evening, right about the time the two main fires converged. They've reportedly deployed their fire shelters."

My eyes filled with tears, and everything began to move in slow motion. I stood, scanning the faces of the men around me, looking for someone who might know where my boys were.

Darby handed me a tissue, and I wiped my cheeks quickly, refusing to think the worst.

"They're okay," one of the firefighters said, patting my arm.

I turned to the television, praying that any second the words scrolling across the bottom of the screen would change.

"Ellie!"

I turned to see Falyn running into the lobby from the parking lot, looking as panicked as I felt. I ran to her and threw my arms around her shoulders, sniffling.

"I just heard," she said. "Any news?"

I shook my head, wiping my nose with the tissue Darby had given me. "Nothing. We arrived just after seven. Tyler drove like a maniac. He's out there with the crews, looking for them."

She hugged me. "I know they're okay."

"Because they have to be," I said, holding her at arm's length with a forced smile. "I heard … about the baby. First Maddox grandbaby. Jim's ecstatic." Falyn's face fell, and my heart sank. "Oh God. Oh, no. Did you … are you not pregnant anymore?"

She stared at me, seeming equally confused and horrified.

"You're right," I said. "This isn't the time. Let's go sit. Trex is getting updates every half hour from his people."

"His people?" Falyn asked.

I shrugged. "I don't know. He just said *his people*."

Falyn sat with me on the sofa in front of the television, surrounded by firefighters and hotshots. As the night wore on, the crowd thinned, but Falyn, Darby, and I remained, waiting for any word other than Trex's updates that really weren't updates at all. The only thing we knew is that no bodies had been found.

Falyn held my hand and squeezed, her body sinking further into the sofa. Darby brought us coffee and a plate of donuts, but no one touched the food.

Trex came over, sitting in the chair adjacent to the sofa.

"Any word?" I asked.

Trex shook his head, discouraged.

"What about the rescue team?" Falyn asked.

"Nothing," Trex said. "I'm sorry. My guys only give visual confirmation, and they haven't seen anyone in an hour. The helos are up with spotlights, but the smoke is making it difficult to see." He glanced at Darby, wishing he had better news. "I'm going to call them in ten minutes. I'll let you know the second I hear anything."

I nodded, and then the lobby doors swept open.

Tyler walked in, his skin black with soot. He removed his hard hat, and Falyn stood and I jumped up, sprinting toward him and hitting him at full speed.

"Oh my God," I cried softly into his ear. "Oh my God, you're here. You're back." I leaned back, seeing the matching clean streaks striping his cheeks. I hugged him again, and he squeezed me tight.

"We didn't find him. I can't find him, Ellie," he choked out.

"We had to drag him out," Jubal said, wiping his dirty forehead with the back of his wrist. He looked exhausted, clean lines fanning out from around his eyes.

"No!" Falyn cried.

Tyler released me and walked over to Falyn, pulling her into his arms. He whispered in her ear as she shook her head, and then her knees gave way, her wails filling the lobby.

My eyes blinked open, hearing the middle of Tyler and Falyn's conversation. She was going to work, unable to sit around and wait any longer.

"Are you going back out?" she asked.

"I'm not sure they'll let me. I might have punched one or two people before they removed me from the area," Tyler said.

"He's your brother," Falyn said. "They'll understand."

Tyler tensed, and I reached up to touch his shoulder. "He's going to walk in that door any second. They haven't found them. That's a good thing."

He nodded.

"Come on. Let's get you a shower." I stood, pulling Tyler with me. He stumbled to the elevator and then down the hall to our room. I guided him in and to the bathroom, where I unbuttoned his shirt, hooking it on the door, and then pulled off his undershirt, and then the rest of his clothes and boots.

I reached over to twist the knob to the shower, checking the temperature before I let him step in. He closed the curtain, but I could hear him crying.

I leaned my head against the wall, closing my eyes, taking in deep, cleansing breaths to ease the stress and the sudden, deep thirst making my entire body ache. I thought about Stavros and how easy it would be to talk him into a beer for Tyler. Just one. I was tired, and afraid, and worried for Tyler, but I had to be present. I had to stay sober. I stood up, refusing to give in. It was the first craving of many, but I only had to get through one at a time.

Tyler turned off the water and I handed him a towel. He dried off his face and then wrapped the towel around his waist, hugging me against the wall. I placed my hand on the back of his neck, kissing his cheek.

"He's coming back," I whispered. "We should get back down there. You'll want to be there when he walks in the door."

Tyler nodded, then wiped his nose, turning to rinse his mouth and dress again. He held my hand as we walked downstairs, stopping when he stepped into the lobby. His brother was chatting with a small group, just as filthy as Dalton and Zeke standing next to him. They were shaking hands and hugging the remaining Alpine crew.

"You stupid dick," Tyler said, stomping over to his brother. They hugged each other so hard I heard their fists pound their backs. Tyler lost it.

My eyes filled with tears, and Trex hooked his arm around my shoulders as we watched Taylor and Tyler reunite. I gave them a moment, and then I walked over to them, inserting myself into their embrace.

"Hey," Taylor said, a tear dripping off the end of his nose.

"Falyn was here," I said.

Taylor pulled away. "What? She was here?" he asked, pointing to the floor.

I nodded. "She waited here all night. Worried sick. You should call her."

Taylor patted his pockets, looking for keys. He pointed to Tyler. "Love you, brother. I gotta see about a girl."

"Get outta here, shit stain. Don't come back 'til she's yours."

Taylor ran to his truck, squealing his tires.

Tyler turned and threw his arms around me. "Fuck," he said, letting out a sigh of relief.

The crew patted him on the back, just as relieved and emotional as Tyler. I hugged Zeke and Jew, and then the rest of the guys while Tyler spoke with a few of the officials.

He came back to me, lifting me into his arms and carrying me to the elevators while the hotshots made ridiculous hooting noises and catcalls.

My eyes were suddenly heavy, and I leaned against his shoulder. The elevator chimed and Tyler stepped inside, maneuvering a bit so I could press the button to the second floor. He carried me to the room, and again waited while I touched the key card to the lock. The door clicked, and Tyler pressed down on the handle, pushed the door with his foot, and then lowered me to the bed.

I snuggled up to his neck, melting against him as he enveloped me in his arms.

"I didn't know Falyn and Taylor were having problems."

"Yeah, they're broken up."

"Even though she's pregnant? I don't see him letting that fly."

"Falyn isn't pregnant."

I sat up, slapping his chest. "Shut the front door! Are you serious?"

Taylor propped his head with his arm. "She broke up with him, and he went to California to see Tommy. He hooked up with one of Tommy's colleagues. I guess she's going to have it but doesn't want to keep it. How weird is that? Taylor is getting full custody."

"Whoa. You think they'll work it out?"

He shrugged. "She was here all night. She has to still care about him. Come here," he said.

I bent down, getting comfortable next to him.

He touched the back of his wrist to his forehead. "Wow. That was intense. I don't know what I would have done if something happened to Taylor. That makes us three-and-oh the last couple of years."

"What do you mean?"

"Taylor, Trent, and Travis have all had close calls."

I buried my face into Tyler's neck. "It's not your turn."

"Well, it damn sure ain't Tommy's turn. He's an ad exec."

"Are you sure?" I asked.

Tyler paused. "What makes you say that?"

"Well … your family thinks you and Taylor are insurance salesmen. What if Thomas isn't what you think he is?"

"What do you think he is?"

"A cop."

Tyler snorted.

"I'm serious. Or something. He lives in San Diego, right? Isn't there a federal building there? He's something. So is his girlfriend. I saw Travis walking to their room the morning after the wedding, early."

"You have quite an imagination."

"Abby knows," I said.

"Abby knows what?"

"About you."

He laughed once. "No, she doesn't."

"Yes, she does. And she knows about Travis, too."

"What about Travis?"

"Whatever he's not telling her. She's smart. I'm smart, too. I'm a photographer, Tyler. I notice things. I'm always looking at people. I knew you were inherently good, didn't I?"

He frowned, unwilling to concede just yet.

"I think your dad knows," I said.

"What?" he said, lifting his head. "Where is all this coming from?"

"I've known. I watched them at Thanksgiving. Abby was asking you all of those weird questions, and she and Jim had a look."

"A look," he deadpanned.

Tyler's phone went off, and he dug it out of his T-shirt pocket. "Huh."

"Who is it?"

"Dad. He texted me."

"What does it say?"

"He's just checking in, asking if everyone is okay."

I leaned up to his ear, kissing his cheek. "Told you."

"No way," he said, tapping out a reply and then putting his phone away.

"He's a former detective. You think he can't figure you out?"

"Why wouldn't he say anything?"

I shrugged. "Maybe he's just letting you think you've fooled him. Maybe he knows there's a reason why you lied, so he's letting it go."

"Since Dad's psychic, maybe he can tell me when you're going to pick a date for the wedding," he said, only half-teasing.

I slipped my hand under Tyler's T-shirt, running my fingertips up his chest. "I thought you said you didn't care."

"Of course I care, baby. I'm just not going to pressure you about it."

Tyler's skin was warm under my hand, his chest rising and falling with each breath. I thought about when we first met, how sweaty and sexy he had been, trading punches in my parents' gallery room. We had conquered heaven and hell, fire and ice, and he'd stuck with me through it all.

"My mother seems to be very concerned about me affording the condo."

"Yeah, but your dad's not worried."

"If Taylor's going to be a dad … won't he and Falyn need their own place?"

"Yeah, wow. I hadn't thought about that."

"Maybe you should give them the apartment, and you move into the condo with me?"

Tyler turned onto his side and propped his head with his hand. "What?" he said, suspicious.

I shrugged. "You can pay half the rent. We can get married after fire season…"

Tyler's eyebrows shot up. "After this fire season?"

"Too soon?"

He cupped my jaw, turning until his torso was hovering over me. "Baby," he said, pressing his lips to mine and sliding his tongue inside. I reached up his shirt, pressing my fingers into the muscles in his back.

"Like October? November?" he said against my lips.

I nodded.

He touched his forehead to mine, already emotional from the day. "Are you fucking with me?"

"I don't need anything fancy, do you?" He shook his head. "Pick a Saturday."

He scrambled for his phone, opening his calendar. "November seventh. That way we're sure fire season is over, and maybe some of the guys will still be around."

"Sounds great."

"November seventh," he repeated.

"Perfect."

"Last chance to change your mind. I'm texting Dad," he said, waiting for me to call his bluff.

I waited, amused.

He held his phone to his chest, closing his eyes. "If you're bullshitting me, it's going to break my fucking heart."

"Tyler Maddox!" I grabbed his phone, typed out the message, and sent it, turning the phone to show him. "It's sent. It's a done deal. I'm your wife on November seventh."

He touched my cheek with his hand, running his thumb along my jawline. "You sure you're ready?"

"What is there to be afraid of? You've already seen my ugly side and loved me through it."

"What if the situation was reversed?"

I bit my lip, staring at his. He was honest, he was strong, he was beautiful, and he was mine. "You're not the only one who would walk through fire for what you love."

He scanned my face, breathed out a laugh, and shook his head, pressing his lips against mine.

THE END.

ACKNOWLEDGMENTS

Writing about something I know nothing about is always a fun challenge for me, most of all finding an expert who is willing to talk to the "author who is writing a fictional book on the subject." I happened to know the expert in this case, but had no idea he was an interagency hotshot crewmember until I complained to my husband one day about how much trouble I was having finding someone to talk to about wildfire fighting. Cowboy asked me why I didn't just message Tyler Vanover. With much excitement (and a smidgeon of doubt), I sent Tyler a message asking if he had, in fact, been a hotshot. Tyler confirmed he had—although he was shocked I knew, apparently not many people do—and shortly after I had eight full pages, front and back of notes.

Tyler, before I can thank you for the hours of stories, tips, and information you shared with me, I have to thank you for your service as a wildland firefighter. After all the research I've done on this subject, I am in awe of anyone who would do this job willingly, much less with enthusiasm fire season after fire season. The arduous physical labor, the long hours, and the minimal sleep hotshots endure earn them the title of elite firefighters. The danger level alone is enough to make me fear for everyone who puts themselves between the flames and someone's home, or farm, or even an entire town. Thank you, Tyler, for helping me with the details of this story, but it is an honor to know a true hero.

Megan Davis began as a reader I met several years ago at the first Book Bash in Orlando, Florida. We took a picture together, and to this day, it's one of my favorites. I remember chatting with her after that photo was taken, and she was so cool in conversation I'd thought that maybe she'd just taken a picture with me because she saw others doing it. Today, Megan is my right hand (wo)man. She is responsible for the chapter containing Ellie's first week with the hotshots. I was going to skip over that part but Megan wanted more. It was because I wrote that chapter that *Beautiful Burn* took a new direction, one that I truly loved, and all because I filled a gap I didn't know was empty. Thanks for all you do for me, Megan, but most of all, thanks for asking for more.

Thank you to Jennifer Danielle for reading the ARC with me in the wee hours of the night, and to Nina Moore for always saying yes to making amazing promotional graphics. A big thanks to Jessica Landers for moderating a large group of awesome readers called the MacPack. I don't know what I would do without any of you!

Thank you to Deanna for assuring me this book was just as addictive as every Maddox book should be, and for helping me with the dreaded blurb. Thank you most for being my best friend, and for listening to me rant and squeal and everything in between.

More thanks goes to Murphy Rae, Madison Seidler, and Jovana Shirley for help in the production of this book, to Hang Le for an amazing cover, and to Bec Butterfield for her help in Australian slang. To authors Kristen Proby and Jen Armentrout, for their support along the way, and to my agent, Kevan Lyon, who came out of 2015 with me with amazing grace and patience.

Finally, thanks to L3 for being my bubble of positivity, and to my squad: Megan, Jessica, Chu, Liis, Deanna, and Misty. You are the butter on my bread.

ABOUT THE AUTHOR

JAMIE MCGUIRE was born in Tulsa, Oklahoma. She attended Northern Oklahoma College, the University of Central Oklahoma, and Autry Technology Center where she graduated with a degree in Radiography.

Jamie paved the way for the New Adult genre with the international bestseller *Beautiful Disaster*. Her follow-up novel, *Walking Disaster*, debuted at #1 on the *New York Times*, *USA Today*, and *Wall Street Journal* bestseller lists. *Beautiful Oblivion*, book one of the Maddox Brothers series, also topped the *New York Times* bestseller list, debuting at #1. In 2015, books two and three of the Maddox Brothers series, *Beautiful Redemption* and *Beautiful Sacrifice*, respectively, also topped the *New York Times*, as well as a Beautiful series novella, *Something Beautiful*.

Novels also written by Jamie McGuire include: apocalyptic thriller and 2014 UtopYA Best Dystopian Book of the Year, *Red Hill*; the Providence series, a young adult paranormal romance trilogy; *Apolonia*, a dark sci-fi romance; and several novellas, including *A Beautiful Wedding*, *Among Monsters*, *Happenstance: A Novella Series*, and *Sins of the Innocent*.

Jamie is the first indie author in history to strike a print deal with retail giant Wal-Mart. Her self-published novel, *Beautiful Redemption* hit Wal-Mart shelves in September, 2015.

Jamie lives in Steamboat Springs, Colorado with her husband, Jeff, and their three children.

Find Jamie at www.jamiemcguire.com or on Facebook, Twitter, Google +, Tsu, and Instagram.